VICISSITUDES OF FORTUNE

BOB SIQVELAND

DEDICATION

Hollywood, Washington D.C., the music world and all the athletic fields produce celebrities; this book however, is dedicated to our Nation's law enforcement, fire fighters, and the brave men and women who so unselfishly serve our country in uniform. These are America's HEROES and to have been a part of this elite fraternity…I am most honored.

THANKS TO ALL OF YOU

"One's virtue is all that one truly has,
because it is not imperiled by the vicissitudes of fortune."

—**Boethius**

AUTHOR'S NOTE

Maybe I should have kept this story to myself. I thought about it, but in the end, it had such a profound effect on me that I had to share it with someone.

I knew all these people—some a lot better than others, and some only in passing, but I knew their backgrounds and the histories that influenced them. Several were real bottom-feeders, but the good ones were at the top of the human food chain. Still, what happened wasn't fair. Yeah, I know. Life's not fair. But there are still a bunch of us who cling to the delusion that at least it can be.

That said, I hate being part of a failed experiment, which it seems that man, in most ways, is proving to be.

CHAPTER 1

Greenwich, Connecticut
2010

Some might say that the fine line between self-assurance and arrogance is one of many criteria defined by, and that define, character. It usually doesn't take gifted intuition to figure out who's got what.

With the affected posture of nobility vaguely reminiscent of an Arabian show horse, Winston Tyler III descended the half-circle staircase, holding the highly polished mahogany railings that topped the intricately carved and shiny brass balusters. He set the keys to his car on the Louis XIV pier table as he headed for the kitchen. A well-trained psychologist would intuit the subtlety in the man's demeanor and body language as perhaps that of someone who was not quite comfortable in his own skin. The ambiance of the house was almost kitsch in its extravagance, but seemingly taken for granted, as is often the case with inherited money.

Tyler said nothing as he entered the kitchen, grabbed a mug from the cupboard, and filled it halfway with coffee. He saw his wife, Barbara, on her knees, retrieving some cookware from a low, deep alcove. For several minutes, the silence resounded like a polka band on a curtain call, only muted.

When it became uncomfortable, Tyler spoke in a tone more pithy than indignant. "So . . . is your brother going to be staying at the house all three days?"

Barbara didn't respond, continuing with her pan-rattling task.

Tyler closed the physical gap and stood over her. "Couldn't he find one of his soldier buddies to stay with? Hell, that's why he's in town, isn't it?" This time he waited.

Barbara slowly stood, picking up a Crock-Pot in both hands and taking it to the sink to give it a quick wash. "Billy loves an old-fashioned stew . . . with veggies and brown gravy."

The non sequitur irritated Tyler. He made a corresponding facial expression, but resigned himself to having had his question answered by her extraneous response. Still, he seemed to feel the need to fire one more shot over her bow. "Well, at least I hope he can stay sober and respect my house rules."

Barbara stopped what she was doing, slowly wiped her hands on a dish towel, and turned to give her husband a penetrating stare. "*Your* house rules!"

Tyler sensed the gathering storm.

"You really think you spend enough time around here to even *establish* house rules? Maybe you would care to share with me your house rules." The slow drip of ridicule was beginning to stream. "Do your house rules also apply to the old man who lives upstairs? You know—your father—the one that requires a full-time guardian? And *who* do you think that might be? Or how about the procession of intrusive, unannounced business and golfing buddies you show up with for 'drinks and a bite to eat?'"

A long silence followed until Barbara made her closing statement.

"Well . . . here are *my* house rules, Winston: you will be cordial and respectful to my brother while he is here." She paused before finishing. "And in case you didn't get the message, he's here for a funeral, not one of your golf tournaments. So how about you just run along and play businessman and leave me to my work?" She turned her back to him and returned to the sink.

Admonished, Tyler set his cup down and went for his keys. He could hear her humming some old '70s song as he left the house.

There was a light drizzle. Tyler stood under the porte co-chere, admiring the silver 2012 Maybach 62 for which he had paid $723,000. Of course, he could have had a chauffeur—and actually, he did have one—but he loved to drive this car. What he really loved was to be seen driving this car, especially in this town.

The ultra-luxury car had been built by hand, to his specifications. Tyler had sleuthed to find a separator, something that told the world that he was cut from a different cloth, and this was it.

The German carmaker had been founded in 1909 by Wilhelm Maybach and his son. At some point, Daimler AG out of Stuttgart bought the company. However, Daimler announced in November 2011 that Maybach would cease to be a brand by 2013, and accordingly manufactured the last Maybach vehicle in December 2012. There had been only 3,000 cars sold since the brand's revival in 2002. For almost a decade, Daimler AG had tried to make Maybach a profitable rival to Rolls Royce and

Bentley, but ultra-luxury meant ultra-rich, and with a base price tag starting at just under $400,000, that was indeed a limited market. There was only one other model in the city of Greenwich, that being a Maybach 57 owned by an award-winning actor, and Tyler didn't mind the comparison.

As Tyler left the long, circular driveway to his mansion, heading to the office, his thoughts returned to Barbara and her brother.

Tyler, at sixty-two, was ten years older than his wife, who was thirteen years younger than her brother, Billy Stone. Tyler's first marriage had been a disaster, short-lived and expensive. Of course, there were exceptions to the basic laws of life, but Tyler wasn't one. If you believed that easy money was detrimental to character development, Tyler was the poster child for that sentiment. If we left the planet for our teen years, figuratively speaking, most of us returned when we left the parental nest, went into the Army, created bills, or simply began to mature—whatever.

But Tyler, it seemed, was still hopping from Pluto to Uranus in his lavish spaceship of ignorance and apathy. From an external perspective, it seemed that his excursion was a good ride. His self-concept, however, stood somewhat at odds with that perception.

Barbara was Tyler's home base. He knew it, but he would never tell her. Like Lassie, he always seemed to come home to her, if only to regenerate his power source and blast off again. Someone had said, "Still waters run deep," implying that somewhere under a banal veneer was real value. But Tyler was little more than a wading pool, shallow and simple. In truth, it wasn't totally his fault. Some blame had to be assigned to Winston Tyler II.

There was gristle in the roots of the early Tyler family tree. Winston the First had stumbled through the halls of Ellis Island in the early 1920s after a two-week torment in the bowels of a transport ship arriving from Liverpool. His relative success for the times was predictable. Ellis Island was like every other gate of entry throughout history. You want in? Show me the money. In this way, "Grease" Tyler, as he was known in the back alleys of Liverpool, had spent nearly a year prepping for his trip. He had a stash of saved and stolen documents and money, as well as the names, profiles, positions, and work schedules of immigration guards and customs officials so that his arrival into New York City would come without incident. After that, life became a bit dicier.

Tyler had formed a wry smile while clinging to the deck rail as his ship entered New York harbor and passed below the colossal green sculpture of *Libertas*, the Roman goddess of freedom. His senses were on overload. As part of his preparation for entry, he had become familiar with the history of this monument and Emma Lazarus's inscription, and he stuffed his cynicism as he recalled the poem.

Most urgently, he *yearned to breathe free*. Actually, he simply yearned to breathe. The stench of the ship's *huddled mass of wretched refuse* was overwhelming. He might have called it mongrel mania. The shouts and cries of his immigrant shipmates came in Greek, Hungarian, Italian, and other languages, and he envisioned the great city in the throes of an eclectic fit. He would need to be prepared for a difficult integration fraught with peril.

He also pondered the intent of this great gift from the French. France had never been big on almsgiving and brotherly love. There was always an agenda. Most likely, France figured that

Lady Liberty would be the world symbol of a lifelong union between the two countries . . . or at least everlasting chumminess. But he was English. He knew the French. Good luck on that one.

As he walked the streets of the east side of the city, he wondered if this was where Darwin had come up with his theory. Here, no doubt, the weak were screwed. Adopting a posture of intense *high alert* would be his only ticket to survival. He saw or sensed guns, knives, and truncheons everywhere, and yet beneath the chaos, he felt great opportunity.

Tyler the First had, early in his life, adopted the mantra that would one day become the acronym KISS, or "Keep It Simple, Stupid," as it made his own life easier and less complicated. He reflected on the gravel streets with laundry drying on ropes; booths of vegetables, meat, fish, and utensils; and street urchins fighting, playing kickball, and carousing. In addition to sustenance, he also considered the other staple of existence: housing. In short order, he came to a conclusion. The one constant was money.

What he found was that the value of money varied from one neighborhood to the next. It was a commodity. Indeed, there was an exchange rate for the numerous currencies, but only a minority understood it and used it. Where you would buy three apples for *two pence* in the British precinct, you could get five apples for equal value in the Hungarian hood for kroners. Simply put, Tyler could open a food stand, buy five apples from the Hungarians, sell three or four apples to the Brits, and either keep an apple or sell it for over a 20 percent profit. And so he did. Within a year, he had learned all the intricacies of commodity trading and currency fluctuation and exchange rate opportunities.

He moved out of the less-desirable wholesale and retail grocery business and into an office. Actually, it was but a strategically located flat in a buffer zone Irish parish. He developed his ano-nymity with guile and canniness. Few knew who he was or what he did. No one was angry with him. No one was resentful or jealous. No one wanted to kill him. Really, no one cared. He was just another customer or seller—hell, just another poor schmuck trying to make ends meet. As an apparition, he thrived.

Juxtapose, if you wish, the first Winston Tyler's story to the hundreds of immigrant success stories that you've read or heard about over the years. He morphed from a gravel road to a brick street, from wood construction to stone, and from second floor in the Irish slum to the fifth floor in the business district. He no longer had "marks," but clients. He made the choice to eschew banking, as it was imprisoned in regulation and litigation, opt-ing instead for the less controlled and wider-boundaried world of financial service, a term that covered a multitude of sins. In the meantime, he got married and had a son, to whom he bequeathed his name.

In the hard world of survival, it is difficult to say if one can truly understand the sensitivity of the word *love*, especially when one has no sensitivity. Winston Tyler the First wasn't exactly stone cold. He was more like stone *tepid*. He was most pleased to have a son, but in line with his conditioning, it fell under the head-ing of ownership, an asset on a balance sheet. He was certainly protective and quite generous, a committed tutor and instructor. The boy was perhaps an enhancement to his own id. To Tyler II, Tyler I was an icon in almost every way—but still, something was missing that related to the whole nature-nurture thing.

In any event, by the time young Winston was fifteen, he was way ahead of where his father had been at that age, at least regarding business and finance. He had been homeschooled, the student of a cycle of his father's accountants, managers, and consultants. He never developed socially because he was never given the chance. He never played kickball—or any sports, for that matter—and as a result, he had no friends. When he finally came to work for his father, physically he resembled a young Woodrow Wilson, if you could picture the older Woodrow as he might have looked when he was younger. With respect to personality and behavior, he was an alter ego of his old man.

Tyler I had spent his service time during the Big War in an office in London. There, he was most valuable and productive, even creative. Initially, he had been attached to a cryptology team of the RAF (Royal Air Force). He had consulted in the ongoing development and employment of radar, without which the predominant language of Buckingham Palace might have become Hochdeutsch.

In January of 1943, the long-established British-US Army relationship regarding diplomatic traffic was formalized, and shortly after, the issue of the Enigma crisis and intelligence took collaborative priority. What happened is history, but being the good Boy Scout that he was, Tyler never spoke about it except to occasionally drop the name of his friend, colleague, and OSS founder William J. "Wild Bill" Donovan, the so-called father of American intelligence.

After the war, it was back to New York, but Tyler soon discovered that, regarding living conditions and working environment, the bloom had come off the rose in the Big Apple. He started to search, and within months found his paradise across the state line in Connecticut.

The city of Greenwich was named after the borough of London in the United Kingdom whose claim to fame was the universal time standard, referred to as Greenwich Mean Time (GMT). It was the signature town of affluent Fairfax County, Connecticut, with a population of just over 60,000. In July 2005, CNN/Money and *Money Magazine* ranked Greenwich first on its list of the *Hundred Best Places to Live in the United States. Money* also ranked Greenwich first in the "Biggest Earner" category. In 2012, Greenwich was listed as having the wealthiest residents per capita in the US

Greenwich was the southernmost and westernmost municipality in Connecticut, and resided just over thirty-eight minutes by express train from Grand Central Terminal in Manhattan. It played home to many financial service companies, as well as some of the most successful hedge funds. For over fifty years, the town had an abundance of celebrities, from actors and movie producers to artists, musicians, models, sports stars, authors, and even a couple of presidents.

In 1950, the nascent development of Greenwich as a prominent city among cities was marked with the completion of Winston Tyler's extravagant home, a mile from the downtown business district. The first car to grace the circular driveway was a red-and-black Riley RMD drophead coupe. Not long after that, Winston Tyler II added his own dark gray Tatra Tatraplan T-600 sedan.

Most people who knew Tyler I . . . scratch that, *everyone* who knew Tyler I called him a control freak. When he designed and built his home, he designed it for two families: his and his son's. However, he didn't bother to tell his son. And then there was his son's wedding. You'd have thought the groom's father was from the Middle East. The boy's nuptials were the closest thing to an arranged marriage since that of Dushyanta and Shakuntala. So, when Tyler II married Marie Dewinter, daughter of George Dewinter, VP of Tyler Financial Services, the reception was an extravaganza for the ages at the Tyler compound. Conveniently, except for a three-night honeymoon at the Fontainebleau on Miami Beach arranged and bought by Dad, the prominent couple was not burdened with all the hoopla and heartache of finding a place to live, and could jump right back into the work schedule.

Within a year, in line with Tyler I's proclamation that he wanted a grandson, Tyler III was born in May of 1952. According to the proud grandfather, it was as important an event as such other events that year as Elizabeth II's succession to the British throne and Dwight Eisenhower's election as America's thirty-fourth president.

Aside from his mentoring, Tyler II was innately precocious in the world of finance matters. Early on, his father deferred to his knowledge and decision-making. He was nearly robotic in his intuitive processing, formulating structures and deals in his head while his father's brain trust spent collective hours only to arrive at the same conclusions. He was much like a human computer when it came to doing his job. Unfortunately, he was much like a human computer in living his life, as well, and like Morris West once proclaimed, "Computers seduce man to blind faith and betray him to his own idiocy."

So it was with Tyler II's life and the damage that resulted from his own self-betrayal. When it came to his family and personal interests, there was a void. What little personality and emotion he possessed was rarely seen outside of a wry smile over a signed contract or a completed deal sealed with a wimpy handshake. He did have the respect of his peers and competitors, who knew that their only competitive advantage was salesmanship and charisma, but outside the office, he was a dullard. At home, he was clueless. If he hadn't been a Winston Tyler, he might have traveled through time unnoticed.

In truth, his marriage was a contract, and accordingly, the parties to the contract were like credible corporations, professionally yet distantly honoring all the terms and conditions. He didn't appear to be mean, selfish, or even self-absorbed . . . just vacuous in the ways of the world outside of work. At company social functions, he was like an old truck in need of a tune-up. His timing was palpably off. For his occasional family vacations and trips with Marie, it was like he wouldn't go anywhere he'd never been before, so they went to the Fontainebleau.

Marie always followed her husband, one step behind and one step to the right. She was the perfect wife and a good mother. The Tyler household may have been different, however, if she had been more assertive, but like the employees at Tyler Financial Services, she deferred to her husband on most all issues.

She came from solid stock, the Dewinter clan having sailed to the new world in the hold of an English merchant ship in 1756. They were from Radnorshire, a historic county of mid-Wales, part of the ancient kingdom of Powys, where a Norman knight, de Winton, was granted vast estates on the English-Welsh border, including Maesllwch Castle. Marie had her framed certificate on the wall of the study, the one announcing her membership in the Daughters of the American Revolution. She never missed the annual gathering of the DAR.

And so it was that within this milieu of non-discipline and ill restraint, the third and last Winston Tyler became older. One would normally say he *grew up*, but in Tyler III's case, that would be an oxymoron. It didn't take a rocket psychiatrist to predict the type of person T-III would become when the primary responsibilities of parental leadership, management, and oversight were left to the kaleidoscopic vagaries of juvenile peers and recalcitrant youth. Like his father and grandpa, Tyler III was blessed with smarts—an interesting amalgamation of his gene pool, brains, and street smarts. Though he had danced around the borderland of law, he had certainly never spent even a night in the pokey.

He smiled at the recollections as he drove the big Maybach toward his office, waving to all who glanced his way.

Barbara watched as Tyler drove away, and then listened for any sounds from upstairs. It was Saturday, and the kids would be sleeping in. The old man wouldn't come down until lunch. Not only did she no longer care that Winston went to his office every Saturday morning, she was relieved. It was her time, so she went to get her coffee and grabbed the ornate bottle of Courvoisier from the cabinet and poured two fingers of the pungent liquid into her cup. In combination with her already fragile state of mind, the smell of the cognac sent her to another place in another time.

It was three years ago—one year before she had sold her successful designer business. She still didn't know why she had done that. It certainly wasn't the money. The business had been her identity, her independence, and her second love. Yes, she had once been in love. The most honest answer might simply have been attrition, but with the sale, she soon knew that it was the time when she first admitted her reality of regret. Up until that fortuitous meeting with the woman stranger, Barbara had failed to recognize her own denial and self-imposed smoke screen of integrity and truth. Ignorance may not have been blissful, but it had beaten the alternative . . . reality.

The show had been in Chicago. As she sipped her coffee, she recalled that unplanned meeting and wondered about the woman.

"I wouldn't have gotten on that plane at Sea-Tac sixteen years ago," Barbara answered in a soft, wistful tone as she stared out at the fog-shrouded runways of O'Hare.

"I don't understand," said the stranger, a woman perhaps a decade older than Barbara.

"Well, it's lucky I don't know you," Barbara said in a flatter tone, the reverie disappearing. Following a deliberate pause, she whispered, "Funny isn't it?" Then, making eye contact with the woman, she added, "It's so easy to be honest with a stranger . . . not much risk."

The two women were sharing a table in the airport bar, their flights delayed due to heavy fog. They'd been passing the time with the usual introductory exchanges that result when strangers are put together, constrained by the bond of inconvenience, when the woman had encroached upon the unspoken boundary of intimacy with the question: "If you could change one event in your life, what would it be?"

The woman had listened to Barbara's answer, her chin resting on the thumbs of her church-steepled fingers.

"People who know me would be shocked," Barbara stated, traces of a coy smile forming on her lips. "Perhaps more by how quickly I answered than by the answer itself." After a nearly un-comfortable pause, she penitently murmured, "It was obviously a whimsical response."

Their eyes met . . . knowing . . . acknowledging the backslide.

Earlier, she had left McCormick Place with plenty of time to return the rental car and get through airport security, so she'd taken South Lake Shore Drive. Something had reminded Barbara of that long-ago weekend in Chicago she'd spent with David. The recollection had segued to random visions she had so profes-sionally and dispassionately packed away in the dark corners of memory, like the forty-foot Morgan that David berthed in the harbor near Seattle.

"Your question caught me in a nostalgic moment." Barbara swirled her snifter, inhaling the robust fumes of Courvoisier. She seemed to become defensive, with an undertone of faux loyalty. "For one thing, I'm quite happy with my life. My husband's a fine man, respected and most successful. I have great kids and an accomplished career."

Yes, she was a celebrated fashion designer. After leaving Seattle, and David, she'd put her heart and soul into achieving her career goals. She'd done that with blind tenacity, blinkers on, full steam ahead, deaf to the sporadic, aching laments of her cri de coeur. She wasn't sure she could have become the woman she was today if she hadn't made that choice and walked through that boarding gate without a backward glance.

"A fine man . . . a respected man . . . interesting descrip-tion," the stranger offered, noting the absence of any passion in Barbara's claims.

Barbara stared at the woman. She absorbed the innuendo, es-chewed the faint rumble of guilt, and opted for the fantasy.

There'd been a midsummer mist on Puget Sound as they'd tacked out of Admiralty Inlet, heading north toward Whidbey Island. She'd marveled at David's control of the wind and sails. They would zoom along on a reach until he pushed out the billowed sail, running with the wind. She'd felt a lustful spasm when he winched in the boom on a close-haul with his muscular arms and fluid motion and shouted "Hard alee."

"I'm a practical person. Love versus career is a textbook approach-avoidance conflict. I made the right choice." Sounding discomposed and less than convincing, Barbara signaled the waiter. Uncharacteristically, she'd downed the brandy quickly. "I can't afford the burden of regret. After all, it seems that regrets would not only negatively affect my karma, but would in many ways invalidate the choices I've made, and what I've accomplished." Barbara looked at the woman, feeling vulnerable, imploring support.

The woman watched Barbara for a while with an empathetic expression and an affirmative nod. "At some point in my life, I stopped critiquing other people's choices," she claimed. "I found that I so despised being judged that I simply removed it . . . even from my responses . . . first, verbally, and over time, as part of my whole cerebral process. I was living my life initially based upon my parents' and family's criterion, and later upon my husband's. Choices should be supported." After a pause, she added, "I understand."

Barbara's time with David had been both easy and deliciously agonizing. Yes, she'd lost herself in some ways, and compromise had come too easily, but that pain of separation was a most wonderful form of masochism. It was only when reality began to creep back into their relationship, hat in hand, before demanding its rightful place, that she'd made her choice, standing tall and strong, not allowing herself to be undermined by the frailty of human nature and emotion. Yes, the choice had been academic and analytical, manipulated by perception, interpreted through the dictates and structures of rules for success and people of influence in her life.

"So, are you in the throes of a . . . choice?" Barbara queried with a glint of apprehension in her eyes.

"I was." The woman sipped her coffee, thoughtful, seemingly nodding to some distant, silent tune. "From the time I found I couldn't have children until my mother developed cancer, I was living in an . . . almost comfortable state of denial. I was never demanding . . . didn't need Technicolor, but I did know what it was . . ." Some far-off memory seemed to prompt a nostalgic escape before she continued. "Basically, we got married because all our friends were married. Their lives were changing . . . ours weren't, and we were being nudged out of the group. It wasn't mean. I don't think it was even intentional, but in subtle ways, it was certainly there. Hard to explain, but it seemed like we were all at the same show, and yet we were the only two without a ticket."

Barbara's expression said she was absorbing, slowly nodding agreement, but she was elsewhere. "Winston's a good man. I have always liked and respected him." The redundancy of that description prompted the woman to give a questioning glance at Barbara, whose protracted shake of the head answered the unspoken question. She wasn't offended.

The woman continued. "When my mother got sick, she went in a hurry. That's when I saw that I was my mother. True, without kids, but less than happy and so little time. So, after some sleuthing, I made a strange call, which in turn initiated a long-overdue discussion with my husband Bill. That was six weeks ago." The woman's mien punctuated the last sentence in a way that stated, "So there you have it."

When the silence finally became awkward, there was disguised pain in Barbara's simple question: "So what now?"

"I'm going to Denver to meet the man I should have married thirty years ago . . . See what happens." She paused. "And . . . I feel the need to thank you."

The women exchanged silent expressions. Barbara didn't ask the obvious question, "For what?" She already knew the answer. She envisioned the blanket of fog over Puget Sound. She felt a chill, guessing that Seattle would probably get rain today.

The two women peered out the tall glass window, lost in separate thoughts, and noticed that the fog was lifting. Barbara checked her wristwatch. Their flights would be leaving soon.

Barbara's recollection of that exchange was eerily vivid . . . and painful. She had compromised both principle and reality. She missed her fashion business. She missed David.

"Hey, Mom, whatcha' doin'?"

Barbara's strained visage melted. Her smile was warm as she watched her little *ethereal elixir* go to the fridge. "I'm planning your uncle Billy's favorite meal, honey," she said.

Shotsy Tyler was eight. She was a fireball of kinetic energy and motion. She reminded Barbara of herself when she was young. Oh, to have that attitude again.

"Goody-goody. When's he comin'? Does he still have his pony-tail? Think he'll bring me something?" Shotsy spouted her questions like a Gatling gun. She grabbed the milk and her Just Bunches cereal, which she always ate in her big blue bowl. Her brother called her the "cereal killer."

Barbara drained her juiced coffee. "Not until next week, honey. I'm just getting some things ready. He probably does still have a ponytail, and I don't know if he'll bring you anything, but don't say anything if he doesn't." After a pause, she added, "You know you are his *little star*."

"Yup . . . I love Uncle Billy."

Barbara grinned and thought, *Yup, at least the two of us do.*

CHAPTER 2

A Week Before
Carlsen Law School Lecture Hall—Minneapolis

"Well, it appears that justice was served after all, but it had nothing to do with the law. It is only related to O. J. Simpson's extreme hubris and idiocy. To quote our enlightened friend, Mr. Gump, 'Stupid is as stupid does.'" Billy Stone raised his upturned palms in the air, the gesture almost daring any of the students to debate the issue. "In the end, the trial was only distantly related to Simpson's innocence or guilt. It was about racism—social injustice—a statement from the black community to the L.A. Police Department. Hell, I've never met a soul, white or black, that doesn't think he's a murderer." After a look around the room, he added, "Rodney King was the epicenter of that trial."

One student raised his hand. Billy nodded.

"So what is your take on the legality of the so-called sanctuary cities?" the student asked.

Billy pondered the question. The room was quiet as he strolled in front of them. "The answer to that is lengthy, subjective, and certainly interpretive. From a strictly legal standpoint, the states and the cities have the authority to protect those residing within their borders. They can't be forced to cooperate with the feds. On the other hand, they can't prevent the federal authorities from entering their domain, making arrests and removing individuals or even groups that have violated the law."

Again he paused, considered, and continued.

"Like the jury statement in the Simpson trial, the reality, however, centers around social and security issues and the power of the citizenry. If, among those being provided sanctuary, there are illegals, perhaps previously convicted criminals, allowed to roam free, and they pose a threat to law-abiding residents, it is the will of the people to protect themselves by protesting and influencing change for the common good." He looked from the students to the faculty. "The people must understand the real agendas of their politicians."

After letting the statement hang, Billy glanced at his watch before his closeout.

"Seems the bell is about to ring. Perhaps we'll continue this discussion at a later date. Thanks for your attention." He smiled at the students and saluted the faculty members in attendance before leaving.

Billy Stone had been a guest speaker at the second-year law symposium. He had received his LLB from the school in 1976. After Vietnam and his discharge from the service in 1970, he had gone off the grid for a while. There were rumors about his fate, a recalcitrant attitude, and his destinations of choice, but eventually his four veteran watchdogs traced him to a small Mexican town between Puerto Vallarta and Acapulco. He wasn't living with a Mexican *puta*. He wasn't a drug addict or reseller. He wasn't in a fugue state of depression. He wasn't even an expat vet nursing latent hostilities. True, he was into the tequila sunrise of a hovel, a hammock, and a stash of funny cigarettes, but to his comrades, his state of mind was simply perplexing. It was more like contemplative suspension.

"Come on, Peter," Billy said to his friend Peter Akecheta. "All those conspiracy theories and Washington rationalizations are bullshit, and you know it. Plain and simple, Nam was Johnson's economic war. He never gave a shit about us, just as the Vietnamese never gave a shit about democracy." He handed Peter a plastic cup of dark rum. "I suppose you also believe that there won't be any more Vietnams. Shit, there'll be four more in the next thirty years."

Peter watched and listened to the most influential and impactful man he'd ever known. After all, he would have been a broken-boned corpse lying in a shallow grave or a tunnel in Cu Chi Province without him.

Peter's gaze followed Billy's, left to right in slow traverse. To see, Billy always had to turn his head farther to the left because of his glass eye. The mountains, or perhaps hills, descended to the white sand beach. Whitecaps rolled through several volcanic spires jutting from the polychromatic ocean of permuting hues of indigo, azure, emerald, and Persian green. The beach in front of them was seashell white and soft as fabric. To the right was a mile of sparkle and pounding surf. Peter felt a mystical kind of harmony, a place one might search forever to find. So, why again did they want to take Billy back? That picture was out of focus.

"You come to any conclusions down here, Gunny?" Reuben James looked at Billy, his smile big and warm, just like the rest of his six-foot-four, 230-pound black frame. *Gunny* was actually a Marine term, but Reuben liked it.

Billy smiled back. "Would it surprise you, Reub, if I told you that every time I get close to a conclusion, it disappears like smoke in the wind?"

"I 'spose not, Gunny. You always been a damn poet." Reuben laughed and hoisted his rum.

"So, who gives a fuck, Billy? Why does anyone need black and white in a gray world? Metaphorically speaking, that is." This from a short, curly-haired guy named Israel Cohen.

"That's why I was here, before you assholes so rudely interrupted my delusional fata morgana."

"What's a damn fata morgana, Mr. Poet?" Reuben asked.

"Like a mirage . . . a pipe dream . . . in Italian."

"So, our warlord is now the monastery monk from Shangri-La?" This question from a lithesome Japanese man named Akio Yamada.

They all smiled and sipped their rum, feeling, smelling, hearing, and even tasting the salty breeze.

"The morphed patriot. That what you're saying, Ack?" Billy shook his head, keeping the smile. He continued, "It's a cliché that anyone surviving a near-death experience will reprioritize, but I'm beyond that. This ain't the love child shit. It's about trying to reconcile the futility of injustice . . . everywhere . . . all the time. And nobody cares . . . so it seems."

They drank in silence before Reuben finally spoke. "Ain't never gonna change, Gunny. You creatin' some bad expectations or something?"

"You've always been way ahead of me in the real world, Reub."

"There's no stronger bond between the five of us, outside of Nam, than injustice," Israel said as he got up to get more rum. "Most people have a perception of what it is. We've all been there."

More silence until Akio said, "Amen."

A few days with his comrades had cleared the cobwebs from Billy Stone's cerebral man cave. He had made a decision to go home. Reuben had hit the nail right on the old noggin. Because of his ingrained value system and spiritual sinew, Billy had allowed a fucked-up world to create and build up a compost pile of illusory expectations that were misaligned with reality. That reality had overwhelmed him. Racism was everywhere. Injustice was rampant. Stone saw the country his grandfather had died for, and his father and he had fought for, in an irreversible backslide. Where there had always been hope, there was now fear. Where there had been unity, there was growing separation—not just philosophically, but of class, religion, gender, and political parties. Where there had been national integrity, there was dissimulation. And certainly, where the country had once been the hypocenter of kindred spirit, it now spiraled in a maelstrom of self-service and greed. His lesson: create new realistic expectations and manage them with single-pointed resolve, right out of a Psych 1 textbook or some spiritual guru's metaphysical message.

Billy was emphatically aware of the breach between justice and law, but he really didn't understand it. He couldn't syncretize it. The terms were far from synonymous, but in theory, that should not be. A successful attorney might laugh at him.

He could almost hear the words: *From what planet cometh thou, oh rose-colored glasses man? Lawyers can't be concerned with justice. They'd all be in the poorhouse.*

He could fathom that in the courthouse, but outside, a group conscience should dictate verdicts regarding children, entitlements of right and wrong, and fairness for all peoples, for that matter. But people were by nature greedy, power hungry, self-serving, and vindictive . . . themselves the center of the universe. But they were also good, caring, empathetic, generous, and moral. And to think that this great dichotomy had all started over an apple in a fictional land called Eden . . . What irony.

Billy's conclusion was that he would go to law school. Where else would this age-old catechism be debated academically and objectively? He would need to secede his experiential judgments for the time it would take to understand the sometime cruelty of fact. On top of that, Uncle Sam would fund his law degree. Lord knows, he'd earned it.

Many soldiers suffered at least some form or degree of anxiety, stress, and anger when reprocessing back into society after the trauma of combat, and Sergeant Billy Stone recognized that he was no exception. He eschewed the Army's psycho-assistance programs, not because of some inner false pride or external machismo mien, but because he knew who he was and what he needed, and what he needed was to fade. He didn't have anxiety or stress, but he was angry—a generic kind of anger, but one that he could deal with. For him, it was "*Hasta luego, gringos.*" In 1970, he donned his figurative sombrero and headed for the land of gardenias, tequila, *señioritas*, and *serenidad*.

Month after month in the milieu of Mexico, Billy processed his life and those of his four comrades. One thing he knew for sure: he had some unfinished family business when he got home . . . and he had help.

Billy's grandfather had been an Army staff sergeant who died on a tiny atoll called Kwajalein, in the Marshall Islands, on January 5, 1944. According to one soldier's account, he had attempted to grab a live Japanese grenade and throw it back at an enemy machine-gun nest. His timing was off by less than two seconds. He received a posthumous medal and left behind a wife and a fourteen-year-old son named Benjamin. Depending on whom you were talking to, the boy had been named after either Franklin, the great American patriot, or Disraeli, the great British prime minister. Unless you were Mr. Gladstone, you were proud of either claim.

When Benjamin was eighteen, two things happened. One, he left his condoms in his jeans when he took his girlfriend to a dance and later to a friend's basement couch for some TV, grab ass, and extended oxytocin eruptions. Two, he joined the Army. In the case of number one, he soon found himself in nuptial bliss. In the case of number two, he soon (relatively speaking) found himself on a line called the 38th Parallel in the country of Korea. The end game in the first scenario was the birth of William B. Stone, and in the second scenario, two Bronze Stars for valor. Seems time passes quickly when you're having fun. Like his son would do one day, Benjamin left the service after the war, in his case the Korean War.

Benjamin bought a house on the GI Bill, south of the Minneapolis city limits. The area would one day be called Bloomington. It was a small two-story with a white picket fence. No, seriously! He secured a contract with Standard Oil and opened up a filling station. Soon he had some top-notch mechanics and was doing well.

Young Billy was a gifted athlete and shone in three sports. When he was thirteen, his parents gave him a special gift: a baby sister who they called "a surprise." They named her Barbara, after Billy's maternal grandmother.

Everything was hunky-dory until the new city of Bloomington took his dad's business through eminent domain or adverse possession—whatever. Didn't matter. They took it. The value of the business was worth many times what he got, and since the land was leased, Benjamin received nothing from that. The word *bureaucrat* took on a foul odor in the Stone household. It was probably the first time that Billy heard the word *injustice*.

Benjamin was angry. He wanted redemption. He spent more and more time at the local pubs, disparaging the city fathers. His spirit was fractured. Life at home got worse for Billy and his baby sister, let alone the escalating episodes of abuse—first verbal, and later, mildly physical—that victimized his mother. It started to tear Billy apart. His father, his hero, was disintegrating. Could it be something other than just the inequity of his business loss? Was there a latent germ of emotional imbalance growing within this iconic pillar of fortitude and stability? His father wasn't a quitter.

In April of 1967, Billy turned eighteen. He was dealing with an uncomfortable quandary. With the ugly war that was mushrooming in Southeast Asia, the country was in a call to arms, and he knew a draft notice would be arriving soon. He had no intention of being drafted, however. His dilemma was, who would be the watchdog at home? With his father's state of being, he worried about both his father and mother, and just as much, his little sister. He addressed both issues by enlisting and planning a confrontation with his father.

One day, after his mother had gone to Mankato to visit a friend and his sister was at school, Billy found his father at home.

"Hey, Dad, I got some news . . . I joined the Army."

His father's knowing smile said it all. "Wondered how long

you'd wait, Billy." He was sitting in his La-Z-Boy, sipping on a Bud.

"Seems the Army needs more guys like you, Dad." Billy sat down across from his father.

"I'm a little past my prime, son. This one's your war." He gazed out the window. "Nothin' conventional about this one, Billy. Sounds to me like it's all choppers and guerillas." After a pause, he added, "Not sure I understand what we're doing over there, anyway."

"Guess we're honoring some treaty. Spreading democracy to some repressed people. Isn't that what America does?"

After giving his son a thoughtful look, Benjamin replied, "Depends . . . Some people want it, some don't. It doesn't necessarily work everywhere." His father looked at him. "Dangerous place, son. Lotta boys gettin' killed."

Billy saw sadness in his father's eyes, knowing he'd been thinking about that. "Not to worry, Dad. I got the tough genes. We're survivors, right?" There was subtle implication in the statement, which segued into the reason for the chat. "I am a little worried about something else, Dad."

There was a long silence before his father spoke. "Worried about me, aren'tcha?"

"Yeah . . . and Mom and sis," he said, trying to water down the implication.

His father stared out the window again. "I found out some stuff, son. Haven't told anyone . . . Been stuffin' it. Goes back to Korea."

Both Billy and his father leaned back in their chairs, with body language of a coming story and a patient listener.

"My platoon was defending a strategic hill. We were part of

the 2nd Infantry Division, defending a line along the Naktong River. It looked like we'd be overrun. I called back for ammunition. It didn't come, and so we had no choice but to retreat. In the process, I came across a private cowering in a ravine three hundred yards behind our line. He had a box of the ammunition we needed, but was too much of a coward to bring it up." Anger was reflected on his face as he shook his head. "Two of my best men died because of him."

Billy remained silent, knowing that his father wasn't finished.

"When things had settled down, I court-martialed the son of a bitch. Turned out, he was from here. Turns out, he had a son, a few years older than you. The biggest irony is that the son is now one of the top dogs on the Bloomington City Council, and he was the one that pushed through the confiscation of the land and my business. According to one guy at the Legion, it didn't have to happen." Benjamin swigged his beer, an angry guzzle. "Then, couple months ago, I get a letter in the mail. All it said was '*Hi from Dad.*'" Benjamin looked defeated . . . drained.

"Isn't there anything you can do, Dad?" Billy said.

"Guess not. I talked to an attorney who said I could submit a petition to the council to lease from the city, but I know where that will go. Still, they are supposed to meet and address the issue within ninety days." Benjamin gave his son a look of surrender before he said, "So that's the deal. I'm trying to cope with it." As he got up to leave, he turned back to Billy. "Don't worry, Billy. I'm done taking it out on your mother." With that, he left the house.

Billy slumped in the chair for a while. He understood now. He could do nothing but provide support for his father, but he was shipping out to Fort Jackson in three days. He still hadn't told his mom or his sister.

CHAPTER 3

Greenwich
2010

"So . . . the little pumpkin seed loves her uncle Billy." The remark was snide, followed with a loud mock kiss. Eighteen-year-old William entered the kitchen, his comportment resembling his father's.

"Well, the son also rises." Barbara tried finesse with her light double entendre, attempting to ignore her son's insolence.

"That's appropriate. The Spanish Civil War, soldiers, killing, which leads right into the question of when does Patton arrive?"

Barbara just looked at her son, absorbing his vitriol before saying, "For every *real* person of letters, there are ten dilettantes. There's a dictionary in the study. If you're going to refer to Mr. Hemingway's works, at least get the right one . . . in this case, that would be *For Whom the Bell Tolls*." She stood up and walked to her son. "You seem to have an attitude this morning, William. Care to explain it?"

"Yeah," said Shotsy.

Her mother gave her *the look*, the one that says, "I'll handle this." William also gave her a look, the one that says, "Mind your own business, you little twerp."

Admonished, William went to the coffeepot. "Just asking when your brother was going to get here."

"He'll get here when he gets here. And when he does, young man, just as I informed your father, you will treat him with respect . . . understood?" Barbara stood firm.

"Whatever." William avoided his mother's eyes, glancing at his sister, who stuck her tongue out from behind her mother's back.

Barbara left the kitchen, followed by her daughter. William sat on a stool at the counter, sipping his coffee. After a short while, he left his cup on the counter, grabbed the keys to the Mustang his father had given him, and went to the three-car garage.

William picked up his girlfriend and drove to an upscale grill.

Melissa Montagne was from another blueblood Greenwich family. Her father had started at an Esso gas station in 1957, and now owned six BPs in the Greenwich/Port Chester area and part of a refinery in Oklahoma. The man was tough and highly disciplined, and one could see the effects in his opinionated daughter.

"Why don't you like him, William?" Melissa asked before nibbling on her spinach omelet, sans yolk.

"I don't know. My dad thinks he's a jerk." William took a big bite out of his double cheeseburger. "Wears a ponytail and some old Army jacket . . . no class."

"I thought he was a war hero or something."

"So my mom says. But you know what they did in Vietnam, killing babies and shit."

Melissa's eyes widened. "You think he did that?"

"I don't know . . . maybe."

They ate in silence.

"Why's he even here?" Melissa asked finally.

"Darned if I know. Some sort of vet thing, I guess . . . losers."

"Doesn't seem that you know much about anything, William. Don't you want to understand him better? Get your mom's opinions?"

"He's her brother, Melissa. What do you *think* she's gonna say? My dad knows what he's talkin' about."

William switched the subject to his new car, and soon they were both disparaging a number of their classmates.

When they left, he smiled and looked at Melissa, saying, "Let's drive around and see what the poor folks are doin'."

While that was going on, William's father sat at a table in the Kiosko Restaurant and Bar in Port Chester, having just ordered his third martini. He found himself there because Port Chester, New York, was only a ten-minute drive from Greenwich, and the drinking age in Connecticut was twenty-one, whereas in New York it was eighteen, and it wasn't exactly like there was a Greenwich border patrol. With him were two analysts and a high-test broker from New York.

"I first came over here in 1969," Winston claimed. "I was seventeen, and had a fake ID like all my buddies. We'd go to Vahsen's Bar, down the street. I had a 'vette, and all my buddies had old beaters . . . Guess who got the broads." He was starting to slur his words. "So, guess who got a 1970 'vette last year. You guessed it, but don't tell my wife. I keep it at the office, drive the Maybach to and from the house." Winston lifted his drink in the air and winked.

His disciples followed his lead with their drinks and salutes to the great man.

"Anyway, here's the inside dope, fellas," he went on. "We're back into energy again." Winston had read a report from one of his own analysts about a tanker company that was, in his opinion, underpriced. His generic claim was uninformed. "On top of that, this president has been a boon to alternative energy, so we have our eye on wind and solar. Give me a call, and I'll tell you our picks. In the meantime, how 'bout one for the road?"

When Winston Tyler pulled out in his Maybach, it was followed closely by the broker in his Lexus. The two analysts watched them go.

"So, what do you think, Jimmy?"

"I don't think he knows his business, for one thing. But on a personal level, I think he's a pompous egocentric. How about you, Rick?"

"I'm more colloquial. I think he's an asshole, but he does have a couple of good analysts over there. From what I hear, they call Tyler 'DAN,' an acronym for *does absolutely nothing*."

The two analysts laughed, shook hands, and departed.

CHAPTER 4

Fort Jackson
1967

As the state capital, a college town, and a place possessed of old southern charm, Columbia, South Carolina, was a beautiful place in the spring. The year 1967 was the fiftieth anniversary of Fort Jackson Army Base.

Ford Mustangs were the rage around town, but there were plenty of Pontiac Firebirds and Buick Skylarks, as well. In April, the streams were on the run, the trees and foliage swollen with new life, and the collage of colors almost ubiquitous. Latent surges of energy and motion elevated children and old folks alike to high-alert status. One just wanted to be part of the celebration of spring.

At Fort Jackson, on the other hand, high-alert status took on a different meaning. By the end of 1967, US troop levels in Vietnam would reach 463,000, with 16,000 combat deaths. President Johnson saw his approval ratings on the upswing, and economic statistics were, too. Hundreds of thousands of new conscripted were scheduled to go, and accordingly, basic training at

Fort Jackson was a controlled form of chaos. Leadership recognition and promotion was accelerated. So it was when Billy Stone arrived in this frantic state of actuality.

An appropriate word to describe Billy's timing for basic training might be *opportune*. *Serendipity* doesn't fit, nor does *auspicious* or *propitious*, as they imply good fortune, and going to war is not normally considered a good thing. However, if accelerated advancement was the goal, the Vietnam War posed opportunity for soldiers in 1967.

That, however, was not the only reason for Billy Stone's quick rise from E-1 to E-5, from grunt to squad leader, and from follower to leader. Yes, he wanted to emulate his father's legacy, but more so, he seemed pushed by the smoldering coals of anger and injustice that burned in the cavity of his soul. For one thing, he was angry at authority figures. A city council megalomaniac, motivated by revenge, had ruined his father. An administration in Washington had created and escalated a conflict that had no definition, little substantiation, and seemingly little to gain, but was killing America's most valuable assets by the thousands. Billy had come to doubt the jingoistic rhetoric about duty. Still, if he was to go, it would be with commitment . . . his way.

It didn't take long for Billy to become a hard-ass, as basic training has a way of doing that to leaders and survivors. There, the weak are culled from the herd. Billy was a quick study on soldiering. He had an elevated intuition. He was strong and athletic. Mostly, he walked a fine line between fearless and reckless. His superiors recognized his leadership skills almost immediately. Once Billy became eligible to be squad leader, his captain called him into his office.

"You should know, Sergeant Stone," the captain said, "you are exactly what this man's army is looking for in this war. And by the way, I call it a war, though the brass refers to it as a *conflict*. They like to put an earring on a pig and call it a pretty girl. I'm not a fan of duplicity." The captain gave Billy a wry smile. "In any event, the problem is, I believe you bring bigger value here for now, getting these 'cruits ready for battle, so I want to keep you for a while."

If the captain expected a reply, he didn't get one. So he continued.

"Oh, don't get me wrong. You will definitely get your chance . . . just not yet."

Another pause.

"So, any response?"

"No, sir. Wherever I can help . . . sir."

This time, the pause became uncomfortable, so Billy stood up and held his salute.

It was returned as the captain said, "That'll be all, Sergeant."

Billy liked training. It provided an element of power and respect that he had never experienced before. He developed quickly, and soon many of the elements of leadership became second nature. He was tough, but fair. He was both liked by his fellow trainers and respected by his men. He was comfortable in his role and his duties. Still, he wanted the *rush* of battle. He could never really know whether he was a soldier unless he was in the arena, as Teddy Roosevelt claimed. How would he react? Would he be brave, or a coward? He felt that he knew, but he needed to be sure.

Historian Liddell Hart once labeled war as the "realm of the unexpected," and so it was in late 1967 that, without preamble, Billy learned that his time had come.

On October 17, 1967, in the Battle of Ong Thanh, a large force of Vietcong ambushed and decimated soldiers from the 28th Infantry, known as the Black Lions. Two weeks later, at the Battle of Dak To, US forces suffered additional losses, and a week after that, the perception of America changed world opinion with the massacre of My Lai. On November 17, President Johnson stated, "We are inflicting greater losses than we are taking . . . We are making progress."

Twelve days later, Robert McNamara announced his resignation as defense secretary. He had been experiencing mounting doubts over Johnson's war strategy. He joined a handful of other staff members who did the same. The following day, antiwar Democrat Eugene McCarthy announced that he would be a candidate for president, opposing Lyndon Johnson, stating, "We are involved in a very deep crisis in leadership, a crisis of direction and a crisis of national purpose . . . The entire history of this war in Vietnam, no matter what we call it, has been one of continued error and misjudgment."

Four days later, 585 protesters were arrested in New York City, including Dr. Spock. In the meantime, recruits piled into Fort Jackson, and the luxury of extended training schedules was lost to more troop demands in "Nam."

In November, Sergeant Billy Stone entered the barracks to meet the members of his newly assigned squad. He would never forget that moment. Only four soldiers remained from the intense demands of the accelerated training. His distracted and diffused mind was working to process what stood in front of him:

a six-and-a-half-foot black man who was built like Atlas, a lithe-some six-foot American Indian, a five-foot-nine-inch Oriental, and a shorter, curly-haired kid that looked to be Jewish.

What the fuck? he thought. *And me, a white kid, a hick, from the Midwest . . . is this an Army experiment in equal opportunity integration?*

"Good afternoon, gentlemen." His gaze swept from right to left and back again. "This should prove to be most interesting . . . wouldn't'cha say?"

The four soldiers stared at him until they seemed comfort-able enough to look at each other. Then, almost in unison, they barked, "Yes, sir."

Billy just stood there, watching them until he muttered, "Seems we have some work to do." With that, he turned and left them holding their salute. He needed some alone time to absorb and process the many challenges that this merry band of diversity posed. Little did he know . . .

CHAPTER 5

Greenwich
2010

Barbara had cut the veggies, diced the stew meat, and toiled over her special concoction of mildly spiced gravy. Her reverie had faded, and with a comfortable buzz from the coffee cognac, she was putting the bowls in the fridge when she heard someone descending the stairs. She shivered as she prepared for the unpredictable. Her own dubiety became palpable as her aura of tranquility vanished.

"I thought Marie was going to get me. Where the hell is she?" The old man was wearing a ragged bathrobe. It had to be fifty years old. Months ago, Barbara had thrown it in the garage and bought him a new one. He had thrown a fit, and after all efforts to appease and convince him otherwise, Barbara had retrieved the old rag. The worn slippers were of the same vintage.

"Now you know that she won't be coming, Grandpa. We go through this at least once a week." Barbara's voice was firm, but with an empathetic tone. After all, though he wasn't the reason for her underlying irritability, he was certainly part of the problem.

But at least she could process the elements that were the cause. Winston Tyler II, on the other hand, could barely process at all. Tyler II's wife, Marie, had been dead for over five years.

Dementia, she knew, was a general term for loss of memory and other mental abilities severe enough to interfere with daily life. It was caused by physical changes in the brain. Alzheimer's, on the other hand, was a progressive disease of the brain that slowly impaired memory and cognitive function. The exact cause was unknown, and there was no cure. After very extensive testing, it had been determined that the gradual decline in Tyler II's functionality was indeed Alzheimer's.

He scowled. "I don't want to argue with you. You weren't my first choice, you know."

Barbara didn't even pause as she got him his coffee. She wasn't offended. She had heard it before, and had decided long ago to give the barb no power. She had never had any meaningful feelings for the man, and so what was once resentment had morphed into indifference. She had been tempted to engage the old man in a war of words, but he was now so vulnerable that there would be no reward from a pyrrhic victory, which in turn would only diminish herself in her own eyes.

"So . . . do you remember my brother, Grandpa?" Barbara waited while he stared into fictional space, perhaps trying to recollect.

"Tough guy? Soldier . . . with girly hair?"

"Times have changed, Grandpa. Lots of *younger* men are wearing long hair these days." Barbara wondered if he caught the jibe. Probably not. "In any case, he will be staying with us for a few days. I'm making a stew for a dinner. I know you like that."

The old man looked at her, paused, and eventually just grunted.

Fourteen miles away, Tyler III drove his Maybach to a medical clinic. He was not in need of medical attention, but was dropping in on one of his clients, a Dr. James Beloit.

Beloit had shown up at Tyler's office about a year ago. In his experience, doctors were not his favorite clients because many of them seemed to feel that their doctorate degree somehow bestowed upon them certain elements of enlightenment and knowledge about nearly everything, including stock market divination. Turned out, Beloit was there for another reason.

"So, Mr. Tyler, I have come to offer you a business proposal, and my first challenge is to convince you that I am a very thorough person who does his homework."

The men studied each other like two wrestlers sizing each other up, anticipating a direction and what was next.

"I have become convinced that you are a man who can evaluate and . . . perhaps seize upon an opportunity. Would I be correct in that statement?"

Tyler chose to be opaque until the doctor provided more clarity. "That has always been our family business, Dr. Beloit."

The doctor church-steepled his fingers under his chin, appearing to be deep in thought before stating, "Perhaps we can both agree that the government wastes millions—correct that—*billions* of dollars every year?" Beloit looked at Tyler, eyebrows raised with an expression of question, and waited for a response.

Tyler felt like a bass lurking in the reeds while Beloit jiggled the bait. "I believe most intelligent people would agree with that."

"Indeed. So now that the country is experiencing Obamacare and is finding it to be a potential economic disaster, and with the Medicare system mismanaged and out of control, I see the opportunity to profit from that, and in the process, bring benefit to our good senior citizens." Again, Beloit let his statement hang.

Tyler found something oily about Beloit. It was subliminal, but his intuition for such things was inherited and had provided him reason for some of his success. It was not as fine-tuned as his father's or grandfather's, but then, it hadn't needed to be, as he had basically let his inherited money *make* money. His forebears had filled the trough.

"Please continue, Doctor. I'm not sure I understand where you're going with this."

Beloit became a bit more cautious as he approached a boundary beyond which it would be difficult to backtrack. "First of all, this might be a bit outside the family business—something that you might like to do on your own, with me as your partner, of course."

Tyler simply waited.

"Of course, we all have our secrets, like a condo or a car . . . private accounts . . . you know."

At that point, Tyler became nervous. What did this guy know about him? Was his statement generic or pointed at him? "You know, Doctor, I'm not into the innuendo game. I like straight on. So, go ahead and get to the point."

"Okay, sorry. No intention to be obscure, Winston. Can I call you Winston? And please do call me Jim."

Tyler just nodded.

"I need someone like you," the doctor continued. "And if that is you, you would need me to make this work. Basically, it is a plan to provide and enhance certain medical benefits that so many need, but they don't know that they are entitled to them. I can provide them, but do need a separate, nonaffiliated entity, an independent location, and some initial funding. You provide that, receive first monies back to repay the funding, I do the rest, and we both make a lot of dough. In simplest terms, that's the deal." After giving Tyler enough time to process, Beloit closed with, "Interested?"

"I will assume that your plan is on the up-and-up. That said, I will need a lot more detail and some kind of business plan before I can make any kind of decision."

"Of course, Winston. I can have that information for you by a week from today."

After Beloit left, Tyler just sat in his chair, the same chair his grandfather had bought in 1946, the one that had been re-finished and re-padded twice since then. He replayed the meeting several times and concluded that this man and his plan were most likely not on the up-and-up. That, however, was not among the critical questions to Winston Tyler III. Rather, the critical questions were how much risk would he have, and how could he protect himself if things went to hell? And could he show up the damned politicians? He felt sure that he was smart-er than Dr. James Beloit.

He was wrong.

After Beloit left Tyler's office, he sat in his car with a wry, knowing smile. *The only thing worse than a fool is an arrogant fool*, he thought. But the worst was an arrogant, greedy fool. As for himself, he might be greedy, but he was neither too arrogant nor a fool. Admittedly, his disclosure had a few holes in it, but as he looked to the future, if for no other reason, attrition would bring out the truth, and by that time, Tyler would have both hands and a foot stuck in the tar baby.

CHAPTER 6

Vietnam
Late 1967

B illy watched as his squad, along with several hundred other grunts, puked their guts out. The Pacific had been brutal and angry for nearly two days. If the storms that ravaged the transport ship were sending a warning signal of things to come, it was not subliminal. Though most troops traveled to Vietnam by air, his unit was on a converted Liberty ship headed for Da Nang Harbor. Billy had heard that US troop levels now exceeded 450,000, while with the infiltration of nearly 100,000 North Vietnamese soldiers and Vietcong down the Ho Chi Minh trail, enemy troops stood at 300,000. His source was credible. He had little reason to believe the media that put their spin on all reports. As always, it was *follow the moolah*. In addition, he couldn't muster much enthusiasm for celebrating Christmas in the jungle, but he'd always been a believer in playing the hand he was dealt.

Billy had been thinking about his dad—flashbacks and images mostly. It was as if he was avoiding sequence and structure in his recollections, fearful of spending too much time on the *happy days* that he knew would never come again. His father, pushing hard and letting him go, for the first time alone, scared to death, traveling at lightning speed on his new red Schwinn. A picture of the soldier, Corporal Stone, on a desolate, frozen butte somewhere in Korea called Triangle Hill, smiling, indestructible. And his last image of a defeated man, lost in a world of distorted injustice. Irreconcilable antagonisms, probably a deflection from the darkness that loomed ahead.

As Billy and his team filed down the gangplank of the transport, he absorbed the mass of human confusion. He pictured moviegoers escaping a burning theater. His thoughts were corroborated with the declaration from PFC Cohen: "What the fuck?" The predominant sound was one he would become conditioned to, the *wop-wop-wop* of UH-1 Huey helicopters.

Christmas came and went. President Lyndon Johnson made a token appearance at Cam Ranh Bay, his last, offering bellicose but untrue claims about success in the war effort, and a week later, what was called Operation Niagara I commenced, mapping NVA positions around Khe Sanh. Simultaneously, 20,000 NVA troops surrounded the American air base at Khe Sanh, entrapping 5,000 Marines, the start of a 77-day siege.

"I don't want any damn Dinbinfoo," President Johnson told the Joint Chief, referring to the 1954 encirclement of French troops at Dien Bien Phu, which ended in their defeat and withdrawal from Vietnam.

It wouldn't be until early April—200 dead Marines and 125,000 tons of bombs later—that the air base was freed. It was the end of January in 1968 when Billy and his squad became ensnared in the barbarity of war.

Perhaps the most popular example of the word *oxymoron* is

jumbo shrimp. That, however, is followed closely by *military intelligence.* Why? Contradictory terms? Really?

On January 31, 1968, 84,000 Vietcong, aided by NVA troops, initiated a surprise attack on hundreds of cities and towns in South Vietnam. It was labeled the "Tet Offensive," and almost remarkably had not been on the military's intelligence radar. Guerilla warfare now separated troops and units in an uncoordinated and uncontrolled fight unlike anything ever seen before.

"I have no fucking idea where the air support is," Billy said. "There's supposed to be two other platoons around us. Shit, I don't even know where the CP is, but you gotta watch every step you take. These little fuckers have planted bombs, grenades, and punji sticks everywhere."

Billy was leading his squad through a thicket of vines and underbrush not far from a long stretch of rice paddies on his left. Less than thirty seconds after that, he heard a click and a whoosh of air when a spring-loaded board with a bamboo stake nearly penetrated his chest. Were it not for his M-14 that he carried at port arms, he would have been impaled. Then a hail of gunfire. They dropped to their bellies and searched to find where the shooters were.

Billy found a sniper hiding behind the fronds of a palm tree nearly a hundred yards to his right. He was hidden from the shooter by a large tree trunk, and had the time to set, aim, and pull the trigger. He watched as his first kill tumbled to the jungle floor. He didn't have time to process that as he turned to face his men. They were staring at the rice paddy. Shots were coming from reed stands. It took a moment to understand that the reeds were moving, camouflage stalks banded on conical hats. Maybe six or seven.

They were mesmerized as Akecheta suddenly stood up with a grenade in each hand and started running like a crazy man, looping, ducking left and right, fast as hell. When he got close enough, he pulled the pin off one grenade, then the other. With Jerry West accuracy, he lobbed them into the moving reeds. One ignited in the air, spraying indiscriminate death. The other submerged and sounded the dull thump that underwater explosions make. In any event, nothing moved in the paddy, and the next sound was Akecheta, bent legs, fists balled in the air, yelling at the clouds the single word, "Fuckers!"

Akecheta returned to the squad, sort of hat in hand, waiting for some response. Billy and the others were just staring at him. Cats had their tongues. As he joined the team, subdued congratulatory remarks and backslaps ensued, the men looking to Billy for approval.

After a lengthy pause, Billy said, "Nice work, Geronimo. We'll talk later." His tone suggested a mix of admonishment and praise. "Let's get going, men. We gotta find the command post before dark."

Billy processed what had happened as he again started down the trail, glancing at the body of the man he had killed. Yes, it had been reckless and needed to be addressed, but he knew that he had at least one very brave soldier in his squad. In addition, if he had ever wondered whether this would become a cohesive team, he wondered no more.

For his bravery, Peter Akecheta received a Bronze Star.

CHAPTER 7

Peter Akecheta

The Pine Ridge Indian Reservation in western South Dakota was a sad and desolate place, one easily ignored by the government—a place that, in the temporal world, stood still. The reservation was made up of about 11,000 square miles, or 2.7 million acres, making it approximately the size of Connecticut. It played home to the Oglala Lakota Sioux, one of the seven subtribes of the Lakota people, who, along with the Nakota and Dakota, made up the Great Sioux Nation.

The other Lakota subtribes consisted of the Brule, the Hunkpapa, the Miniconjous, the Sihasapa, the Itazipacola, and the Oohenupa. The Dakota, or Santee, were made up of four bands: the Mdewakanton, the Wahpeton, the Wahpekute, and the Sisseton. The three bands that made up the Nakota were the Yankton, the Upper Yankton, and the Lower Yankton. Some of the greatest military leaders and warriors, many of the wisest and most respected political and spiritual figures, and numerous iconic men in American history came from the Great Sioux Nation, but sadly, history failed to present them with proper integrity and give them the recognition they deserved. History books, too, have always had their flaws.

Perhaps at some point in the future, sociologists, anthropologists, and historians would collaborate in the quest for truth and justice, strip out the jingoistic and racist influences that made up the pages of nineteenth- and twentieth-century history as they had depicted this country's first Americans, and properly juxtapose the character, the skills, the leadership abilities, and the benevolent and empathetic response to their peoples, between the white man and the red man. Remove the prodigious advantage of advanced education, and one would be challenged to choose Abraham Lincoln over Chief Joseph as to leadership ability. Could anyone, without prejudice, say that Ulysses S. Grant was a better military tactician than Geronimo or Sitting Bull? Given the times and circumstances, could one argue that Hillary Clinton was a more skilled ambassador than Chief Red Cloud? Men like these emerged from the dust and the frozen tundra, the bowels of poverty, the incessant quest for survival, and they developed in adversity.

And so it was that in a hovel, in the spring of 1947, within the Pine Ridge community, Peter Akecheta was born. He came early, and as a result weighed in at just under six pounds.

In 2007, within the confines of the Pine Ridge Reservation, the infant mortality rate was three times the national average. One in four infants were born with fetal alcohol syndrome or its effects. In 1947, the numbers were worse. In addition, only Haiti had a lower life expectancy rate than Pine Ridge. The chance that Peter Akecheta would survive and become a man were minimal.

Peter Akecheta beat those odds, and they were not the only adversities on the reservation where Peter was born and grew to manhood. One need only interpolate the present-day statistics with what existed over sixty years ago, understanding that regardless of medical, economic, and social advancements, there had been little change. The present unemployment rate was 80–90 percent, the per capita income $4,000. The United States' rate of diabetes was eight times higher at Pine Ridge, where they also suffered five times the national rate of cervical cancer, twice the rate of heart disease, and eight times the rate of tuberculosis. The alcoholism rate was estimated as high as 80 percent, the suicide rate at more than twice the national figure, and the teen suicide rate four times the national average.

With such numbers at play, how could young Peter, or perhaps any young person born and raised in such adversity, beat the odds? In addition to luck, one answer was sociologically generic: loving and caring parents.

The word *akecheta*, in the language of the Sioux, meant *warrior*. Ben Akecheta was born around the turn of the century, 1906. He would have been a brave warrior, if the timing would have been different. As it was, by 1900, America had established itself as a world power. The West was won, and the frontier was no more. The continent was settled from coast to coast. Geronimo and his Apache band had surrendered in 1886. The massacre of the Sioux at Wounded Knee in 1890 had brought the Indian Wars to a close. By 1900, the Indians were on reservations, and the buffalo were gone. Homesteading and the invention of barbed wire in 1874 had brought an end to the open range. The McCormick reaper had made large-scale farming profitable, and by 1900, the US had become the world's largest agricultural producer.

Next came the first transcontinental rail link, completed in 1869. Three decades later, in 1900, the nation had 193,000 miles of track, with five railroad systems spanning the continent. The Central Pacific Railroad traveled from Sacramento, California, tunneling through the Sierra Nevada Mountains to Promontory, Utah. The Union Pacific Railroad was constructed from Council Bluffs, Iowa, to meet the Central Pacific Railroad with the golden spike at Promontory. These two lines became known as the First Transcontinental Railroad.

The Northern Pacific Railroad operated in the far northern United States, from Minnesota to Washington, connecting the Great Lakes to Puget Sound. The Southern Pacific Railroad was founded to connect San Francisco to San Diego in California, but was bought by the Big Four, who merged the company into the Union Pacific. The Southern line ran from California to Texas, and the Atchison, Topeka, and Santa Fe Railway traveled across the southwestern United States from New Mexico to Kansas and then Colorado.

Once the free spirit of the Native Americans had been extinguished, there were few options as to what the warriors and their families could do. In the new American economy, there was no place for the Indian. To classify them as POWs would not have been inaccurate. They had no formal education. They had few labor skills, and they were, in any event, persona non grata, as prejudice and racism prevailed. In the cynical view of Washington, DC, they were a problem.

It would have been hard to imagine that any of these warriors could have had a positive attitude in that environment, but Ben Akecheta was the exception. In an earnest attempt to emulate and amalgamate into the American way of life, and with an eye toward providing for his family—which at the time consisted of two sisters, a brother, and his mother, father, and grandmother—Ben tried his hand at farming. Despite his resolve, the effort proved futile.

The topography of the Pine Ridge Reservation included the barren Badlands, rolling grassland hills, dry prairie, and areas dotted with pine trees. The soil and water conditions were, at minimum, challenging. Even if he had had the agricultural know-how and the proper tools to plant and harvest crops, it was doubtful that he could have made a go of it, but as it was, his siblings and aging parents barely survived. Although his older brother, Two Bears, saw himself as a victim and displayed his resentment and recalcitrance in self-destructive behavior, he did find some reward and energy in Ben's next project. His sisters were passive, but always willing to pitch in.

Ben pictured the wisdom and reward of doing something that could merge the new and the old. One event that prompted his idea was the access to acquiring wagonloads of barbed wire. He was convinced that he could raise a herd of buffalo.

Three years after Ben Akecheta was born, the Pine Ridge Reservation went into mourning. Chief Makhpiya-Luta, better known as Red Cloud, died at age eighty-seven. His mother had been Oglala, his father, Brule.

Red Cloud was more than just a warrior. He was a statesman. His success in decades of confrontations with the US government provided a legacy as one of the most important Lakota leaders of the nineteenth century. He gained enormous prominence within the Lakota nation for his leadership in tribal territorial wars against the Pawnees, Crows, Utes, and Shoshones.

Beginning in 1866, Red Cloud orchestrated the most successful conflict against the US Army ever fought by an Indian nation. Red Cloud's strategies were so successful that, in 1868, the United States government agreed to the Fort Laramie Treaty. Among the provisions of the treaty was a mandate that the United States abandon its forts along the Bozeman Trail and guarantee the Lakota their possession of what is now the western half of South Dakota, including the Black Hills, along with much of Montana and Wyoming. Through later revisions, this became the modern Pine Ridge Reservation.

After the massacre of the Lakota nation at Wounded Knee, Red Cloud continued to fight for the needs and autonomy of his people, only now as a statesman, not a soldier. Throughout the 1880s, Red Cloud was engaged in a struggle with Pine Ridge Indian Agent Valentine McGillycuddy over inequities and graft involving the distribution of government food and supplies. He was eventually successful in securing McGillycuddy's dismissal. Red Cloud cultivated contacts with a number of sympathetic eastern reformers and politicians, especially Thomas A. Bland (who in 1885 founded the National Indian Defense Association), to achieve his ends.

Red Cloud possessed an intuitive and legitimate fear about the Army's presence on his reservation, and knowing that war was no longer an option, he adopted the role of reformer. In this way, he continued to fight to preserve the authority of chiefs such as himself, opposed leasing Lakota lands to whites, and vainly fought allotment of Indian reservations into individual tracts under the 1887 Dawes Act. Red Cloud died in 1909.

With Red Cloud's death came a more ubiquitous and devastating death, that of hope, pride, and the Native American spirit. Red Cloud was an icon outside the boundaries of the Lakota reservation. He was one of the last great chiefs that represented the Native American's resistance to the white man's impugnable belief in manifest destiny, the convenient rationalization to conquer and appropriate territories occupied by the Indians. The future of the Native Americans, as a people, was dim as that chapter of history faded away.

There was a law of nature—or to some, theology—that said that when something was needed, it appeared. And so it did.

As Red Cloud journeyed to "the happy hunting ground," the nascent but soon-to-be-burgeoning reputation of another Native American came to the world. Wa-Tho-Huk (Sauk), translation meaning "Bright Path," turned twenty-one in 1909, and three years later, would win gold medals in the decathlon and pentathlon for the US Olympic team. In a poll of sports fans conducted by ABC Sports, out of fifteen athletes that included Muhammad Ali, Jesse Owens, Babe Ruth, Wayne Gretzky, Jack Nicklaus, and Michael Jordan, James Francis Thorpe was voted the greatest athlete of the twentieth century.

Jim Thorpe was actually a hybrid product of Native American and European ancestry. His father, Hiram Thorpe, had an Irish father and a Sac and Fox Indian mother. His mother, Charlotte Vieux, had a French father and a Potawatomi mother. He was born in Indian Territory in 1888 near the town of Prague, Oklahoma. He attended the nearby Sac and Fox Indian Agency school with his twin brother, Charlie, until Charlie died from pneumonia when they were nine. He became depressed and ran away from home several times before his father shipped him off to an Indian boarding school called the Haskell Institute in Lawrence, Kansas. Two years later, his mother died, and again he was emotionally distraught. He became estranged from his father and went to work on a horse ranch.

When Thorpe turned sixteen in 1904, he decided to attend the Carlisle Indian Industrial School in Pennsylvania. Under the tutelage of "Pop" Warner, one of the most revered and influential football coaches ever, Thorpe's prowess as an athlete began to be recognized. Unfortunately, later in that year, Thorpe became orphaned when his father passed away, and he again dropped out of school and farmed for two years before returning to Carlisle.

In a 1961 speech, President Dwight David Eisenhower said, "Here and there, there are some people who are supremely endowed. My memory goes back to Jim Thorpe. He never practiced in his life, and he could do anything better than any other football player I ever saw." Eisenhower played for West Point in the 1912 game in which Army suffered a 27–6 drubbing at the hands of Carlisle. Carlisle did go on to win the national championship that year, primarily due to Thorpe's efforts as he scored twenty-five touchdowns and 198 points, and for the second year in a row, was voted an All-American. In the previous year, Carlisle was 11–1, which included an 18-15 defeat of Harvard, a top-ranked team in those earliest days of the National Collegiate Athletic Association (NCAA).

1912 was certainly a magical year for Jim Thorpe. Few if any men ever had his versatility and athleticism, which he certainly proved in the 1912 Summer Olympics held in Stockholm, Sweden.

Track and field aficionados would appreciate these statistics. Jim Thorpe ran the 100-yard dash in 10 seconds flat, the 220 in 21.8 seconds, the 440 in 51.8 seconds, the 880 in 1:57, the mile in 4:35, the 120-yard high hurdles in fifteen seconds, and the 220-yard low hurdles in twenty-four seconds. He could long-jump twenty-three feet and six inches and high-jump six feet and five inches. He could pole vault eleven feet, put the shot forty-seven feet and nine inches, throw the javelin 163 feet, and throw the discus 136 feet.

Thorpe encountered little resistance in winning his gold medals, taking first place in eight of the fifteen individual events comprising the pentathlon and decathlon. In the decathlon, he placed in the top four in all ten events, and his Olympic record of 8,413 points would stand for nearly two decades. In an interesting anecdote, Thorpe was able to accomplish his achievements despite the fact that someone had stolen his shoes just before he was due to compete, and he found some discarded ones (not even a pair) in a trash bin. It was with these shoes that he won his medals. One shoe was bigger and required him to wear an extra sock. As the medals were presented, several sources recount that, when awarding Thorpe his prize, King Gustav said, "You, sir, are the greatest athlete in the world," to which Thorpe replied, "Thanks, King."

The multi-talented Thorpe decided to play baseball in 1913. He chose to play for the 1912 National League Champion New York Giants, and with his help, they repeated that status in 1913. Between 1913 and 1919, Thorpe played for the Giants, the Cincinnati Reds, and the Boston Braves, accruing a respectable record in the process. His earlier baseball career, however, was the cause for controversy that stripped him of his Olympic medals, which were not reinstated until 1983, thirty years after his death.

His least documented athletic achievements were on the basketball court, but in 1926, he became the main attraction of the World Famous Indians (WFI) of LaRue, Ohio, and toured the Eastern Seaboard for several years. By that point, where Jim Thorpe showed up in an athletic uniform, so did the crowds.

His first love had always been football. In the same year he was playing baseball for the New York Giants, 1913, he also started his professional football career. In 1915, Jim signed with the Canton Bulldogs. His team won titles in 1916, 1917, and 1919. During his professional football career, he received many awards, including first-string all-pro, and in the inaugural year of the Football Hall of Fame in 1963, a decade after his death, he was inducted into the hall along with sixteen other players. He ended his career in 1928 with the Chicago Cardinals at the age of forty-one. In the stands on the day of his last football game was one of his greatest fans, twenty-two-year-old Ben Akecheta.

On March 28, 1953, Jim Thorpe died in a trailer home in Lomita, California. He was an impoverished and broken man. He had been an alcoholic for many years. When he was admitted to the hospital for the final time by his third wife, she pleaded for help: "We're broke . . . Jim has nothing but his name and his memories. He has spent money on his own people and has given it away. He has often been exploited." Among those recipients of Jim Thorpe's generosity was the Oglala Sioux Ben Akecheta.

The winters on the Pine Ridge Reservation were cruel. Longfellow spoke of coming winters in his tale of Hiawatha. He spoke of Kabibonokka, the wild and fierce north wind:

But the fierce Kabibonokka
Had his dwelling among icebergs,
In the everlasting snow-drifts,
In the kingdom of Wabasso,
In the land of the White Rabbit.
He it was whose hand in Autumn
Painted all the trees with scarlet,

Stained the leaves with red and yellow;
He it was who sent the snow-flakes,
Sifting, hissing through the forest,
Froze the ponds, the lakes, the rivers,
Drove the loon and sea-gull southward,
Drove the cormorant and heron
To their nests of sedge and sea-tang
In the realms of Shawondasee.

When the north winds brought the snow and froze the tundra of the reservation, there was little that could be accomplished out of doors. It was the time of the Great Depression that lasted almost ten years, 1929 to 1939. It didn't seem to be very different on the reservation, however, as depression, both economic and emotional, was always the status quo.

Just as in the olden days, the tribal families would keep the fires burning and hunker down to cold nights and stories. It was Ben's grandmother who was the primary source of history and stories, and when sub-zero temperatures came, friends and neighbors would show up at the well-built and insulated Akecheta home with food and drink and share their memories, cultural heritage, legends, and passed-down accounts. It was in this milieu that Ben's brother, Two Bears, first developed his well-deserved but unhealthy and destructive resentments.

Sparrow Song was a cousin to one of Black Kettle's children. She lived nearby, and was Grandmother Akecheta's friend. She had married a Cheyenne who was with Black Kettle in the fall of 1864. He died on the banks of a stream called Sand Creek.

Black Kettle was a wise and pragmatic leader of the Southern Cheyenne. He was considered a peacemaker. The tribe had complied with the terms of the Treaty of Fort Laramie, but when the Pikes Peak gold rush started in 1859, once again the white man abandoned their promises and violated another treaty. They displaced the Indians from their land, and now, without water and game, conflict again ensued when the tribes attempted to defend their survival.

Two years later, however, despite the unfavorable terms, Black Kettle believed that he could protect his people. Along with the Arapaho, he surrendered to the commanding officer of Fort Lyon and agreed to the new Treaty of Fort Wise. The two tribes were sent to the Sand Creek Reservation in Colorado, forty miles from Fort Lyon, where no crops could grow, no buffalo roamed, and no deer and antelope played. The tribes were forced to raid white settlements for food and supplies, and this again prompted the bellicose US Cavalry, bent on the annihilation of America's indigenous peoples, to justify their savage response. In the process, the US Army produced a Himmleresque colonel named John Chivington.

"So what happened, Sparrow Song?" asked Two Bears, huddled with his siblings around the fireplace.

"In the time of the red leaves," Sparrow Song said, "Black Kettle went to the white Fort Weld for final peace. He returned with his message that the people could sleep in peace. But it was not so." Sparrow Song stared into the fire, the flickering flames reflecting on her wrinkled face and the lone tear that slid down her high cheekbone. "In the morning of the first snow, the devil and his blue coats came to our sleeping camp on thunder hooves, and after, for many moons and many seasons, it was a dark time for our people."

Sparrow Song was minimizing. The three decades, 1860 to

1890, were indeed a dark time for Native Americans, which in turn produced a darker stain on those pages of the history of the United States.

It was the ultimate irony that John Chivington was a Baptist minister. Behind that title, however, was a diabolical and twisted racist. He defined himself and made his intentions clear with his statement, "Damn any man who sympathizes with Indians! . . . I have come to kill Indians, and believe it is right and honorable to use any means under God's heaven to kill Indians . . . kill and scalp all, big and little; nits make lice."

In 1864, Chivington attacked the sleeping village near Sand Creek that was supposed to be under treaty protection, even disregarding the American flag, and a white flag that was run up shortly after the soldiers commenced firing. To use the word *massacre* would be understatement. In total, about 25 braves and 110 women and children were slaughtered. In the atrocious aftermath, he and his soldiers scalped many of the dead, regardless of whether they were women, children, or even infants. Chivington and his men dressed their weapons, hats, and gear with scalps and other body parts, including human fetuses and male and female genitalia. He then proceeded to put them on display in Denver's Apollo Theater and other public saloons.

Similar acts became a trademark of his military career. He was never punished or even censured for his crimes. Eventually he resigned from the military and led a quiet, untroubled life until his death many years later. A town in Colorado was named after him.

At the same time, another military megalomaniac was achieving levels of fame, one who would eventually have not just a city, but a county and a national park as well as a small hillock above the Little Bighorn River in Montana named after him. In many ways, George Armstrong Custer was a more clever and duplicitous evil twin of Chivington, most contrary to the elevated status he would come to hold in American history. If there was truth in symbolism, some historians concluded that he was a rapist who never listened to anyone. When his body was found after the Battle of the Greasy Grass (the Lakota name for Battle of the Little Bighorn), there was an awl in his ear and an arrow shoved into his penis.

After an ineffectual career at West Point, where he graduated last in his class, Custer achieved his highest success as a soldier in the Civil War. That was short-lived, however, as in 1866 he was assigned to the infamous 7th Cavalry. In 1868, Custer commanded a raid upon the Cheyenne that was a repeat of Chivington's massacre at Sand Creek. In November of 1868, Black Kettle had settled his tribe on the Washita River in Oklahoma. He and Little Robe, the son of Geronimo, embarked on a trip to Fort Cobb to again propose a peace treaty, but the commander, a Colonel Hazen, refused to accept their offer.

Right after the chief's return, Custer charged the Cheyenne village at dawn, killing more than a hundred members of the tribe, including Chief Black Kettle. Custer reported that 103 fighting men had been killed, when in truth, it was only eleven. The other ninety-two were women, children, and old men. The slaughter took only minutes, but Custer then killed all the tribe's horses and mules, nearly 800 of them, which took hours.

Custer's duplicity was again apparent when he met with a demoralized group of Cheyenne at the lodge of Chief Medicine Arrows. There, he smoked the sacred pipe of peace and promised never to attack them again—another promise he quickly broke. During this time, Custer abandoned his troops and was court-martialed and convicted on eight counts of abandonment and other offenses. In the following years, he was relieved of his command by President Ulysses S. Grant, this time for corruption. Far and away his most egregious crime, however, was the act of total disregard for the lives and safety of his men at the Little Bighorn. Hubris, poor leadership, and incompetency brought about the massacre of these soldiers.

So how could history paint such a different picture of this man? Once studied, the answer is easy: General Philip Sheridan and Custer's wife, Libby. The first, a man blind to Custer's shortcomings who wanted a soldier who would kill the enemy, would do whatever was required to keep Custer's services. The second was a woman who showed little love but much loyalty to her husband's legacy because it made her very rich. And of course the media gave it their spin—Custer as hero, the Indians as the devil incarnate.

The nadir of the relationship between the military-political complex (to coin a phrase) and the First Americans came during the last days of the year 1890, near another river like the Washita and the Little Bighorn. It was a creek, a tributary of the White River in South Dakota. In Lakota, it was called "Chankwe Opi Wakpala," which in English translates to "Wounded Knee Creek."

The commander of the military division of the Missouri was Major General Nelson A. Miles. Had he been on-site that fatal day, perhaps things would have been different.

Miles was one of those rural, meat-and-potatoes kinda guys. Born on his family farm in Massachusetts in 1839, he studied and nurtured his passion for military history and tactics, and in the fall of 1861, volunteered his services to the Union army. It took only seven months for Miles to rise from lieutenant-grade to colonel in the 61st New York Volunteer Infantry Regiment after proving his leadership ability at the Battle of Antietam.

In the subsequent battles of Fredericksburg and Chancellorsville, he was wounded four times and received promotion to brevet brigadier general. For his valor at Chancellorsville thirty years later, he was awarded the Congressional Medal of Honor.

His post-Civil War career took him to the Great Plains, where he played a leading role in many of the significant battles in the Indian Wars. He was a field commander in the force that defeated the Kiowa and Comanche along the Red River in 1874–75. After the Battle of the Little Bighorn, he was responsible for forcing the Lakota and their allies onto reservations. In the winter of 1877, it was Miles who intercepted Chief Joseph and his Nez Perce band, prompting the iconic chief's historic claim of surrender: "From where the sun stands in the sky, I will fight no more forever."

After a brief stint of fighting the legendary Apache chief Geronimo with questionable success, Miles was posted to Rapid City, South Dakota, in 1890, where one of his authorities was commander of the 7th Cavalry.

On the morning of December 19, 1890, General Miles sent the following telegraph to General John Schofield, commanding general of the United States Army, and another Medal of Honor recipient for Civil War gallantry:

The difficult Indian problem cannot be solved permanently at this end of the line. It requires the fulfillment of Congress of the treaty obligations that the Indians were entreated and coerced into signing. They signed away a valuable portion of their reservation, and it is now occupied by white people, for which they have received nothing.

They understood that ample provision would be made for their support; instead, their supplies have been reduced, and much of the time they have been living on half and two-thirds rations. Their crops, as well as the crops of the white people, for two years have been almost total failures.

The dissatisfaction is wide spread, especially among the Sioux, while the Cheyenne's have been on the verge of starvation, and were forced to commit depredations to sustain life. These facts are beyond question, and the evidence is positive and sustained by thousands of witnesses.

Today, Schofield is remembered for a lengthy quotation that all cadets at the United States Military Academy at West Point, Officer Candidate School at Fort Benning, and the United States Air Force Academy are required to memorize. It is an excerpt from his graduation address to the class of 1879 at West Point:

The discipline which makes the soldiers of a free country reliable in battle is not to be gained by harsh or tyrannical treatment. On the contrary, such treatment is far more likely to destroy than to make an army. It is possible to impart instruction and give commands in such a manner and such a tone of voice as to inspire in the soldier no feeling, but an intense desire to obey,

*while the opposite manner and tone of voice cannot
fail to excite strong resentment and a desire to disobey.
The one mode or other of dealing with subordinates
springs from a corresponding spirit in the breast of
the commander. He who feels the respect which is
due to others cannot fail to inspire in them respect
for himself. While he who feels, and hence manifests,
disrespect towards others, especially his subordinates,
cannot fail to inspire hatred against himself.*

There is no historical evidence of a reply before the events that
took place nine days later.

On December 28, 1890, Chief Spotted Elk (Big Foot) of the
Minneconjou (Sioux) was leading his band of 350 to the Pine
Ridge Reservation. They were suffering from starvation and cold.
He was lying on drag poles behind a horse because he had pneumonia and was too ill to ride or walk. He was informed that four
companies of the US 7th Cavalry had arrived. The commander,
Major Samuel Whitside, demanded his unconditional surrender,
and Big Foot did not argue. He and his people were then escorted
to a settlement of sorts near Wounded Knee Creek, fifteen miles
east of the Pine Ridge Reservation. There, four more companies
and the overall commander of the Seventh, Colonel Forsyth, also
arrived. The eight companies numbered nearly 500 armed men.
They had with them four Hotchkiss, state-of-the-art, rapid-fire
light artillery guns that fired high-explosive two-inch shells.

Bigfoot and his meager band of starving followers encamp-
ed south of a low plateau. Of their numbers, 230 were women
and children. Forsyth positioned the four Hotchkiss guns on the
plateau above them. For all intents and purposes, they were at

that point POWs. Throughout that evening, the soldiers drank a cask of whiskey. Angry epithets and cries of "remember the Little Bighorn" were shouted down at the frightened captives.

In the morning, Bigfoot was brought out and seated in front of his tent. He was told that the Indians would be disarmed. Accordingly, they stacked their guns in the center, but the soldiers were not satisfied, and proceeded to go through the tents, bringing out bundles and tearing them open, throwing knives, axes, and tent stakes into the pile. The women and children were pushed to the ground, as they had been separated from the men. Then they ordered searches of each individual warrior. There were five armed soldiers for every unarmed warrior.

The search found only two rifles, one brand new, belonging to a young man named Black Coyote. Black Coyote was deaf, and when the soldiers tried to take his rifle, he raised it over his head, claiming that he had spent much money for it. The soldiers grabbed him. At this point, a shot was heard. It was never determined where or who fired the shot, but that was when the killing began. At that point, the only weapons the Indians had were what they could grab from the pile.

The Hotchkiss guns opened up, and the shrapnel shredded the tents, killing women and children indiscriminately. They tried to run, but were shot down. In the opening volley of rifle fire, the soldiers shot nearly half of the unarmed men, including Big Foot, who had been separated into a group. The soldiers were in a ring surrounding the 230 women and children, and continued to shoot them. Some ran and sought shelter in a ravine, but were pursued by soldiers and cut down. Some women and children managed to make it over a mile from the camp before they were shot. Many of the dead women were found with shawls or blankets over their faces, sometimes with a child inside, shot at point-blank range. Only a few found places to hide.

One final insult affirmed the mindset of those behind the guns. Even after the shooting had abated, the soldiers searched the dry ravine for survivors. A group of young boys was lured into the open from their hiding place, only to be riddled with bullets.

When the mass insanity of the soldiers had ended, nearly three hundred of the captives were dead. Twenty-five soldiers were dead, and thirty-nine wounded. It was later determined that the vast majority of soldier casualties was the result of crossfire from the ring that the soldiers had formed and the positioning of the Hotchkiss guns. In the subsequent investigation, General Miles officially criticized Colonel Forsyth for this tactical disposition of troops. The survivors, four Sioux men and forty-seven wounded women and children, were loaded on wagons, taken to Pine Ridge, and left in the bitter cold until Episcopal mission volunteers provided shelter.

The Army hired civilians to dig a mass grave, and on New Year's Day of 1891, the bodies of the Sioux were shoveled into the excavation, much like was done at Auschwitz.

Hugh McGinnis, Company K, 7th Cavalry, later provided this account:

> *General Nelson A. Miles, who visited the scene of carnage, following a three-day blizzard, estimated that around 300 snow shrouded forms were strewn over the countryside. He also discovered to his horror that helpless children and women with babes in their arms had been chased as far as two miles from the original scene of encounter and cut down without mercy by the*

troopers . . . Judging by the slaughter on the battlefield it was suggested that the soldiers simply went berserk. For who could explain such a merciless disregard for life?

General Nelson Miles denounced Colonel Forsyth and relieved him of command. An exhaustive Army Court of Inquiry convened by Miles criticized Forsyth for his tactical dispositions. The Court of Inquiry, however, was not conducted as a formal court-martial.

The secretary of war reinstated Forsyth to command of the 7th Cavalry. Some testimony (most likely from Medal of Honor candidates) had indicated that, for the most part, troops attempted to avoid noncombatant casualties. Miles continued to criticize Forsyth, whom he believed had deliberately disobeyed his commands so that he might destroy the Indians. Miles promoted the conclusion that Wounded Knee was a deliberate massacre, rather than a tragedy caused by poor decisions. This was later whitewashed, and unbelievably, Forsyth was promoted to major general.

Frank French, a civilian who helped bury the dead Indians after the massacre, described the soldiers of the 7th Cavalry as "a rotten type of human beings. Some of the soldiers in them days was outlaws and ruffians caught by the law. They were given their choice of going in the Army or going to jail. They always took the Army. It was a disgrace to invite them to a private home or to a public gathering."

There were twenty-three Congressional Medals of Honor, the most for any battle in US history, awarded for the massacre at Wounded Knee. A number of the recipients were from Germany and other foreign lands. A number were described as "drunkards" and "flunkies." Some were convicts serving their sentences as soldiers. A number ended up committing suicide. The descriptions for all their citations for receiving the MOH were sparse and nonspecific, some only two words. Most were not recommended by their commanders for the award, but rather by each other. Several were recommended *not* to receive the award. In the end, General Miles, as the commanding officer of this troop, and the Congress of the United States of America and the president of the United States all individually and collectively passed legislation, signed resolutions, and went on official record as claiming that Wounded Knee was not a battle, but officially a massacre.

One Medal of Honor recipient was John E. Clancy of Company E, First US Artillery. He received his medal on January 23, 1892. His citation stated that he had rescued wounded soldiers. This was a man who was court-martialed *eight* times during his career, twice between the massacre at Wounded Knee and the receipt of his medal. A letter from his commanding officer, Lieutenant Hawthorne, stated that he was *not* recommended for a Medal of Honor or even honorable mention.

Another recipient, Private Mosheim Feaster, Company E, 7th Cavalry, was recommended by an officer who was over a quarter mile away at the time of his "heroic action." Ironically, the three men who signed affidavits attesting to his acts were close friends of his, and in turn, all three of these witnesses also received Medals of Honor.

One recipient manned a Hotchkiss at the end of the ravine where the unarmed women and children sought protection, and he slaughtered them, while another received the award for chasing down a mule that had run away from the conflict.

At the site of the massacre, there was a ravine often referred to in the MOH citations. This ravine was found to be filled with the frozen bodies of unarmed women, babies, and young boys in the site surveys and investigations that followed.

Such were the stories that Sparrow Song told to her family around the fire of their hut as the icy north wind, Kabibonokka, whined and howled through cracks along the windows and doors.

Ben Akecheta was wise beyond his years. In 1937, he was thirty-one years old. He understood the ways of the white man, and the nature of the red man and his plight. Mostly, he understood things about mankind on a deeper level. On the surface, all men were different, and they worked hard to be so. On a deeper level, they were vulnerable and even insecure. On the deepest level, a spiritual level, they were alike. Ben believed in the Great Spirit. He knew that the trick was to understand the attitudes and behaviors needed to survive and grow on the surface. He worked incessantly to become physically, emotionally, and spiritually strong.

Ben's two sisters were much alike—salt of the earth, obedient, and stoic. They were always there, helpful, supportive, and loyal. He never once worried about them. Ben's older brother, Two Bears, however, was a different story. Ben never *didn't worry* about him.

In 1928, after Jim Thorpe's final football game in Chicago, Ben was one of a number of fans that waited outside the locker room to get an autograph. He wanted to be last, but hoped the icon would not run off at the first chance he got. Ben was not disappointed.

"Hello, young brave," the world's greatest athlete said with a smile. "Tell me your tribe."

"Lakota from Pine Ridge," Ben replied, offering his hand. "Ben Akecheta."

"Life is not easy where you live, Ben." Thorpe shook his hand firmly.

"The Great Spirit smiles on me wherever I sleep, Mr. Thorpe." Ben didn't want to let go of his hand. He was in awe.

"I believe you. My Great Spirit is called Jesus, and I, too, am much blessed." Thorpe gave a kind smile to Ben, an undercurrent of camaraderie.

Ben remembered reading that Jim Thorpe was Roman Catholic.

"Do you work on the rez?" Thorpe asked.

"I tried farming crops, Mr. Thorpe, but nothing grows on Pine Ridge but the appetite."

They both smiled.

"I am going to try raising buffalo when I have enough to buy some barbed wire. I have much to learn, however."

"First of all, please call me Jim. Secondly, I have a source for your wire. I will give you my telephone and address. Contact me in two weeks, Ben Akecheta."

"Oh thank you, Mr. Thor—er, Jim. Thank you."

They shook hands again and Ben walked away, forgetting to get the autograph.

Jim Thorpe watched Ben leave. He wasn't that familiar with barbed wire, and he certainly had no idea how to get some, but he liked Ben Akecheta, and he knew he could find the stuff some-where. He looked skyward and smiled. He truly had been blessed and felt the need to give back. One day, it would be his downfall.

Two weeks later, Ben made the call. Two weeks after that, four wagonloads of barbed wire showed up at the house with a note that said, *Don't need payment, Ben Akecheta. You provide four buffalos for tribal members. —Jim Thorpe.* Ben got his autograph, after all. He wrote a thank-you note and promised to keep his idol informed. Unfortunately, the snow had come by then, and the project had to be put off until spring.

It was another cold winter, and for Two Bears, it became one of discontent. The stories told by Grandmother and Sparrow Song around the fire that winter had created anger within Two Bears, which, by the time the streams were running again and the frost line had thawed, had turned to rage. Were it not for the barbed wire and Ben's project, something tragic would have happened that spring. As it was, the tragedy was postponed.

"The white man has created his own story," Grandmother Akecheta said. "The white man tells of fighting and battle. The white man has given honor to many blue coats for shooting the sick, the old, the women, and the children, as well as the few braves to protect them, but none had weapons to defend. Chief Spotted Elk had surrendered as he was dying from the sickness. The blue coats were screaming, 'Remember the Little Bighorn,' as they shot Spotted Elk while he lay on his buffalo hide and poles. Their guns were loud and shot many bullets. The blue coats were not brave. Their own chief Miles called it a massacre, but they still honored many shooters with medals. I still don't understand what kind of people they are."

Grandmother Akecheta did not speak in angry tones, only shook her head with a confused and sad visage. No one asked questions. Ben watched his older brother and saw the dark shadow of things to come.

Ben Akecheta had studied the whole history of injustices throughout the so-called Indian Wars. He despised all forms of injustice, but his intuitive and almost enlightened understanding of human nature was beneficial to him in processing proper prioritization and directing his emotional energy in the most productive ways. He kept abreast of current events both nationally and internationally, and was aware of the unrest in Europe. More poignant to his life, he felt that Franklin Roosevelt was a good and compassionate man, and that he would bring this Depression to an end. Unlike so many tribal members who didn't believe that better economic conditions would benefit Pine Ridge, Ben instinctively knew that if the white man had more money, he would spend more money, and any hardworking and creative person could get some of it.

A plurality of reservation residents languished in a "victim" mentality. Alcoholism was prevalent. Hopelessness was contagious. The old leaders were gone. The reality was that the great chiefs were like Churchill, whose value seemed to dissipate when peace came. A new breed of Native American leader was needed. He would have to be a visionary, a captain of industry, an economics manager, a motivator, a politician with influence, and blessed with a personality to obtain capital, grant money, and support. There would be no magic wand. "Ghost dance shirts" couldn't stop bullets. Progress would take time and hard work and commitment. The whole attitude and thought process of Native Americans would need to change. As good as the elders were as people, change was only going to happen through the young and the children. It seemed that the line of demarcation separating the changeable from the unchangeable ran between Ben and his older brother, Two Bears.

Ben knew for certain that the white man had made money on the buffalo hides—after all, they had slaughtered hundreds of thousands of them, skinned them, and left the meat, carcasses, and remains to rot on the prairies. Their perception seemed to be that the buffalo was inferior to their cattle.

Ben knew better. The American bison, or buffalo, was probably the most utilitarian and efficient animal in all of history. The Indian used every part of the buffalo, from stem to stern, even including their excrement, called buffalo chips, which provided fuel for their fires and ceremonial smoking. The tails were used for flyswatters, decorations, whips, and medicine switches. The stomach lining would harden into cups, dishes, buckets, and other containers. The bladder was softer, and was used for pouches and medicine bags, while the hooves were used for glue and rattles. The thick, curly hair was the source for halters, headdresses, ornaments, pillows, and rope. They strung their bows with the muscle sinew, which was also a source of glue and thread. The beard provided ornament for clothing and weapons while the horns were used for cups, headdresses, ladles, powder horns, spoons, and toys. The bones were made into spear handles, needles, knives, paintbrushes, clubs, scrapers, and toys. The skulls were prayer objects and ceremonial decorations. The brains provided a coating for tanning the hides. The tough leather hides provided bedding, belts, cradles, dresses, gun cases, leggings, moccasins, shirts, winter robes, and teepee covers, while the soft, untanned hide was made into armbands, belts, pouches, rope, buckets, containers, headdresses, knife cases, moccasins, medicine bags, saddles, shields, splints, and stirrups. Most importantly, of course, was the meat. The ribs, the rump, the tongue, and the organs were considered the best meat, while the rest was dried and provided jerky and pemmican. Even with much of the use becoming obsolete, Ben was convinced that every buffalo would provide sustenance and product revenue.

Thankfully, the claim that the buffalo were gone was somewhat exaggerated. Taming the wild and skittish rogues and cows that remained, however, would be challenging. From 1929 to 1937, with the country in economic chaos, Ben, Two Bears, his two sisters, and numerous part-timers who took buffalo meat for service developed a buffalo farm. In keeping with his promise to Jim Thorpe, each season, Ben provided buffalo to those in need.

In the early years, there were many mistakes and setbacks. Initially, rounding up several dozen of the animals was most frustrating. Ben had found a good location with natural rock barriers that provided almost 70 percent of the needed corral, with the remaining 30 percent being barbed wire. Ben had received from the elders what would today be called a use permit. At first, the small herd would run over and through the wire fencing, but with the creation of wolf and man scarecrows, eventually it was under control, and the domestication process had begun. Proper food had to be brought in, and knowledge about certain veterinary skills was needed. Much to Ben's surprise and pleasure, his sisters developed a more than adequate proficiency in this area—some through reading, some through an innate sense of motherhood, and much from finding the contacts and gleaning information from native medicine men and whites that lived on the reservation.

Best of all, Ben found that Two Bears was fully engaged in the business. Credit for that came from Ben's nurturing and supportive attitude and management skill, but in a subtler way, Two Bears was an anachronism, acting out a subliminal desire to regress and revert to a more glorious and romantic time when the Indian was engaged in war and buffalo hunts. Whatever it was, he worked from dusk till dawn, drank his liquor, and passed out on his bunk by nine o'clock every night, seven days a week.

Today, the benefits of buffalo meat are factual. Grass-fed buffalo is lower in calories, fat, and cholesterol than even chicken and fish, and provides 40 percent more protein than beef. Today, people order buffalo steaks in restaurants and buy frozen buffalo burgers in most grocery outlets. These nutritional facts were not only unknown in 1937, but no one cared. Again, Ben suspected, however, that he could, through salesmanship and competitive pricing, create a market for the meat. By the fall of 1937, though regional only, Ben Akecheta had not only accomplished that goal, but had established almost a dozen retail outlets for his trinkets and other wares made from the buffalo in the purest of Native American tradition.

In 1938, Ben's business was operating successfully, and without major incident. In the years after 1939, however, four incidents occurred that would change Ben's life, and they would happen in the following order: Ben's near-death injury, his introduction to Barbara Moon Owl, Germany invading Poland, and the murder of his brother, Two Bears.

Severe weather was as integral to life on the High Plains as was supper, swallows, and cracker-barrel bullshit. Thunderstorms, tornados, and high winds were the rule, not the exception. What most panicked a herd of cattle or buffalo, however, was intense thunder and lightning. And so it was on one late evening that Ben Akecheta went to check on his stable.

When Ben had not returned from his herd check in a reasonable amount of time, his sisters became worried, and so they rousted Two Bears from his mild stupor and pushed him out the door to find his younger brother. What Two Bears found was an empty corral, broken fence posts, and scattered barbed wire. Under the wooden gate was the battered body of his brother, who must have been in the path of a stampede. The wooden gate had saved his life.

Ben was alive, but broken. It took months for him to recover to the point where he could attend to his business. Two Bears and other volunteers had rounded up the herd and mended the damage. Along with his sisters, they kept the business going, but at a reduced productivity level.

When Ben did return, he did so in a diminished capacity, and would thereafter walk with a permanent limp and constant pain. Interestingly, of all the consequences that gave him anguish, at the top of the list was the fact that the Army rejected him for duty when America went to war in December of 1941. He felt crippled—physically, of course, but emotionally, as well. Had it not been for Barbara Moon Owl, he would have withdrawn into a deep depression from which he might never have recovered.

Love at first sight has always been a misnomer. Anyone who has been around knows that love develops with time. Infatuation, hormonal rushes, and star-struck excitement, however, is indeed a reality. For the young, it happens all the time. In Ben's case, it happened when he was in bed—a hospital bed.

One afternoon, he awoke and wasn't sure whether he was still dreaming. There was an angel fixing his intravenous drip. She had long, straight black hair, sculpted facial features, and a heavenly smile outlining straight white teeth. He searched for her wings, straining to see her back.

"Hold it there, cowboy," she said, and even her voice was angelic. "What do you think you're doing? Relax."

"Am I dead?" Ben said in a groggy tone. "The only good news would be that I made it to heaven."

"And what makes you think this is heaven?"

"You. If you're not an angel, I'm not Lakota." Ben smiled.

The nurse giggled. "Actually, you're at the Rapid City Army Air Base medical facility, and I must confess that I can't fly, though I dream about it on occasion." After a pause, she said, "I hope you're not coming on to me."

"Lotta good that would do me." Ben nodded to his arm and leg casts, smiling.

The nurse's angelic smile returned. She finished hanging the drip and turned to him. "My name is Barbara Moon Owl, Mr. Akecheta, and I'm Oglala." And with that, she left.

For the next six months, Ben slowly grew back together. When the casts were removed, he began a painful program of rehabilitation. Nurse Barbara was with him most of the time until he was well enough to leave. He went home in the intense, dog-day heat of August 1939, and on September 1, Adolph Hitler and his Wehrmacht, the mightiest armed force in the history of the world, invaded Poland, and life on Planet Earth changed forever.

For the next two years, America seemed to float in a state of colloidal suspension, half-committed, half-directed, and half-prepared to join the side of right in the defense against tyranny.

During that interim, the country was in recovery from the Great Depression, and would now begin another sideways adjustment. Factories began a process to convert to wartime production. A serious military war machine needed to be built in preparation for the inevitable entry into what would be the last *conventional* war, ever. It appeared as though the Conscription Act of 1917 would need little enforcement, as the line that separated the good from the evil was clear and indubitable, and volunteers would, in the months following the duplicitous Japanese sneak attack on Pearl Harbor, crescendo into a stampede. America's women would become an integral force in the contribution, and hidden within this national endeavor was a most subtle phenomenon: never again would Americans be so indivisible, integrated, and united as a people, yet in this process, Ben Akecheta was left behind.

"Ben, please understand that your frustration is mired in a misdirected guilt," Barbara told him. "Your intentions are clearly admirable, and to my way of thinking, overly patriotic. You must accept the reality of your limitations. You cannot be a soldier, and it is not your fault." Barbara's stoic, yet intense expression was intended to be empathetic. She saw the need to provide Ben with support and direction.

"My brain hears you, Barbara, but my heart's not listening. I hate sitting on the sidelines, watching the game, knowing I could contribute."

It was February of 1942, and Ben and Barbara were having dinner in Rapid City. Ben had worked hard to become as physically fit as he would ever again be, but he still walked with a noticeable limp.

"Well then, Mr. Benjamin Akecheta, how do you categorize the significant food and materials donations that you've been making over the past eighteen months? Huh?" Barbara's visage was a big question mark.

"Least I can do, but it felt good to receive a letter of gratitude from the State Department."

Over a third of Ben's food inventory was going to the war effort. Full resource utilization of the buffalo was again atavistic in nature. As had the Plains Indians of decades ago, the government used the hides, the hair, the soft leather, and certainly the meat. Contrary to her cynicism, Barbara did her part by donating all her overtime to the Army medical facility.

"So, Ben, let's talk about where this relationship is going."

Ben gave Barbara a surprised look before saying, "Okay."

"I love you, and it seems you feel the same." Barbara let that hang.

"You don't question that I feel the same, do you?"

"No. What's not to love? But you've never talked about marriage, or kids."

Ben's reply was delayed. She saw a shadow of sadness cross his face as he stated, "I'm a cripple, Barbara, and I sometimes feel you deserve more."

"Really?" She looked hard at him. "And you somehow think that that is your decision?"

"A feeling, not a decision." Ben held her gaze.

After a while she said, "Ben, you're the finest man, let alone person, that I've ever known. You do more with a limp than most men do with two good legs. I can't imagine not having you in my life to lean on. So if you have a legitimate reason for not wanting to marry me, spit it out. Otherwise, let's move this train out of the station."

Though there were many reasons that Ben loved Barbara, one stood out: her direct and forthright approach to everything.

"Forgive me for not attempting the impossible and going to one knee, but Barbara Moon Owl, will you be my wife?" Ben waited.

Barbara made him wait until she couldn't hold her laughter. "Of course, you dummy, but it has to be a traditional Oglala ceremony."

Ben nodded, and they laughed together, something they would do often over the ensuing fifty years.

"War is hell." So said William Tecumseh Sherman, a man of pure sinew and granite. He succeeded Ulysses S. Grant as the Union commander in 1864. If you went to the movies or watched TV, you had an idea of what it was like, but contrary to the spin that most Hollywood producers created, and contrary to the romantic songs, war was a torturous, bloody bitch.

The casualty count of World War II spoke to the enormity of the war, but it was only part of the story, as it was in all conflicts. If you counted the war-related diseases ending in death, the number approached 85 million people, or about 3 percent of the world population, but the damage ran deeper. Ask the grunt that survived Tarawa, the Brit who came home from the Bataan Death March, or the Jews who couldn't walk out of the pens at Auschwitz without scars you can't see. Ask wives and children who each day peeked through their curtains to see if a staff car would stop in front of their house. Ask your parents and grandparents, and most will decline to talk about it. Those scars had been gathered and stuffed into boxes, taped shut, and stacked away in the innermost sanctum of their souls.

The last momentous decision of the war was left to a diminutive Missouri native who could have in some ways been a clone of General Sherman, Harry S. Truman. He told the Japanese emperor about the bomb and the damage it would cause if the Japanese didn't surrender. The emperor told Harry to go fuck himself, and Hiroshima disappeared. Harry repeated the same caveat with the same demand several days later. The response was the same, and *poof*, no more Nagasaki. History does not explain why the Japanese didn't believe President Truman the first time, or believe him the second time, given the indisputable evidence, but the prodigious tragedy and aftermath of those bombs once again changed the attitudes and philosophies of mankind.

In American neighborhoods, one of hundreds of subtle changes reflecting that metamorphosis was the gradual disappearance of the corner savings and loans. Realizing how quickly life could be snuffed out, the next generation would live in the now. Why save for a future that might not be there?

"I'm pregnant," Barbara said to Ben as he nailed in the last board of the new porch.

He stopped and stared at her for a full minute before the wide smile appeared. "Well, I guess I better get some more boards and turn my office into a room for the *chikala cink* or *cunk.*" Ben thought he had correctly recalled his grandmother's term for little boy or girl.

"You need to brush up on your Oglala, Mr. Akecheta."

"Okay, Miss Moon Owl. Tonight we will discuss names." Ben's smile faded as he recalled the previous year. "I don't know if you ever knew that Two Bears had an American name, as well. He chose to be called by his traditional name, which we respected, but anyway, it was Peter." After a pause, he added, "Maybe we can consider it if it's a boy."

"I just did," Barbara said, "and it will be Peter."

"You're an angel. I still peek at your back for wings. Does the Great Spirit know you snuck out of heaven to have a baby?"

They smiled and hugged, but Ben's thoughts soon returned to Two Bears. In retrospect, the way Two Bears died may not have been inevitable, but it was predictable.

The Axis powers surrendered on May 8, 1945, and Japan followed on August 15, three months later. The world celebrated, and in the streets of American cities, it was a lovefest.

Returning soldiers felt a certain entitlement to some time off before getting back into the grind of jobs, responsibilities, and pressures. Many rewarded themselves with the gift of unrestraint, a well-earned and well-deserved behavioral pass, and for some, it wasn't just through the expression of joy and relief, but rather, pain, resentment, and anger.

In every human being, there is a dark place. It's part of the deal, part of being human. For most, it is rather benign—degrees of benign, actually—like small pieces of the seven deadly sins or similar such shortcomings and frailties, but venial in nature. But no one gets a free pass, not even Mother Teresa, though for people like her, it may be but a tiny speck that is a darker shade of gray.

For others, it is more baleful, with more serious results and consequences. People like that, those who commit felonious transgressions, are often exercising a predisposition to criminal behavior. Many are recidivists and become incarcerated, while many never get caught, and go unpunished. Some seem to operate in the opaque world of amorality, neither aware of nor caring about results or consequences.

Then again, there is a class of human excreta that floats in the septic tank of the severely demented and immoral. These are men who, from irrational and unfathomable reasoning, commit the kinds of crimes that define the worst of the species. They're called psychopaths. Adolf Hitler, Pol Pot, and Joseph Stalin come to mind, and it is their inhumanity that plants deep seeds of fear, anguish, resignation, and hopelessness in every human being, and provides the spiritual initiative that Francois-Marie Arouet, commonly known as Voltaire, referred to nearly three hundred years ago when he claimed, "If there were no God, it would be necessary for man to invent him."

The death of Two Bears was simply an unfortunate set of circumstances and ill timing.

During the Christmas season of 1945, Two Bears and a friend drove to Deadwood. The historic town was a magnet for fun and excitement. Prostitution was legal, and gambling was still king for another eighteen months before it would officially close in 1947. Though it was fact that Jack McCall shot Wild Bill Hickok in the back of the head in No. 10 Saloon in 1876, the original bar had burned down in 1879 and moved, and several other bars put claims on some piece of that incident.

Two Bears and his friend found a place at the bar of the Bullock Hotel, which was loud and rowdy. After several beers, a nearby patron, wearing a service cap and seemingly inebriated, spoke up. His comment was directed at Two Bears and his friend, but the vet was looking at his drinking mates.

"So where do you guys think Sitting Bull and Geronimo were stationed during the war? Germany? Pacific? Or was it at their local watering hole?" He pointed to Two Bears.

There was immediate tension, but the two Indians chose to ignore the racist slight. Soon, however, the insults continued.

"Seems the cat got their tongues, huh? Don't defend our country—don't defend themselves." Again silence, until he added, "These redskins sure like their firewater, huh? Think they know the ghost dance? I think they should do it for us. Whaddya say, boys?" With that, there was muffled laughter.

Two Bears was beginning to boil with anger. He knew what was coming, and fingered his knife. He knew that their only chance to avoid violence was to leave. He stood up and grabbed his friend by the sleeve.

"Hey, Chief, where the fuck you think you're going? You ain't leavin' till you do the dance, got it?" The man had walked behind Two Bears, attempting to block his retreat.

Just as one winces as a physiological reaction to a needle, so can a psychological stimulus produce a physical response. Two Bears was six feet tall and 210 pounds. He was not only tough, but lightning quick. In the blink of an eye, he had the man by the neck, and the blade of his knife was touching the skin just under the man's jaw.

"We don't dance for no drunks. We're leaving now. We don't want no trouble. Are we agreed?"

The man's eyes were big as golf balls, screaming with fear. He nodded up and down very gingerly.

Two Bears motioned for his friend to leave. When he was at the door, Two Bears slowly pulled the knife away and headed to join him. At that point, the man pulled a gun, aimed, and shot

Two Bears in the back. There was silence throughout the bar, except for the sounds of pain coming from Two Bears as he lay on the floor, his blood leaking into a growing pool.

"He tried to kill me!" the man screamed as he looked around for support. "You all saw it. The redskin almost killed me!"

People just stared at him, except for a woman who rushed out, mumbling about finding a doctor. The man continued to look for affirmation from his pals and anyone else. They just stared at him, a collective visage of disgust, until a tall, lithesome man wearing his unit fatigue jacket and lid walked over to him, stopped, and spoke.

"Take off that uniform hat, you coward," he said before slowly walking out.

Two Bears was buried on the reservation. Apparently, the man who murdered him was not held for charges, as enough people testified that Two Bears had threatened him with a knife. The man left Deadwood alone. Ostracism and humiliation had their own form of punishment.

The Akecheta household was devastated. Grandmother Akecheta's mantra had always been, *Be happy with who you are and what you got*, but try as she might, she had spent her life as the victim of racism, and in the end, until her death in 1949, she could only talk about the injustices perpetrated by the white man.

Ben responded on the outer reaches, the borderland of his tolerance levels, accepting the injustice as he had so many others, and directed his energy into moving his family forward. Vindication, he knew with certainty, had never worked. He was a man who would never know his own sagacity, his gifted intuition, and his magic. He absorbed the tragedy because he had no choice. He was the leader. He was the unrecognized Chief Joseph.

He was the quiet messiah, and what Ben looked forward to was having a son.

The child was not named Peter. You shouldn't name a girl Peter.

"Her traditional name will be Weayaya," Barbara said. "'The setting sun.' But we agree that we will call her 'Sue,' a play on words." She hugged her hero.

"Once again, you have sprouted wings, my love," Ben said. "Why does the Great Spirit not give me the gift to see them?" He was high, feasting on the thought that another angel would live in his house. Ben's little papoose was so like him that he didn't recognize the similarity.

In the autumn of 1946, Barbara told her husband that Weayaya was going to have a sibling, and in May, when the prairie began to green, the animals awoke from their long hibernation, and the flocks of vacationing geese returned to build camouflaged stick nests near the pond banks, Peter came into the world, wide-eyed and screaming to behold its magic and wonder.

By 1948, the buffalo herd had expanded to include cattle. Ben was providing food and products to fourteen outlets. His operation had become too big for him to handle, but fortunately, his sisters had both married solid men of character, to whom Ben had given substantial ownership, and with their help, business was strong.

Myth has it that there is a place where time stands still. Pine Ridge was no myth, and as the years passed, conditions remained the same and people continued to struggle. The Akechetas were an exception. Not only was their business expanding, they were providing supplement to other reservation families, as well. Ben Akecheta was the most respected member of his tribe.

When young Peter was not helping his father with the family business, he was developing his passion. He loved to run. In 1962, when he was fifteen years old, he was the fastest runner on the reservation, and was equally accomplished at long-distance trials. Ironically, it wasn't Peter Akecheta, but his hero and mentor, another Oglala Sioux from Pine Ridge, who was getting all the attention.

In 1938, only months before Ben Akecheta's accident, Makata Taka Hela (Respects the Earth) was born only miles from Ben's corral. His American name was Billy Mills, and he would go on to become an American icon, but in 1962, he was a Marine lieutenant.

After attending the Haskell Institute for Indians, like Jim Thorpe before him, Billy Mills went to the University of Kansas on an athletic scholarship. By the time he graduated, Billy had been named an NCAA All-American cross country runner three times, and in 1960, he won the individual title in the Big Eight cross country championship. The University of Kansas track team, coached by Bill Easton, won the 1959 and 1960 outdoor national championships. Billy graduated with a Bachelor of Science degree in physical education.

Upon graduation, Billy turned his attention to the military, and was commissioned a lieutenant in the US Marine Corps. He could not, however, abandon his love for running, and after training for a year and a half, he qualified for the 10,000 meters and marathon events on the American Olympic team. The 1964 Olympic Games were held in Tokyo, Japan.

Billy's qualifying time was almost a full minute slower than the favorite's, Ron Clarke of Australia. The pundits were all focused on Clarke and his highly anticipated duel with Mohammed Gammoudi of Tunisia. Billy's intriguing story was certainly newsworthy, but as a contender, he was completely discounted. The field for the 10,000-meter event included former Olympic gold medalists and world record holders. No American had ever won the 10,000-meter race in Olympic history, and no one expected that to change in Tokyo.

There have been few more exciting Olympic calls than the finish of that race. Billy Mills would later state, "The ultimate is not to win, but to reach within the depths of your capabilities and to compete against yourself to the greatest extent possible. When you do that, you have dignity. You have the pride. You can walk about with character and pride no matter in what place you happen to finish."

Billy did indeed reach deep to mount a final charge that sent him first across the finish line almost fifty seconds faster than his previous best time. In the process, he set the Olympic 10K record at 28:24.4. As of fifty years later, no American has duplicated his feat.

In the years that followed 1964, Billy Mills would receive many awards and accolades as an athlete, as a Marine, and as a great human being. With each award, Peter Akecheta would cut out the articles and tape them on his wall. Like his idol, Billy Mills, Peter Akecheta knew at an early age that he wanted to distinguish himself as a Native American representing his family, his people, and his country. That he would do.

Though no one could ever deny that Peter grew up in adversity—and on a comparative basis, poverty—it was also true that he did have the best of a bad deal. His father was a great man, and had worked hard to provide. His mother was the hardwood trunk of a family tree with a canopy of strong branches. Peter was loved, and as a result, loving. He had inherited the best of his parents' genes and personalities. He understood the concept of life being hard, but from that came character and value. Things that came easy had little value. In addition to excelling at the reservation high school, Peter was homeschooled every night by his mother. He took nothing for granted, and so, soon after his nineteenth birthday, and against his mother's wishes, Peter joined the Army.

"Ben, have you been reading about this conflict in Vietnam?" Barbara asked. "For God's sake, our son could be killed."

"We do not control the choices of a nineteen-year-old, only influence. He's doing what I wanted to do over thirty years ago. I'm sorry, my love, but I can't intervene. The choice is his." With that, Ben walked away.

CHAPTER 8

Fort Jackson
1967

It was as if a spaceship had stopped at Pine Ridge, picked up Peter, and dropped him on the red planet. He had heard of South Carolina, even seen pictures in a magazine, but the world of Fort Jackson was a far cry from the reservation. Not many Indians. White kids, blacks, even Orientals, but not many Indians. On top of that, the place was named after a guy who was not listed on the Native American list of most admired. He had heard the handed-down stories about the Trail of Tears from his grandmother, and Andrew Jackson was the bad guy in that operation, yet the white guys looked at him with great admiration. Most, however, didn't know about the Trail of Tears. One guy Peter spoke to about it thought it was a rock group.

Few recruits were in the kind of shape Peter was in. For most, the physical rigors of basic training were very taxing. For Peter, it was a light workout. After all, his whole life had been one of basic training—running, hunting, tactics, and survival. He was the highest-rated recruit in his class after six weeks, followed distantly by a Jewish kid from a place called Greenwich, Connecticut.

The Jewish kid was a bit of a physical putz, but made up for it with an intense commitment and an extreme degree of hard work. Peter could see that he was trying to prove something with his steel-willed determination, but nevertheless, the kid had earned his respect. Peter thought it was somewhat humorous that his name was Israel. Peter had tried to befriend some of the other recruits, but probably out of jealousy or some other shortcoming, they kept their distance. Still, he sensed something in the Jewish kid that prompted him to try again.

Peter had never met anyone like Israel. True, Peter had lived in a cocoon, the enclosed environment of Pine Ridge, and though there was a smattering of white people, they were poor or inter-racially mixed, and few were his friends. His father's teachings and example had prevented Peter from absorbing the deep and emotional dislike for white people that permeated the reservation. On the other hand, he couldn't avoid the imbedded feelings of distrust, which, though unspoken, Peter knew his father shared. History had proven that the white man was not entitled to the trust of Native Americans. Israel, on the other hand, was different.

"Did you enlist, Israel?" Peter asked as they sat together on chow break.

"Yes, I did." His short answer implied a tightness that attempted to close the door on conversation.

After a bit, Peter tried again. "So, why did you volunteer?"

Israel took a long time before he replied. He seemed to be solemnly processing the question. Eventually, he set his food down and looked at Peter. "My father got me into Yale and secured a draft deferral. I planned to go along with it, but went on vacation instead. I sort of found out who I was, or at least who I wanted to be. I needed to enlist." He took a deep breath. "The group I'd hung around with was like me. Arrogant little rich kids born with the proverbial silver spoons, living off the fat of the land, with influential families who manipulate the system and bow to the gods of money and success. I looked at my life. I was a nothing, a zero, a taker. I had no character. Nothing was of value to me. I was a spoiled, scared little Jew who was his father's pawn, and in the end, I was a draft dodger. So, Peter, how 'bout them apples?"

Peter silently regarded Israel.

Israel was almost out of breath. He shrugged in relief as if jettisoning a great burden. He wasn't looking for a reaction, certainly not patronizing support. After a quiet delay, he added an epilogue. "I can't believe I said that. Seems there's something about you I trust. Maybe it's a feeling you won't judge me. Regardless, it feels good to have told someone." Israel smiled in relief.

Peter smiled back. "Seems that your intensity for honesty is on a level with your determination to excel. Thank you for your trust, Israel. You have my respect."

That was the first of their exchanges, and after that, the conversations flowed easily, like air from a punctured tire.

CHAPTER 9

Vietnam
1968

The Tet Offensive was war at its worst. Check that, the Civil War was worse, but it was bad. What am I saying? All war is bad.

Anyway, Billy's squad was part of an infantry battalion defending Saigon, this based on a hunch by Lieutenant General Fred C. Weyand. Amid this union of the uncoordinated, this was a lieutenant general who did have his shit together. A veteran of World War II in the Pacific, he was later nicknamed the "Savior of Saigon." Without that hunch, Saigon would have been overrun.

"These assholes are on a mission to occupy the Imperial Palace," Billy whispered to his squad as he walked the line. "NVA are farther east. We got the Cong . . . sneaky bastards."

There had been sporadic mortar fire and occasional potshots, but as yet, no fusillades of rifle fire. Billy had a bad feeling that they were being set up. It got eerily quiet for about ten minutes, and then the shit hit the fan.

The terrain was more conducive to a frontal assault than it

was to a defensive position. Rises and hillocks dotted the forward positions with trees and jungle to the west and the flank. Billy and his men were third squad, third platoon Charlie Company. Their mission was to protect the left flank and prevent any attempt to encircle the unit. As a result, there were two forward sentries spaced fifty yards apart.

It started with mortar fire, quickly followed by hordes of "screaming banshees," droves of dancing conical hats, black robes with toothless apparitions, skinny legs, and bare feet, armed with Russian rifles with one objective: kill or be killed. At first, they fell like small, dead trees in a tornado, but the sheer numbers just moved the line of fallen enemy soldiers closer and closer to the defenders.

Billy could see the captain yelling into his VRC, and thought he heard, "Bring it on. We're pulling back." Billy knew there was a battery of 105 howitzers a half mile to their rear, and figured that their CO was calling in artillery fire as they withdrew. The lieutenant gave that order.

As they started to pull back, Billy saw PFC Reuben James sling his rifle, and in a crouched position, head into the conflagration. "What the hell are you doin', James?" he called after him. "Get back here."

James just ignored him, and continued his suicide mission to nowhere. That was when Billy looked out at the battlefield and saw that the two sentries were lying near their posts. One was writhing in pain. The other wasn't moving. His squad didn't retreat, but instead fell to the prone position and set down a sheet of fire toward all enemy combatants in the general area they occupied. They saw James take a hit, stumble, and continue toward his fallen comrades. He picked up the first man and turned to the second. That was when he took a second hit, but continued with his mission.

The men could see that he was bleeding, and their fire intensified. Through the smoke and fire, they saw James turn toward their position, a man under each arm, their adrenalin-induced Samson, limping, bleeding, but intractable in his commitment to rescue. He took a third hit, again stumbling, nearly falling, and that's when the fires of hell exploded.

The smoke and high-explosive artillery rounds began to fall. The attack came to a standstill, and the troop of Vietcong dancers began their retreat. At the same time, PFC Reuben James came into their camp, dropped his two passengers, and like a big, dead red pine, fell to earth.

"Medic!" Billy bellowed. "Goddamn medic! Find a fuckin' medic! Hurry!"

Turned out that the one sentry was dead. The other was going to live. PFC James had three bullet holes, one in his arm, one in his shoulder, and the last in his ass. When his squad came to visit him in the field hospital, it was Cohen who said, "Hey, Reub . . . your heroics sure were a shot in the ass for the whole unit. Oops, sorry man, that was a bit cheeky. Ah man, I need to cover my butt before I get in trouble."

The whole squad was suppressing their giggles.

"Look, you little squirt," Reuben replied. "You better watch it. I could still jump outta here and tear you a new asshole." It took a moment before his own slip registered, and Reuben started to laugh.

Then they all did, except Billy, whose eyes watered as he turned away.

For his bravery, Reuben James received a Silver Star, and for his injuries, a Purple Heart and clusters.

CHAPTER 10

Reuben James

T he name rings of history, heroism, and myth, with a later song by Kenny Rogers that was most germane to our lesser-known "sharecropper's son," a soldier of distinguished character and courage. Until his own death, Sergeant Billy Stone would hum the tune and speak the words, "Reuben James, you still walk the pearly fields of my mind. I loved you then and I love you now—Reuben James."

Alabama's first residents were the Paleo Indians, but they didn't stick around. The Choctaw, Chickasaw, and Cherokee were more prone to hunker down for a spell, but they got moved out by the European settlers. Then came slavery, Civil War clashes, economic recessions and depressions, and, *whoa*, seems the Paleos mighta had the right idea. However, regardless of the conflicts and defeats, Alabama survived.

In 1817, the era of steamboat transportation on the Alabama River began to play an important role in the economic development of the state, and the town of Selma (which in old German and Arabic means "Helmet of God") was incorporated one year after Alabama became the twenty-second state of the Union in 1819.

In 1861, Alabama became the fourth state to secede from the Union. With its central location and river and rail connections, Selma became a major military munitions and supply-manufacturing center during the Civil War. In the years following Lee's surrender, the economy of the state of Alabama slowly improved with continuing industrialization, but Selma was hit particularly hard by the defeat. In addition to the destruction of Army arsenals, navel foundries, and factories, many parts of the retail and residential areas had burned to the ground. It would take Selma many years to recover from the devastation, and it brought widespread displacement, poverty, and hunger to both white and black residents.

It seemed that if one chose to plug one's nose to relieve the stench of the Civil War's surviving body of ignorant, hard-core racists, the intellectual pygmies that still cohered to their Paleolithic concept of white supremacy, that certain men of substance and vision did reread the part of the Declaration of Independence that addressed the self-evident truth that all men were created equal. In 1868, black men voted for the first time in Alabama. By 1874, several African Americans emerged as political leaders. Benjamin Turner, Jeremiah Haralson, and James T. Rapier were among the most notable, having served Alabama in the US Congress. But the heavy wheels of the freedom wagon moved slowly, even with the high energy of reformists.

In 1940, Ezra and Esther James were party to two big events in Selma. First, they got married, and second, they attended the opening of the Edmund Pettus Bridge, which would become of historical significance twenty-five years later.

For those who relish in the greatest ironies of history, Edmund

Pettus was a Confederate general during the American Civil War, who, upon retiring from the military, became the grand dragon of the Ku Klux Klan. The bridge's continued existence and significance in the fight for civil liberties seemed to imply an "in your face" somewhere. Perhaps a nagging prevention of eternal serenity for the racist general?

It is interesting that in the first half of the twentieth century, lots of parents jumped on the biblical name bandwagon. Theosophists might try to tie it to the fact that in tough times of struggle and war, people needed a direct line to "the Good Book," but then again, was there ever not a period of tough times of struggle and war? Whatever—still, Ezra and Esther were both recipients and proponents of the fad.

Ezra James and Esther Wilson were solid to the core. Their respective folks had sharecropped the farms in the surrounding area. Farming ain't easy—just ask a sharecropper—but one can conclude that the agrarian life will most always produce "solid to the core" people.

After high school, Esther had earned a teaching certificate and taught fifth- and sixth-grade English at a nearby school for blacks. There was love all around, to quote a Beatle. Esther loved her work, and she loved her kids. The kids didn't love school, but they loved their teacher. Esther loved to sing, and she sang in her Baptist church choir, which she also loved, next to a man with a deep base voice who also loved his church, loved to sing, and shortly after joining the choir, loved the pretty soprano that sang next to him. Ezra owned the deep voice, and often sang to the other workers on the Selma docks as he welded steel for the ships. He was an imposing man, but a gentle giant, who was—yup, you guessed it—loved by his fellow workers.

So, in the summer of 1940, E and E loved each other enough to bless the ties that bind. The wedding was big—dockworkers, teachers, kids, family, church people, and stragglers—a real lovefest.

They bought a house near the school. They bought a big brown Hudson so Ezra could get to the docks, and for six years, they worked their butts off to build a little nest egg.

Then, one day in 1946, Esther said to Ezra over dinner, "Guess what, Ezra? I'm pregnant."

The love cycle would start anew.

Unfortunately, however, I should mention that from 1942 to 1944, Ezra had to leave town. He went to an ugly African desert and worked for a very competent megalomaniac named Patton, driving a big old tank, and during that period of employment, there wasn't much love. Ezra came home from his tour of romantic Casablanca, Sicily, home to the Cosa Nostra, up the boot of Italy, and was released to return home as the Third Army approached the border of Germany. He was never injured, at least on the outside, and the dockworkers, the teachers, the kids, the church people, and a throng of stragglers again threw rice at his homecoming.

Ironically—sort of—on the morning of December 7, 1946, an eight-pound hunk of fightin' blue steel came charging out of Esther James. Like his folks before him, he would inherit a biblical name.

Long before Kenny Rogers's song, and long before Kenny Rogers, there was a boatswain's mate who served on the Navy frigate USS *Constellation*, and later the frigate USS *Philadelphia*, which was captured during the Barbary Coast wars in 1803, during the presidency of Thomas Jefferson. His name was Reuben

James, and the story goes that while the ship was aground in the harbor of Tripoli, there was some hand-to-hand combat during which young Reuben interposed himself between his commander and an enemy combatant, taking a sword to the head and saving his commander's life. James didn't die, and actually returned to serve in the Navy until 1836. I must, unwillingly, submit to iconoclasm by adding that many believe it was another sailor, not *our* Reuben, that was the real hero. Whatever, I'm goin' with Reuben James.

Apparently, the Navy went with Reuben James, as well, and more than a century later, named a four-funnel destroyer after him. Unfortunately, as his unlucky streak continued, on Halloween of 1941, a German U-boat sank the USS *Reuben James*, the first United States Navy ship sunk in World War II. In tribute, Woody Guthrie wrote a song, "The Sinking of the Reuben James," which is also still performed today to the tune of "Wildwood Flower."

In any event, with all that hoopla, E and E named their son Reuben.

There are two almost contrasting biblical interpretations to the name Reuben: "He has seen my misery," and "He will love me." In the case of our future soldier, both would be true.

When people first laid eyes on Reuben, they said, "He's either a fullback or a middle linebacker." What would you expect? It was Alabama.

There was something special about baby Reuben. He was strong and he was tough, but what was special was a cerebral thing. He didn't cry or fuss with the usual baby accidents and frustrations. He almost seemed to process them through an advanced form of analysis. If he did cry, you could be sure that something was wrong. If he should have cried, it was like a dog with pain—you just couldn't measure severity. His motor skills were freakish. He was doing things at five that most eight-year-olds couldn't do. He fell from the backyard apple tree when he was six and seemed to go into a mild funk. When his happy face hadn't returned in a week, his mother took him to the doctor, where x-rays showed a simple fracture of the ulna. By the following day, he was back at play with his new toy: his cast.

Regardless of his very protective parents, Reuben couldn't be completely sheltered from discrimination.

Where Native Americans are much more passive by nature, especially regarding the battle against injustices and inequality, to their credit, blacks are not and were not. Competent leadership was being developed within the infrastructure of the civil rights movement. In 1951, eight-year-old Linda Brown's father sued the state school board of Topeka, Kansas, over "separate but equal" schools. It took three years, but in 1954, in the Supreme Court case *Brown v. Board of Education*, the court decided that "separate but equal" schools cannot be equal and are inherently unequal. This Supreme Court decision made any legal school segregation unconstitutional. This was a landmark case, and a leap forward for America.

In November of 1955, segregation was prohibited by the Federal Interstate Commerce Commission on interstate trains and buses, and later that year, Rosa Parks, a heroine of the movement, refused to give up her seat to a white passenger on a bus in Montgomery, Alabama.

In 1957, Martin Luther King Jr. assisted in founding the

SCLC, or the Southern Christian Leadership Conference. The purpose of the organization was to fight for civil rights, and Martin Luther King was elected as the organization's first president. And in the same year, Orval Faubus, the governor of Arkansas, blocked the integration of Little Rock High School by using the National Guard to prevent nine students from entering. President Eisenhower, however, overrode the governor and instructed federal troops to integrate Little Rock High School.

The most significant legislation passed by Congress was the Civil Rights Act of 1957. This act created the Civil Rights Commission, and also authorized the Justice Department to look into cases of African Americans being deprived of their voting rights in the South.

The three years of 1959 to 1961 were filled with civil rights legislation and protests. Martin Luther King was arrested and sentenced to hard time for protesting without a permit in Georgia, but Attorney General Bobby Kennedy obtained his release on bail.

A group of *Freedom Riders,* black and white, traveled from Washington, DC, through heavily segregated southern areas and were attacked by the Ku Klux Klan. They were arrested in Montgomery. President John Kennedy stepped in to enforce more penalties and regulations on facilities and buses that refused to integrate. He did this through the Interstate Commerce Commission.

In the fall of 1962, the Supreme Court ruled that the University of Mississippi had to admit James Meredith, an African American veteran and student, which only happened after President Kennedy ordered United States marshals to the campus to ensure his safety.

In the summer of 1963, Martin Luther King, along with many other civil rights leaders, marched to the nation's capital for jobs and freedom. Here, in front of nearly 250,000 people, he delivered his famous "I Have a Dream" speech.

On November 22, 1963, President Kennedy was assassinated, but the desegregation momentum continued, and his successor, Lyndon Johnson, passed more civil rights legislation, riding the wave of the country's anger and JFK's legacy.

The next year, Congress passed the Civil Rights Act of 1964. The act banned discrimination in public places and in employment. At the end of 1964, the Nobel Foundation awarded Dr. Martin Luther King the Nobel Peace Prize.

In March of 1965, the civil rights movement returned to Selma, Alabama. At that time, and in that place, was nineteen-year-old Reuben James.

Those Alabama pundits that had seen baby Reuben had been right. In 1961, at age fifteen, he had won the starting fullback position on his all-black high school team, and he was only a freshman. He was six feet tall, 185 pounds, and ran the hundred-yard dash in just over eleven seconds. By mid-season, recruiters from northern and West Coast colleges were attending his games. And the residents of Alabama were football crazy. Bear Bryant coached the 1961 Crimson Tide to an undefeated season, a Sugar Bowl win over Arkansas, and the first Associated Press national championship. Still, it would be a decade, 1971, before the first black football player, John Mitchell, would play for Alabama. In the meantime, Reuben's high school team would win six games and lose two.

"Sure would be easier if we didn't have to travel so far for games." Reuben was talking to Wesley, an older defensive end.

"Yeah, bro, but we go where the black teams are, or we just play ourselves."

"How 'bout the schools with black and white kids?" Reuben asked.

"Don't see no black ballplayers, do ya, kid?" Wesley gave a look that told Reuben he was an idiot. "You can go there now, but you won't play ball."

"We could beat 'em," Reuben said.

"Don't make no difference. Blacks don't play with or against whites."

"They gotta someday, right?" Reuben's question was more of a statement.

"The Tide don't got none either. You won't be playin' for them, Reub."

"Yeah, well, maybe I don't want to." Reuben's reply was quiet, resigned.

"You don't wanna play for the Bear? What, you nuts?" Wesley looked surprised.

"Don't think so, if that's how he is."

Reuben's team lost one game the next year, and was undefeated the following two.

On a spring morning in 1963, Reuben sat with his father and another man with curly hair and a round face. He spoke with a southern accent. He was from Tennessee. The man addressed both Reuben and his father. His name was Murray Warmath, and he was the coach of the University of Minnesota's football team.

"Not only did we win the national championship three years ago," Warmath said, "but we had two black All-Americans, Bobby

Lee Bell and Sandy Stephens. And Stephens was the first African American All-American quarterback in division one. You could be the next one, Reuben." The coach broke into a wide smile.

"I sure do hear what you're saying, Mr. Warmath," Reuben said. "But truth be told, I would like to play for Bear Bryant." The young man's face was kind, and so honest.

"Well, I'd like to play for Bear myself, Reuben, but I'm too old." Same smile. "He's a terrific coach and a fine man. When this racial business does get straightened out, you can bet that Bear Bryant will be leading the charge. But until then, you and your family need to choose what's best for you. Minnesota is a great school of learning, son, and I just want to say that we'd sure be proud to welcome you up there."

"I want to thank you, Mr. Warmath, for coming to see me, and I will sure keep your offer in mind." Reuben offered his hand and went inside to his mother.

"You've raised a terrific young man, Mr. James," Warmath said to Reuben's father. "And if we're lucky enough to have him head our way, I can promise you we'll take good care of him."

Warmath and Ezra shook hands. As Warmath left, he thought to himself, *Whoever gets that young man will probably win it all.*

Minnesota was only one of many football schools that gave Reuben their pitch. In the end, and added to life's long list of things that might have been, Reuben would never play football again after high school.

For three years in a row, Reuben had been elected captain of the football team. He was also class president his senior year. He was voted "best liked" and "most admired" in the senior legacies. In addition, no one in the district, including parents, was more versed on the issues and developments surrounding the civil rights movement.

"The great man will be here next week, Dad," Reuben told his father in early March 1965.

"I know you think I'm a moron, son, but I can read the paper, and your mother and I are joining the march. It'll be part of history."

"Since you're going to need protection, I'm going with." Reuben sounded lighthearted, but on a deeper level, he was worried about his folks. He was now six feet three and 220 pounds, with Olympic speed.

"So, you already got your parents in a nursing home, huh, smart aleck?" Ezra said with a grin.

"Really, Dad, it *will* be historic, and I want to experience it with the two people that mean the most to me."

"Wow, you got to my soft spot, Reub." Ezra was touched.

After Reuben absorbed the moment, he asked his father, "White folks sure are different up North. How you figure that?" He wore his serious expression.

"There are lots of good white people down here, Reuben. They're just the quiet ones. It's the Klan and other racists that make all the noise, and they scare the good people. You see those film clips of Dr. King's speeches? There's plenty of white folks in the crowds, even some standing with him." Ezra searched his son's face for a reaction. "You wait and see who's in the march."

"People like Mr. Warmath? He's from Tennessee." Reuben showed a hint of hope.

"Yup, there are lots of 'em, son. Lots of 'em."

In 1965, there were a couple of black folksingers named Joe

and Eddie. They sang a song titled "Hey Nellie Nellie," written by Shel Silverstein and Jim Friedman. It was a powerful song about equality, and the last verse included the lyrics,

Hey Nellie Nellie, come to the window
Hey Nellie Nellie, time to make a row
I see white folk and black folk walking side by side
They're marching in a column that's a century wide
From Selma to Soweto we're turning the tide*
I feel things changing now
It's been a long and a hard and a bloody ride
and it's 1965
*This line added by Susanne Kalweit

On March 21, when Ezra, Esther, and Reuben showed up at the Edmund Pettus Bridge, there was an aura of danger that had been building for almost two weeks. They had to park some ways away.

"You know that boy died, don't you?" Esther said to her husband and son.

"Yeah, Mom. He was just a voter registration worker. Jimmie Jackson. He was a good guy. Police shot him in the stomach." Reuben showed an atypical anger. "And not only that, but Sheriff Clark locked up over a thousand protestors."

Jim Clark was the sheriff of Selma in 1965.

"I've heard some big-time musicians will be on the march," Ezra stated, trying to steer away from the nascent anger.

"Pete Seeger and Joan Baez is who I heard," Esther said. "And I really believe that the music works. It provides unity and spiritual hope, and it's certainly symbolic."

"They're calling what happened two weeks ago, 'Bloody Sunday.'" Reuben's anger hadn't gone away. "In addition to guns, you heard the police used cattle prods, billy clubs, and tear gas?"

"That's true, Reuben, but now Dr. King got a court order. There shouldn't be any police interference." Ezra spoke with a calm authority, and Reuben calmed, but got the last word.

"You believe that?"

From a historical perspective, many consider the Selma to Montgomery march the grandest and most significant of the civil rights demonstrations. It started on Sunday, March 7, when some six hundred marchers headed east from Selma on US 80. When they got to the Edmund Pettus Bridge, they were attacked by the local lawmen and had to disperse.

Two days later, Martin Luther King led what could only be called a symbolic march to the bridge. At that point, Dr. King sought court protection for his full-scale march to the state capitol in Montgomery. Federal District Court Judge Frank M. Johnson Jr. ruled, "The law is clear that the right to petition one's government for the redress of grievances may be exercised in large groups . . . and these rights may be exercised by marching, even along public highways."

On March 21, the march began again. Despite the possibility of danger, Dr. King attempted to garner support from well-known musicians that he knew were sympathetic to the cause. Over 3,000 marchers started from Selma and took US 80 all the way to Montgomery. They tramped through the cotton fields, not on the highway, as the court order was clear, but that didn't prevent state troopers and the White Citizens Council from driving past and harassing them. They were joined by Pete Seeger and John Stewart (Kingston Trio). The collective voice of the crowd that moved along the fifty-five-mile trek at thirteen to fourteen miles per day, sleeping in the fields at night, could be heard singing "We Shall Overcome," for miles.

Just outside of Montgomery, they were joined by Peter, Paul, and Mary, Harry Belafonte, and Joan Baez. By that time, the crowd of demonstrators had reached about 30,000 strong.

On the whole, the march was without major incident, but danger was always just a spark away from ignition. As John Stewart would later say, "In Selma, it was like being in a war zone in your own country." In the aftermath, a woman demonstrator named Viola Liuzzo was shot by a Klansman while driving away.

Within five months of the march, President Johnson signed the Voting Rights Act of 1965. In 1996, that road along which the march took place was designated by Congress as *The Selma-to-Montgomery National Historic Trail, an All-American Road.*

"There's something that happened to me on this march," Reuben said to his parents when they got home. "It's a spiritual thing that I can't really describe."

"I think everyone felt that way," his mother said.

"This is different, Mom. What I thought was important, isn't, and I can feel a real change about where I need to go from here. Can you understand that?"

"I believe I can, son," his dad intervened. "The conscience of an individual must be shaken before that of the nation can be roused." Ezra spoke to his son as his eyes watered and his pride swelled.

Reuben had a job commitment that he felt obligated to finish, as well as certain other responsibilities, but just after his twentieth birthday, and the dawn of 1967, he told his parents that he was going to enlist. It didn't matter to him that his number in the draft hadn't come up.

Like all mothers, Esther was ready to protest, but Ezra had a quiet chat with her about men, their obligations and destinies, and his own history, and she held her emotions in check. She did try hard to talk him into a noncombat branch, but Reuben told her he was qualified for the infantry, so that was where he was headed.

Norman Rockwell should have had his paints and easel when the train left the Selma station for Fort Jackson. It was a classic picture of hugs and farewell between parents and son.

CHAPTER 11

—⁓—

Vietnam
1968

And the war in Vietnam continued. Unlike that truce on Christmas Eve in 1914, when German and American soldiers crossed into no-man's-land to drink and share for one night before returning to the killing fields, the sentiment of this conflict was not as benign. There was no hint of even subliminal respect, no empathy for the enemy, no desire for truce. Just fear and hatred. Most soldiers never knew what for, and in retrospect, perhaps the rancor was not so much single-pointed as it was generic . . . the disassociation of the controlling establishment from the individual on the front line. "Old men start the wars. Young men fight them." Though moral reconciliation was underway back in the States, for the soldier, it came years later.

The Vietnam War was just an ugly, tenuous chain of 10,000 days linked together by fear, pain, and death. In the end, ninety-nine out of a hundred will tell you that the war was a complete waste of time, money, resources, and most grievously, of the world's most precious assets, the lives of hundreds of thousands of our young. The loss of lives was almost unforgivable, but that 1 percent knew better regarding whether there was victory or total defeat.

"Victory has a hundred fathers and defeat is an orphan." So said JFK after the Bay of Pigs fiasco. In the case of Vietnam, the orphan had a legitimate argument. For the ninety-nine, they could give credit for that perception, and for the result to the media, and once again to the military-political complex. Billy Stone would one day revisit the orphan's argument.

To some degree, most everyone has a touch of claustrophobia. There is, however, a unique breed of men that have no such fear, and they came together in this war. These guys not only didn't have nightmares about confinement, but according to Peter Gorner, "were cocky members of a spit-and-polish clique who kept to themselves, ridiculed rank, disdained drugs and self-doubts, and exulted in jobs that no sane man would do." And they did their perilous work with few tools—knives, flashlights, and pistols. They were called "tunnel rats."

In the defense of Saigon, soldiers like Sergeant Billy Stone and higher-level leaders, all the way to Westmoreland, would claim in wonder about the Vietcong, "Where the hell are these guys coming from?"

It took years before they got it, and the mystery really never became clear until almost four years after the US withdrawal. What Billy didn't know during the Tet Offensive was that the underground tunnels housed thousands of enemy troops. Just twenty miles north of Billy's position was the district of Cu Chi. Again, to quote Gorner, "A network of small access holes (two feet wide by three feet deep) led to communication tunnels that, via a series of cleverly hidden trapdoors, zigzagged up, sideways, and down as far as eighteen feet. These passageways led to a labyrinth of caverns and caves that snaked through as many as four separate levels for 200 miles, stretching all the way to the Cambodian border.

"Air, sanitation, water, and cooking facilities were sufficient to maintain a primitive but reasonably safe existence. In the subterranean mazes (few of which were more than six feet high), the Vietcong built sleeping chambers, air-raid shelters, latrines, hospitals, kitchens, stages for political theater, conference centers, and print shops. They stored huge caches of rice, precious water buffalo, and captured American artillery (they even entombed an American tank)."

Everyone in Billy's squad was claustrophobic, but they had a situation. During one of their night patrols, they had come across two trapdoors that were in close proximity. Billy wasn't sure what it was, exactly—a hiding place, storage space, or something more. If it was something more, they had to know, as it could present a threat, the size of which depended on what was down there. Although he could have ordered one of his men to go in, he didn't feel right about doing that. He couldn't really lead his men if he wouldn't do what he asked them to do. So he sent Peter Akecheta to cover the second hole.

As he began to take off his backpack and belt, PFC Yamada spoke up. "Hey, Chief, I'm the best man to do this. Although I'm not going to tell you why, I have had some experience in tunnels, since I was a kid."

Billy and the others just looked at him. Yes, he begged the question, but no one asked, and they wouldn't.

Eventually Billy said, "You don't have to do this, Private. It's my responsibility."

Yamada replied, "Understand, Sarge, but I got this one." With that, he dropped his gear, grabbed his flashlight, shoved his .45 into his back, and checked his leg for his knife. He was cautious. He attached his belt to the handle of the trapdoor and handed the end to Cohen. "Stay back and pull it open when I signal," he whispered.

He kneeled beside the opening, out of the line of fire, raised his hand, and pointed to Cohen. When the door flipped open, there was only silence. Yamada slipped the flashlight over the edge and turned it on. After several seconds, he peeked over and looked into the shallow abyss. It was about five feet deep. Seeing nothing and hearing nothing, he jumped in. Upon further inspection, he noticed a much smaller hole in the corner. He held his hand up to the squad, finger to his lips for silence, got on all fours, and disappeared. Whoever said that the number one human fear is public speaking either smokes funny cigarettes or hasn't entered a two-foot-by-two-foot black hole wherein someone who wants you dead is waiting.

Yamada inched along on his elbows. If he suddenly needed his knife, he would never be able to react in time, so he stopped, wiggled his knife from his leg, and held it in his right hand as he continued down the tunnel. His standard issue Army knife was six inches long. He stared at the blade, and when a vision began to appear, he quickly retreated from his developing imagination. Fear avoidance comes in many colors, and Yamada's color at that moment was a screaming bright red. He was petrified, but he stayed focused and kept going, stopping every few feet to listen. After several zigs and zags, the hole got bigger.

Outside, Billy was nervous, as were the others. The jungle sounds were periodic. Birds, frogs, monkeys—they didn't know—but they would flinch whenever they heard a sudden squawk.

Billy had jumped into the hole with his ear to the smaller opening, but heard nothing. He convinced himself that *no sound is
good sound,* or something like that. His patience was being tested.
He somehow preferred battle sounds to this silence.

Yamada heard muffled voices as he continued to crawl. As
he got closer, the opening widened, and the sound he heard was
banter . . . in Vietnamese. As he turned a corner, he saw light. He
was in shadow, and as long as he was quiet, he didn't think he'd
be detected. He surveyed the room. It was almost twenty feet
long and somewhat less than that wide. Along the left side were
munitions and stacked rifles, mostly M-14s, but also boxes of
explosives and a few bags of rice and water. In the far-right corner
was a low-wattage bulb, the soft hum of a generator coming from
somewhere, and the faint smell of fuel. There was a small, wicker-
type table on which was some kind of game board, seemingly
checkers or chess . . . maybe mah-jongg.

Across from each other sat two small men. One seemed older
than the other, but then again, the age guessers at the carnival
would lose a lot of teddy bears to these guys. They wore ragged
black silk, bare feet, and the usual Cong hats of braided reeds and
conically shaped. They made a giggle each time they moved a tile,
fully engaged in their game.

Yamada held the element of surprise, but knew that firing a
gun could cause an explosion. He would need to be positioned
right. He slipped his hand back for the .45. "Shit," he said to
himself. Panic. It wasn't there. *It must have come loose in the tunnel somewhere.* But he couldn't turn back, as he was too confined.
Only one-way traffic.

He processed the situation. He didn't see any firearms near
the table, but that didn't mean they didn't have them. He did see

that they had knives attached to their skinny legs. Could he get to that stack of rifles before these guys could? Probably not. So, two against one. He'd been there before, and he was still standing.

He bit the bullet and jumped into the room, charging for the guns. At first, they didn't move, only watched him with golf ball eyes and gaping mouths.

When they did move, it was lightning quick. With drawn knife, the closest man blocked his path to the guns. The younger man held his knife in both hands and slowly circled to the right, more hesitant. Yamada knew that his only chance was to take down the first soldier quickly, before the warier, younger one reacted.

He juked toward the rifle stack while deftly flipping his knife from the left hand into the right. While his attention was momentarily deflected to movement on his right, the first man made a slashing stroke toward his eyes. The knife swipe missed his eyes, but sliced a four-inch cut across his forehead. It wasn't as painful as it was an intrusion, when a spurt of blood poured into his right eye.

With his arm extended, the man opened up his lower right side. Yamada took his knife and swung upward, just under the man's armpit, and the man fell to the sound of something like a high-pitched blackboard screech. The younger man had been frozen, watching the fight. By the time he recovered, it had become a one-on-one.

Yamada sensed that the boy had never been in a knife fight before. He just danced around, reminiscent of Ali in the Liston fight, but he didn't sting like a bee. Instead, he skedaddled. He dropped his knife and ran to another hole near the table, where he disappeared. Yamada didn't chase him—just said, "Good riddance," and sat down in one of the table chairs, which immediately collapsed under his weight. He was having a bad day.

The anxiety level was high when Yamada poked his head out of the entryway. He looked like a Japanese Kabuki dancer with his blood-red face and white eyes.

"What the fuck? That you, Yamada?" Cohen's usual smartass remark to these things.

"No, shit-for-brains, I just wanted your take on my new Halloween outfit."

Billy administered a gauze compress to Yamada's forehead before getting a debrief. Not sure how to handle the weapons cache, Billy radioed the captain, who would send a separate recovery team.

For his bravery, Yamada received a Bronze Star, and for his injury, a Purple Heart.

CHAPTER 12

Akio Yamada

Once again, I will dangle a choice morsel of irony for all of you ironyphiles, which spellcheck tells me is not a word, but you know what I mean.

In March of 1942, three months after the Japanese attack on Pearl Harbor, Lieutenant General John L. DeWitt, head of the Western Defense Command and Fourth Army, issued the first of 108 military proclamations that resulted in the forced relocation from their residences to guarded relocation camps of more than 110,000 people of Japanese ancestry from the West Coast, the great majority of that ethnic community. Two-thirds were born in the United States. Japanese Americans who were born in the United States to immigrant parents were called Nisei. At the time, per presidential Executive Order 9066, all Americans of Japanese descent were prohibited from serving in the military. There have been books written about this topic, so I will shortcut this story and jump to the conclusion: it was racist. It was typical knee-jerk government reaction. It was a stigma on the United States of America, but in some perverse way, it may have provided an incentive for what was to be.

After a great deal of initiative and pressure, on February 1, 1943, the US government reversed its decision on Japanese Americans serving in the armed forces. It approved the formation of a Japanese American combat unit, and that unit became the 442nd Infantry Regimental Combat Team, almost exclusively soldiers of Japanese descent whose parents were living in internment camps. To the date of this writing, the 442nd Infantry Regiment Combat Team is the most decorated military unit in US history. Few things can bring this man's eyes to tears, but I'm unabashed that this does.

The 442nd became known as the "Purple Heart Battalion" because of the casualties it suffered. The original 4,000 Nisei who initially came in April 1943 had to be replaced nearly 3.5 times. In total, about 14,000 men served, ultimately earning 9,486 Purple Hearts (many earning double and triples), 4,000 Bronze Stars, 1,200 Oak Leaf Clusters added to the Bronze Star, 560 Silver Stars, 28 Oak Leaf Clusters to the Silver Star, 52 Distinguished Service Crosses, 15 battlefield commissions, and 23 of America's highest decoration, the Congressional Medal of Honor. Unlike the 7th Cavalry soldiers at Wounded Knee, these were deserved.

Akio Yamada's father, Daisuke, served for nine months with the 442nd. He received a Purple Heart in the Battle of the Lost Battalion.

Against the advice of his senior officers, Major General John E. Dahlquist committed the "Texas Battalion" to an engagement. The battalion was cut off by the Germans, and attempts by the 36th Division's other two battalions to extricate it failed. The 405th Fighter Squadron of the 371st Fighter Group airdropped supplies to the 275 trapped soldiers, but conditions on the ground quickly deteriorated as the Germans continued to repel US forces.

The final rescue attempt was made by the 442nd Regimental Combat Team. The 442nd had been given a period of rest after heavy fighting to liberate Bruyères and Biffontaine, but General Dahlquist called them back early to relieve the beleaguered 2nd and 3rd Battalions of the 36th. In five days of battle, from October 26 to October 30, 1944, the 442nd broke through German defenses and rescued 211 men. In the process, the 442nd suffered over 800 casualties. I-Company went in with 185 men. Eight walked out unhurt. K-Company began with 186 men, and seventeen walked out. Additionally, the commander sent a patrol of fifty to fifty-five men to find a way to attack a German roadblock by the rear and try to liberate the remainder of the trapped men. Only five returned to the "Lost Battalion" perimeter. Forty-two were taken prisoner and sent to Stalag VII-A in Moosburg, Bavaria, where they remained until the POW camp was liberated on April 29, 1945.

When Daisuke Yamada returned to California after the war, he did not suffer from PTSD. He was not embittered or resentful. Remarkably, he was energized. He was indeed a man of strong fiber. Unlike the way his son would be treated by America upon his return home from Vietnam twenty-five years later, Daisuke received a hero's welcome. After all, Saint George had slain the dragon. Now only the temperature would change. The intense heat of the atomic bomb would begin to cool, and a subtler conflict would morph into a cold war with the primary combatants being the United States and the Soviet Union.

Daisuke, with help from the GI Bill, was able to buy a relatively large corner lot and home in Bakersfield, California. He started to sell used cars on his lot. Desotos, Plymouths, Hudsons, and the newer rage, a Ford product that fit nicely between Fords and Lincolns, the Mercury, adorned the new streets of towns and cities up and down the California coast. America breathed rarified air for a decade following the end of World War II. There was love everywhere. There was respect. There was opportunity. People didn't lock their doors because they didn't have to. Kids played kickball in the streets until nine o'clock at night . . . without parental guards. Savings and loans were popping up everywhere, as were family-owned grocery stores and hardware stores, and "Ike" was running the show. Life was good, and those that deserved benefit were rewarded.

Somehow Chevrolet heard about "a Japanese guy in Bakersfield that is absolutely sellin' the shit outta used cars." It wasn't long before there was a big white building along the busiest street in Bakersfield with flagpoles flying Chevy flags, and dozens of suited salesmen that resembled carnival barkers makin' the big bucks and spending even faster. It seemed the country had received a subliminal message that life is brittle and, "Hell, we could be gone tomorrow from an A-bomb. Gotta let'r rip."

Daisuke was managing the dealership. He could control his domain from his fancy office with knee-to-ceiling windows. He had picked up the game of golf, and sponsored a tournament for needy families that had lost loved ones in the war. He even played with a Masters champion. His life got even better when nine months to the day of his return from Germany, he and his wife had a son, who they named Akio.

Akio would never have the dubious luxury of becoming a spoiled brat. His environment was strict, both because of his father's experiences and his mother's gene pool. However, few parents escape the challenges of recalcitrant youth, and so it was with the nouveau riche Yamadas in 1958.

Every parent should probably take at least one psychology course before having kids. They should at least be able to understand and recognize that point in a child's development when peers become more influential and important than they are. Duh! It's one thing to lose your focus, and another to lose your memory. Parents are idiots, while kids are brilliant. Whatever. Akio joined a gang of hoods. (Should any Millennials happen to stumble across this book and read it, a hood was a kind of bully that wore his jeans low, smoked Camels, and intimidated the vulnerable. Basically, they were assholes.)

So, there was an Esso filling station (another couple of anachronisms) just off the main drag in Bakersfield that hadn't updated to a cement floor, just dirt. It was owned by a farmer. His wife and a mechanic ran the joint. They weren't too concerned about security, at least at that point, and left the money in an old Dolls House National cash register all week until their Friday deposit.

One day, when thc hoods got their "buck's worth" of gas, they noticed that the register was chock full of ones and fives, and their thoughts turned to the nefarious. They cased the place for a week, and came to the conclusion that Thursday night was probably the most lucrative time to rob the joint. After numerous rather illiterate discussions about how to do it, it was Akio who came up with the brilliant idea of tunneling in.

Only one side of the station wasn't fully visible to either the farmhouse or the road. On the east side of the building stood a large Monterey cypress that provided cover from night shadows.

"Two of us will dig," Akio instructed, "the other will be the lookout." He was, at least for this operation, the kingpin. His self-appointed kingship was primarily due to his sense of survival, as he had some time ago concluded that his two cohorts were idiots.

He avoided the deductive reasoning that would conclude with "Thus, he was an idiot," a compromise he was seemingly willing to make to be the kingpin.

While he and one of the idiots dug the hole, the other idiot, a guy they called "Shucks," thought it would be a good time to relax and enjoy a doobie, African broccoli, cabbage, curly-wurley, or whatever the latest slang for cannabis hitting the charts around Bakersfield. No matter what they called it, it was illegal, as was robbery . . . kind of a twofer for any ambitious young member of the Bakersfield gendarmes trying to make his mark. And with the growth that the town was experiencing, there was a plethora of newbies on the force.

Bryce "Fitz" Fitzbern may have been the cop after whom Barney Fife was created, only a fatter version. He was the designated driver of the slick black-and-white Ford coupe cop car that patrolled the east side. He had seniority, as he often reminded the "young whippersnapper" academy grad that rode with him, Artie Carroll. Artie's dad had fought in the Pacific—a "bilge rat," as sailors that worked in engineering spaces were called. He'd been injured when a kamikaze hit his ship, the USS *Curtis*, at Kwajalein. He hated the "Japs," and naturally, that sentiment transferred to his son. Artie graduated number two in his police academy class, and wanted to please his father as an up-and-comer in the Bakersfield Police Department, so he not only showed commitment to every training regimen for new officers, but volunteered for every opportunity that afforded extra credit. The other cops called him "Sparky," short for "Spark Plug."

On that certain evening, while the idiots were smokin' and diggin', Barney and Sparky were cruisin'.

Akio was nervous. If something went wrong, he would be royally screwed. His folks would kill him. He knew that his dad had paid a big price to gain the position he held, and more importantly, the reputation he had so passionately developed against the subliminal forces of prejudice was a point of pride for him. Compared to the Oriental philosophy, where nothing was more important than honor and reputation, Americans were almost cavalier in that regard.

The ground was pretty soft near the cypress tree, and it didn't take long to dig a hole under the old wood-frame siding.

"Fats, you help Shucks watching for trouble," Akio said. "I'll get in, get the cash, and then get out as fast as I can."

They called idiot number two "Fats," for the obvious reasons. When he moseyed over to join Shucks, he saw that his pal was lying on his back, looking at the stars, humming some Roy Acuff song, seemingly skipping through poppy fields toward the merry old Land of Oz.

"Shucks," he whispered, "got any more of that shit?"

"Fats, my man, how's the diggin' goin'?" Idiot One lifted his head with a shit-eating grin.

"Akky's in grabbin' the dough. So gimme a drag, huh?"

Shucks handed the stogie to his friend as he stared at the black-and-white coming down the road. He pointed and said, "Shit, man, I love the looks a that car. That's the kinda car I'm gonna get if we get enough bread outta this joint. Whaddya think?"

"Yeah, it's cool, man," Fats said, staring at the car as he took a big drag. As the car pulled up, he finally processed. "Know what, Shucks? That's a damn cop car."

With that, they both got up and took off, running past the new hole, yelling, "Akky, it's the cops." They kept going.

"What the hell?" Fitz said, turning on the flashing lights and slowing down.

"Pull over, Fitz. Those guys are running from something."

Artie was out of the car, starting to chase the two runners. Fitz was trying to get out of the car—actually, he was trying to get his newfangled seat belt undone.

Ford had been the first car company to offer seat belts as an option in 1955. Others didn't follow for three years. The Bakersfield Police Department made it mandatory for their officers to wear them. It was an insurance thing, but it also set a good example, or so they thought. Sometimes the mechanisms didn't work so well. Sometimes those who wore them didn't work so well. Fitz often had a problem.

By the time Fitz became untangled, the two perps and Sparky were nowhere in sight. Damned if he was going to run after them. Hell, he was all tuckered out from the gosh-danged seat belt, so he strolled over to the front of the station to sit on the bench and wait for his partner.

Akio had heard the warning sounds of his compadres as they ran by. He'd had little trouble breaking open the cash register, but left it and went to the window, which was reflecting a flashing blue light. He watched the uniform run past and felt it could give him a chance to get away, but shortly after that, another cop headed toward the station. He looked like an older version of Fats—an out-of-shape dude who waddled up to the front and plopped onto the bench.

He was trapped. "Fuck."

Artie Carroll returned along the east side of the building and spotted the hole. He got closer and drew his pistol. He called out, "Fitz . . . where the hell are you?"

Fitz hurried around the corner. "I been checking things out . . . Deputy" It was a defensive reaction to both inferred admonishment and guilt. "You get those guys?"

"Too much of a head start, but look at this." Artie pointed at the hole and the shovels. "Could be someone in there?" Fitz grabbed his gun as well as they examined the dig.

"Anybody in there, come out with your hands up . . . Police!"

They listened and waited.

Inside, Akio slumped in resignation. He didn't want to die. He couldn't get away. No option. "I'm coming out. I don't have a weapon. Don't shoot."

He went to the hole, got in, and saw a vision of the worst day of his life as he crawled out. He wondered if death just might be a better choice. He climbed out of the hole and raised his arms. The two cops had their guns pointed at his chest. After a short pause, the younger one formed a menacing smile before saying, "Well, Fitz, what have we here? Looks to me like a fucking Jap, huh?"

Old Samuel Clemens put an interesting twist on an old saw: "The lack of money is the root of all evil." In his inherited wisdom, Daisuke Yamada understood the concept. It just might be his saving grace.

After receiving a call from Chester Samson, chief of the Bakersfield Police Department, he sat down with his wife to provide a watered-down version of what had happened. Against her insistence, he told her that he would handle the situation. He needed a short respite to compose himself—some accelerated meditation might work. Disguising lividity was an art form, especially in discussion with a police chief. He couldn't afford to fantasize about various forms of torture he could impose upon his teenage son. Instead, he needed to keep his composure and a keen mind. He prepared himself on the drive to the city jail.

"Mr. Yamada, I have to say that I'm surprised," the chief said. "You are much admired in this community for your business contributions. Those of us that know your service record have an added level of respect. So how is it that your son has strayed from the path of discipline I know you and Mrs. Yamada have taught him?" The chief grabbed a smoke, giving Daisuke some time to process.

"If you will permit me to commiserate with you," Yamada said, "that has been foremost in my mind since you called." He was shaking his head in the negative. It was a genuine gesture, not for show. "May I ask if you have found the other two boys? I ask because he has not been a rebellious child, or at least never displayed such behavior at home." Daisuke paused to see if he would get an answer.

"I really can't discuss that with you, sir, except to tell you we are investigating it. But your son refuses to give us their names, and of course that would help."

Yamada processed that. Loyalty ran deep in family heritage and teaching, but these boys did not seem to deserve such loyalty. "Perhaps I can speak with the boy and get a better understanding of what happened." Daisuke's words, "the boy," were a subtle intention to distance himself from his son, almost implying that he and the chief were in consonance with their thinking.

"I think that would be in order, Mr. Yamada."

After being escorted back to the cell, Daisuke just stood and stared at his son. It was in some ways surreal. His anger returned. What more could he have done for the boy? He had been almost pampered, certainly when compared to his own upbringing.

Where had he and his wife gone wrong? Did most parents ask themselves this question at some point? And everything he had worked so hard for . . . could it disappear like an echo in the valley?

To say that his son looked distraught would be minimizing. He looked drained of emotion, lost, as if in a fugue state.

"Akio, who were the other two boys?" Daisuke's tone was fervid.

For a long time, Akio just stared at his father, a visage of shame and sadness. Eventually, he simply said, "I'm sorry, Father. I'm sorry for what I did. I'm sorry for having dishonored you. I'm sorry for everything, but understand, I can't snitch." After a pause, he added, "I will take what's coming to me, but I won't snitch." With that, he hung his head, elbows on his knees, face in his hands.

Daisuke absorbed his son's statement. Initially he wanted to scream and punish, but he knew the apology was genuine. Akio had accepted full responsibility. He knew it was not a visceral, defensive statement to lighten any perceived consequences—after all, the boy had had hours to formulate. His own genetic conditioning was based upon honor, and his son had inherited it. Daisuke knew his son would "never snitch," and he felt a small sense of pride . . . misguided though it was.

There was nothing to say at that point, so he returned to the chief's office. He knocked, and was given the hand signal to enter.

"Chief Samson, I would appreciate you hearing my thoughts on this matter." He again sat down and waited.

"Of course, Mr. Yamada." Samson lit another Lucky Strike and leaned back in his chair. It seemed an afterthought, but he leaned forward, offering Daisuke a cigarette.

"No thank you, sir. I gave them up on V-E Day." Daisuke's body language implied a sense of supplication. He needed to be very careful in what he was about to say. "First, I understand this crime is being called a robbery, and two things occur to me. One, it was not an armed robbery, and two, nothing was taken. Perhaps it was in reality . . . a break-in." He quickly added, "Please know that I am in no way minimizing or making excuses, simply searching for definition."

The chief gave no reaction—just pulled on his Lucky.

"Secondly," Daisuke continued, "he will not give up the other two names. For him, it is a question of honor, and he is prepared to take the full punishment for the offense. Actually, I expect that your department will not take long to find the two boys, anyway, but that is beside the point. Thirdly, if after you evaluate the degree of this crime, I can provide assurance that whatever punishment he is given by the law, it will pale in comparison to what I will be doing, included in that would be any kind of community service you and your department can provide."

Again, Samson chose silence, not sure if his guest was finished. He wasn't.

"Finally, in some way, our meeting is coincidence, and I want to be very clear that what I'm about to say is in no way misunderstood or misinterpreted. Our monthly dealership management meeting was two weeks ago. At that meeting, I proposed that we provide the Bakersfield Police Department with a new Chevrolet Impala . . . black and white with all appropriate decals and markings."

Samson's eyebrows raised.

Yamada knew that could mean many things, but to eliminate any thoughts of bribery, he continued. "Understand, Chief

Samson, this is a decision that was already made, and of course, anything we talk about here today has no tie whatsoever to this contribution. The decision was made in recognition of the service that your department provides our community. You will receive it within thirty days"

Technically, Daisuke had not lied, as the idea had been brought up, more or less in passing, but had also quickly been tabled. Now, with its timely resurrection, it was a fait accompli. He would have some work to do, but he would get it done. He was gambling with his intuitive opinion of Chief Samson's character. A man of integrity would not compromise his values or the law, but history had always proven that the law was interpretive and flexible when needed. A break-in was a misdemeanor, not a felony like robbery. No one hurt, nothing taken. If the chief could feel that appropriate punishment was being dealt and his department could benefit from community service, then perhaps in his mind justice would be served. Whether he felt any sense of obligation to Yamada for the new police car was Daisuke's wager.

"Are you saying that this decision on the Impala was already made?" Samson's expression was a question mark.

"Yes, Chief. It was already decided. This is really the first chance I've had to speak to you, and unfortunately, it has come under this dark cloud. I hope you and your department will be pleased with the dealership's show of support, but again, it is unrelated to this other matter."

Samson stared at Daisuke, trying to read the truth behind this development. "Indeed, they are separate. So in relation to the car, I would like to thank *the dealership* on behalf of the Bakersfield Police Department. A most gracious gift of support." He moved quickly to the second item. "Regarding your son, I need to process what happened in more depth. I have no doubt that a man of your character and discipline will provide reason for your son to never forget what he has done. I will let you know tomorrow what we are going to do. He will, however, spend tonight as our guest. Are you fine with that, Mr. Yamada?"

"I certainly am, Chief Samson. I have the highest respect for your department, and will honor your conclusions, whatever they may be."

After Yamada left, Chief Samson had one more smoke. His thoughts were cycling. He was convinced that the boy's father was a good man, a decorated soldier, and a real boost to the community. The kid had been stupid, but came from strong, honorable bloodlines, and although he refused to help with the investigation, Samson felt a conflicted admiration for someone that young that would fall on his sword for friends, regardless of their low value to the citizenry. In court, any attorney worth his salt would certainly label this crime as a break-in, and it was true that no real harm had occurred. He also agreed that he could always use some help with community work.

And then, there was the brand-new Impala. He would drive that car. He had to give Yamada high marks for his cleverness in creating the tacit obligation. The only real thorn would be Fitz and his prejudiced young partner, but then, he was the chief, and he hadn't gotten there by being a wimp.

For most of us, there comes a time in our later years when we will pause to reflect on the *long and winding road* that we have traveled, which really ain't that long. If we take the time for introspection, have the courage, and make the effort to do what AA members call "a fearless moral inventory," or engage in what the mystics refer to as meditation, or maybe it just happens, a moment of enlightenment when we can identify an event, or perhaps a person, or something we read or saw, we might recognize and comprehend an experience that changed the direction of our lives. For some, it becomes a beacon for success, an overt or even subliminal reference point that guides us to be a contributor and a giver. For others, it is an ember that smolders with resentment and burns with hatred, and those misdirected souls come to the end in a fusillade of lead bullets, martyred for some opaque and misanthropic cause. For most, it is something in between.

For Akio Yamada, this moment took place sometime after his return from Vietnam. Once the metaphorical, leather-tethered cat-o'-nine-tails with which he had self-inflicted his guilt-ridden punishment for having forsaken his parents had finally deteriorated beyond use, he forgave himself and moved on.

His father's message had been simple: "When you come of age, you will join the Army." Yes, he had been punished in other ways by his parents, but never anything that resembled a vindictive spirit, and always a life lesson. In the end, after all was said and done, his arrest was a gift. Not only did he end up doing cleanup work on the streets of Bakersfield, but directed by Chief Samson, he performed numerous chores and tasks for the farmer who owned the Esso station. He cleaned the station after school for a year, and with his father's help, spent one weekend putting in a concrete floor. He was often invited to eat with the farmer's family.

On occasion, Chief Samson would fill up his Chevy Impala police car with gas and get a report on how the Yamada kid was performing. The only drawback was the occasional encounter with the two officers, Fitz and Sparky. Officer Carroll would pull him aside, use derisive slurs, and threaten him.

"Tell you what, you little bonsai bastard, I'm prayin' you fuck up again. Next time will be *very* different."

Fats and Shucks were never charged. They were at the top of the suspect list, but without Akio's testimony, the cops had nothing. As a result, Akio was a hero among Bakersfield's less desirables.

"Akky's da man . . . he don't snitch."

CHAPTER 13

Greenwich
2010

D r. Beloit had indeed done his homework. His entry into the intriguing world of white-collar crime had been innocent enough. He had prescribed a sophisticated home heart monitoring device for a Medicare patient that was returned to him when the patient died. He had already been reimbursed for the cost, with all the usual markups attached. When another patient needed a similar device, he simply rebilled the government for the equipment—essentially double-dipped—and was quickly paid.

Hell, that was easy.

So, he played a streamlined version of double-dip for about six months until he saw the ease with which he could expand his newfound corruption with negligible risk. One conclusion was that a guy could probably make a quick killing submitting claims for dead people, but sooner or later, they'd catch on to the fact that it might make sense to cross-reference Medicare cards with the obits.

He, however, thought of himself as a long-term investor, so he concentrated on scams that he figured were under the radar of the appropriate governmental agencies, CMS (Centers for Medicare and Medicaid Services) and the Inspector General for the Department of Health and Human Services (HHS). "Be smart and don't get greedy" was his mantra . . . Simple.

The Medicare scammers that had been caught were "hit-and-run" artists and they were greedy. Unlike himself, these guys hadn't put the effort into studying all of the system's subtler inefficiencies. The government was now promoting the claim that it would be nearly impossible to hoodwink the updated and upgraded system, but that was pure bovine defecation. The Medicare/Medicaid behemoth was far too big for the limited personnel running it, with 4.5 million claims and $1 billion in payments a day.

Their claim, at least as he saw it, was beneficial to his cause—even a cover. Anytime an enemy gives you their battle plan, maps, and time schedules, you know you are going to win, and the current Washington administration had honed that practice to perfection. What he now needed was a patsy, or more appropriately, a "cat's paw" that would provide layers of insulation, and he found just the guy. Before that guy, however, he needed an insider . . . an informant within the inner circle of the CMS.

Most people are someone else. In Clinton Hilliard's case, it was not a clinical thing. It was neither multiple personality disorder nor dissociative identity disorder—his other someone was more of a romantic thing, really, the guy he wanted to be, thought he should be, pretended to be. And that was a guy like Richard Branson. In the Bible, Mark claims in Chapter 9, "To be the greatest, you must be the least."

When that was read at a corporate retreat, Clint giggled out loud. He had no interest in the second part of that verse. *Mark musta been a bean counter.* What he did every day was boring. He worked with boring people. They all had a job, as did he, but he wanted an opportunity, not just a job. He deserved it. He'd paid his dues. Clint was sick and tired of Clint. He wanted to be Richard.

He worked in the Centers for Medicare and Medicaid Services. He was an actuarial. Right. Like when he was a little kid and someone asked him what he wanted to be when he grew up? *I'm really settin' my sights on bein' an actuarial.* He was one of three guys that worked directly under the director of Program Integrity, who also happened to be a putz. He spent his days reviewing processed claims from *weirdos and nearly-deads*, looking for red flags. He was a pretty compliant fellow at work, *like the rest of the dildos* in his workspace, but at night, he was a social media freak. Facebook and Twitter mostly, but eToro and Exploroo, as well. *Never know who ya might meet on there.* Although he was pretty careful with his opinions online, it didn't take a rocket psychiatrist to read old Clint. He was a man who kept his options open, and always kept his eye out for the big break.

In his efforts to develop his plan to swindle the Medicare department, it wasn't so much what Dr. Beloit learned *to do* as it was what *not to do.* Billing Medicare for claims from dead people was out . . . and stupid. Same with identity theft. False claims and misrepresentation were tricky, and would have to be evaluated case by case. Telemarketing and phone solicitations left a paper trail, so that was out. Nonmedical transportation was out, but that could be covered with a new van purchased through his practice. How he paid for it was a different story. *Maybe lease it back on a high per-mile rate?* As long as the power wheelchairs and scooters met Medicare qualifications, that could add to his revenue stream if done right. He would avoid smart patients, only low IQs and people that didn't check on everything. Culling that herd would mean evaluations from personal interviews. He also knew that he could create receipts for expensive drugs and get reimbursements from the pharmaceutical salesmen that would never see the light of day. He knew he would be limiting his market with these rules, but more importantly, he would be limiting his risk. He would still be able to bring in between $5,000 and $10,000 every week or so without appearing on the CMS radar . . . maybe more.

It may have taken a few years more than Orwell imagined, but then again, he might have shared the claim, along with Al Gore, of having invented the Internet if he'd stuck around. Actually, the nascent seeds of the Internet began in the '60s, about fifteen years after George Orwell's dystopian novel *1984* was first published in 1949. Almost coincidentally, the Advanced Research Projects Agency Network, or ARPANET, adopted TCP/IP in early 1983, and the formation of the "network of networks" had begun.

But aside from that useless piece of trivia, Dr. Beloit believed that it was the greatest invention of all time, mostly because it led him to his victim. All right already, Zuck, Facebook gets some credit, too.

In any event, Beloit had to first get a list of employees at the top of the Medicare department food chain. Then he had to investigate them to see which of those were approachable. Then he had to really watch his ass.

Beloit knew a guy. The guy was a burnout for whom he had once written a prescription, a '60s guy who still called marijuana "shit." "Got any shit, man?" "Hey dude, this is really good shit." Visualize. So, the guy was named Ernie, and Ernie considered himself a hacker. Real hackers wouldn't call Ernie a hacker, but he could hack well enough for Dr. Beloit, who could pay him enough to get some fine shit, so Ernie went to work for "da main man."

There was little challenge for Ernie to find a list of personnel within the Medicare facility. Same with CMS. Profiling and intuiting any vulnerability, however, required a much wider investigation. He checked police records and court records, though he didn't expect to find anything interesting, as these people would have had to be vetted to some degree, but places like Google and MyLife could sometimes provide interesting disclosures. Ernie wasn't the kind to get discouraged. That was how guys like him were wired. Tidbits of interest began to appear once he got into the social media world.

First of all, anyone who is a big social media player may have some issues. For the gregarious crowd, it is perhaps entertainment. Then you have the nosey folks and the curious. Some are imagination voyeurs, some with little else to do, and certainly, many are just connecting out of loneliness.

Unfortunately, there is a huge contingency of pleasure-seekers with dishonorable intent, and of course, the hunters and stalkers who prey upon the naïve, the weak, and the wounded. Sometimes you may encounter someone who is just a bigmouth, someone who uses the Internet soapbox to express their bottled-up resentments, emotions, and opinions. They might even succumb to hubris and forget they're being watched.

When Ernie found such a guy, he back-checked and found where the fellow worked and his position. He double-checked before he whispered, "Bingo."

Ernie leaned back in his ergonomic chair, inhaled deeply, exhaled slowly, and looked out the window at the blue sky. It was transcendental, slow-mo and halcyon, soft and inviting, and it took him to a calm and serene place, a place that titillated his meditative spirit. He visualized a bag, a beautiful bag, a bag of Grand Daddy Purple Grade A+, the best and most expensive *shit* on the planet.

CHAPTER 14

Vietnam
1969

There's backstory and then there's backstory—like 2,500-years-ago-backstory. But don't fret, we'll catch up quickly.

Though some historians argue that he was a fifth century BC *fictional* character, it seems a guy named Sunzi—more commonly known as Sun Tzu—a Chinese military strategist, wrote what has come to be considered the bible of combat, *The Art of War*. The text is composed of thirteen chapters, each of which is devoted to one aspect of warfare. This work has had an influence on Eastern and Western military thinking, business tactics, legal strategy, and beyond. One of Sun Tzu's statements was "Know thyself, know thy enemy. A thousand battles, a thousand victories."

In the Vietnam War in 1969, only one of those four propositions was true. Sadly and detrimentally, it was the third one, "a thousand battles." The other three were lost in a ganglion of chaos. It appeared as though President Lyndon Johnson and Private Reuben James had no idea what was going on, and I should add that that included most everyone in between.

The precept "know thyself" appears on AA medallions as a personal code. On a much more generic level, the country did not know itself in Southeast Asia as that conflict progressed. There seemed to be no real purpose within the administration, no end game, no understanding, and if there was, Washington certainly wasn't passing it along to the people. Hundreds of thousands were protesting this war, some leaving the country for places unknown. Regarding "know they enemy," the military chiefs appeared to lack direction and strategy. The military seemed an anachronism. Conventional warfare was but a World War II memory—and to some extent, Korea—but guerilla warfare was a conundrum, and those in charge simply shook their heads in frustration and misdirection.

Yes, there were *a thousand battles*—actually that by a geometric number—but *a thousand victories*? That would only be heard in the political rhetoric coming out of Washington.

In late 1968, Johnson halted all bombing of North Vietnam, hoping to resume peace talks. To that point, over one million tons of bombs had been dropped on North Vietnam, about 800 tons every single day, with nearly 1,000 US aircraft having been shot down and 300,000 sorties flown, all this having almost no effect, and in retrospect, apparently the opposite effect. Richard M. Nixon was elected in November as the thirty-seventh US president. As the fifth president involved in coping with Vietnam, he accepted the title of "peacemaker." In February, the Vietcong attacked 110 targets in South Vietnam, including Saigon.

Billy and his squad were hunkered down on the edge of a

dense forest. Fighting and killing had been torrid. Even the fittest had been challenged to survive, because the numbers were so big. Some pedant would probably call it quantitative analysis and Darwinian exceptionalism. Frontal assaults, encirclement, snipers, and pincers, lots of dead bodies. They were split from the rest of the company. They could hear them, but couldn't see them. They had to shout directional locations of the enemy based on the imaginary clock—noon being north, the primary concentration of the Cong.

"Gooks at seven o'clock."

"Sniper, two o'clock."

Billy had radioed the 118th Helicopter Assault Team to send a chopper. It would be their only chance to survive this herd of screaming Hun. The chopper would have to make a hot landing about 600 meters to the rear of their position. They'd have thirty to forty seconds to load on and take off. For his men to traverse the open terrain, he knew he would have to stay in position and use the M-60 to provide them cover. Otherwise, they'd all be killed. Private Cohen was their machine gunner.

"Izzy, how much ammo you got? Save the rest." Billy shouted the question and command to Cohen as he surveyed a path of retreat, at the same time listening for the *wop-wop-wop* of a Huey.

"Only about three belts left, Chief, and I need 'em," Cohen replied, his look one of disbelief.

"Grab that Thompson we captured from the gooks and use up that ammo. Give me the sixty." Stone yelled the command as he grabbed the machine gun and the belts. "When I give the signal, you four haul ass along the tree line and head for that small rise behind us. You got that?" He screamed the order, staring and daring each man a rebuttal.

After another minute of heavy fire, he heard the angelic trumpet of the Huey.

"Okay, go . . . *now* . . . *go!*" As his men took off, Billy set the M-60 on the small hill and surveyed his field of fire.

They came at him in fours and fives, from noon, two o'clock, and ten o'clock. He took a bullet in the shoulder—a through-and-through, no bone. As he smacked the cover latch down on the second belt, he looked back at his squad. They would stop, shoot, run, stop, and shoot again. He smiled and continued to fire. The onslaught seemed unstoppable.

He could feel the cold fingers of death. His thoughts turned to his dad, his mom, and his sister, the sweet little girl he adored. Still, he couldn't be captured. He thought about using his M-16 on himself.

Billy's eardrums almost popped as the rotor blades of the chopper sounded about fifty feet over his position, coming in low from behind him. Billy watched as first one and then a second Folding Fin Aerial Rocket (FFAR) streamed toward a platoon of Vietcong soldiers, sending bodies into the air. That was followed by cannon fire as the UH-1B made a quick turn and took out more soldiers from behind.

The charging troops were suddenly in disarray, and that gave Billy the time he needed to abandon his post and attempt to join his team. He knew the helicopter would now disengage, having depleted its armor. He used up the ammo and broke off the cover latch to disable the weapon as best he could. He would have to leave it.

As he stood to run, he was hit in the thigh. He also couldn't see out of his right eye, as it had been penetrated by a piece of shrapnel. The pain was intense, but he continued to hobble in retreat as best he could.

After about a hundred yards, Corporal Reuben James stepped out from behind a tree, scooped him up, and carried him like a ten-pound gunnysack to the LZ.

The extraction was successful. By the time the Cong had recovered from the damage inflicted by the Huey Slick, as the troops called it, Billy and his men were aboard and the chopper was headed to the base camp. Other than Billy's wounds, a bullet had grazed the gluteus maximus of Corporal Reuben James. It was a flesh wound that stung like hell and would earn him another Purple Heart, but he didn't give a damn about that. He was more concerned about the shit he knew he would get from Cohen about his big ass.

"Thanks, Chief," Billy shouted to the pilot, a first lieutenant with a quiet smile. "Damn nice flyin'. You saved my bacon."

Cohen had wrapped Billy's shoulder and thigh—no excessive bleeding from either wound. Billy felt he wouldn't be out of action for long. Reuben, lying on his side, kept giving furtive glances at Cohen while trying to hide his wound, but then he caught Izzy's impish giggle. *Shit.*

Apparently the pilot had broken off from a "Snoopy mission" and picked up a loner, a sergeant who had a prisoner with hands tied behind his back. He was an old man whose visage of terror showed helpless confusion. The soldier was bending the fingers of the prisoner and screaming at him. The cargo doors were open, and the noncom was pushing the old man toward the open space as the chopper skimmed the jungle treetops. When it appeared as though he was going to push the old man out, Billy grabbed his collar.

"We're not barbarians, Sergeant. If you do what I think you're planning to do, I can assure you that you'll join him."

They stared at each other in icy defiance before Billy let go, saying, "A word to the wise."

Except for the beat of the rotor blades, there was silence until the Huey landed at the base camp. Until their individual deaths, many years in the future, the four men in Sergeant Billy Stone's squad would never forget that incident. It would be a life lesson like very few that they would ever again experience.

For his bravery, Billy received a Silver Star, and for his wounds, a Purple Heart.

CHAPTER 15

Greenwich
2010

Sometimes, deep in the fecund soil of corruption, the seeds of delusion germinate because the corruptor finds reason to believe God is on his side. Not uncommon really. "Cause" people and serial killers claim the same.

Dr. Beloit found that rationale to be a convenient support system as he reviewed his upcoming phone call with Clinton Hilliard. With Ernie's input, Beloit couldn't believe his luck. Could there be a more perfect candidate? Now, if only Hilliard also believed in divine intervention.

After mulling over a number of scenarios relating to how to get Hilliard to respond and connect in an environment with very low risk, Beloit concluded that maybe Ernie should make initial contact. Ernie would provide insulation and tacit deniability. The other thing was, Ernie was good at bullshit and could perhaps dangle a tempting enough carrot to lure Hilliard to the next level.

Ernie didn't like to waste time, so he called directly into the

Centers for Medicare and Medicaid and asked for Mr. Hilliard. *Start with simple, not complicated.* Ernie was a fan of a computer systems guy named John Gall, who claimed, "A complex system that works is invariably found to have evolved from a simple system that worked. A complex system designed from scratch never works and cannot be patched up to make it work. You have to start over with a working simple system." That was Gall's Law.

What the hell, Ernie thought. *If it works for systems, why not everything else, including getting someone to meet with you?*

"Hello, this is Hilliard." That was his usual, short, bored, and boring pickup.

"Good morning, Mr. Hilliard. My name is Ernie Slopes, and I'm calling on behalf of the Beloit Clinic here in Connecticut." He paused, but not long enough to let Hilliard speak. "The clinic has made the decision to bring in a speaker—an expert, if you will—to address the employees about the many changes, and frankly, what have been problems within the Medicare system over the past six months or so. The clinic wants its employees to be informed." Again, only a short pause. "It seems your name was on a list of experienced Medicare executives, and since the clinic is offering a very generous fee for this presentation, I have been asked to inquire as to whether you may have an interest." Ernie smiled, pleased with the creativity of his bullshit. He especially liked his anonym, Ernie Slopes, a spin-off of the old Cubs shortstop. It sure beat "Ernie Financialinstitutions."

After a minute, Hilliard responded. "First of all, let me say that I would be honored to speak to the clinic. Perhaps you could expound on the 'generous fee' that you mention, which I assume includes any minor expenses. Secondly, if you could tell me about the proposed arrangements, I will check my calendar to see if I am available." Clint was having a hard time playing it cool. His prayers may have been answered. He pictured himself speaking to not just a single clinic, but many, and hundreds of people clapping at his insights. Mainstream television? He and O'Reilly bumping knuckles?

His reverie was interrupted.

"The fee for your presentation would be three thousand dollars, and of course, all expenses would be paid, as well as other arrangements. However, there is a sense of urgency to schedule, so Dr. Beloit would like to meet you for lunch this Saturday. You are approximately a five-hour drive from Washington to Greenwich. He would like to meet you at the Homestead Inn on Field Point Road at one o'clock. Will that work for you, Mr. Hilliard?"

"I will arrange my schedule to make it work, Mr. Slopes."

With that, Ernie again settled back in his comfy new chair and said out loud, "It's a beautiful day for a ball game. Let's play two."

The Homestead Inn was a luxury boutique hotel and four-star contemporary French restaurant located in the prestigious Belle Haven residential area, just minutes from Dr. Beloit's clinic. Perfectly placed on 2.7 lushly manicured acres, this timeless, architecturally significant hotel was brave and bold, effortlessly blending the old world with the new. Contemporary artist's paintings, and forged iron and bronze sculpture were reminiscent of Garouste and Bonetti. Their website stated, *It is said the difference between real life and the movies is that real life has bad lighting*

and no score. The owner claimed that "all that changes as one enters the manicured gardens of Homestead Inn."

Dr. James Beloit agreed. He loved the place, and knew the effect it would have on Clinton Hilliard.

Beloit arrived early and talked with his waiter before Hilliard got there.

"If you'd care for a glass of wine," Beloit said after Hilliard sat down, "the selection is fantastic. If you like, I would be happy to choose."

"That would be most welcome, Doctor. I trust your choice." Clinton Hilliard knew nothing about wine, except maybe sangria.

Beloit watched Hilliard surveying the décor. He guessed that the man didn't get out much, at least to places like this. The doctor was a master of positioning, and not too bad at manipulation. He began to steer Hilliard toward the web.

"So you know, Clinton . . . may I call you Clinton?"

"I do go by Clint, Dr. Beloit, and if you like, I can call you James, or maybe Jim."

"Call me Jim, Clint." He smiled at Hilliard. "So, as I was saying, Clint, it appears as though Washington has gone into the construction business . . . in this case, building mountains . . . mountains of regulation and paperwork. Forgive my cynicism, but do you agree?"

"No sh . . . kidding, Jim. It's ridiculous. The expansion in the amount of time to process, the ever-increasing number of forms . . . time, money. Yup, you're right-on, Doctor. My talk to your people will probably fall under the category of a training session as much as just being informative. That way, *you* will save both time and money." Hilliard gave Beloit a big victory smile, like Lassie waiting for a well-earned doggie biscuit.

Beloit's return smile was not so much agreement as it was confirming that when he handed this guy a shovel, he would be able to dig a nice hole for himself.

"Well, I'm glad to hear we're on the same page, Clint." Beloit stroked his chin in thought before continuing. "So, what would you think about some kind of, should I say, consulting arrangement where you could provide me with updates in your department? You know, ways to shortcut some of this bureaucracy?" The two men looked at each other in silence, each trying to read the other until Hilliard spoke.

"Can't say I totally understand what you mean, Jim, but I could be interested in helping you out . . . based on the arrangement, of course."

"Of course."

Again, there was a period of quietude. Picture Muhammed Ali and Joe Frazier sizing each other up. Beloit thought he sensed an opening, and he pursued it.

"I do, of course, want to do things right, but we shouldn't have to be punished for providing valuable services to the program. We want to serve, but also profit. And, Clint, I don't want to create boogiemen where they don't exist. So, as I see it, if your department is investigating things that probably aren't going anywhere anyway, you could give us a heads-up. That make sense?" Beloit was being purposely opaque in trying to set his trap.

Hilliard's response told him that he had succeeded. "I can't see any problem with that, Jim. I'd just be helping everyone in the process and making a few extra shekels for old Clint while helpin' out. Everybody wins . . . right?" The Lassie grin again.

"Right," Beloit answered out loud, but the word inside his head was *Gotcha!*

"Okay, so tell me about the consulting proposal." Clint Hilliard was picturing himself behind the wheel of a 2010 Mercedes Coupe. Bright red.

Dr. James Beloit was picturing his next visit with Winston Tyler III, the final piece to his puzzle.

The waiter brought a second bottle of wine. The two men continued their conspiratorial discussion about peripheral topics that seemed to merge their interests while at the same time enjoying the lavish delicacies of gougères, foie gras, boeuf bourguignon, and madeleines for dessert. When the cognac arrived, their individual visions of sugarplums danced.

CHAPTER 16

Israel Cohen

Sergeant Billy Stone had asked Private Cohen during Army basic, "Just out of curiosity, Cohen, when did you first become a smartass?"

Cohen, who actually thought the question was legit, and not rhetorical, remembered that in sixth grade, a substitute teacher had sent him home with a sealed note that said, *Mr. Cohen, your son is an intelligent boy with much potential, but he's a smart aleck. Any ideas?*

His father had given him a strong lecture and sent a sealed reply to the teacher. Israel had opened the envelope and read the words, *Thank you. I have addressed the issue with my son. If it happens again, let me know, please.*

Israel wrote his own note and put it in another envelope. *He's not always a smartass. Sometimes he's asleep.*

The sub just looked at him and shook his head, saying something about not falling far from the tree, and never returned.

Cohen's reply to Sergeant Stone was short. "Sixth grade."

Israel had grown up near the Belle Haven Club in Greenwich,

Connecticut. *Grown up*, was, semantically, an exaggeration. It would not be until he volunteered for military duty that he began to show signs of maturation. Where he acquired his attitude was anybody's guess. He would later conclude that it probably related to his high IQ and cynical world view at an early age, or his privileged environment, probably the combination, but nevertheless, it was his signature characteristic.

His father was very wealthy, as was his mother. Both members of eastern blueblood families, they had inherited several millions of dollars. His mother spent her money on extravagant things like cars, clothes, trips, jewelry, parties, and such. His father had been extremely shrewd with his investments: Standard Oil, Ford Motor, General Electric, as well as getting in on the ground floor of the computer industry with Control Data and HP, to name a few.

Less than sixty miles to the north of Greenwich was the town of Wallingford, on the Quinnipiac River. Of course, it was quaint. It was established in 1667, when the Connecticut General Assembly authorized the "making of a village on the east river" to thirty-eight planters and freemen. Hell, it was so quaint that those guys could still be hanging around today, along with another 45,000 freemen and ladies, of course.

In 1890, Wallingford resident Mary Atwater Choate founded a highly disciplined girls' school called Rosemary Hall. Six years later, her husband, Judge William G. Choate, established a school for boys on the same grounds. It was simply called *Choate*. The standards, discipline, and mission statement for the two schools coincided. They operated separately until merging in 1974. Recognizable alumni include Adlai Stevenson and John Fitzgerald Kennedy, Michael Douglas and Glenn Close, and all sorts of other notables.

Notably missing from the esteemed list, however, is one Israel Cohen. Whereas students ordinarily list their accomplishments in the yearbook when they matriculate to schools of higher learning, Israel Cohen's list was brief, and did not include the primary reason that he graduated from Choate at all: a $1 million contribution to the scholarship fund from Albert Cohen, Israel's father. After that, Israel decided to eschew matriculation altogether. He decided to make some money instead.

Israel had learned about finance and the stock market from his father. From his father's generic discussions and opinions, he gleaned an understanding that, with a most assiduous commitment to further study and absorption, as well as an innate intuition, led him to a conclusion that the relationship between the business cycle and the stock market was distant at best. There may have been some method to the madness of the market, but really, it was simply a reflection of the mood and the emotion of the investment community. It clearly operated on greed and fear, underscored by optimism or pessimism.

He felt that his father didn't understand that art form in his world of scientific analysis. Not that his father wasn't an extremely successful investor—after all, he must have been gifted with prescience to so often be a ground-floor player in companies and industries that sometimes exploded, but almost always grew in arithmetic and geometric progressions over time. Thing is, he was only a buyer, and what Israel found to be fascinating was what was happening *during* that time. Israel's interest was in the field of graphs and charts, and he came to see the intractable patterns of predictability with his father's successful holdings. On a long term, the graphs would trend up, but it was the path of two steps up and one step back where Israel saw opportunity. Risk was a function of predictability, and that path was predictably redundant. So, Israel concluded that you could make money both going up and coming down. The two things that were mandatory for success with this strategy were a good growth company and volume of trading.

Israel started with four stocks, two NYSE and two NASDAQ. He bought them and held them until they reached a threshold. Then, depending on volume evaluations, he would sell them short, hoping they would go down to, or below, his down threshold, protected by stop losses. In a steady market, he was making money both ways on the same stock. He would lose profit if he got out early, in either direction, but he was sometimes in and out and back in several times a month and sometimes more often than that, profiting from almost every trade.

Yes, he had a high metabolism, and yes, the adrenalin rush kept him on high rev. But then one day he reached burnout. He didn't feel comfortable with what was close to an addiction, as well, so he cleared out his account and put $97,000 into a savings account. Then he drove to San Francisco, where he hoped to find his new icon, Ken Kesey.

Okay, so most people know that excessive regrets may not be a sign of top-tier mental health, but most of us have a couple, anyway. Years later, as Israel paged through the book of his life, there was one that still stung: he hadn't been one of the 400,000 people on a dairy farm in mid-August 1969, near the small town of Woodstock, New York. On the plus side of the ledger, however, he had stood on the corner of Haight Street and Ashbury Street in "Frisco" three years before.

In the 1950s, the equivalent of today's Millennials were called the Beat Generation. As a member, you might have been referred to as a "beatnik," a stereotype who displayed the more superficial aspects of the movement—but I'll tell you, these guys used some crazy cool lingo. A well-dressed person was *a shape in a drape*, while if you listened carefully, you would *focus your audio*. If you were thinking, you were *interviewing your brains*. If you were aware, you *knew your groceries*. And if you were out of control, you were *slated for crashville*. A used car was *a lead sled*, and your personal space was called your *Mason-Dixon line*.

These characters morphed into the hippies of the 1960s, a liberal counterculture of lovefests, cheap guitars, and peace . . . *Yeah man, a bit off the cob, but really Kumbaya*. The mores of mainstream American life were to hippies, *craptastic man, yeah, lamesauce, and cronk man*. But Israel was a smart kid who knew his groceries, and for his little hiatus from the real world, he wanted to interview the brains of Kesey and his merry band of pranksters. Israel's favorite book was *One Flew Over the Cuckoo's Nest*, and he wanted to talk to *the man*. He supposed that if he had to participate in a lovefest or two along the way, he could put up with it.

A "sanctuary," in its original meaning, is a sacred place, such as a shrine. In 1966, San Francisco was a sanctuary city for the love movement. Today, it is a sanctuary city for criminals, where crime and fear rule the streets.

I'll go with the first one, where Israel arrived in his lead sled on July 3. First thing he had to do was *jungle up* (find a place to stay). He found a cheap motel. Next, he had to go where the hippies were, and from what he had read, that was Haight-Ashbury. When he got there, he was disappointed. No crowds, not lotsa hugs goin' 'round, only one weirdo sitting on the curb strumming a strange stringed instrument he obviously didn't know how to play.

Now what? He decided to drive to the famous Golden Gate Bridge and find something to eat, catch some sights, kill some time, and come back in a few hours. So he did. Three hours later, he returned, and the expectations he had been managing for the past three hours were met with great surprise. The place was hummin'. Seemed there was a poetry reading several blocks away when he had first arrived, but now, like the cows at suppertime, the hippie hoards had returned home.

History shows that the fertile loam of the Haight was where the seeds of acid, a classic music niche, peace, love, and protest grew into a movement that stopped a war, a war in which Israel Cohen was almost killed. But on that day, nothing could have been farther from Cohen's reality. He walked around, watching artists and artist wannabe's as they painted and drew childlike pictures. He listened to poets read to groups of threes and fours, followed philosophers, students, and panhandlers, and stopped to watch a band called the Charlatons, a band that would one day be the legendary acid-rock-western band that would inspire and spawn some of the biggest names of that era. He was in the zone.

For several days, Israel found himself to be in a world the likes of which he had never been in before. His world had been that of eastern aristocracy, hoity-toity condescension, prim and proper. The students at Choate were prioritized by parents who had been conditioned by their parents, and those priorities were perhaps more external than internal. Character development, discipline, achievement, global perspective on cultural, social, political, and environmental issues were seemingly noble ideals, but underlying was the offset, a strong influence toward financial and power positioning, an elitist and material recognition designed to separate the "great" from the "great unwashed." This was an establishment that worked hard to develop its veneer of success.

To a degree, Israel had eschewed that dogma. Now he was suddenly whirling round and round in a maelstrom of indiscipline and a very different set of mores. Although his visit would precede by a year the so-called Summer of Love, 100,000 youths, and Scott McKenzie's song, "San Francisco," the girls actually did wear flowers in their hair, and they were a far cry from the debutantes from Rosemary Hall.

In their belief that they were part of an enlightened community, these kids were not totally delusional. In their belief that the world could collectively join hands and sing "Kumbaya," they were. After all, one cannot void or avoid the frightful universality of the frail human element. Aside from the detriment of drug misuse, the psychedelic window of peace and love through which the beautiful people innocently and verdantly gazed, there was a wonderful kind of revolution. Sadly, and with historical redundancy, it would become just one more interfering nudnik that the political machine couldn't afford, and like those flowers, the movement would eventually dry up and die.

Israel fell in love twice in his first three days. The first time was simply infatuation. The second was the deep stuff, until the object of his affection kissed him on the cheek and left with her new lover, perhaps a deeper and more committed relationship. He saw her later with another guy, but by then, he had gotten over her and had found someone new. Still, they remained friends. Banter aside, Israel absorbed that there was a genuine collective love affair, without possession and jealousy . . . kind of a *sharesy* type of thing.

On the fifth day, serendipity came. It came like an apparition down Haight Street, up from Kezar Stadium, through Downey, Ashbury, and Delmar Streets toward Buena Vista Park. It was covered in kaleidoscopic graffiti and painted many colors, like Joseph's coat, and with similar symbolism. It was an International Harvester school bus. The driver pumped his fist in the air and shouted to several people he recognized, all the windows open. One girl waved and screamed, "Hail to Hopalong Cassidy."

The sign on the front that normally signified a destination simply had the word *FURTHUR*, apparently a misspelling, or so Israel thought. Sitting on top was a man in a chair, a well-built fellow wearing a cardboard crown. He was playing a role, waving to his cheering subjects. Israel just watched. When the bus had gone past, he turned to his current squeeze, a girl with straight, long, braided hair, a plain face, and a cherubic smile, and said, "Who the hell is that?"

She looked at him as though he had just arrived from Pluto. "You've never heard of Ken Kesey?"

Every once in a while, a writer is born with the sole purpose to tell, or maybe to remind people, that there is something of extraordinary value that needs attention in the human spirit. Kenneth Elton Kesey was perhaps such a man. A counterculture figure, Kesey considered himself to be a link between the Beat Generation of the 1950s and the hippies of the '60s, yet there were no definitive lines in his transition, as he didn't have definitive lines in his life.

A farm boy born in Colorado in 1935, he attended the University of Oregon, where he distinguished himself as a wrestler and actor. He later received a writing scholarship from Stanford. While attending Stanford, he volunteered as a paid experimental subject in a study conducted by the US Army in which he was given mind-altering drugs and asked to report on their effects. In 1968, a rather dapper Virginian named Tom Wolfe would write a nonfiction work titled *The Electric Kool-Aid Acid Test* about these experiments, and Ken Kesey's and his pranksters' quest to achieve intersubjectivity (the psychological relationship between people) among the masses.

Kesey could preach and captivate listeners like "Brother Love and his travelin' salvation show." He despised injustice, and after working as an aide in a psychiatric ward, wrote his classic novel, *One Flew Over the* Cuckoo's Nest, in which he examined the abuses of the system against the individual. His next work, Sometimes a Great Notion, focused more on questions of individuality and conformity. Some consider this his greatest work, and like *Cuckoo's Nest*, it became a major motion picture. At one point, in typical Kesey form, he was charged with marijuana possession, faked a death note, and fled to Mexico, only to later return and serve half a year on a work farm. In most ways during this age of the transcendent psychedelic lifestyle, he was an icon.

Israel and Moonbeam, his latest girl, followed the bus to the park. There was a crowd around the bus, and it was the driver that was the most animated, with a throng of followers.

"I love Neal. You know who Neal Cassady is?" Moonbeam beamed. "He's crazy fun, and dreamy looking. You gotta meet him."

When the crowd thinned and they got close, "Mooney" gave Cassady a long hug and kiss. Cassady smiled. Actually, he hadn't stopped smiling.

"Cass, meet my new friend Izzy."

They shook hands. Cassady smiled, looking around, apparently waiting for more hugs and kisses.

Israel smiled back, looking to the top of the bus before asking, "Will Mr. Kesey be coming down?"

Cassady's smile was instant incredulity before it became a raucous laugh. "*Mr.* Kesey? You kiddin' me? No one's ever called him that." He kept laughing until he said, "Shit man, he's *gotta* meet you."

Neal Cassady was like a Kesey doppelganger in many ways, only he wasn't really a writer. He thought he was, and even wrote five books, but they were grade-B attempts. His claim to fame in literature, however, was that his wild spirit immortalized him as the key character in Jack Kerouac's classic book, *On the Road*. He would die from drugs two years later.

When Cohen was finally introduced to Kesey, he was disarmed by the man. The merriest prankster was soft-spoken, and he processed Israel's questions before answering. He was neither dismissive nor arrogant. Israel liked him. It is often the case that the insecure are the ones that camouflage with bluster, but Kesey seemed comfortable in his own unapologetic self, palpably satisfied with his unique but perfect imperfections.

Israel was fulfilled with having accomplished his goal. Along with that, he had adapted his persona and demeanor to the Haight experience. He was in transition, and he saw both the world and the future through a new and much mellower lens than he had ever imagined. He was wearing his best smile when he arrived at his motel room. It would disappear in the next ten minutes.

Israel had told his parents that he was driving to California to take some time off and see the famous Golden Gate Bridge, and that he would be back "in a few weeks." He had been surprised to see the message taped to his door, and when he returned his father's call, he endured the chastisement for not having been more specific, as his father had to hire an agency to track him down.

After the short exchange of pleasantries and not-so-pleasantries, his father said, "A draft notice came for you the day before yesterday." There was a long, punishing silence before he continued. "I will take care of it. Actually, my good friend Senator Babbs will take care of it, but I need you to head back right away. We'll talk when you get here."

With that, his father hung up. Israel sat on the bed with the phone in his hand for nearly five minutes.

CHAPTER 17

Greenwich
2010

T he old man, Winston Tyler II, had been having a strange dream. He and Marie had been walking on the beach. They weren't holding hands—they never had—but it was most pleasing, even appealing to him, and few things were. There was a breeze, with lazy, white cirrus horsetails drifting across a deep blue backdrop. The sound of the curling waves pounding the wide, sandy beach, crashing and reaching to extreme before their silent withdrawal, provided a metronomic beat of antediluvian music, unchanged since primordial dugouts first landed on these shores.

He watched parents corralling their children, some with unleashed dogs. They were staying at a nice place. He couldn't remember the name. Something Blue, but it was in Florida. They'd been there before, a long time ago.

He had never liked his dreams. They were mostly hard and gray and alarming. For the first time since he could remember, he tried to go back to sleep and recapture the moment, but it proved futile, so he got up. As he walked down the hall, he could hear voices from the den. He heard his son talking to someone. He leaned against the wall and listened.

"Understand, Doctor, the money is only a small incentive for me. I don't need it. It's the goddamn system. The system is a farce. It's broken, and I want to prove it." Tyler spoke with a passion that belied his personality. "I'm not even offended by governmental corruption. It's expected, and maybe it couldn't even operate at all without it, but it's the outrageous incompetence that's offensive. 'Never ascribe to malice that which is adequately explained by incompetence.' So said someone with a brain."

"Well, don't be offended, Winston," came the reply. "But although I happen to agree with you, not all of us have the luxury to be indifferent to the luxury of cash."

"Regardless. But the one thing we can't be . . . *indifferent* about is our mutual commitment to never compromise our activity here . . . might I say our *omertà*. *Capisce*?"

"Honor among thieves, the age-old concept of self-protection. *Capisce*."

The old man knew he had overheard something he wasn't supposed to. He stifled his urge to confront his son and ask what was going on, but some element of self-preservation held him back. He was very confused. Who was this doctor? He had to think about what he had heard. He quietly returned to his room.

For Tyler, this deal had never been motivated by money. It was peanuts. For him, it had for some time been a building resentment for the so-called establishment. His country, his father's and his grandfather's, was but a distant memory. Capitalism was a dirty word. There were no statesmen anymore, only self-serving politicians, corrupt and incompetent, irresponsible and without regard for the populace.

And the media, they were worse for operating under the pretense of journalistic truth. What a joke! Follow the money. The distant relationship between the truth and media integrity had only widened. If the truth didn't sell papers and increase ratings, so what? "Put some goddamn spin on the story. Lie if you have to. But *sell*."

Tyler knew he couldn't beat 'em, so he had joined 'em. He had a number of local politicians and several federal-level cats' paws in his pocket, and so he would humor himself and play his game, make a mockery of the irreconcilable Medicare program. *Idiots!*

Beloit may have underestimated Tyler. In retrospect, to think that Tyler was motivated by monetary incentive was naïve, and certainly a mistake. Yes, he had gotten what he wanted—a front, credibility, money, and resources.

The Home Healthcare facility was in the same center as his office. It was impressive, with new furniture, contemporary design and wall décor, several nurses, and a receptionist. Exceptional camouflage, the key being that the operation was overlaid with legitimacy. Of course, legitimate patients, legitimate equipment, even legitimate bills. Beloit had planned well, and in the end, Tyler had bought in.

The hidden agenda, aside from achieving their individual objectives, was a most interesting one, as it was personal: Who was more brilliant, shrewd, and duplicitous, Dr. James Beloit or Winston Tyler III?

CHAPTER 18

Israel Cohen

For someone with the advanced cognitive skills that Israel had inherited and developed, his mind was in turmoil. The forces in his personal world were engaged in a war of choices and ethics, each battling to influence his decisions on the proper course of action.

The drive home had been much faster than the drive to California, not because of the speed with which he traveled, but because of his preoccupation with those upcoming decisions. The trip was robotic, with sights, towns, and countryside blending into a haze of unawareness. He didn't even feel a sense of urgency to get home, and in some ways, he was feeling the wishful avoidance of seeing his father, though that wasn't a choice.

Yesterday's drive had been one of deep introspection. The idyllic world of the Haight was certainly a nice place to visit, but regardless of its attraction, he couldn't live there. The regimented life of his father's house was where he had always lived, but he now knew he couldn't live *there* anymore either.

Though most of the quarrels he had with his father were sub-liminal and unspoken, the life of two-faced detente was like much in recent weeks, a thing of the past. In another con-tradiction of terms, the man was a passive demagogue. But Israel's choice of lifestyle was of very secondary importance on his priority list today.

Though his own father had not served in the armed forces during the war, almost all of Israel's friends' fathers had done so. He never knew for certain how his father had escaped the draft, but he certainly had his suspicions. Israel had been born close to V-J Day, and had read and seen pictures about the celebration. Those fathers had been icons to the rest of the country, and Israel sorely remembered how embarrassed he was when others would ask which branch or which theater his father had been in. He had also seen the military cemeteries and understood the price those men and their families had paid to be free. He had been a recipient.

And now there was Vietnam. Draft notice or not, Israel be-lieved his father. He didn't have to go and get killed. A smart man would waste no time on such a dumb decision. I mean, *really?*

Okay Mr. Cohen, you have two choices. You can choose to live an amazing life, or you can choose to be shot or blown up and die. You have five seconds. Which one will it be?

In his mind, Israel pictured the fuckin village idiot saying, *Oh gosh, let's see. Dang it, that's a real mind-bender, man. Can you give me a little time to think about it? It's not as easy as you think, man. It could be a trick question, maybe.*

But that really wasn't the question, was it? Not for a person of character.

When Israel pulled into Greenwich, he stopped at a restaurant and went to the pay phone. He located the address of the Army Recruitment Center in the phonebook and drove there. He volunteered, filled out the paperwork, and got his date. After understanding all instructions, he went home to meet with his father.

CHAPTER 19

Vietnam
1969

At this point in the war, the laws of action and reaction were in full swing on the battlefield and on the home front. Like a bad marriage, or a defective ménage à trois, the politicians, the military, and the American people were engaged in a dysfunctional and antipathetic relationship that was heading for divorce court.

On March 4, 1969, President Nixon threatened to resume bombing North Vietnam in retaliation for Vietcong offenses in the South. On the Ides of March, US troops resumed offensive action inside the demilitarized zone for the first time since 1968.

At the same time, President Nixon authorized Operation Menu, the secret bombing of Cambodia by B-52s, targeting North Vietnamese supply sanctuaries located along the border. By April, US troop levels peaked at 543,000. There had now been 33,641 Americans killed, a total greater than the Korean War. Meanwhile, back home, 300 antiwar students at Harvard University seized the administration building, removing eight deans and locking themselves in. They were later forcibly ejected.

The New York Times broke the news of the *secret* bombing of Cambodia. As a consequence, Nixon ordered FBI wiretaps on the telephones of four targeted journalists, along with thirteen government officials to determine the source of the leaks.

Only days later, 46 men of the 101st Airborne were killed, and 400 others were wounded during a fierce battle on what was called Hamburger Hill. After the hill was secured, the troops were then ordered to abandon the position by their commander. Enemy troops then moved in and took back the hill, unopposed. After such reckless strategy, it seemed as though Americans had had enough.

Churchill described the Battle of Britain postwar status as, "Perhaps the end of the beginning." The Hamburger Hill fiasco was perhaps the beginning of the end for America in Vietnam, as Washington subsequently ordered the overall commander, General Creighton Abrams, to avoid all such encounters in the future. Hamburger Hill would become the last major search and destroy mission by US troops during the war. Only small-unit actions would be used thereafter, of which there were many.

Sometimes bodies would pile up so quickly that they could not be recovered immediately. Battle lines were so ephemeral that cleanup could be too treacherous. Coordination was unbridled, and troops were often unaccounted for.

Billy Stone's squad was supposed to be on the left flank of the company patrol. His men were thought to be in a line at 100-foot intervals, but who knew? There was almost no control. They were in a jungle so thick you couldn't see fifteen feet in any direction.

Billy, now recovered from his wounds and wearing an eyepatch, had instructed his men that any communication would be low-volume radio, and only in emergency. The only sounds were birds and monkeys, with occasional gunfire. Intelligence claimed that the area was saturated with Cong, but intelligence had been less accurate than weather forecasters. NVA troops had been reported two miles to the north.

Israel had to sling the M-60 over his back, as he needed both hands to get through the foliage and vines. He was a washrag dripping with sweat. Suddenly he froze and shivered as he stared at a stack of bodies, GIs. He figured they had been gathered for transport back to base, but must have been interrupted. He quickly said a *kiddush hashem* for them, and when he turned back on his path, nearly tripped on a large tree that had fallen. Elephant ear leaves had partially hidden the trunk. As he slid over the tree, he saw movement through a hole in the forest. More movement. Black vests and pants. Green hats and tan cones. Gibberish and short commands. And . . . rifles. They were coming toward him. They would be on him in less than a couple minutes. He silently mouthed his usual and most appropriate and spontaneous exclamation: "Fuck."

Israel knew that in a Mexican standoff, he was a dead duck, so he had to run or hide. If he ran, they could shoot him—or worse, capture him—so he had to hide. He looked around, removed the M-60, shoved it as far under the fallen trunk as he could, and covered it with leaves.

He then did something he would never forget and would always shiver with the recollection: he buried himself in the pile of dead bodies, burrowing as close to the bottom as he could. The smell was horrific. He breathed through his mouth, but very slowly, so as to limit even the smallest of movement. The bodies were bloated from the heat and wet from . . . who the hell knew what. He heard the green flies and saw squirming movement in the white mound near his face . . . *Holy fuck . . . maggots.*

Maybe he should have run, or done the Mexican jig—anything but this. Now he was getting sick. Shit, he was cooked. Dead bodies don't puke. They would discover him. He closed his eyes and thought of Moonbeam. Why Moonbeam? He wasn't that hot for her. How about his fifth-grade teacher? He used to jack off thinking about her. *Please, any kind of distraction, dear God.*

Then they were above him, speaking Vietnamese and laughing. One of them kicked a body and laughed again.

After about two months, or so it seemed, the noise faded. He guessed they were gone. He waited a few more minutes before digging out of his larvae-infested mound of rotten flesh. Then, as quietly as possible, he did the colon explosion in reverse, blowing lunch, breakfast, and maybe every meal he had ever had. Finally, drained, he looked heavenward and spoke to God . . . "Really?"

Israel now processed his new circumstances. He was behind enemy lines. *Now what?* In the movies, the guys behind enemy lines would run around and blow up ammo depots and set traps and gather intel and walk out heroes. But this wasn't Hollywood, and he wasn't Steve McQueen riding his Schwinn through the little streets of the French countryside, waving to German soldiers. These guys were freaky-deaky, popping out of holes in the ground and suddenly showing up like apparitions in the mist. Again, he figured he was pretty well fucked. Still . . . *Think, you smartass preppy from Choate . . . you hot dog short-trader from Greenwich . . . you newly converted hippie from the Haight . . . Get it together and think.*

He got the M-60. He had two belts of 7.62 mm rounds that could fire over 500 rounds per minute, so he knew he wasn't goin' down without putting some big damage on these little pricks.

Speaking of pricks—yes, this was an emergency, so he could use the radio to contact his team, and they could find him. That was a great idea, only he didn't have a radio. Sergeant Stone had the "Prick 25." The AN/PRC 25 weighed twenty-five pounds and was too cumbersome for the machine-gun carrier. He continued to talk to himself. *Good one, Izzy.* Finding a solution through process of elimination would mean he could be here until the new decade. Jesus, his head was whirling. *So, what if they come back?*

Israel set up the M-60 on the tree trunk, got a couple of elephant ears for cover, and took up a defensive position. He waited. He thought. At this point, thinking was bad, so he stopped. Now he was using his other senses. He stunk of death and puke, so he stopped that, too.

Then he heard gunfire, and soon, the rustle of leaves and people running through the forest. *Whoa Nellie,* they were coming back.

He was itching to start shooting, but in the heat of this death-threatening crisis, Israel suddenly recalled a history class at Choate. It was a study of the American Revolution, and in particular, the Battle of Bunker Hill. He had been proud. The commanding general was one of the great Connecticut icons, and he was his namesake, Israel Putnam, whom historians called "Old Put." He remembered the lesson.

Israel Putnam first established his reputation at twenty-two, when protecting a herd of sheep. He entered a wolf den, and according to legend, "killed the last wolf in Connecticut." As a member of "Roger's Rangers" during the French and Indian

War, Old Put first distinguished himself as a soldier. Captured on August 8, 1758, by the Mohawk Indians during a military campaign near Crown Point in New York, he was saved from being ritually burned alive by a rainstorm and the last-minute intervention of a French officer named Francis Parkman.

In 1762, he survived a shipwreck during the British expedition against Cuba that led to the capture of Havana. Putnam is believed to have brought back Cuban tobacco seeds to New England, which he planted in the Hartford area. This reportedly resulted in the development of the shade tobacco called Connecticut Wrapper.

In 1763, during Pontiac's Rebellion, Putnam was sent with reinforcements to supply relief at Fort Detroit, where he was hailed a hero.

Putnam was among those who most strongly resisted British taxation policies, and around the time of the Stamp Act in 1766, he was elected to the Connecticut General Assembly, and was one of the founders of the state's chapter of the Sons of Liberty. In the fall of 1765, Putnam threatened Thomas Fitch, the popularly elected Connecticut governor, over this issue. He said that Fitch's house, "will be leveled with the dust in five minutes," if Fitch refused to turn over the stamp tax paper to the Sons of Liberty.

On April 20, 1775, Old Put was plowing his fields near Pomfret, Connecticut, when he received word of the fighting in Lexington and Concord that started the war the day before. He left his plow in the field and rode over a hundred miles on horseback, reaching Cambridge the next day, where he immediately offered his services to the patriot cause.

In the early days of the war, Putnam was regarded by Washington as one of America's most valuable leaders. His courage, leadership, and planning were prominent in the victory at the Battle of Bunker

Hill, which was the reason that Corporal Israel Cohen had had his flashback in the first place. When the British were attacking the hill, Putnam had allegedly commanded, "Don't fire until you see the whites of their eyes."

When the Cong first came through the trees, Israel didn't see any whites in their eyes—only black holes. They were carrying their guns at port arms, jogging and making strange sounds in a strange language. Their faces were obscured in masks of hostility, and maybe fear. There were about a dozen.

He was noticeably shaking, but like Old Put, he waited, and when the front-runners were about thirty yards in front of him, he opened fire.

The M-60 spat bullets in a torrid stream of unsparing brutality. The first half-dozen soldiers were nearly dissected, stomachs and chests of instant red sickly ooze and goo. Some of the others veered off at a run and were cut down from behind.

Israel was on adrenal overload, so much so that he lost awareness of his available ammo. He held his finger on the trigger like a highway engineer on a jackhammer. His upper body vibrated. He'd put down all but three when he ran out of ammunition.

The last three had fallen to a prone position, and when they saw that he was out of ammo, they looked at each other, stood up, and charged him, screaming as they ran. Israel had enough time to pull out his .45-caliber pistol and shoot one in the stomach and another in the shoulder. The third was on him with a knife. Israel had fallen on his back and couldn't get off a shot, so he dropped the pistol and tried to grab the man's arm.

A knife thrust barely missed his head, but caught his ear. He felt the warm liquid on his neck. They were about the same size, and Israel was surprised at the strength of the skinny Vietcong. Their faces were only inches apart. The man's breath was foul with a smell not unlike the earlier odor of dead decay. When Israel went for the enemy's knife, it sliced deeply into his palm, but at the same time, threw his attacker off guard, and Cohen's knee came up to his groin with piston-like fury.

The man crumpled, giving Israel enough time to grab his own knife, strapped to his shin, sinking it deep into the man's head through the soft palate under his chin. The Cong's eyes appeared to solidify, like liquid into ice, instantaneously, and he expired to a sound like a punctured tire. Israel rolled to his side. He heard the other injured men groaning. His ear and his hand both stung with pain.

And then he heard more bodies coming at him from the forest. He couldn't move, he was so exhausted. He was out of ammo. He resigned himself to the imminent big hurt, a bigger sadness and the biggest loss a soldier can suffer, but damned if they wouldn't know he'd gone down fightin'.

Israel muttered a prayer that sounded Yiddish, and laid back on the soft jungle earth. He was embarrassed by his tears. When the soldier appeared over him, he blinked twice, and then heard a voice.

"Jesus, Preppy, you look like shit . . . as usual." Peter Akecheta saw the tears and felt the pain of his friend's resignation, but he just smiled.

Israel's smile was both genuine and a defensive effort to cover his immense relief. He absorbed the moment before responding with one of his signature retorts, "Suck my dick, Cochise. You ass-licks been on lunch break or somethin'?"

For his bravery, Corporal Cohen was awarded a Bronze Star. For his wounds, a Purple Heart.

Sergeant Billy Stone and the men of his squad were *short-timers*. They would rotate back to Conus (Continental US) in three weeks. The squad had given the Army, and in turn their country, everything they could give, and with five Purple Hearts with two doubles, three Bronze Stars, and two Silver Stars, no one could ever say otherwise. Their company commander, Captain Ryan O'Flaherty, had also received a Bronze Star with cluster, and by default, he was included in their shared, perdurable bond.

It had been O'Flaherty who had told Stone that his tour was done with his eye injury, but Billy had nearly fought him to stay with his squad. The captain had reluctantly given in. He met the squad as they returned from the field. He had a medic ready for Corporal Cohen, with whom he shared another link, having grown up in New Haven, Connecticut, not far from Greenwich.

He then shook the hands of Sergeant Stone and each member of his squad, speaking to each with a hug. Billy found that to be warm, but certainly a rare breach of military protocol. He wrote it off to Irish emotionalism.

At that point, O'Flaherty took hold of Billy's arm and walked a short distance away. He spoke for several minutes before Billy's head bowed and the captain put his arm around Billy's shoulder. His squad was watching, and they showed a collective concern.

When they returned, the captain said, "Sergeant Stone will be leaving tomorrow."

CHAPTER 20

Greenwich
2010

Barbara Tyler had noticed a change in the old man. She couldn't tell if it was the progression of his Alzheimer's or the nascent signs of depression. Some days, she thought it could even be a bipolar or manic-depressive thing, but she had no qualification to diagnose, so she decided to just keep a closer tab on his behavior. She had seen it again in their exchange this morning, and later, he appeared to be giving an animated lecture to a phantom audience as he walked the hallway.

"Don't you dare to cloud the good name of this family . . . You understand me?"

For most of today, however, she had been busy getting things ready for her brother's visit. Shotsy was on high rev, helping her with preparation and periodically asking, "When's he gonna be here, Mom?"

Son William, on the other hand, hadn't been seen since he had squealed out of the driveway that morning.

Winston Tyler III had gotten into the habit of driving past the healthcare center on his way to work. What may have appeared to be due diligence was really hubris. He would park the Maybach in a prominent spot and make sure he was seen. Of course, it was disingenuous, but his arrogance was masking vulnerability and potential harm that he just couldn't see and for which he would one day pay a price. Arrogance is the cloak behind which insecurity hides, and Tyler was one of those really intelligent people who was really dumb. Now that contradictory statement is like a Rorschach test, or that picture of Jesus that you have to look at for a long time before you see his face. Then again, it might simply be something Yogi Berra would say.

Dr. Beloit was making progress. His primary efforts were directed toward eliminating risk, and proper billing and good records were the keys. He understood the tenet that risk increases with the number of people that know about a plot, but he still needed one more bit player in his scheme: a bookkeeper, if not an accountant, but they had to be corrupt. His guy Ernie found her.

Though she had been fired by a Wall Street firm, her record was clean. She had made that deal when she let the HR dude know that she "owned the cemetery."

"What the hell you talking about? We can press charges and you'll never get another job." So said the HR dude. "So, what's this cemetery shit?"

"Why don't you just let your boss know that a cemetery owner knows where all those bodies are buried." Her tone was most cordial. "I'm only asking for a small severance, and I will sign a release. I'll wait for ten minutes before I leave for lunch with my new friend. I think his name is Woodward . . . or is it Bernstein? Oh phooey, I just can't remember."

When Beloit met her for breakfast, she still had thirty grand in her checking account.

Since he knew that she would know—would actually *have to* know—he leveled with her from the start. "You're a smart woman, Mildred . . ." Beloit paused, his face a question mark. "Not to offend you, but is that your real name?"

The woman laughed. "I appreciate your candor, Doctor. Of course it isn't, but you're the only interviewer that's ever had the politically incorrect chutzpah to ask what they're all thinking. As an accountant, however, *Mildred* may have helped get me hired in the past."

Again, she laughed. This time, he joined her.

"It's actually Sunny . . . for real."

"Okay, Sunny it is. I like that better. So, as I was saying, you're a smart lady, and if you believe as we do that the government is literally throwing our tax dollars away, you can join us in our venture to make money while servicing the out-of-control Medicare program. The way we see it, we can provide needed medical assistance, and at the same time, put some of those irresponsibly wasted dollars into our own pockets. That make sense?" Beloit was going to let her process the innuendo, but she was already ahead of him.

"Not sure I'm a lady, Doctor, but thanks for the compliment, anyway. So, without a coat of sugar, if I read between the lines, you need a billing system and a set of books that show full compliance. But you also need the proverbial second set of books. And I participate in the profits. That about sum it up?"

Beloit laughed at this caricature of flimflam. "You're a quick study. Looks to me like you'll fit in here very nicely, Sunny."

CHAPTER 21

1969

Billy took a MAC (Military Airlift Command) flight from Tan Son Nhut Air Base near Saigon to Travis Air Force Base in California, where he caught a mail plane into Saint Paul. From there, he hitched a ride to Bloomington.

It had been an emotional whack-a-mole trial for him since he had spoken to the captain. Assorted images and emotions would haphazardly pop up, and his attempts to beat them down had been in vain. Eventually, he stopped trying.

"Billy, I'm sorry to give you bad news, but your father has died," the captain had said. "I was told not to tell you this, but it appears he may have taken his own life. I didn't think it was fair not to tell you what I know."

Captain O'Flaherty was solid, and Billy appreciated his integrity, but the shock was harder than anything this fucked-up war could deliver.

As he got out of the car, he spoke to the E-8 who had given him a ride home. "Thanks, Top."

"No problem." The man's eyes were sad. They had been here

before. "Sorry, kid. And thanks for your service." The top dog NCO had noticed the Silver Star and Purple Heart. His heart was heavy when he pulled away.

Billy tried to brush the wrinkles out of his uniform as he stood in his driveway, but it had no effect. He gazed at the house he had grown up in, and more memories flooded back. He was pulled out of his meditative state when he heard his name . . . and suddenly his little sister was hugging him, her eyes filled with tears. He didn't want to cry, but he lost that control. He pulled lightly on her ponytail . . . God, how he loved her.

"How are you doin', Button Nose?" Billy had called her that for years, ever since she had broken the black button nose of her stuffed Snoopy when she was eight.

"Oh God, Billy, it's so hard. Thank goodness you're home." She hugged him harder, and more tears came.

He held her face in his hands. "How's Mom taking it?"

"Not good. She's blaming herself . . . cries all the time. You gotta talk to her."

They held hands and walked to the front steps. The screen door opened. His mother's visage was a blank stare for almost a minute.

"Hey, Mom," was all that Billy could say.

She looked thin, her face drawn, her hair lackluster and straight. Her spirit was gasping for life. Billy held her. She didn't cry. She said nothing, and almost seemed to have fallen asleep.

"Let's go in."

Billy shouldn't have been surprised at the number of cars in the funeral procession, and still, they only represented about half of those who attended the church service. Lots of legionnaires, cops, ex-employees, neighbors, guys from the bar, friends of his mom, Barbara, and of course his own friends.

In the past year, Billy had seen a lot of dead bodies, some very gruesome, but his father's was so different. He was having a hard time with that difference, unable to truly process it. The soldiers weren't just younger. It was that *they wanted to live.* They saw the whole earth, and their country with its vast expanse of mountains, plains, and the sea, and the peoples, so different yet so alike, and they didn't understand it, but wanted to explore and find its meaning. They had barely started to lust for it before their beacon burned out. They wanted to be part of it, to make a mark, to sing in a choir and to sing solo, and experience rage so that they would know what love was. They wanted to stand at the foot of their destination, only to look toward the distant beyond which could and would be theirs. They wanted to live . . . but they hadn't been granted the chance.

He knew that, in his youth, his father had been that way, too, but then he wasn't anymore. *So, fuck you, Dad. You stole some of me and my dreams when you did this, so, fuck you.* Even a drunk like Thomas Wolfe understood reality, one who fought his demons with a pen, a six-foot-four-inch Jew who told the world you couldn't go home again, but still understood reality. *Man is born to live, to suffer, and to die,* he wrote, *and what befalls him is a tragic lot. There is no denying this in the final end. But we must deny it all along the way.*

But you couldn't deny it all the way, Dad, so, fuck you. I can't cry for you . . . I'll cry for the soldiers.

Billy's preoccupation and emotional commitment had been to his mother and sister. His father would have to wait.

The tumultuous transition from adolescence to manhood has been called a rite of passage. When a father dies and the oldest son inherits his position as head of household, it is simply a phase in the cycle of life. When the oldest son dies, and the father lives on, that is an aberrant diversion from the norm. Children should never die before their parents. In Billy's case, it also was not the norm, and every time he tried to reconcile what had happened, his internal wires would spark like a circuit on overload.

Barbara was so busy doing her whirling dervish caretaking thing, that except for occasional looks of adoration for her older brother, she was mired in preoccupation and self-protection thanks to her wall of denial. Billy wondered if his Button Nose would ever put her own interest ahead of, or at least on a par with, the needs of others.

Billy's mom had fallen into a fugue state, sometimes defined as a "rare psychiatric disorder characterized by reversible amnesia for personal identity, including the memories, personality, and other identifying characteristics of individuality." How much was a result of guilt producing depression? Billy wasn't sure. He was sure that she would recover—after all, it was from her genes that he had inherited his strength and character. For now, he would be her bulwark, her strong shoulder to lean on.

The earliest headstones in the Fort Snelling cemetery were dated 1870. As the long procession passed through the gates of the vast graveyard, Billy looked to the heavens. Could he intuit any message from the Higher Power, or at least the woman in lesser command, Mother Nature? If so, they didn't seem to be of the happy kind. There was a dark gray thunderhead moving in from the west, and the white and lighter gray cumulus tints were disappearing quickly, heading for Wisconsin.

A big white canvas-covered tent had been constructed around the open grave, the apparent work of some clairvoyant planner. Billy sat on one of the white foldout chairs, his mother on one side, his sister on the other. It had started to drizzle, and those who could not squeeze under the tent remained in their nearby cars.

The lugubrious old pastor droned on about "a valley of death" and "the greatest of these," but Billy's thoughts were in a far-off place where punji sticks could bring a different kind of pain. When the seven rifles shot three consecutive blanks into the low-flying clouds, and the first refrain of "Taps" sounded from a distant bugler, the muscles on Billy's cheek twitched. Something had now been lost . . . forever.

At the Legion Hall, Billy sat with his mother at a corner table and methodically got drunk. Barbara ran around hugging and crying, and his mom sipped red wine as mourners came by with vapid but well-meaning wishes and stories. When it was over, they went home, where Billy couldn't help but feel the presence of an uninvited wraith. He did have to return to Fort Jackson for many reasons, not the least of which was to be officially released from active duty, but he would have to see some strength return to his mother first.

After two days of melancholy inactivity, he saw what he needed.

"Well, my darling hero," she said, "are you just going to hang around like a lazy lout, or do something useful? Enough of that mournful frown. It's affecting my karma." She gave her son a knowing smile.

Billy's bigger smile didn't call for a reply, other than, "Love you, Mom. I gotta clean my uniform and head south to get my discharge from this man's Army."

When Sergeant William Stone walked into the barracks at Fort Jackson, his squad was already there. All the short-timers had rotated back, and a bunch of green inductees had already taken their place in Vietnam. Collectively, their emotions were a mixed bag. The biggest and most intense piece of their lives would soon be over. What they had developed and what they felt about each other transcended family, as only combat can do. The word *love* was almost inadequate. When every day for two years, you become closer, more trusting, more dependent upon each other, and one day say together, "We served our time in hell, so, the victory is ours because we were willing to pay the price," individually and collectively, then only a small number can ever expect to achieve such a level again.

As Billy looked at his team, he knew they were the best of the best. Indeed, they hated war, but this strange collection of Americans loved their country. He recalled a statement from J. R. R. Tolkien: "I do not love the bright sword for its sharpness, nor the arrow for its swiftness, nor the warrior for his glory. I love only that which they defend."

They watched their leader as he came into the barracks. They were expressionless, not knowing what to say. Interestingly, it was Yamada who finally spoke.

"You should think on this, Sergeant Stone. My ancestors claimed, 'Duty is heavier than a mountain, dying lighter than a feather.' That said, I offer you my condolences for your father's passing."

"Thank you, Ack Ack, and I will do that."

With that, his squad gathered around him and expressed their thoughts, as well.

It was only later when Billy was alone with Reuben that he asked, "So, Reub, what do you think Ack Ack meant with that mountain statement?"

As always, Reuben thought for a while before responding. "I think he was saying duty's tough, dying's easy."

Once Billy processed that, he knew what Yamada was saying, and once again, he was angry at his father.

Several days later, they departed for their homes to the South, the East Coast, the West Coast, and the Midwest. These guys were tough, and their only hugs were in their expressions. They pledged their commitments to reunions and get-togethers, but needed time to reacclimatize first. They had life decisions to make and relationships to rebuild. Each felt the mammoth loss of something when they left, but just couldn't put their fingers on it. As with everything, time would provide them clarity.

CHAPTER 22

Greenwich
2010

D r. Beloit's program was off to a good start. He had played
his hunch about Winston Tyler to a T. What he'd heard
from the rumor mill about Tyler's criticism for government regulation, fees, and obtrusive interference was true. The man was angry. He was sure that he was being targeted by certain politicians
that he had publicly criticized over the past year. In turn, he had
been audited—not once, but twice—by both the IRS and the
SEC. In a smug and condescending statement, two of the political hacks informed Tyler, and the investment community, that it
was the political establishment, not the financial elite, that dealt
the cards. Their abusive and flippant dismissal of Winston Tyler
had ignited a vengeful brushfire that could burn out of control.

Friedrich Nietzsche said, "It is impossible to suffer without
making someone pay for it; every complaint already contains revenge." Such would be the cause. Confucius, on the other hand,
addressed the consequence: "Before you embark on a journey of
revenge, dig two graves."

What Beloit knew was that, without this agenda of Tyler's castigation and subsequent derision and mockery, the man was much too smart to have assumed the risk inherent in this plan. Part of the risk, to Beloit, was that he also knew that Tyler couldn't be fully requited without rubbing their faces in public excrement. Could he control that risk? Still, he had gotten what he wanted, the straw owner, a legitimate storefront from which to operate and insulate his own risk.

The storefront was an essential part of the scheme. A physical address was a must, but as more and more Medicare scams were being uncovered, having an empty space was an absolute giveaway. An investigator would drive by, see an empty location, and it was over. Beloit and his little team had learned the art of subterfuge, and that by putting in equipment—a phone and a body or two—unless the investigator was a budding Colombo, they would simply make a checkmark on their sheet and move along. The cost, Beloit found, could be offset by providing shoppers with blood pressure readings and health consultations for a nominal fee. Cash on delivery, of course.

The energy and skills that Ernie and Sunny brought to the party had far exceeded Beloit's expectations. They had become a combination of old married couple and standup comedy team, with that touch of competitive spirit that had them continuously trying to outdo each other.

Sunny's billing system was a thing of beauty. Once it was in place, Beloit submitted the application and the nominal fee needed to become a Medicare provider. The design of the system was sophisticated to the point that it would require a CPA to investigate and find corruption, primarily due to the layers of paperwork needed to penetrate validity. In actuality, the government had, as was often the case with their piles of unnecessary regulation, structured the titanic Medicare program for self-destruction.

Ernie was able to match Sunny's program with his own high-test billing software needed to match phantom diagnoses to phantom procedures and medications. The synergy between these two was a strange phenomenon, one of those equations where one plus one equaled three.

The biggest challenge, and the most vulnerable risk, was the accumulation of patients and doctor IDs. The poor and the indigent were certainly a source, but they had to be vetted. The unworldly, low-tech Medicare thieves had ended up in the pokey because they didn't do their homework, were too arrogant, and didn't understand that Medicare was a political issue and at least a rudimentary effort to police it was a voter issue. Vetting the ne'er-do-wells was not that difficult, and a core of these people were legitimate and could be a big profit source.

There was bigger potential in the Clinton Hilliards of the world, corrupt pharmaceutical, hospital, and insurance-company employees that had access to IDs, numbers, and other Medicare data. Beloit was getting referrals from Hilliard every week. Just as important, Hilliard was monitoring the areas of investigation and where the current emphasis was regarding specific corruption disclosures and practices. Beloit's team was able to stay ahead of that curve.

Some of these lists could be purchased from brokers on the black market, but again, those contacts needed to be scrubbed. The quality of these lists was an imperative measurement. The risk factor increased geometrically if doctors and patients were dead, incarcerated, or deported, so Ernie's software was designed as a double check.

The final piece was to initiate the program of sending in the bills. It was expected that some bills would be rejected for one reason or another, but with 4.5 million claims and $1 billion in claims paid every day, the miniscule resources of the Centers for Medicare/Medicaid Services (CMS) didn't have anywhere near the capacity to investigate the rejected claims. The administration, the healthcare-related department spokesmen, and the politicians would occasionally puff out their chests and sound tough, but the reality was that they were just one more governmental paper tiger buried in regulation and paperwork.

Beloit's machine was well-oiled and running like a top by the time the first checks were deposited. It didn't take long to discover that Dr. James Beloit had greatly minimized his projections.

CHAPTER 23

1969

No matter how tough the soldier, reintegration from combat into a normal life—assuming there is such a thing as normal life—is not seamless. The exercise is integral to managing expectations, starting with the illusion that there is stability in human affairs. In combat, like Pavlov's puppy, a soldier becomes conditioned to salivate when the bell rings, only it is far more lethal. Instead of a bell, it is gunfire. Instead of saliva, it is sweat. And the reward is not a biscuit, but a corpse, ideally that of the enemy. When the mind is a high-tension wire for a year, the kilowatts have to be slowly and methodically drained to afford a fine and sensitive pathway to equilibrium. When there is disruption to that process, the cerebral professionals call it post-traumatic stress disorder, or PTSD.

Of the five members of Billy's squad, only two showed any signs that their assimilation back into society, as they pictured it and expected it, would be a bumpy road. Neither would ever need counseling, as both would have that ingredient that was necessary to avoid it . . . recognition. What they recognized was that their priorities and their lives had forever changed, and that both they and those around them would have to make certain adjustments, emotional and behavioral, or those relationships would wither and die.

The other three would ease back into the milieu of their lives with little difficulty. Only years later would they better understand the reasons why. The most simplistic explanation was hidden within the claim of M. Scott Peck: "Life is difficult. This is a great truth, one of the greatest truths. It is a great truth because once we truly see this truth, we transcend it. Once we truly know that life is difficult—once we truly understand and accept it— then life is no longer difficult. Because once it is accepted, the fact that life is difficult no longer matters."

The lives of Akio Yamada, Peter Akecheta, and Reuben James had been difficult before Vietnam, so what was to change? Israel Cohen and Billy Stone had seen the world through the proverbial rose-tinted spectacles, and their rude introduction to reality had been an iconoclastic punishment. Therein was a societal message of deep substance.

Israel's return to Greenwich was greeted with tension. After the first evening with his parents, Israel surmised several things. His mother was unchanged, still chasing windmills in her quixotic world of delusion. His father nursed the perceived scars of his son's rejection from a couple of years ago. His mother, Israel amusedly thought, looked younger, and he searched for the hidden signs of plastic surgery. His father had aged, especially his eyes. He was cordial, but the message he was sending to his son was "You're on your own, kid. Don't look for any help from me." And that was just fine with Israel. He wanted no part of dependency on his father, and could actually feel the relief.

"So, what are you going to do now, Israel?" There was condescension in his father's tone.

"Not sure yet, Dad. Lots of choices." Israel's insouciant response had the appropriate effect.

"Perhaps it's time to become responsible, don't you think?" his father replied with a subtlety of miff.

"Seems to me that responsible people respond to their country's call to duty, don't you think?" Israel's determined stare muffled any further discussion. The line had been drawn.

Most evident in Israel's maturation was a certain intolerance for injustice that he had developed. His cavalier attitude had faded, and a wiser and soberer one had replaced it. Contrary to his father's perception, he did feel the weight of responsibility in regard to what his contribution toward humanity should be.

It didn't take long for him to absorb the many issues that surrounded the protest movement. On a day that he had worn his fatigue jacket to the grocery store, he felt the derision in the eyes of some shoppers and heard disparaging remarks from others as he went to his car. He was torn between antagonisms toward the critics whom he considered to be unappreciative recipients of democracy's benefits without risking a thing, and the beauty of youthful idealism that felt universal love was an obtainable goal, though certainly an illusion.

He recalled the words of Teddy Roosevelt:

> *It is not the critic who counts; not the man who points out how the strong man stumbles, or where the doer of deeds could have done them better. The credit belongs to the man who is actually in the arena, whose face is marred by dust and sweat and blood; who strives*

valiantly; who errs, who comes short again and again, because there is no effort without error and shortcoming; but who does actually strive to do the deeds; who knows great enthusiasms, the great devotions; who spends himself in a worthy cause; who at the best knows in the end the triumph of high achievement, and who at the worst, if he fails, at least fails while daring greatly, so that his place shall never be with those cold and timid souls who neither know victory nor defeat.

The road to bitterness would have been an easy, though a self-righteous one, but Israel eschewed it for other reasons. It was a path fraught with resentment and self-destruction. His own father had fit the mold of the critic without investment, but his reasons had been self-serving. At least this *army of love* was responding to a genuine belief system. Who knew? Maybe *that army* really could become something more than a pipe dream.

Israel had begun to play the game of elimination: what he didn't want as opposed to what he might want to do with his life. In the end, it was a news item he saw on TV that sent him on his new course.

In 1969, the *Huntley-Brinkley Report* ran an NBC Special Report on a new alleged threat to the country, claiming that, "The Black Panther Party (BPP) is a black extremist organization founded in Oakland, California, in 1966. It advocates the use of violence and guerilla tactics to overthrow the US government. Recently, the FBI's Charlotte Field Office opened an investigative file on the BPP to track its militant activities, income, and expenses. It is unclear how much of a threat this organization is now, or could become."

After hearing the collective conjecture of the media, the

politicians, and law enforcement, Israel decided to apply to the Federal Bureau of Investigation.

As the crow flies, it is about 4,000 kilometers from Greenwich, Connecticut, to Bakersfield, California, but who uses the metric system outside the military and foreign countries? Back in the real world, it's miles, my good man . . . *miles* . . . like 2,400 miles. Nobody was talkin' metrics on the streets of Bakersfield, and they sure as hell weren't talkin' metrics in the Blackboard Café, Bob's Lucky Spot, the Clover Club, or Tex's Barrel House. No shit, man, you heard other sounds, like Cousin Herb Henson, Jelly Sanders, and Johnny Cuevelo, and maybe Buck Owens and the country's favorite ex-con, Merle Haggard. Yes, sir, sounds belching out of all the smoke-filled honkytonks in and around Bakersfield. *Whoa Nellie* . . . the Bakersfield Sound.

Steinbeck's classic novel *The Grapes of Wrath* told the story of where the Bakersfield Sound originated. It came from the migration of Okies from the dust bowl to California. Those migrants were simple but powerful people who understood desperation, worked their asses off, and achieved their goals no matter the roadblocks and deterrents. Simple and powerful . . . just like the music, and Akio Yamada loved it.

The dictionary defines "sinew" as a piece of tough, fibrous tissue uniting muscle to bone. There is, metaphorically, mental and emotional sinew . . . even genetic sinew. The Japanese are a people of sinew. If that doesn't make sense to you, humor me, because I'm sticking with it. Yeah, I know that they have stumbled along the way, just like every other race and country that ever lived, but they are a proud, honorable people, rich in history and tradition, and really tough . . . like sinew. Who wouldn't want to go back in time and be a samurai?

From his unpropitious beginnings, Akio Yamada had become a samurai.

Some guy named *unattributed author* once said, "Terrible he rode alone, with his Yemen sword for aid; ornament it carried none, but the notches on the blade." And so it was with Akio and the five-inch scar on his forehead. He could have had some cosmetic work done, but there was no reward in a pretty face, especially when you could have real character with a battle scar. Akio, like his *brother* Israel, a continent away to the east, was also an object of ridicule just by being a Vietnam vet, but not with the vitriol of the East Coast. California was more laid back, and the scar of American imperialism was less acidic out there and more BFD (Big Fuckin' Deal). Also, with Ack Ack, he and his family had heard it all before, so he had developed a thicker skin.

Akio's father was making money hand over fist, and had preserved a spot at the biggest car dealership in Bakersfield for his son. Akio, however, wasn't that big on the whole concept of materialism and getting ahead of the Joneses, and he could see the downside more than the alleged rewards. The disingenuous and tawdry veneers of his rich acquaintances gave him an oily feel just by association. A soldier from Texas had described such friends as "big hat, no cattle." The war and his squad had provided him the value of substance, of true character, and of contribution. He wanted to leave a meaningful legacy.

So, as irony so often makes an unexpected appearance, while Israel was watching Chet Huntley, Akio took his new main squeeze to Alfred Hitchcock's *Topaz*, and he was hooked. He put together an impressive résumé and applied for a job with the Central Intelligence Agency.

Peter Akecheta had been on a high for several days. He had pictured the looks on the faces of his family when he would unexpectedly appear out of nowhere and say, "Surprise, I'm home." He knew there would be tears and hugs, and the Indian telegraph system would alert the rez to his homecoming. There would be a traditional powwow with pig on a spit, a cauldron filled with sweet corn, beer, and whiskey, and dancers with painted faces and primal music sounding to the redundant beat of skinned drums.

But the elation waned on the drive from Rapid City as the timeless desolation of stagnation, even retrogression, was painful to observe while the old Packard pounded the battered roads of the Pine Ridge Reservation. He spotted several old, rusted carcasses of 1950s Fords and Chevys in drainage ditches and familiar rock piles spray painted with graffiti. He tried pushing the embittered thoughts aside, replacing them with positive visions, but they wouldn't go away. The country he had fought for, risked his life for, had abandoned him and his people. The government didn't care, so why had he? Because he was a product from the genetic mix of his parents, that's why—people who did care, who knew right and wrong, and instilled in their children and all those around them that responsibility was in the individual. Responsible individuals created a responsible collective, like his Army unit. Thank God for the men of his squad, who had confirmed what his parents had taught him.

"You've become pretty quiet, Peter," his oldest friend, Tommy Brand, said, glancing at him as he drove.

Tommy had wanted to enlist, but his mother and two younger sisters had no one to take care of them, and he had been exempted.

One should know that no stronger commitment to armed service ever existed than that of Native Americans. War Department officials have stated that, during World War II, if the entire population had enlisted at the same rate American Indians did, Selective Service would have been unnecessary. According to the Selective Service in 1942, at least 79 percent of all eligible Indians, healthy males aged twenty-one to forty-four, had registered for the draft. Throughout the Vietnam era, American Indians enlisted in the military to the tune of more than 42,000. Ninety percent of them were volunteers, with the others serving through draft selection. Almost two dozen Native American soldiers have received the Congressional Medal of Honor.

"So, tell me, Tommy, why is there so little change on the reservation?" Peter asked, not taking his eyes off the bleak terrain.

Tommy took his time to process the question. "Well, old friend, couldn't you come up with an easier question after not seeing you for nearly two years? Like maybe, 'Who are the hot chicks?'" Tommy continued to ponder after a shared snicker. "Unfortunately, it would be way too easy to just blame Washington for our woes, though that might be the short answer. But if you want my honest answer, and I know you do, the tribe needs to take a big part of the blame."

Peter waited for his friend to continue.

"How about I start with leadership, or lack thereof, and opportunity, or lack thereof?" Tommy went quiet again.

As the old Packard chugged along, Peter was transfixed with

the stark landscape of his homeland. He was seeing it through a very different set of eyes than he had in his youth. There were so many images cycling in his head. He recalled the earliest photographs of this land that his father had shared. They were called daguerreotype, images formed on a highly polished silver surface. Two of those early photographers were Frank Fiske and Edward S. Curtis. Fiske had lived among the Plains tribes for over fifty years. He had known and photographed Sitting Bull and Gall, among many others.

But for Peter, the most poignant were several by John C. H. Grabill, those depicting Indian life about the time of the massacre of December 31, 1890. He didn't know about deer and antelope playing, but he did know about the lifeblood of the plains, the buffalo, and the buffalo roamed no more. He remembered the pictures of the piles of buffalo skins that the white hunters were transporting back East for sale to the rich and curious, while leaving the hundreds of thousands of carcasses of meat and valuable remains to decay and waste in the prairie sun. He recalled a picture of scantily dressed warriors on saddleless, drooping horses on a hill overlooking the campsite of dozens of teepees, the long poles wrapped in buffalo skins, the black-and-white photos faded to yellow.

"My simple mind divides life into two categories, mathematics and the human element." Tommy finally broke the spell with his statement. "Leadership is the human piece, while opportunity is just math.

"Look around, Peter. We're an enclave . . . an island. Might as well be in the middle of the Mojave Desert. You see opportunity? You see traffic?" Tommy let that sink in. "Our reservation has resigned itself to reliance . . . not self-reliance, because there is so little opportunity." Another pause before Tommy continued. "And that segues into leadership. So, before you tell me about your father and how he created opportunity, understand that there are few men like him. If there were more, perhaps things would be different." Tommy released a heavy exhale, one that depicted frustration, and more so, acquiescence.

Peter knew that his oldest friend was right. The discussion hadn't lifted his spirits.

After a while, Tommy added, "You should know that, as of today, only a very few members of the tribe are as qualified as you are to understand the true qualities of leadership. You should think about that."

Peter remained silent. Was Tommy pushing an agenda? Was there a new pile of responsibility waiting for him when he got home? Was Tommy right in his analysis? Peter's shoulders suddenly got heavier, and he didn't want to carry this conversation any further, so he pretended to sleep, like that was going to happen.

But it did. Peter awoke to a nudge from Tommy. "Almost there, old friend."

Peter looked around. There was little activity in the streets. He felt a lift of energy from the nap, the aura of despondency having receded with sleep. His house looked empty. Tommy parked the car, and they walked up the old log stairs that his father had built so long ago. Peter had an uneasy feeling as he opened the door. Not a light and not a sound.

"Surprise!" The lights flashed to the chorus of cheers.

Peter almost had a heart murmur. His father limped over to him with a bear hug, and his mother followed. She held his face between her hands, tears in her eyes, and just held him. His sister joined the fray, followed by others. He saw the cherubic smile on Tommy Brand's face. He'd known. Hell, Peter should have known. Ben Franklin said, "Three may keep a secret if two of them are dead." Tommy had done it well.

"Come on, folks. I make it through a war only to die of fright. You would have had to contend with the wrath of my spirit." Peter laughed along with the group.

That night, during the festivities, one of the tribal elders, a man named Hotah Mato (Strong Bear), spoke to Peter. "You have answered the call from your country, Peter. Now you must answer the call from your people."

Peter Akecheta had a vision, and knew that his freedom of choices had been drastically reduced.

On April 4, 1968, Reuben James had been with his unit defending an ammo dump twenty-three miles southwest of Saigon. They would hold that position until April 8 before returning to base camp. That was when he would hear the news that Dr. Martin Luther King had been assassinated. That would be the first and only time that Billy Stone would ever see Reuben James cry. The other squad members would see that happen one more time, many years later.

It wasn't until Reuben had come home to Selma and his parents that he would have the opportunity to grieve for the prodigious loss of the great man. Aside from his mother and father, Reuben was the man he was in large part due to the impact that Dr. King had on the development of his character.

His return from Vietnam was received very differently in Selma than that of the two coasts. He had left Selma as a hero and returned a bigger hero, and being the quiet, unassuming man he was, that was almost uncomfortable for him. And he wasn't just a black hero, he was Selma's hero. On the docks and in the school, both Ezra and Esther bathed in their son's celebrity, as well. They were so proud, while the introverted hero shied away from the spotlight.

"Look, Mom and Dad. I just did my duty, like you, Dad. I appreciate the fuss, but it's time to move on." Reuben hoped they wouldn't be offended, and in typical parent fashion, they looked at each other and smiled, looked at their son and smiled, and gave him another big hug.

Reuben simply shook his head. "So, I talked to Chief Withers yesterday, and he really wants me to join the force. He said he could get me into the upcoming academy class."

Paul Withers was the Selma police chief. Reuben's father knew him from the VFW.

"You sure you want to be a cop, son?" his father asked.

"I think so. I believe in law and order."

Things had settled down in the Stone household in Bloomington, Minnesota. Barbara was back fending off boyfriends, and Billy's mom was expanding beyond a healthy social schedule and finding reward in volunteer work.

Billy's father had left a surprisingly valuable bequest in the form of a stock portfolio. Since his life insurance didn't pay for suicide, it appeared that Benjamin Stone may have been planning his death for a while. He had been picking up shares in a company only several miles from his house, one his pals at the "V" had told him about, a computer company called Control Data, and another one over in Saint Paul called Minnesota Mining and Manufacturing. Both had done quite well.

Billy's financial relief came with knowing his mother's financial relief. As for Billy, he didn't need or care about money. Money always somehow showed up for him, and it always would. He would never be rich, but he would never miss a meal or not have a bed. So everyone was fine . . . except for Billy. In his mind, he was a guardian, not a caretaker. Guardians take care of their brood, but who takes care of the caretaker?

Billy's mind and his body needed a sabbatical. What he didn't need was any kind of pressure. He had just left pressure. He needed time alone. Hell, he hadn't really processed his father's death, let alone his own volatile psyche and priority list. He wasn't suffering—he knew that—he was just tired and needed to recharge his batteries . . . alone. So . . . why not Mexico?

Tequila may not be the nectar of the gods, but as an elixir for expats, it was a great substitute. Billy had flown into San Diego, where he found a motel room near the beach. Actually, it was a dog beach, and was just what the doctor ordered.

Billy had never had a dog, but his friends did. He had always wanted a dog, but his parents had just never understood their value, and had in retrospect overvalued a dog's needs. Billy could feel true joy sitting on the beach, just watching the dogs, and he could intuit their reality. They loved their masters more than they loved themselves . . . No other creature did that. He understood the truth of Will Rogers's claim, "If there are no dogs in Heaven, then when I die, I want to go where they went."

It was like a slow leak in a tire for Billy. The pressure seeped away, and the warm sun penetrated his taut muscles, tensions soothed by the soft breezes blowing in from the Pacific. His patient was his anger, and he nursed his patient with care and worked hard at understanding the pain and the scars from the surgeries his patient had suffered. His anger was a brittle and delicate specter, more like a demon that taunted and tempted him whenever he felt the gentle hand of forgiveness and what he perceived as love. And he was an equal-opportunity employer with his anger. It wasn't just the Vietcong, it was also his own country and all the politicians and government agencies and military egomaniacs, including Lyndon Johnson and Richard Nixon and all the idiots that drank their Kool-Aid. And now the war protesters that were takers, not givers.

And where was God in this mess? An age-old philosophical question about how does an all-forgiving, all-loving God let this kind of shit happen? And was Sergeant Billy Stone so arrogant to think there was any originality in these thoughts? Fuck . . . When Adam got his ass kicked for taking an innocent bite of a fucking apple, was that justice?

Whoa, Billy, where's the nurse? You did it again. Mellow out, my good man. Attend your patient. You sure as hell ain't cured, Stone. You need time, the great healer, time.

Other than his passport, Billy didn't need much—maybe a backpack with a few digs. He befriended a couple of college girls that were headed to Puerto Vallarta for vacation, and they were happy to have him tag along. He made them feel safe. Sweet serendipity, he didn't want the noose of a car, and on top of that, the girls were cute and fun.

So when they got to Puerto Vallarta, they were a triumvirate.

No one was possessive or jealous. It was still the '60s, and there was love everywhere, so why not join the party? They drank, they smoked weed, they danced, they made love. Billy figured it was a bit more than a prelude to heaven, maybe even an answer to his disparaging thoughts about the Higher Power insinuating himself into the natural course of things. It didn't matter, though, because it was cathartic and a week-long rehab program. Even their good-byes were natural and easy, and in a most subtle way, they took some of Billy's anger away for their farewell present, as well. Time and memory, one going north, the other south.

Billy was starting to adapt to a temporal world in slow-mo. It was a luxury he had never really experienced before. Indeed, he knew that it was but a hiatus, but because he didn't have to, he eschewed the whole idea of a schedule, any schedule, and when the time came, if it ever did, he would again pick up the pace along this strange path of life.

But for now, and for no reason that had anything to do with anything, he decided he would be a bartender. True, he didn't know a Singapore Sling from a Klondike Cooler, but he could read a book, or talk to an experienced "tender." But bartenders got to talk to people, all kinds of people—pretty girls, arrogant young lions in the business world, down-and-outers, maybe even Mafioso and real dirtbags. Who knew? Who cared? But timing is everything, and when he was told that a job had opened up at one of those cabana-type bars on the beach of Puerto Vallarta, he got the job, and for the first couple of days, his biggest worry was that someone would order something other than a Cerveza or a Bud.

"Hey, new guy, *que pasa*? How 'bout a strawberry daq, my man?" The guy looked like "Shaggy" Rogers from Scooby-Doo.

"Comin' up, my good man," Billy responded. "What's in your

queue this lovely day, Señor?" Billy wondered if his hippie lingo would pass muster. Probably didn't matter to this guy who was definitely not having his first strawberry daq of the day.

"Just cruisin' an' gazin', my shaman . . . cruisin' and gazin'." Shaggy was mellow-yellow as he gazed at the rolling surf.

Billy handed him his drink with a genuine smile, envious of the man's 'tude, nary a care.

The guy plopped down a ten-dollar bill, smiled, and said, "You, my man, are entitled to pocket the balance as reward for your *preternatural* magic trick." He held up his drink, a toast and evidence of the miracle.

Wow, thought Billy. *Five dollars for the drink, five dollars for the tip. Not a bad gig.*

Shaggy took his plastic cup and started to mosey, but first he sipped, smiled, and said, "Should I find my field of saffron, I shall return. If not, my sacred sorcerer, *vaya con Dios.*"

Billy's day was pretty much in line with that first exchange. By noon, his domain was teeming with downloaded tourists and adrenalized college students, sexual tensions on high alert. Outfits and apparel ranged from burqas to bikinis for the ladies and tanners to thongs for the men. The ambient mix of language and accents blended into a rather pleasant thrum of white noise, broken by drink orders and greetings. The topics and conversations were mostly benign, squabbles minimal, and altercations limited to a pushy few line-barging for drink orders.

Eventually Billy got reinforcement from an attractive Mexican *chiquita* who could have won the bartender of the year award. Long black straight hair, short shorts that displayed a pair of legs that would have made Grable jealous, Mitzi could make drinks two at a time and didn't need an instruction manual. The throng of customers shifted quickly from Billy's side of the cabana to hers. That was just fine with Billy—less pressure and a chance to watch her as she worked . . . a twofer.

In the late afternoon, things slowed down enough for Mitzi to leave. Billy thanked her, and she gave him a smile to die for. He was smitten, and as he later learned, so was her weight-lifter boyfriend, but *c'est la vie*, he would become more like Shaggy Rogers with that Dali Lama attitude. And speaking of Shaggy, along about cocktail hour, who should be wandering back down the beach, but the man himself. Oh, how life is but a circle. First to come and last to return, the seeker of the saffron fields.

"Aha, Merlin, my main man. Know ye that my heroic Homer spoke of Elysian fields but neglected to tell me they were so elusive. But perhaps it is like Dorothy and Scarecrow and it was always here anyway and I never had to leave. However, lest ye forget, there is sorrow in leaving, but great joy in the return." Shaggy took the stool closest to Billy. "So, share your thoughts, friend, while you again create your magic potion."

Billy felt a kinship with this ersatz philosopher. He was certainly on something more potent than strawberry daiquiris, but he was harmless as a new puppy. When he went for his money, Billy raised his hand. "On me, my friend."

"Blessed are the wizards, for they shall inherit the beaches." Shaggy raised his glass.

Billy's Puerto Vallarta days would meld together in a comfortable and depressurized vacuum of time and space, nothing lost and something gained, like soft, white, collapsing sand filling his heavy, burdensome footsteps along the beach.

And then one day he had the urge to move on. Yes, life is but a series of beginnings and endings, and so his time had come again.

This time, he walked. Sometimes a car would pull over and offer him a ride, and if they passed his litmus test of "nonthreatening," he would get in for a few miles. He had a plastic rain poncho from Nam that he had stuffed in his backpack, and he used it at night, on the beach, but the weather was nice most of the time. He spent a few days in Manzanillo just lounging around, and spent one day on an open trolley tour of the city. It was overpriced, but the tour guide was funny.

After getting back on the road, he soon came into Lazaro Cardenas, the largest seaport in Mexico, named after a Revolutionary general who later became president. He was called "Mr. Clean" by some, as he was one of the most honest and hardworking leaders in the history of Latin America. But the city was too busy for Billy's taste, and he again put on his walking shoes.

At one point, Billy found himself humming an old German song, "The Happy Wanderer," and he knew that something had happened. As he wandered down the old road that eventually went into Acapulco, he tried to give some meaningful definition as to what it was, but found that exercise frustrating, and that was when his enlightenment occurred. *Voila!* He didn't have to *try* any more. His newfound serenity was just happening, all on its own, without effort. Simple.

He had become so familiar with anger and resentment that letting it go was an unknown, and all people have a subliminal fear of the unknown. On top of that, he had paid the fee and earned his anger, so why should he give it up? It was like the unforgiving divorcee, but the anger had bound his spirit, and to loosen those binds, he had inappropriately set himself up in a psychic world of mind-fuck. People think too much. How much of his thinking had been tied to guilt? He had killed. No matter the justification, and yes it was survival, but still, he had killed. And guilt was simply anger directed inward.

As for his resentments, they were perhaps a gift from the Higher Power as a built-in defense mechanism to safeguard against injustice, but at a point, if they weren't jettisoned, they would slowly and methodically kill you. In a short, unintended lesson from Shaggy, if only by osmosis, a certain peace of mind had nudged its way to the front row. In the end, Billy Stone realized that he didn't have and didn't want any control.

Billy never made it to Acapulco.

CHAPTER 24

Greenwich
2010

The old man was on his knees, searching under the bed. Where the hell was Marie? He needed her help. He'd been trying to figure out who the people were that were in his house. Damnation, this was his house, and people were coming and going without his permission. He thought that if he could find some paperwork in a shoebox or files somewhere, he could figure it out. It had to be here with names on it . . . somewhere.

He did know that his son was in his den, as he could hear him. He recalled that his son was doing something wrong, but he didn't understand or couldn't remember what it was. And who was the other guy? And mostly, his father had started the company and he had carried it on, developing a respected reputation for integrity.

I'll be damned if anyone is going to harm that image and those decades of hard work. Damnit, Marie, where are you?

The old man was in a hyper state of frustration. He left his room and walked down the hallway to the den. He didn't knock—hell, it was his house—and opened the door. Tyler III was at his desk, and he immediately stood up, trying to cover his work, but he wasn't quick enough. His father came over to the desk and saw the stacks of hundred-dollar bills.

"Well, Father, it appears as though you don't show the courtesy of knocking on closed doors." He was trying hard to snuff his anger as he tried to create a barrier between his father and his desk.

"It's my house, young man, and I shall do what I wish." He stared at his son with obvious indignation. "And what the hell are you doing with all those hundred-dollar bills? Where'd they come from? Did that man who was here have anything to do with this?" The barrage of questions seemed to meld together.

Tyler grabbed his father's arm as gently as it took to direct him toward the couch. As he sat him down, he said, "How about I answer your questions one at a time, Father? Would you like a cup of coffee?"

"Don't you dare treat me like a child. I am still the head of this household."

Tyler walked over and shut the door. He knew that Barbara was in the kitchen. When he returned to the couch, his temperature had cooled, and he spoke to his father with feigned sincerity and calm.

"First of all, understand that you do not own this house anymore, Father. I bought it from you seven years ago." Tyler let that statement sink in.

"The hell you say? We never did that."

"Indeed, we did, and if it will alleviate your stress, I will be happy to go over the documents with you. I think you just may have forgotten." Tyler could see that his father's mental deterioration was getting worse. He didn't think he was a threat.

The old man held his head in his hands, apparently trying hard to recall the sale and other things. He was too proud and too confused to demand proof.

Tyler continued on. "As for the hundred-dollar bills, I have several people that are doing some work for me that have asked to be paid in cash. Their price is good, and if they choose to avoid taxes, that is not my responsibility, and the man you saw was one of those people. There is nothing underhanded going on, Father." Tyler put his hand on his father's shoulder. After a moment, he said, "How about I make your favorite, a grilled cheese sandwich, and bring it up to your room while you relax?"

His father said nothing, stood up, and walked back to his room. He seemed to age with every step.

Tyler finished counting the money, made an entry into his booklet, and put the bundle in the safe. He noted that the safe was running out of room, and that he would need another storage box soon.

Barbara had not been in the kitchen. She had been in the dining room near the bottom of the stairs, and had heard the exchange right up to the moment Tyler had shut the door. She was trying to process what she had overheard. The old man was going crazy, but he was not yet insane. Some old country song she recalled. His cognitive skills had certainly worn thin, more so every day, but he still absorbed what he heard and saw, for some period anyway, and there was no reason for her to be totally dismissive about those things.

So what was this pile of hundred-dollar bills her husband was hoarding, or some strange man who had been here when she wasn't? She might have to have a chat with the old man.

Across town, Beloit was in his office with Ernie and Sunny. He had met with Tyler yesterday and given him a check for $9,900 for rent and numerous reimbursements, fiction and nonfiction. Tyler was headed to his bank to cash it, alleging that there would be no red flags if the withdrawals were less than $10,000.

Beloit knew better. Any investigator worth his salt would follow through on a series of cash withdrawals in large amounts. Future checks would have to be more sporadic, and in varying denominations.

He had also had a lunch with Hilliard on Saturday, and in his case, there was no check, just greenbacks. Hilliard had provided some valuable information, however, and Beloit was finding great value in his "inside" man. He handed a copy of his notes to Ernie and Sunny.

In the first year or so, the Medicare system had been ripe for fraud, primarily because of the soft underbelly of vulnerability. It was an open system, and any provider that met the base set of requirements could enter the program, treat patients, and bill for those services. However, in the past six months, a high number of the amateur fraudsters had been caught due to a combination of their ineptitude and new rules and increased surveillance through a beefed up CMS . . . They were becoming organized.

"One big development, folks, is that the CMS reviews—or at least a percentage of them—are now being done on a prepay basis, before claims are automatically paid. This allows them to suspend one hundred percent of a provider's payments. Also, Hilliard says that they are now working with private payers in data exchange in order to identify common vulnerabilities and a list of providers of concern. Hilliard has given me those lists so we can take preventative steps."

"Looks to me," Sunny said, sticking her glasses into her bundle of hair held together with pins and clips, "like the big push is finding the unlicensed doctors, and now they've been given new authority and new tools to do that. Hilliard says that they have now connected over a hundred different databases at both state and federal levels to look specifically at medical licensure." She looked first at Ernie, who gave her a supportive nod, and then to Dr. Beloit.

"Good point, Sunny, but we're well-protected in that regard, and Hilliard will earn himself a nice bonus when he gives us the list of those databases and Ernie can see if we come up."

Beloit and Sunny looked at Ernie for a response.

Ernie looked at them, wondering what he was supposed to say, so he threw out a non sequitur. "Yup, they're just another government agency whose incompetence is incomprehensible." He smiled.

Beloit and Sunny gave him a silent, "Huh?"

CHAPTER 25

Mexico
1969

M exico! Land of beauty where gardenias grow, across the border into Mexico—olé! Well, except for the crappy roads, the trash, and maybe the slum barrios and the highway-men, drugs, murders, and squalor. Except for that stuff, it was *muy hermosa, Señors y Señoritas.*

Somewhere south of Lazaro Cardenas, Billy got off the roads, opting for the scenic route. Out in the middle of nowhere, the roads could be perilous, and he really didn't need that. He had warmed up to the whole idea of siestas. Under a big, shady tree, with an ocean breeze, the smell of salt water, and a good view, what's not to like about a siesta?

Billy's neck no longer ached from having to turn his head way to the right in order to see to the right. He smiled as he sat down and leaned back against the palm. He was amused at people's reac-tion to his glass eye, even his family's. His mother had simply held his face in her hands, her eyes watering with a mix of anguish and empathy, making an offering, "You are such a handsome boy."

He had smiled, almost giggled, and replied, "I've still got another one, Mom."

She cried and hugged him for a long time.

The doctor had done a good job with the cosmetics. He could see his sister's discomfort as she looked from one eye to the other as she talked to him, like she wasn't sure which one was which. That, too, made him laugh, but it also made him feel less conspicuous.

He thought about his men, what they were doing, and how their mental state was acclimating to the *real world*. He thought about Nam and what was happening over there. He thought about what he was going to do with the rest of his life. He had good vibes about his mom and his sister. And once again, he avoided thinking about what he had been avoiding thinking about for the past month . . . his father. Good time for one of those Mexican siestas.

In his dream, he had been captured. Toothless, black-clothed apparitions were kicking him, their feral, heinous expressions only inches from his face. Their screams were silent, but their breath was foul and overwhelming. They had knives poking at him, but without penetration. Another soldier sat next to him, and they were attacking him, as well. The other soldier wore Army-issue fatigues, but of another vintage. His face showed great strength. It brought calm to Billy, and he absorbed that strength and certitude.

Across the room was a bamboo cage, where Reuben James, wearing only a loincloth and bleeding from a thousand cuts, was trying to get out. He needed to help Reub, but he couldn't, so he looked to the other soldier for help, and that was when he saw that it was his father, a younger man, his uniform that from the Korean War. Now he felt the thousand cuts.

And he awoke, his hands and arms covered in ants. He jumped

up, brushed them off, removing his pants to get them all. Sweat was dripping from his forehead. It took several minutes to come around. His heart was pounding. He stripped and went to dive in the roiling breakers, and soon his metabolism began to slow. *What the fuck? Where'd that come from?*

Two hours later, Billy was on a beach with white sand as far as the eye could see. The only sound was the crashing of waves and the euphonious cries of seagulls chasing imaginary morsels through the air. He believed they were greeting him. *Welcome to our secret place, friend.* Maybe it was his soul, but his limited spirituality only allowed the concept of *good angel*, and she spoke to him. The voice was kind, nurturing, and told him that this was his secret place, as well. He felt strangely complete. Somehow, this was meant to be his realm, and he had a synesthetic kind of reaction, a sense impression that produced colors of blues and greens. *Was this what happened to Saul?*

He came upon an abandoned hovel listing slightly toward the sea. It was kind of like an upside-down wooden box . . . a big one, with two glassless windows on each side. Maybe it would only be for one day, but Billy Stone was home.

CHAPTER 26

Greenwich
2010

Barbara was alone in the house with the old man. Lethargic old people who lie around and watch TV, read if their eyes work, sleep off and on, and occasionally miss the toilet are easier to take care of than those who have anxiety issues.

Barbara had noticed that old Tyler had developed a behavioral change. He had become even more restless and irritable than normal, which was irritating enough. She hoped like hell that he wasn't developing an anxiety disorder of some sort. That and dementia would not be a combination that she would be able to handle . . . the bad news. The good news might be that he would have to be moved to a care facility, and she could get her life back. One thing for sure was that her husband would now have to take responsibility for his father.

She went to the old man's room and knocked on the closed door. After a minute of no response, she figured she had been too tentative, and knocked harder. This time, he opened the door and just looked at her, lacking recognition.

"Is everything okay, Grampa?" she asked. In the early years, she had addressed him that way, and he had almost seemed to enjoy it. At least he had never said otherwise.

"I'm not your damned grandpa."

Barbara ignored the attack and said in a calm tone, "I thought you might like some coffee and maybe toast and jam."

The ice melt was palpable as he shook his head and turned back into the room, mumbling, "So did the kid go to work, or did he go to get more money?"

Barbara was confused. She assumed "the kid" was her husband and the reference to "more money" was related to the conversation she had overheard. "Yes, Winston has left for work, and perhaps you can tell me about the money."

The old man was sitting on the edge of his bed. Barbara sat in the nearby chair.

"I don't know. He has stacks of money. Lots of hundred-dollar bills. And that man he meets . . . calls him a doctor. They argue, you know." The old man kept rubbing his hair and looking at her for answers.

"It's probably just work, but if it would make you feel better, I will see what I can find out. In the meantime, come down to the kitchen and have a nice cup of coffee with me." She gently lifted his arm, and they went to the stairs.

There was definitely an element of bipolar behavior, but the anxiety seemed to be related to this issue about the doctor and the cash. She didn't dare confront her husband about this, but she would talk to her brother about it when he arrived.

Beloit was becoming increasingly irritated by Winston Tyler's interference. For one thing, the money was pouring in on a scale he had never anticipated. Beloit was shortchanging his partner to the tune of thousands of dollars every week, and he had Sunny working overtime on a third set of books, just for Winston's review. Both Ernie and Sunny had been incentivized with a piece of the pie that they could slice out of Tyler's cut, while assuring that he wouldn't discover the deceit.

More importantly, the man was coming to the location nearly every day. For what reason, Beloit wasn't sure, but he would sit out front or come in and disrupt the operation. His behavior was becoming strange when they did talk, and the visits could be increasing the risk of detection—or at minimum, arousing the curiosity of some meddlesome investigator. He now faced an unanticipated problem, and would have to address it.

Ernie and Sunny had met for an early breakfast. After ordering coffee, bagels, cream cheese, and jam, Sunny said, "You know, Ernie, I have some mixed feelings about the good doctor. Yes, I like the bonus program he's giving us. Who doesn't like more cash? But he's stealing it from his partner." She let that sink in before continuing. "If he can screw one partner, he can screw another."

"So, what are you saying?" Ernie seemed a bit deflated.

"I'm simply saying we need to watch the guy. Don't you agree?"

Ernie nodded, processing the disclosure.

Winston Tyler was going to the office less and less. He was missing scheduled meetings. People in the office were wondering what was going on, especially his secretary. When he did come in, he was short-tempered and evasive. He would shut his door and go out for long lunches. If he did return, he was two to four sheets to the wind and usually angrier than when he had left. He said things like, "The public should know how stupid and corrupt their so-called leaders are. I'm going to show them, and you can take that to the bank."

Instead, *he* took it to the bank. He took his secret checks to the bank, and got hundred-dollar bills, sometimes twice a week. And the tellers and bankers who had never even seen Winston Tyler III before wondered why.

Because this money seemed so immensely important to this man, who had millions, one could only surmise what was happening here, and it was most abnormal. He was bewitched, perhaps not clinically disturbed yet, but there were signs of paranoia and schizophrenia. His facial expressions were often a caricature of anger one minute and achievement the next. He was no longer the namby-pamby grandson of a tyrant. Unlike Casey, he had redefined himself as a hero of Mudville.

William Tyler had been picked up for a DUI. When stopped, he had gotten out of his Mustang, contrary to the cop's instructions, and proceeded to make several inflammatory remarks about cops and threats relating to who his father was.

Officer Wilson was a professional, and whereas he wanted to grab William by the balls and say, "Open your fuckin' mouth again, you little shit, and you won't be fucking for the next three years," instead, he said, "You're already in trouble, young man, and talking will only make it worse." His threatening stare had the appropriate effect.

Officer Wilson shook his head at the reality of how political correctness had opened wide the door that was leading to lawlessness and chaos. That snowball continued to grow as it rolled down the hill of civil disobedience, parental permissiveness, and legal promiscuity.

William didn't call his mother. He called his father's office.

CHAPTER 27

Mexico
1971

As relaxing and serene as is the world of meditation and *let life happen*, at some point another phenomenon begins to take root. The body develops a thirst and a plea for nourishment, the need for food and water. When neither is nearby, one must do what is needed to obtain such items. Ancillary products like soap, a toothbrush, and clean clothes may also come into play, and one finally becomes motivated to *get up off your dead ass, go to town, and get the shit you need, you lazy bum.* Such was the cycle of Billy's thoughts after hours of beach time.

Billy needed transportation . . . if not an old beater, at least a bicycle. He thought there must be a store between where he was and Acapulco, miles to the south. He would need fire. He would need a weapon to defend himself. He needed some tools.

Reality really sucks, he thought. And then, a good thought . . . *Maybe a bus will come down the road.* A not so good thought . . . *Where is the road?*

From the hovel, the road was almost a half mile to the east, through trees and brush via a narrow footpath. There were no signs on the road inviting visitors to see the beauty of the hovel beach, a good thing for Billy and his hope for inactivity. Could he really have been so fortunate as to have stumbled upon a desolate paradise? Time would tell.

As he walked to the road, Billy counted out $300. He had a balance of $1,900 hidden within the lining of his backpack. At some point, he would want to find a more secure place for his trove, but until he felt more comfortable in his surroundings, if ever, it would have to do. If he could find a throwaway with some ammunition, that would be a deterrent against what he pictured as a marauding tribe of banditos. On the other hand, now that he was *tranquility man*, maybe he could just brush up on his diplomacy skills . . . or not.

After a hot and frustrating fifty-two minutes of standing on the side of a poor man's highway, a smile came to Billy's face, partly because a bus was finally coming, but mostly because of the bus itself. It was a replica of every bus that ever appeared in a movie about Mexico. Decorated in multicolored graffiti, rocking on worn-out shocks with the quintessential overflowing storage rack on top, its driver gave him an exaggerated smile and greeting from under a sweat-soaked, straw sombrero.

"Señor, I am guessing you speak-a-dee-Eeng-lish. Heh?"

Billy stepped aboard. There was no door. "*Sí, como esta, mi amigo?*" Billy smiled back.

"Aha, thass wat every gringo say . . . mi amigo. Where you go to?"

"The closest place that has food, drink, and clothes. Am I on the right bus?"

"*Sí, Señor.* You sit down there." He pointed to the closest seat.

"And I get you to a *muy* good place to get that things." Another huge smile portraying about sixteen of one's normal twenty-eight teeth.

The next stop was about fifteen minutes of bumpy ride, and to Billy's welcome surprise, it was his destination. This would certainly bode well for ease of future supplies.

"Did I not bring you right to your door, Señor? And it cost only a leetle, heh?" "Señor Smiley" was less subtle about a tip than the doorman at the Hilton.

The ride cost a dollar. He tipped his amigo a dollar. He would be seeing this man again, so pay it forward. With this smile, Billy actually got a view of the man's tonsils.

"*Gracias*, my friend. I will pray for you good health, and to give you another ride."

Billy waved as he drove off and said to himself, "I bet you will."

After walking half a block, Billy started looking around for Marlon Brando and the "scum-suckin' pig" John Saxon, a livery stable, and a shootout at high noon. The place was an anachronism, or maybe a Hollywood set. So he moseyed past the hitchin' post and into the general store and figured he would get help from a gal named Kate. Turned out to be a young Mexican kid with long hair and a "Don't fuck with me" scowl.

Billy got everything on his list, except a pistol. That could wait. He would while away another hour before catching a bus back to the hovel beach. The old bicycle rode up top, and he pedaled from road to hovel in an easy seven minutes after a different driver dropped him off. This fellow was more of a curmudgeon, and so not much conversation, the one smile coming at the price of a fifty-cent tip.

Holy shit, Billy thought as he set the grocery bag down next to his make-believe fridge, *look at that sunset*.

And so he did for the next hour. Only once did his mind get caught up in thoughts about Nam, that being when a flock of pelicans did their dive-bomb thing not far offshore, snapping up the surface fish as they submerged and taking off again with gunnysack chins full of wriggling appetizers. They would circle and come back for more, the first batch probably still wriggling in undigested stomachs. In any event, it sparked the vision of diving Douglas A-4 Skyhawks strafing the jungles with napalm, and in the heat of the day, he shivered.

And so tomorrow became today while certain events that happened yesterday lost their clarity and faded into a bigger and more generic time frame called *the past*, slipping away like grade school best friends forever, whose names and faces become harder to remember, while strangely, one might recall the faces of the parents. Time has been called a thief, but for the dispassionate, it's but a pickpocket. For those who lust from the very depths of their spiritual marrow for connection to every grain of life's essentia, time is a mugger, and Billy had always been a person of passion.

If there were dog days of summer in Mexico, they were different from the Northern Hemisphere intensity, and for Billy, they were metaphorically "puppy days," soft and warm and fuzzy, with eyebrows that said a hundred things, and nights when sweet pup breath and a pink tongue seemed to lick the wounds of a survivor in a loving effort to bring solace. A little at a time, it did. Still, like puppy tails, Billy's mind was in constant motion. The only truth Billy knew for sure was that he had lived, others had not.

Though Billy had experienced no sleeping problems since returning from the war, that had changed. He didn't think it was

fear, guilt, or anxiety. Of course, he hadn't slept well in Vietnam—
no smart soldier did. Fear controls some kind of subliminal alarm
system during situations of unrelenting stress . . . no batteries
needed. But he wasn't afraid now. Could it be that the quietude
and solitary space that he was finding was cause for some kind of
cognitive rejection, a foreign interlude without having completed
the transition process yet? If so, his insomnia would fade with
time. Not to worry—less sleep, more time for life absorption.

There is a certain comfort when routine and patterns develop,
and so it came to Hovel Beach, as Billy had named his temporary
home. He found that "Smiley" was the bus driver going south,
while "Surly" drove it north. Billy's discussions with Smiley were
mostly redundant, limited by language and other reasons, but always happy. At the same time, the non-discussions on the return
trips were also redundant, but never unpleasant, just introverted
and always ending with the appreciative smile for the fifty-cent
tip. Turned out that the "Don't fuck with me" kid at the general store was also an asset, as he supplied Billy with a pistol and
ammo—for a healthy fee, of course. They found an unspoken
kinship, as the kid was intuitive and street-smart and knew that
Billy was like himself and that he'd "been there."

The shanty had been stabilized and with nails, hammer, and
boards, upgraded from a ten, on a scale of one to ten, all the way
to maybe an 8.5. In other words, it was livable, especially with the
hammock. The most crucial missing piece was a refrigerator, or
some facsimile thereof. Luckily, his juvie friend had given him a
source for dry ice and ice blocks, so he bought a cooler. For two
days, it had worked just fine, but there would have to be more
S&S (Smiley & Surly) time. As contractor and interior decora-
tor, Billy could only do so much with his shack, so he decided

the time had come to ruminate about the issues surrounding his father's suicide.

Benjamin Stone had been raised in much the same way he had raised his own son. After his father was killed in the Pacific, he was raised by his mother. He was fourteen at the time. His mother taught him strong family values, the importance of taking responsibility, making good choices, and all the good stuff that builds character. Ben had been a fine athlete, and in his senior year was selected as an all-conference middle linebacker.

When the Korean War started, Ben was one of the first to enlist. He received two Bronze Stars for gallantry with the 2nd Infantry Division in fighting around the Naktong River. When he got back, he took a risk and showed great initiative in starting his own business, which he built into a real success. He had been a good husband and a great father until the day all that changed.

Billy recalled the story his father had told him, and his emotions broke from their newfound passive environment like wild mustangs loose from the corral. Anger, confusion, and frustration cycled around his conclusions of injustice and the vindictive son of a coward. His father didn't deserve to be bushwhacked by a heartless and vengeful bureaucrat who would destroy a good man, just because he could, and for unjust reasoning. His father had been a patriot. The coward had been a traitor.

The note his father had left was brief: *Whatever you think, I do love you.* Certainly generic and wordless, but also opaque, and Billy knew his dad could have said a great deal more about loss of self-concept and the pain of a hopeless future, but his father was a proud man and avoided excuses.

For that reason alone, Billy's personal pain intensified, as did his lust for retribution. Yes, Billy had learned that anger was a violent emotion, as harmful to the giver as to the recipient, but his passion for revenge would never be removed by logic or the platitudes about the glory of forgiveness. Billy also knew that there would be far less satisfaction in implementing physical penalty when compared to the same kind of mental and emotional anguish that drove his father to do what was so discordant with his character. Revenge, as a dish best served cold, entailed the torture of fear with the fatal thrust, unexpected.

For the moment, however, Billy smoothed the ruffled feathers of his karma and committed to providing justice when the time and opportunity were right. For certain, it would come.

CHAPTER 28

Israel Cohen

The bank was on the corner. It was next to the post office, which was next to a dry cleaner. The bank was wood, kind of gray in color, and certainly plain. Security on that Tuesday morning seemed lax. It was overcast, threatening rain. There was that uneasy stillness that sometimes is prelude to violence.

Israel had ducked behind a 1965 Chevy Impala. There was a sudden flash-bang from inside the bank, and Israel took off at a run. Halfway across the street, a 7.62 mm bullet entered the back of Israel Cohen's head, and he died within seconds, fifteen feet from the bank's entrance. As the smoke cleared, a voice was heard.

"Seems your smart mouth didn't save your ass this time, Cohen."

Israel turned and faced his assassin, who was getting out of an older Ford Coupe. "Well, if I didn't have to call you sir, I'd probably tell you to go fuck yourself . . . sir."

The FBI tactics instructor just shook his head, the hint of a smile. Charlie "Chan" Hachiro had been training FBI recruits for seven years. He was a legend, with scars and stories to prove it. He had never quite seen a recruit like Cohen, who he credited with a certain brilliance and a high level of intuition. He was in good physical shape, and was a quick study in all phases of the training program. His shortcomings, however, were that he lacked patience, he had a tough time playing nice with others, he had his own rules, and he had an ostensible lack of control over his big, fat trap.

"If I have to review my *boundary lines* speech again, Cohen, the consequences will not be pleasant . . . You hear what I'm saying?"

"Yup, gotcha, Mr. Instructor, sir." His tone had a light coating of sarcasm, more humorous than mean. Israel actually liked *Charlie Chan*—admired him, as well. His response had been that of frustration. He hated not scoring at the highest level in all phases of the training program, and when he didn't, it showed.

The bank was part of a Hollywood set that had been temporarily constructed behind the FBI Academy building on the Marine base in Quantico, Virginia. The old building hadn't changed since 1940, when the Marines had first allowed the FBI to construct a firing range and classroom for the growing numbers of police academy and FBI trainees. It would be two years before the new expanded facility would open. Talk about a major upgrade: the complex included more than two dozen classrooms, eight conference rooms, twin seven-story dormitories, a 1,000-seat auditorium, a dining hall, a full-sized gym and swimming pool, a fully equipped library, and a new firing range. In addition, it included much-needed enhancements like specialized classrooms for forensic science training, four identification labs, more than a dozen darkrooms, and a mock city classroom and crime scene room for practical exercises.

Fifteen years later, the temporary bank where Israel had been killed would become a permanent brick-and-mortar tactics training facility, and the Bank of Hogan would become only part of Hogan's Alley, *the Baddest Town in America*.

Israel was hard on himself. The training was nearly finished, and he was ranked number three in his group at the time of his *greatly exaggerated death*. With time and maturity, his instructors agreed that he would be a most valuable asset. He would graduate in two weeks. After that, things would change.

CHAPTER 29

Akio

"I never would have agreed to the formulation of the Central Intelligence Agency back in 1947 had I known it would become the American Gestapo." So said Harry Truman in 1961. Many of the enlightened have applauded Harry's *straight-talkin'* ex post facto assessment even fifty years later.

In 1970, on the other hand, the CIA was blossoming under the political creation and exploitation of national paranoia. Joe McCarthy had already proven how effective that blueprint for manipulating perception could be, especially as the American audience was the most gullible on the planet. In 1970, the culprit was South America—not just the "commies."

Akio was wearing a disguise, and he looked exactly like a young Japanese guy with a goatee. Actually, he had simply grown a goatee, mostly because he wanted to, but the goatee added to his self-created aura of intrigue. He was feeling especially CIA-*ish*, all decked out in Chilean garb as he walked the streets of Santiago. He was part of a covert action against the elected government of Chile, led by Marxist Salvador Allende. These were politically tumultuous times in Chile, and the mysterious death of René Schneider, minister of defense, was allegedly integral to Akio's intelligence assignment.

After his many months of training and the shroud of secrecy under which he operated, he knew for certain that his handler's instructions contained cryptic messages that might determine world direction. "Walk around, observe, take secure and accurate notes, and wait to be contacted by me. Check your messages every morning, and if there is a ten-digit number, call that number in reverse."

Holy shit, it was Hitchcock, Michael Caine, and *Topaz* all over again. So he walked around, observed, took detailed notes, and waited for the message. And he waited. Then he waited some more.

Finally, he was contacted, a ticket back to Washington, DC, where he was debriefed by a newly hired college grad and heard nothing more for about five years. That was when he discovered the hidden meaning behind his instructions, "Walk around, observe, take good notes, and wait to be contacted." There was none. Seems they had forgotten he was there. At that point, he said to himself, *No wonder the Bay of Pigs was such a clusterfuck.*

The CIA training program was done at a location not far from Williamsburg, Virginia. Specifically, the location is at an unincorporated community in the census-designated place of McLean in Fairfax County, Virginia, called Langley, that name most often used as a metonym for the CIA. Initially, when Akio had used that name, he said it in a kind of whisper. After learning the truth about Chile, the bloom was off the awe.

There was a lot going on in the CIA in 1970. The Federal Law Enforcement Training Centers (FLETC) was set up in Brunswick,

Georgia. These facilities were set up to serve as an interagency law enforcement training body for what became more than ninety United States government federal law enforcement agencies. The stated mission of FLETC was to "train those who protect our homeland." Initial CIA training for agents and analysts was often conducted there, but in its first year, it lacked organization. Some have said it never did achieve that elusive goal, "elusive" perhaps the operative word for the agency. Agents have always taken pride in their moniker of *spooks.*

The training is comprehensive, but the agency must, by its very essence, be a flexible organization in an ephemeral world. The threat of terrorism is very different today than it was forty years ago. The Internet and social media didn't even exist in 1970, at least as we know it today. In 2002, the CIA University was established, and the curriculum of classes was impressive. Today, they work in partnership with the NIA, National Intelligence Agency. Subjects taught at the school have included chemical weapons manufacturing, communication skills, defensive driving, dirty bombs, geography of critical regions, information technology, intelligence community, money laundering, project management, terrorism, weapons of mass destruction, weapons proliferation, and weapons training. Additionally, sixteen language courses are taught at the school. The school's faculty consists of professional educators, along with intelligence experts drawn from within the agency.

Again, in 1970, the major efforts of Langley, in addition to Vietnam, Laos, and Cambodia, were concentrated on guerilla and terrorist organizations in South America. Their involvement was vast, including the countries of Argentina, Brazil, Bolivia, Costa Rica, Guatemala, and Mexico, in addition to Chile. In 1970, the career of Pablo Escobar was just beginning in Colombia. In the 1980s, the man would become the wealthiest criminal in history, in some years making $22 billion in personal income from international cocaine sales, but in 1970, the CIA had bigger fish to fry, an intended double entendre.

There were over a dozen intelligence offices within the Directorate, and Akio's training covered two of them: Latin America analysis and the Crime and Narcotics Center. After his Chile snafu, he became entrenched in an office within the Langley complex, where a whole new internal story line of conspiracy and stratagem was developing. Like Churchill's 1939 description of Russia, "a riddle wrapped in a mystery inside an enigma," not only was a KGB defector involved, but so was James Jesus Angleton, J. Edgar Hoover, and even John F. Kennedy. At the center was politics, personalities, and the uncooperative relationship between intelligence and law enforcement agencies, especially the FBI and the CIA.

Okay, folks, admit it, there really wouldn't have been much of a story if David had been the same physical size as Goliath. Where would be the life lessons? Not great material for motivational speakers and football coaches, huh? "Not the size of the man in the fight, but the size of the fight in the man." Nope, back-page article in the newspaper of history. Metaphorical giants of history, at odds with each other, however, provide a redundant narrative of great interest, substantial historical influence, and impactful consequence. So it was with "Wild Bill" Donovan and J. Edgar Hoover, going back to December 7, 1941.

Donovan's Office of Strategic Services was the forerunner of the CIA. William Donovan was a World War I combat vet while Hoover was in Washington, DC, building intelligence files and setting up the General Intelligence Division (GID). The GID took files from the Bureau of Investigations (later renamed the Federal Bureau of Investigation) and systematized them via index cards that allegedly covered nearly a quarter-million people.

By 1939, Hoover had more than ten million people indexed in the FBI's domestic file system. The FBI indexes were a series of personnel databases used by the FBI before the adoption by the Bureau of computerized databases. They were used to track US citizens and others believed by the Bureau to be dangerous to national security. The indexes generally had different "classes" of danger the "subject" was thought to represent. On the question of constitutionality, Wild Bill, along with others, objected to the indexing (today called "profiling"), and the practice was allegedly shut down. Hoover was duplicitous, however, and continued to expand the index system, and those files of untold numbers of Americans are still accessible today.

Included in the numerous catalogs are the Reserve Index, with influential people to be "arrested and held" in case of a national emergency; the Custodial Index, which included 110,000 Japanese Americans that were held in internment prison camps during World War II; the Sexual Deviant Index; the Agitator Index; the Communist Index; and certain files on Native American and African American liberation movements during the 1960s and 1970s, as well as Vietnam War protesters and other college students. Whether this unconstitutional index system was folded into the present-day national security terrorist watch list program is unclear.

Orwell's *1984* may have been inspired by this program (author's opinion) as it was a template for the concept of *sub rosa* totalitarian control. To the point, the program involved creation of individual dossiers from secretly obtained information, including unsubstantiated data, and in some cases even hearsay and unsolicited phone tips, and information acquired without judicial warrants by mail covers and interception of mail, wiretaps, and covert searches. While the program targeted primarily Japanese, Italian, and German "enemy aliens," it also included some native-born American citizens. The program was run without Congress-approved legal authority, with no judicial oversight, and outside of the official legal boundaries of the FBI. A person against which an accusation was made was investigated and eventually placed on the index, and was not removed until the person died. Getting on the list was easy. Getting off the list was virtually impossible.

In any event, what prompted President Roosevelt to allow the creation of a new intelligence agency, against the resistance of Hoover, was the FBI's intelligence failure surrounding the surprise attack on Pearl Harbor. In 1941, a Serbian double agent for the Abwehr, a man named Dusan Popov, related having informed the FBI on August 12, 1941, of the impending attack on Pearl Harbor. For whatever reason, either J. Edgar Hoover did not report this fact to his superiors, or they, for reasons of their own, took no action. As a result, Donovan was put in charge of a new *centralized* intelligence group.

Donovan's group was more freewheeling in structure and hierarchy than the FBI. They worked with communist agents and formed a loose-knit alliance with the Soviets. Hoover was abhorred. He was a monarch, and ran his agency with an iron fist. Regarding the Russians, like Patton, Hoover believed the Soviet empire would become the "next enemy" after World War II was over. In that regard, he later boasted clairvoyance.

After JFK was assassinated in November of 1963, the Cain

and Able relationship flared up again. Team FBI championed their Soviet informant, Yuri Nosenko, while Team CIA advocated information provided by their KGB defector, Anatoliy Golitsyn, as to the truth behind the assassination. Nosenko insisted that Moscow had nothing to do with the crime, while the CIA was sure that he was lying, and in the end, it may have been the inter-agency conflict that not only impeded the investigation, but resulted in the Warren Commission's report that eschewed valuable arguments, contained multiple mistakes, and may have prompted certain cover-ups that would soon provide the inspiration for con-spiracy theorists to imply government complicity in the shooting.

The agency chasm continued to widen under the conspirato-rial and paranoid presidency of Richard Nixon. In line with that, here was how the game was being played: Hoover felt he was closer to Nixon than was Jesse Helms, the CIA director, so he cut all ties with them when they asked for his help. "Screw you." But Hoover was wrong, and privately, Nixon considered the FBI a bust, as they couldn't even find the communists behind the anti-war organizations he believed existed.

So the White House recruited three guys named Curly, Moe, and Larry, from both agencies, dressed them up as "plumbers," and encouraged them to encroach on each other's turf. Eventually this group of comedians landed in the midst of the Watergate scandal, some cover-ups, and Mr. Nixon becoming the first presi-dent ever to resign from office.

Akio had reached his nadir of disenchantment. It was a job, no longer an exciting opportunity, and he kept his eye out for some reason to go somewhere away from the obscenity that was Washington, DC, and Langley. Serendipity being what it was, *voila*, it happened.

CHAPTER 30

Reuben James

It was a beautiful day for an awards ceremony. Only sporadic shadows traipsed across the city, light gray blankets that were veiled from the bright sun by slow-moving fleecy white cumulous clouds in a warm and welcome motion.

The presentations were taking place in front of the Selma police station. Chief Withers was adjusting the microphone on the old wooden lectern while the other cops were talking in threes and fours, all dressed in their blue uniforms. Several dozen guests were either sitting in the folding chairs or renewing relationships with those they recognized. Ezra and Esther James were also dressed to the nines, smiling and chatting with Al and Muriel Bredeson, the parents of Officer Robert Bredeson, who was receiving the Selma Police Lifesaving Medal. Their son, Reuben, was receiving an award, as well, the Selma Police Medal of Valor.

"First of all," the chief began, "we want to thank you for coming here on this gorgeous day to honor the men and women of your Selma Police Department. Law enforcement is a two-way street. The fine officers you see here today, and all of the administrative personnel that support them, thank all of the people of our great city for the support that you give us. No police department can do their job to the very best of their ability without community support, which is what makes this partnership work. So, thank you."

The chief paused for the rather enthusiastic applause.

"Today is a very special day for this department and the city of Selma, Alabama. Not only are we honoring two of the department's finest for their performance above the call of duty, but we are celebrating an even higher achievement, as well." Chief Withers paused to look over the crowd and let his statement sink in. He had not become police chief through tenure and longevity alone. He was a man of intuition and forward-looking, a man who had earned and held the highest respect from his men, as well as the community.

"It wasn't long ago that the eminent Dr. Martin Luther King led a contingency of thousands of Americans, both white and black, that believed in a dream of true equality, across our bridge, and I say again not just *our* bridge, but across that *one great symbolic bridge*, to close the gap of acceptance, of respect, and of the truth of equal creation. And today, we honor two heroes, one white and one the first black police officer in our city's history to receive the Medal of Valor."

Again, the chief paused, this time to a standing ovation, until he could continue.

"To Officer Reuben James, medals are just old hat." The chief showed a big smile. "All they do is add to his collection of Silver Stars and Purple Hearts. But although we are honoring these two individuals, again I want to applaud the collective." Withers raised his arms, palms up, to present the Selma police force to another round of clapping.

Bredeson had saved a child from drowning in the Alabama River when the high waters had nearly swept the boy away to a sure death. Reuben James had pulled four members of a white family from a single car crash while it burned and eventually exploded. Now he sat on a stage, almost embarrassed by the attention, wishing he were anywhere else. His mom and dad made up for his introversion with their huge smiles and multiple hugs to all the well-wishers, which embarrassed Reuben even more.

When the ceremony ended, Reuben tried to sneak away, but that attempt was futile, so he just grinned and bore it. What meant the most to Reuben was that he was given a genuine hug from every member of the Selma Police Department. If he blushed, it was lost in his big, kind, strong black face. His body language, however, could not hide the message: "Aw shucks, fellas. It weren't nothin'."

Life was good until later that night, when he got a call from Peter Akecheta.

CHAPTER 31

Peter Akecheta

I f people think US presidential elections are a mucky, slimy affair, which they are, you ain't been to a tribal election. Not much political correctness goin' round. Election subversion entails things much more hostile than faulty chads or lost IDs. If there is a self-serving agenda—and there often is—a corrupt tribal faction may form to undermine elections with a laundry list of dirty tricks. They may create a dispute within the tribal leadership—sometimes fictitious—exploit the weak and weak in character through bribery, and seize the assets by force if necessary. If the tribe has a casino, that will be the objective.

Some will exploit the tribal code of silence by leveraging media contacts and threats of exposure. The threat of tribal disenrollment is another tool to lever, and as unethical as it may be, creating disputes over tribal membership will gain collateral, as well. In the end, perhaps the lying and duplicity is really just an overlay of all political elections, but the opportunities are always greater with smaller numbers. But the old rule to *follow the money* will usually be at the heart of the matter. Accordingly, these kinds of plots and political combat gained a new level of intensity in 1979.

So here is a short *once upon a time* story with a Rudyard Kipling flair to it, about how Indian casinos came to be. Certain credit must go to Wikipedia.

In the early 1970s, Russell and Helen Bryan, a married Chippewa couple living in a mobile home on Indian lands in northern Minnesota, received a property tax bill from the local Itasca County. The Bryans had never received a property tax bill from the county before. Unwilling to pay it, they took the tax notice to local legal aid attorneys at Leech Lake Legal Services, who brought suit to challenge the tax in the state courts.

The Bryans lost their case in the state district court, and they lost again on appeal in a unanimous decision by the Minnesota Supreme Court. They then sought review in the United States Supreme Court. The Supreme Court granted review, and in a sweeping and unanimous decision authored by Justice Brennan, the Supreme Court held not only that states do not have authority to tax Indians on Indian reservations, but that they also lack the authority to *regulate* Indian activities on Indian reservations. Hence came the term *sovereign immunity*, and all the subsequent laws and regulations that followed.

As Gaming Law Professor Kevin K. Washburn has explained, the stage was now set for Indian gaming. Within a few years, enterprising Indians and tribes began to operate Indian bingo operations in numerous locations around the United States. Under the leadership of Howard Tommie, the Seminole Tribe of Florida is considered to have been the first to establish an Indian casino in the country, in 1979. Unfortunately, in looking forward, it was geography that would basically prohibit the Pine Ridge Reservation from ever building a cost-effective casino.

For Peter, the past eighteen months had been a frustrating hardship. He was like his parents in the sense that they were rational, logical problem-solvers and the preferred spice was always honey before vinegar. He had spent a good deal of time looking at the reservation from a high-flight view before analyzing the metaphorical ground-level state of affairs, and had reached certain conclusions. His father's experience and sagacity were paramount to his analysis and vision.

It would be quite some time until the next elections, and Peter needed a respite. He had been thinking a lot lately about his other family, especially the father figure, Billy Stone.

When he did finally find the telephone number, it was Billy's sister, Barbara, who answered. Peter introduced himself. Barbara was overjoyed to meet him, and reviewed a few stories Billy had told her. Peter could see immediately why Billy so treasured his little sister. She was like an excited child, innocent and transparent. After a bit, Peter asked to speak to Billy.

"Peter, I miss him like crazy."

"What do you mean?" Peter's confusion was a tinkling symbol. His concern was a sounding brass.

"It's been over a year. I'm worried, but I really miss him."

In the silence, Peter heard her sniff. "Barbara, start from the beginning. Where is he? When did he leave? Why? Help me clear up my confusion . . . okay?"

For the next fifteen minutes, Barbara told Peter everything she knew and what she could recall from her last conversation with her brother before he had left.

"So, he didn't mention a specific place—just that he was going to Mexico?"

"Yes. He said he had some money, but he only took a backpack."

"How's your mother doing?"

"Better than me. She says Billy needs some time alone, and he can take care of himself." After a moment, she added, "I just really miss him, Peter."

"I understand. So do I. But let me ask you the most important question: What was his state of mind when he left?" Peter knew that whatever it was, Billy would never have given Barbara cause for concern, but her response might have some value.

"He was mellow. He was tired, of course, but he was good as far as I could tell. Said he was just looking forward to some vacation time." There was a comfortable quiet before her pleading question. "So, are you going to try to reach him?"

"Let me see what I can find out, okay? I promise you I'll get back to you with any news. In the meantime, you keep your chin up." Another pause. "I just want you to know that your brother talked about you all the time. Called you his little button or something . . . We'll talk soon."

"Thanks . . . Love ya, Peter." She hung up.

Peter thought about his own sister. She was a little button, too.

"Hello."

Just hearing the familiar, mellifluous voice made Peter smile. He tried to imitate their old first sergeant's voice. "You missed reveille, Corporal. What's your excuse?"

There was a long pause before Reuben replied, excitement in his tone. "Peter! Peter, where you been, my friend?"

"I miss you, too, big mon. Catch me up-to-date, you old walrus."

For the next twenty minutes, the two comrades compared notes and filled in the holes. Peter didn't mention the elections, and Reuben didn't mention his award.

"I bet you haven't talked to Billy." Peter waited. He expected the silence. Reuben rarely spoke without processing.

"You're right, but why you put it that way?"

Peter proceeded to fill him in on the conversation with Barbara.

"I got some vacation," Reuben said. "Let's go find him."

Peter got a small lump in his throat. Reuben's first thought, as it had always been, was about what he could do for his friends. The Great Spirit didn't make 'em like that anymore. Reuben's priorities never changed. Peter said a quick prayer of thanks as he looked heavenward for being this man's friend.

"I'm with you, big mon. I'll talk to Ack Ack and Izzy and get back. Hugs, old friend."

"Hello" This voice was a lot different from the warmth of Reuben James. It was cautious, as well as feminine.

"May I speak with Israel."

"Who is this?"

"My name is Peter Akecheta." The wait was almost uncomfortable.

"Are you that Indian friend that Israel spoke about?"

"Well . . . I am Native American, and I am a friend, so perhaps that is accurate." The subtle admonishment and sarcasm were in response to the irritating question and tone.

"I see."

Peter was glad she hadn't missed it.

She backpedaled. "Well, he did speak quite highly about you, but Israel has moved into his own place. Would you like the telephone number?" She gave it to him, and he disconnected.

When Peter called Israel, he got an answering machine. Because he was feeling playful, and because it was Izzy, he left a message. "Good afternoon, Mr. Cohen. This is Credit Fixit, and we were calling you in regard to your dishonorable discharge from the United States Army. I will ring you again this evening. Have a great day." Peter giggled at his own skullduggery and his cheesy British accent. He looked forward to the evening call.

Peter had talked to Akio about six months ago. Akio had called him when he had a one-day seminar in Rapid City. Connecting had not been too difficult, as Peter was living with his parents, and Akio had no problem getting the number from directory assistance. The number Akio had left him was for his parents' home in Bakersfield.

"Good afternoon. Yamada household. May I help you?"

Peter hoped they didn't get a lot of calls, because that greeting could wear you out. The woman had a sweet voice and a slight Oriental accent.

"Good afternoon. This is Peter Akecheta, a friend of Akio's."

The sweet voice got even sweeter. "Oh, Peter, I want so to meet you. Akio tells us of you, and yes, you are great friend. I am Akio's mother."

"Thank you, Mrs. Yamada. I will look forward to meeting you and Mr. Yamada, as well. Can I speak with your son?"

"Oh Peter, we cannot even know where Akio is. He is in CIA, and we only talk to him when he calls."

"How often does he call, Mrs. Yamada?" Peter wasn't really surprised. He seemed to remember Akio talking about that six months ago. He doubted that Akio couldn't call when he wanted to, but he did have a built-in excuse if he didn't want to call home all the time.

"He calls us on Sunday nights. I could give him your telephone number if you wish."

"I would appreciate that, Mrs. Yamada." Peter noted that it was Friday. Ack Ack would call him after talking with his parents.

For the rest of the day, Peter spent time with Tommy Brand, riding horses and talking about the state of affairs on the reservation.

"You know, Tommy, I'm not sure that I really know the difference between what is junk and what is symbol. Is there something about the old, abandoned cars and graffitied rock piles that is sacred? I don't want to sound sacrilegious, but I see a junkyard."

The two sat on a bluff overlooking the tattered landscape.

"You sound like a white man, Peter."

"And you sound like Red Cloud, stuck in outdated thinking that doesn't help the lives of our people. Times have changed." Peter was frustrated with what he perceived as anti-progressive thinking based on tradition and recalcitrance.

"I am a reformist compared to most," Tommy said. "Our people love this land, and yet it is a place lost in time, seemingly off the government's radar, really . . . another country. Periodically, the tribe gets a token check from Washington, but like table scraps for the mutt, it just keeps him hanging around . . . a most subtle tool to control the restless natives." Tommy shook his head, a visage of defeat. "Reality is a bitch, old friend. There are other priorities, don't you think?"

"Prioritization is at the top of my list," Peter said. "I look at the tribe, Pine Ridge Reservation, and the future, and I see that a plan is needed. Housing, schools, quality teachers, government assistance programs, solicitations for tax-deductible donations, someone to run that program. So much to do, so little time, so many roadblocks. I am overwhelmed, Tommy . . . and I'm tired." Peter stared at the setting sun. "I think by making a referendum of these issues, they become a priority whether I'm elected or not."

"You're making an impact, Peter. I'm proud of you, and for the first time in years, I am truly hopeful."

Peter had set up an office in his parents' house. He shut the door and made his call with a thick British accent.

"Good evening, Mr. Cohen. This is Charles Burberry from Credit Fixit and—"

The interruption was loud and scathing. "Who the fuck are you dickheads, and where are you getting your defamatory misinformation?"

Peter could tell that Israel had been boiling since he'd heard the message. He couldn't disguise his laugh. There was a pause.

"Who the hell is this?" Another pause.

"Seems I reached Moshe Dayan." Again, Peter laughed. "What, you lose your eyepatch?"

"That you, Cochise? You asshole. You know I'll get you." The anger vanished, and Peter could hear the joy.

Like two old teammates at a high school reunion, they traded stories and giggles for almost half an hour. Peter alluded to his talk with Barbara.

"Listen, Izzy, Reuben and I are going to find Billy. You got any vacation coming?"

No hesitation. "You know I'm there, brother. Just let me know where and when."

Peter spent the weekend with his mom and dad, walking and riding the reservation and taking notes.

"It may surprise you, Peter, but there are some who resent that I have a successful business off the reservation," his father admitted. "Some kind of abandonment thing perhaps. In some ways, I can understand the feeling, but in reality, it is a collective shortcoming, like one suffers, we should all suffer. Individual initiative is not part of team play, so it's frowned on." His dad looked to his wife for support.

"The real challenge," his mother said, "is the need to change the culture. The old ways are ingrained. Fighting the existing reality without a new model is futile." His mother looked from one to another before continuing. "I recently read a quote by George Bernard Shaw. He stated, 'The reasonable man adapts himself to the world: the unreasonable one persists in trying to adapt the world to himself. Therefore, all progress depends on the unreasonable man,' and therein lies the quandary."

"We all agree that, without deviating from the historical norm, we will not see progress." Peter spoke with conviction.

It was ten-thirty Sunday night when Akio called.

"I didn't check this phone for bugs, Ack Ack, so be careful what you say." Peter smiled and waited.

Akio made a beeping sound on his end. Peter heard him snicker. "Just what I need, Chief, another cloak-and-dagger joke. So, how they hangin', buddy?"

They went through the same routine of catch-up and Peter's recap of his conversation with Billy's sister.

"You're not worried?" Akio asked.

"Nah. If I know Billy, he's just doing his forty days and forty nights gig, only ten times as long. Shit, Akky, we need a reunion, anyway, so block out some time and we'll meet in San Diego and surprise him."

"I shit you not, my friend, you have provided me with an excuse to get away from this bullshit for a while. Put the schedule together with Groucho and Harpo, and I'll call you again next Sunday night."

Two weeks later, four of the five members of the most highly decorated squad in the Vietnam War met at a bar on the beach in San Diego.

CHAPTER 32

***

"Hovel Beach" Mexico
1971

Amazingly, only two incidents had interrupted the Henry David Thoreau experiment of Billy Stone's life on Hovel Beach. One was bad and one was good, so let's save the good for last.

About a month after Billy's first trip to town, he had a couple of visitors.

Billy had built a small sand dune near the water. It was shaped like a lounge chair, maybe a hundred yards from his humble dwelling. He would sit and watch the sunsets with a plastic cup of tequila and a wedge of lime. He had become part of the environment. The quietude had been a special gift. Occasionally, on weekends, a Mexican family would come down the path with assorted beach accoutrements, but the milieu was always one of comfort, sharing, and respect, not unlike the harmony of grazing herds of wildebeest, zebras, and antelope on the Serengeti. Kids would splash and play and squeal as they made the memories that would soon be lost to survival instincts and baser competitions.

They were usually gone by mealtime, sometimes with a friendly wave.

Some evenings were windless, with placid water and sounds that would carry from a great distance, but Billy most loved the onshore breezes and the sound of crashing whitecaps. He had begun to learn the language of the birds, especially the seagulls, like Dylan Thomas who once claimed he could hear them call his name . . . *Dy-lan* . . . *Dy-lan*. There were other birds with deep, throaty burps, and every once in a while, a pod of bottlenose dolphins would skim the shores, their blowholes spewing tiny fountains of mist and treble squawks of warning. Often, this soothing harmony of susurration would lull him into a soporific abstraction, but his dreams still melded into nightmares that drifted to the humid jungles of perdition.

One night he awoke to find his plastic cup upside down, a lime wedge on his stomach and his bathing suit still wet from the spilled liquor. His sleep had been deep and his dreams benign, but his sensitive warning system was still operational, especially to muted voices in another language.

With assistance from the light of a three-quarter moon, Billy rolled on his side, and from the cover of his sand chair, he saw two men lurking near his shack. He had developed the habit of keeping his backpack close at all times, as it contained his survival necessities, money, and pistol.

The two men wore jeans, colorful shirts, and what appeared to be brimmed straw hats. One of them nursed a knife, which told Billy this was not a housewarming call. They were so preoccupied with scouting out his hovel that they didn't notice as he approached.

"Nice night, huh, fellas?"

The two men turned toward Billy with frozen looks of surprise.

"Hey, Señor." Big smile from the tall man. "We like to—"

Billy had the pistol pointed at the tall man's chest. "Shut the fuck up and drop the knife, or you'll see a hole in your stomach." Billy said it quietly, but with controlled ferocity.

Tall-man dropped the knife.

"What-are-you-doing?"

"Señor, no speaka dee English," Tall-man said, his unctuous body language belying a trap.

Billy noticed Short-man drifting away. He motioned with the gun for Short-man to move next to his cohort.

"If I were you, I would learn it very quickly." Billy straightened his arm, pointed the weapon at Tall-man's stomach, and pulled the hammer back.

"Oh no, no, no, Señor. I mean I speak a leetle English, not a goood English."

"I'll ask once more and count to three. What are you doing? One . . ."

"We are just looking at your leetle house, Señor." Tall-man looked at Short-man for confirmation.

"Two." Billy waited. "I warned you . . . Thr—"

"Okay, okay, Señor. We are poor *hombres* that need *dinero* for food, and we were to try to take some from you. We make a beeg, very beeg mistake."

Tall-man and Short-man looked at each other and nodded, and nodded some more.

Finally, Short-man said, "*Lo siento Señor, muy siento.*"

Tall-man repeated the apology, and added, "We go now and never come back, Señor." He grabbed Short-man and they started to leave. Tall-man looked to the ground, where his knife was sticking in the sand.

Billy figured it was probably the biggest asset on the man's balance sheet. "Take the knife. If I ever see you again . . . you're dead."

Tall-man scarfed up his weapon and gave Billy a servile grin, still nodding,

"Sí, Señor. You will not see us again."

Billy knew that would be the case. Petty thieves were a far cry from black-pajama Cong soldiers. He actually laughed as he returned to his seaside seat and a refill of the local tequila brew. It reminded him that a real-life tequila sunrise wasn't far away.

CHAPTER 33

San Diego
1971

"**M**exico's a big fuckin' place, Chief. You know something we don't?" Israel was in his happy-curmudgeon mood.

"Mexico? What's Mexico got to do with anything? This is a surprise party for Reub. Am I missing something?" Peter gave a mock questioning look to the group.

Reuben looked sad. "What about Billy?"

Peter suddenly felt bad. He sometimes forgot how serious Reuben could be when it came to serious issues. "Hey, Reub, I was trying to be light. Remember, this isn't a rescue mission. There doesn't appear to be anything alarming . . . We're together and we're going to find our friend."

"I gotcha, Peter. Sorry." Reuben hung his head like he had done something wrong.

Peter felt worse, so he clapped his hands together and said, "All righty then, so this brain trust—and I use that term loose-ly—needs to formulate a plan. What we do know is that Billy got a ticket to San Diego, and was then, at some point, going to

Mexico. As far as anyone knows, he'd never been there before. Did he ever say anything to any of you guys that would hint where he might have headed?"

There was a long silence, each waiting for someone else to bring forth a nugget of value.

"Okay," Akio said. "So, at one point we were talking about what we were going to do when we got out, and Billy said he wanted to take some time to just walk or ride a bike and see the sights. I think he put it, 'Someplace where I don't have to think,' or something like that." Akio looked to see if that was of value.

"That fits, Ack Ack. For me, when facing such conundrums, I try to identify with the perp—sorry for the FBI lingo, gents—and imagine what I would do in their place under the same circumstances. And in Billy's case, I'd walk until I found my, might I say, *comfort place*, and if we assume Mexico's Pacific coast, which I think we can do, the first destination would be Puerto Vallarta."

Israel turned to Reuben for his thoughts. As always, Reuben processed, passing things through his cerebral filter, a thoughtful expression accompanying.

"Well, men," Reuben said finally, "I'm a cop, and we always start with motive and opportunity. It seems Billy's motive is to enjoy a nice long walk, but one doesn't just walk fifteen hundred miles. Too much downtime. Too much unenjoyable time with industrial areas, detours, desolate areas, you know. So, opportunity, right?"

They all looked at him, nodding, engaged.

"So, he wouldn't get a car. Too many problems. But he would get a motorbike, a bicycle, or he'd hitchhike. Right?"

They nodded again, waiting for him to continue, but he didn't. He was done.

"Good thinking, Reub," Peter offered. "So, where does that leave us?"

Now all four of them processed.

It was Peter who spoke again. "We could grab a taxi to Tijuana, and there, we could get motorcycles and take our time down the coast to Puerto Vallarta, first stop, and then follow our noses. Whaddya say?"

"Sounds like a plan," Akio said.

The rest nodded.

CHAPTER 34

"Hovel Beach" Mexico
1971

Billy had taken a couple of trips to Acapulco. He found that a lot of coastal tourist towns had something in common. From an ocean view, they were beautiful, clean, shiny, and bustling with beautiful people. Rich people. But the farther inland one traveled, the shine dulled to rust and the clean turned to dirty, and the people were less beautiful and the bustle was more criminal. Not really different from most tourist attractions worldwide, he supposed. He hung around the beach, he hung around the bars, and he hung around the shopping meccas, but in the end, he preferred the little Old-West-style town where he bought his groceries, with the gravel streets, hitching posts, the general store, and Alejandra.

Alejandra looked like Sophia Loren. She worked with Billy's buddy, *Don't-Fuck-with-Me*, at the Almacen General Store. She was the checkout girl. Billy checked her out the first time he did his checkout, and he had done a lot of checking out since then. She didn't speak much English. He fell in love, so he asked Don't-Fuck-with-Me how to say, "Will you marry me?" in Spanish. Between the hardware section and the checkout counter, however, he thought she might think him too forward, and might ask for more time to think it over, and so he held his tongue and fantasized instead.

Over the years, Billy had dated a few neighborhood girls, even one on-again, off-again girlfriend, but never anything serious. He had never had time. When he wasn't engaged in sports, he was working part time as a stacker at a local grocery franchise. In other words, he didn't know a damn thing about the fairer sex, and what he thought he knew . . . was wrong. How could it not be, considering that the information came from his immature, jock, prima donna teammates? Garbage in, garbage out.

Billy didn't think Alejandra liked him. He didn't understand that the fact that she ignored him and his obvious interest in her meant that she liked him, because from the male view, that seemed illogical. Oscar Wilde was clear: "Women were made to be loved, not understood." So, Billy tried humor that came off like a dunce, and he tried "cool," which came off as "not-so-hot," and he compromised in other ways that all led to confusion and frustration. Finally, fed up with his own bullshit, he tried something really different in his approach: he was just himself. Oddly, that worked.

It had been four days since he had been to town. It was dusk, and he had a charcoal fire in his pit. He was heating up a can of chili con carne—or at least some facsimile thereof—and a bag of Fritos. His bachelor diet wouldn't be listed among the top ten in any health magazines, but it worked. The sunset was the usual, redundantly gorgeous, and the pelicans were back with their dive-bombing routine.

Billy heard a soft, angelic voice singing and humming. The song bordered on mournful, but it was nice, and fit the moment. It was coming from the path, which he couldn't see from his position. He stood up and walked around his abode. The scene was like one might view in the theater: sun reflection on long black hair flowing in the breeze, a light blue knee-high cotton dress draping the barefoot, athletic body of the seraphic Alejandra. Billy stood there, speechless, unable to respond as a normal.

"Hallo, Meester Beely," the angel spoke. "I think you might need some theengs."

Billy, the dumbwaiter, put his hand out to take the basket she carried, simultaneously trying to formulate a cute and clever greeting, which he eventually came up with.

"Hi." He absorbed what he must look like to her: a weenie, supported by his weenie greeting. "Really great to see you, Alejandra," was his weenie recovery attempt. Maybe, he thought, that's what he really was . . . a weenie.

"I make for you my very special cheelee. You like cheelee?" She smiled like Sophia, her beautiful teeth sparkling in the last rays of sunlight. Then she spotted the pan of chili con carne and the smile disappeared.

Billy followed her sight line and knew why. He gave her a weenie grin and came up with a retort that might have qualified for the lame hall of fame. "I absolutely love chili, Alejandra. I love it so much that I even get this kind of chili," pointing at the pan, "for this stray mutt that visits me." Then he did a super weenie thing, and looked around for the mythical hound and even gave a dog whistle, like some four-legged furry savior would come bounding down the path. It was an embarrassing bit of drama that almost prompted him to say, "Welcome to Weenieville," when she saved his ass with a dazzling, mischievous grin. At that point, he knew she knew.

After a moment, they both started giggling. When it started to die, Billy looked around again and whistled again, and spasms of laughter broke out again.

The language barrier was not a problem. Everything just took longer. They comfortably waded through the usual introductory background checks, history, family, interests, and schooling. In that regard, Alejandra said that she was waiting for a possible scholarship to a high-test school in Rio. The school was a breeding ground for students interested in a career in the hospitality business.

"With a personality like yours, Alejandra, you will be most successful in that industry." Billy's warm smile was magnetic. He had abandoned weenie for genuine.

Comfortable silence is a sign of a healthy relationship, especially in its early stage. They sipped tequila and watched the nocturnal transposition as traces of stars against a fading backdrop magically turned into sparkles against a nearly black curtain.

Billy leaned over to point out Orion's Belt, and Alejandra leaned her head against his. She smelled of mint or patchouli. And then they did what young lovers have done since Adam did it with his main squeeze, Eve, a long time ago.

CHAPTER 35

∼∼∼

Tijuana
1971

Peter and his buddies might have pictured themselves as Marlon Brando and his rebels from *The Wild One* as they tooled down the streets of Tijuana, but in fact, they looked more like the Ringling Bros. clowns that always rode those miniature motorcycles in the circus. Timing is everything, and it happened that the shop in Tijuana had a crackerjack deal on Vespas. That would be older, used Vespas.

With the agreed-upon policy of what's good for one is good for all, they headed south, Reuben representing the most prominent caricature in the bunch. When they rode behind him, they struggled to stifle their laughter.

Israel lagged behind the others as they rolled along the scenic route. It was intended—easier to control his thoughts—like a hen and her ducklings. The wind seemed to muffle the cacophony of expected road noises: occasional car horns, the rhythmic vibrato of exhaust pipes, and the stationary sounds of places and events that came and went along the route.

His feelings were mixed as he inventoried his life. He found it too easy to dismiss certain pieces that were supposed to be most important according to that imaginary overseer of moral code, like his relationship with his parents. He recognized the implied debt that all children owed to their parents, but for there to be real substance, it was like any relationship, the difference between *want* and *need*. Need implies a dependency while want implies a desire, and most people desire *not to need*. Interpretation and semantics aside, *I need you* . . . a sure fire indication of an unhealthy relationship if it discounts affection and love . . . those from the *want* category . . . and in the end, a choice. "I have no choice" is a claim that implies a need, but really, it's just a convenient excuse. Guess what, Bozo, you always have a choice.

Israel recognized his subliminal guilt. He wasn't sure he loved his parents. On the other hand, he loved these guys on the Vespas, and perhaps he needed them, too.

Peter was riding in the lead of Team Vespa. He was pleased with his self-concept, and he owed it to his parents and the men he was cruising with, especially the one they were going to find. It had taken a crazy war to confirm the strength of his character, but the real confirmation had come from the support and love of those most dear to him. He wasn't under any delusion that he had the makings of a Chief Joseph, a Sitting Bull, or his personal icon, Red Cloud---after all, the opportunity for that kind of leadership and idolatry had died with the Wounded Knee Massacre, but still a more subtle, and yes, cerebral kind of leadership had replaced it. Respected Native American teachers and writers, politicians and social leaders, business and military men and women had emerged in the new world, and he was there, the right place at the right time, and he felt secure in stating . . . the right guy. But, for now, his thoughts were in the moment.

No greater bond can form than between those that serve together in combat. Both the physical and the emotional components of man rarely reach the level of brittleness and high alert that they do in combat. No trust levels are higher, no dependency levels are higher, and with some exception, no loyalty levels are higher. In all ways but blood, Peter's squad was his family. As long as any or all of them were still alive, he would go to sleep and wake up knowing that there was someone that would, under every circumstance in life as he knew it, be there. *So . . . where are you, Billy?*

Akio had worn a smile all day, starting with buying this silly little moped or whatever it was called. Then he watched Reuben buy one, too, and when the big mon did a test run, it reminded him of the elephant that sat on the little stool at the circus. He had to run to the bathroom to keep his serious friend from being offended. Akio had forgotten that uncontrolled laughter made you cry. He cried for five minutes.

Akio was gifted. It wasn't intellect—although his IQ was high—it was his elevated intuitive instincts. He was prescient in the world of human behavior, and could sense coming events, usually smaller in scale but most often spot-on. He was introverted by nature and kept most thoughts like that to himself. The gifts had served him well in Vietnam, and now, in his work. No one was a highly successful CIA agent that didn't have such survival instincts.

He thought about how he had fucked up as a teenager, and whether in the *large photo* of life, it had been a bad thing or a good thing. He had been a rebel and a spoiled brat in many ways

. . . a bad thing. He would probably have become an arrogant and self-serving "young lion" in the business world, scaling the ladder of success built by his father . . . a bad thing. But, his fuckup had provoked his father to enlist him in the Army . . . a good thing. Vietnam had provided him the circumstance and perhaps the providence to discover who he really was . . . a good thing. And he had met some of the finest human beings he would ever have the opportunity to know . . . the best thing. So, with the aid of his self-developed casuistic evidence, he concluded that his fuckup was a good thing. His smile returned, and he put the pedal to the metal of his mighty Vespa and roared past his comrades at a top speed of thirty-one miles per hour.

Reuben James wasn't smiling, but then, neither was he frowning. He was thinking, and he was thinking about his mom and dad. He loved them dearly, as well he should. Anyone who is the product of a gene pool of such elevated quality should love the producers. He so exemplified who they were—dignified, high morals, hardworking, honest, brave, and so very lovable. But he would never describe himself in such terms, only shy away with genuine modesty.

He was thinking about what they might need and how he could help them, while at the same time, his law enforcement mind was working hard. He would notice any shops along the way that might sell bicycles. The place where they had bought their motorbikes had not seen a man resembling Billy, as Reuben did have a military picture of him that he had brought along. At one point, he signaled the team to pull off the road to check out a bike shop, but it produced no recognition from the proprietor.

The other three looked at each other with knowing smiles. Akio's clairvoyance kicked in, and though he stuffed the thought into his memory bank, he knew he was looking at the future police chief of Selma, Alabama.

It was a late afternoon when the gang of Hells Angels thundered into Puerto Vallarta. Okay . . . okay, so don't get your undies in a bundle. Yes, that may have been a touch of hyperbole. Still, the Vespa boys putt-putted into the city in early evening and decided to find a fun bar that served nachos and tacos.

"Sure you got enough, Reub?" Izzy looked at the half-dozen tacos and gave furtive glances to the others.

"Looks like it, Iz, butcha never know" was Reuben's serious reply, his mouth full. As usual, he had missed the sarcasm.

They all sipped their Modelos.

"So," Akio offered, "I'd ask what the plan is for tomorrow, Peter, but first I'll ask what the plan is for tonight."

Peter thought about it before replying. "Where do the homeless sleep in San Diego, partner?"

Akio knew where this was going. "Under the stars, on the beach, just like us, right?"

"We'll call it a camp-out, like we used to do in the jungle."

They all looked at each other and shrugged.

Alejandra had driven her old Volkswagen back to her parents' house last night. It seemed she had a curfew. Also, she had to work today.

Billy walked the beach and lay around like a lost Romeo. He wasn't a romantic by nature, so this feeling was foreign to him.

It made him feel uncomfortable, out of control, and he wasn't sure he liked it. Strangely, he found the infatuation pain welcome, however, and if he correctly recalled his senior year English class, that was called "masochism" . . . Or was that a sex thing? Whatever . . . It felt good.

Manage your expectations. It makes good sense in a business deal, where it is usually an art form. One has a pretty good idea of what's going on, who's got leverage, who's bluffing, and if you don't get the right price and terms . . . walk away.

On the other hand, if you're a first-timer who's been smitten by the arrow of cupid, you don't know *jack-shit*, no leverage, no bluff, and then you can't just walk away.

Alejandra didn't come by that night or the next day. Billy wasn't managing his expectations or his emotions very well. So the following day, he rode his bike to town with a devil-may-care attitude that belied his anxiety.

Alejandra wasn't at work. *Don't-Fuck-With-Me*, whose name was Miguel, told Billy that she had gone to Acapulco with her father, but he didn't know why. This, of course, spurred a new round of angst with ghosts and paranoid illusions. What had he done wrong?

An ebullient Alejandra walked down the path to Hovel Beach around dinnertime with the same picnic basket. Luckily, Billy hadn't started to heat his chili con carne yet.

"Oh, Beely, I have the good news. I have been accepted to the school in Rio."

Billy produced a big smile that was not genuine. He was

already losing his angel, who would be flying to South America. "Wow, Alejandra. That's great news. When do you leave?"

"Not for three weeks, and then the school, eet is two years."

"Wow, that's great," which it wasn't. On top of that, his redundant reply was back to Weenieville again.

This time the basket had ham sandwiches. They talked a bit, but it was subdued by the news that hung above their conversations. Billy wondered if this was how love worked . . . push-pull, up-down, forward-backward. Is sorrow the price one pays for love? But if he really cared for her happiness, he had to let her go. Sadly, she wouldn't know his dilemma. But still, he did have three weeks. He suspected they would fly by quickly, like winged angels heading south.

Peter awoke with sand on his cheek. His sleep had been deep. He was in a comfort zone, so his cerebral alert system had been turned off. He stared at the sunrise and looked around. Israel was leaning against a palm tree, also watching the bright, golden fireball peeking over the Pacific. An oil tanker was silently working its way north.

"I think Billy had the right idea. Think we should interfere, Peter?" Israel spoke while perusing the beach.

"If he wants to stay, his choice," Peter mumbled.

A half hour later, the team was revving up their scooters and heading for a place that served breakfast. They covered the red, white, and green tablecloth with huevos rancheros, breakfast chorizo, egg tacos and chicken chilaquiles. They were high on life this morning.

"Olé!" they cried as they remounted the Vespas and headed for the beach, where they sat, walked, and waded until the hordes of *touristas* appeared. Around noon, to no one's surprise, it was the Pride of Selma that found the first clue in their treasure hunt.

"That guy was my guru, man. Not for long. He was gone like ocean mist, but he had an aura, man."

Reuben just stared at the long-haired hippie like he had been dropped from a UFO. He put Billy's picture back in his pocket. The extraterrestrial sat on the end stool of the beach bar.

"Did he say where he was going?" Reuben asked.

"He was Dao to the core, man. He was going to the har-mony—not like you, man. I see it in your eyes. I think he came from the north, going south, but spirituals like him have no real destination."

Reuben was trying to make some sense of this, but there was a language barrier.

E. T. continued. "You, my good man, are like Atlas. You're in my environment, man, a big, strong caretaker holding the bur-dens of our world on your shoulders. My advice . . . Just *let it go*, man." The guy returned to sipping some fruity-looking drink.

Reuben found the other three at a table under a large um-brella. "The only thing I know for sure is that Billy was here and probably went south. The guy I spoke to is really loony tunes, but at least we know we're heading in the right direction. You'd have gotten along well with him, Izzy." Reuben laughed and ordered two beers.

Izzy gave him the finger.

Billy had no choice but to rein in his feelings. Alejandra had unintentionally sent him a message. Things had changed, in subtle ways, like the delicate changes in Mexican weather as the winter months approached. One sensed it in the temperature and saw it in the arrival of flocks of northern birds whose temporal circuits had told them it was time to head south, and like the birds, the intrusion of reality had come to Billy, unnoticed and uninvited. As much as he had developed a proprietary kind of love for Hovel Beach, was it time to migrate north? Perhaps the time had come to put some marbles back in the jar.

Although he had backed off emotionally from Alejandra, the attraction had grown. Her beauty almost overwhelmed him, but it was her unbounded energy, her untethered excitement and belief in the future, her touchy-feely need to share, and her spontaneous articulation about whatever popped into her head, without hidden agenda, that made him both happy and sad. Sad, because Billy knew that such innocent naiveté must invariably encounter the ugly face of the human element sooner or later, most likely in many ways, and sadly, with redundancy. Illusion or not, reality can be cruel, an intractable truism that might one day cause her to abandon those illusory dreams.

Alejandra had quit her job, and so the days following became just warm, fuzzy, fun times of lazy, carefree companionship. Under the euphoric veneer, however, lived a troll with a minacious grin. He was called *time*, and the young lovers were aware of his presence.

"I swear I've seen this place before. It must have been in a movie or something." Israel was wide-eyed as the Vespas rolled down the gravel main street. "Talk about a time warp."

Reuben noticed a repair shop with several bicycles out front. He pulled in and brought out Billy's worn picture. The other three wanted snacks, and walked to the Almacen General. Izzy shouted, "Hi-ho, Silver," as he pretended to wrap an imaginary set of horse reins around the hitching post.

For five minutes, the three browsed the shelves of the general store.

Then Reuben plowed through the entrance with a big smile. "He's close by, you guys."

Israel almost blurted out a smart-aleck response, but quickly stuffed it. He didn't want to drain the big man's excitement. "Good job, Reub," he said instead. "Let's show the picture to the guy in back." Israel grabbed Reuben's arm and dragged him back to the Mexican kid with the surly expression. "Hey, you speak English?" Israel asked the kid, perhaps a bit too assertively.

"Sí, Señor, I-speaka-dee-Eenglish." A snide retort to go with the surly look.

"Yeah, *chico*, so if your eyes work, have you seen this man?" Izzy was getting on a roll.

The kid looked at the picture, then looked at Izzy and rolled his eyes around in circles. "Eet looks like my eyes don't work so good, huh, meester beeg mouth?" The kid folded his arms across his chest in defiance.

"You eat out of that same filthy mouth, you little shit?" Izzy rolled close to the edge.

Reuben had been watching the exchange. Two things struck him: first, he needed to mediate, and second, these two were a lot alike.

"Izzy, let me talk to the young man, okay?" Reuben said, placing his big hand on Izzy's shoulder.

Izzy and the kid glared at each other before Israel went to join the other two.

"Listen, young man, he lost a close friend, and we're trying to find him. We could sure use some help." Reuben was disarming, as well as intimidating.

"Yeah, you guys look like you only need a cholo to win a culture mix of the year award." The traces of sarcasm had lost some steam. After a pause, he said, "So, is that guy in the pitcher in trouble?"

"Not at all. We just need to find him 'cuz we're worried. So, have you seen him?"

"Yeah." He had mellowed. "Well, he's kinda my friend, too, so I tell you, but not that *boca de pedo*." He punctuated the words by jabbing a finger at Israel.

On October 26, 1881, in Tombstone Arizona, Tom and Frank McLaury, Billy Claiborne, and Ike and Billy Clanton were hunkered down near an old livery stable called the OK Corral. They watched and waited for their chance to shoot and kill three brothers and a dentist. Now, the five guys in the stable were basically dickheads.

Four men suddenly appeared, threatening, walking in line.

Dr. John Henry Holliday was more than a dentist. He was a scalawag, a gambler, a gunfighter, and an occasional deputy. His close friend was a deputy that day, as well, Wyatt Earp. Wyatt's brother Morgan was also a deputy, and his other brother Virgil was the marshal. They were the good guys. Long story short, the good guys *kicked ass*, but this rather extensive non sequitur only relates to a romantic image.

So now picture a day on a Mexican beach, where distant images are blurred because of intense heat rising off the sand. Four men are walking toward you, but you can't recognize them, so you squint and strain, and your eyes water. There is something daunting in their approach, and your apprehension causes a protective response. They get closer, and suddenly your fear is gone and relief turns to jubilation. So it was with Billy Stone on that late September day in 1971.

CHAPTER 36

Greenwich
2010

Billy would be here in three days. Barbara had prepared his favorite meal already, cooked and frozen, an indication of her anticipation.

She thought about her family. Billy was her idol, and she loved him. Winston Tyler II was her father-in-law, and though she was empathetic toward his condition, she didn't like him. Winston Tyler III was her husband, and though she bore the weight of some out-dated religious guilt, for him she felt indifferent at best. Someone had once used a term about "quiet desperation." William Tyler was her son. She loved him out of duty, but again, in her moments of fearless truth, he was like his father, and she really didn't like him. And then there was Shotsy, her precious little pumpkin, as Billy had called her.

On scale, it was a plus, a paradox, but such an inventory was a place she usually avoided. It was dangerous and really wasn't healthy, so she leaned toward the ostrich theory of self-analysis, just stick your head in the sand and hope the bad thing goes away. Not responsible and not mature, but it kind of worked.

She went upstairs when she heard a commotion. The old man was in a frustrated state, riffling drawers, crawling, peering under the bed.

"What's the problem?" she asked him.

"I can't find my . . . my . . ." He pointed to his wrist. "Damn it, you know, my . . . arm clock . . . that Marie gave me." He kept fingering his wrist, his face red.

"Your watch?" Barbara went into his bathroom and returned with the item. "Here it is. You left it on the bathroom sink." Barbara's frustration and tolerance levels were being tested again. She had to get away from it, at least for a while. But the old man had to go. Winston could put him in some assisted living place or nursing home, but he had to go. It was him or her.

She called her husband and told him to get home and babysit his father, because she was going shopping. "I think he might harm himself if he's left alone." She didn't wait for a reply, pressing the red button on her Samsung.

Shotsy was spending the night with her friend Melissa, and William was . . . who knows where? She went to shower and dress for a Macy's visit.

The express train from Greenwich to Grand Central had taken about an hour. As Barbara walked from the station, she concluded that the paperback novel she had read on the train may not have been what her frame of mind was telling her she needed. Instead of a book about spirituality, meditation, motivation, or a number of offerings from the self-help section, she had opted for a Nicholas Sparks romance novel. Escape, her magical elixir. Ostriches should read Sparks—less sand in their hair.

Two bags of stuff and three hours later, Barbara finally rolled into Macy's. That was when it happened.

CHAPTER 37

Goodbye, Hovel Beach
1971

Billy had made the transition from "loosely wrapped" to "on-point" in two days—two of the most memorable days he would ever experience. It started when, after hugs, greetings, and smiles, Israel turned to Reuben and asked, "Did that little prick really call me a 'fart mouth?'"

"According to that Mexican guy as we left town, '*boca de pedo*' means 'fart mouth,' so yeah, that's what he called you." Reuben had a big-ass grin as he looked at Israel and then everyone else.

"I'm going back there to teach that kid some respect." Izzy was pissed.

Everyone else was amused.

When they told Billy the story, he said, "Izzy, he's a good kid. Kinda reminds me of you, actually."

"Well, fuck ya very much, Stone," he answered with resignation and a slight smile.

Catching up with his closest friends was special. Billy hadn't realized how much he missed these guys. There had been no weakening in their bond. Once again, five became one in metaphorical math.

Each spoke about their life choices, their families, and interesting and memorable events since their discharge, and much about Vietnam. Israel had an interesting story about their former company commander, Captain Ryan O'Flaherty. They all had a high regard for the man.

"I had dinner one night in Port Chester with Ryan," Izzy said. "He started a company that provides job opportunities for Vietnam vets. It grew like crazy in the first year, and was bought out by a large employment agency. He put a chunk of cash in his pocket and stayed with the firm as a VP of marketing. He's married with a couple kids, and being a Mackerel Snapper, he'll probably have another half dozen."

That opened the door for Billy to talk about Alejandra. Reuben had a sheepish reaction, like it was too private for group discussion. Both Akio and Peter had smiles, glad that their hero had found romance.

Israel couldn't help himself. "'Good night, good night, parting is such sweet sorrow.' *Romeo and Juliet*, for those members of the ignorant masses." Israel looked at the four members of the ignorant masses.

They said nothing until Akio spoke.

"'Quotation is a serviceable substitute for wit.' Oscar Wilde." Akio looked at Israel with a knowing smirk.

The others joined the smirk-fest.

That night, under a full moon, Reuben, Akio, and Peter walked the long beach. Billy and Israel sat near the hovel. Billy had picked up some pot from his pal Miguel, and the two reminisced while mixing cannabis and tequila. They both knew that their straight-laced cop pal would be disappointed about the drug, so they had waited. They would rather be shot than disappoint Reuben.

"Thought I'd let you know, Billy," Izzy said, speaking in that funny way pot smokers do while holding their breath, "I'm being assigned to the Minneapolis branch for six weeks after I get back. We can spend some time together if you end up going home. I'm not encouraging you to do that. This place is paradise. But at some point, I know you, and even paradise loses its charm if you're not challenged."

"Always thought Ack Ack was our only psychic, Izzy . . . already made the decision." Billy sipped tequila. They watched the moon dance on the surf. "Thought I'd go for a law degree."

"Didn't think you were a fan of the legal beagles."

"Best way I know to figure out why I'm not. Plus, Uncle Sam picks up the tab."

"So maybe we catch a Vikings game, huh?"

When the three explorers got back, they watched as their two naked buddies dived into the Pacific, roiling and shouting like kids. Reuben laughed. Peter and Akio exchanged glances, their suspicions agreed to with knowing nods.

"You can't believe all the crabs and critters." Reub was in high spirits. "Those crabs got big pinchers. Don't think I'd be swimmin' in the buff."

It had been a night to remember. Around noon the next day, Alejandra showed up. The four newcomers nodded their approval, each exchanging quips with her and jabbing Billy with mock jealousy.

The Vespas had been lined up behind the hovel. Goodbyes shouldn't be painful unless you'll never say hello again. So say the

French. But still, even if the spirit didn't weep, their hearts got a little misty-eyed as the motorbikes pulled up the path to head back to Tijuana. Billy knew he would be doing the same on his bicycle in the next two weeks, but he would treasure his remaining days with Aly, which he did.

CHAPTER 38

Macy's
2010

"Serendipity" is such a beautiful word. It flows and bounces when you say it. *Sarun-Dip-a-Dee*. And, the definition is alluring and welcome. "Phenomenon of finding valuable or agreeable things not sought for; pleasant surprise; fortunate happenstance." Lovely. Give me some of that serendipity.

Barbara had her two bags and was on the up escalator. At nearly the halfway point, she did a double take and her heart jumped. The gentleman on the down escalator did, as well.

"Barbara?" he asked as they passed.

"David?" she replied, her head turning and watching him descend.

When she got to the top, she hurried to loop onto the down escalator. David did the same at the bottom and they were both laughing at the halfway point as they again passed one another.

"Stay at the bottom," she said, overlapping his comment to "Stay up there." Again they laughed. And they both stayed until she waved him to stay put. When the comedy routine ended, she stood in front of him on the ground floor.

"My goodness, you are prettier than when I last saw you." David's gaze was close to adoring.

"Don't I get a hug?" Barbara tipped her head from side to side, a cutesy sort of thing.

There are courtesy, greeting hugs and then there are other hugs that send a message. They both held the hug way past courtesy. They looked at each other, saying nothing—the kind of nothing that says a whole bunch.

"Been a while, David . . . I think of you." Barbara stuck her toe into the risk pool and waited, but not long.

"Want to go for a sail?" David's toe got wet.

Barbara laughed. "Isn't the romantic expression about *off into the sunset?*"

"Don't tempt me, Barbara. It wouldn't take much." They absorbed the hidden meaning. "Have you got time for coffee?"

"Took you long enough, sailor."

After two pots of coffee, they had caught up on all things external and a few of substance.

"So, I heard you got married some time back. Any kids?" David looked down as he sipped the now-tepid coffee.

Barbara's thoughts were at the bar in O'Hare Airport, long ago, and how she had compromised her feelings.

"A boy and a girl." No expansion.

After what became an uncomfortable pause, David went for the jugular. "Are you happy?"

An even longer wait time.

"I'm not prepared to answer that, David, and I hope you're not offended, but can we meet again sometime? I really miss our talks."

"Like I said, I still live in Seattle, but I come here about once a month on business." He reached into his shirt pocket and withdrew a business card. "Please, take this and call me. We'll have dinner next time."

On the train ride back to Greenwich, Barbara held the business card in her hand, rubbing it between her fingers from time to time, wondering about that woman from O'Hare.

CHAPTER 39

───～～───

Bloomington, Minnesota
1971

Billy had always loved Minnesota in the fall. It was art in its highest form, watching the green cover of the land transition to reds and yellows before turning an ugly brown that seemed to offend the sensitivities of the west wind that made it all go away in a two- or three-day effort. It was football and heavy sweaters, highways of cars dragging boats back from the cabins, and of course, the cheese curds and foot-longs at the Great Minnesota Get-Together, the state fair.

Billy walked the midway with his mom and sister. He wasted his money on a sneak peak of the world's tallest man, alligator man, the world's fattest lady, and the two-headed cow, all subject to litigation for misrepresentation, but Barbara marveled, so it was worth it. He avoided the dangerous-looking double Ferris wheel, afraid his stomach might reject the curds, but he did win teddy bears for mom and sis, needing to compensate for the purposely misaligned rifle scope. It seemed the poets weren't wrong. Absence had made his heart grow fonder.

The waters of Billy's life had calmed, with one exception. Below the surface was the persistent yin and yang of an injustice not reconciled. He didn't look at it as revenge. Billy saw it as honor, his father's, and his duty to restore it. H. L. Mencken said, "Honor is simply the morality of superior men."

Billy had a long list of things to do. He had to apply to law school, be accepted, find a place of his own, and make some money to fund it. He had already missed the start of classes for this year, but that was just fine with him. Mexico had taught him that schedules and rigid timelines were overrated. Outside of being in the crosshairs of a Vietcong rifle scope, Billy felt that stress was the most lethal cause of abbreviated mortality, and accordingly had chosen to avoid it.

He had been sleuthing. Through Army records, Billy had found the name of the private his father had court-martialed in 1952: a Lester Binger. Subsequently, he found that an Anthony Binger, who had been on the council for a number of years, was expected to be elected president of the Bloomington City Council next month. From his limited resources, he had found nothing that was damaging to Binger.

"Hello," Billy answered his home phone, expecting another of his sister's suiters.

"Billy, it's fart mouth."

Billy laughed so hard he dropped the phone. When he could reply, he asked, "Is that your undercover nom de guerre now?"

"Nah . . . term of endearment. So, take me for some of your famous walleyed pike . . . I buy."

Time with Israel was like a day at the circus, a calliope, and clowns. His personality filled an empty balloon mood with helium that sailed to the clouds.

"It's mostly bullshit, Billy. The agents in this office think Eliot Ness is still around. I'm helping to update their training." Izzy crunched an onion ring and sloshed it down with Blue Ribbon.

"I'll be going to law school next fall, but in the meantime, I'm trying to heal an old wound." Billy proceeded to share his father's story and what he had so far.

"I'll snoop around with the locals and see if there's any dirt." Izzy took another bite of fish. "This really is some fantastic shit. Let's go fishin', man."

Billy smiled as he thought of Shaggy and the beach bar.

On a late Friday afternoon, when Billy got back from a bookstore in Dinkytown, there was a message from Israel . . .

"We got the prick."

CHAPTER 40

Greenwich
2010

Beloit had had it with Tyler. The SOB was off the deep end, and if something wasn't done, his golden egg could turn into a brown turd, and he would be wearing a most unattractive orange jumpsuit.

Tyler was acting like a man possessed, and now he wanted an accounting. Sunny had gone over the third set of books with him, and he had shown a lot of apprehension. She got nervous and told Beloit that they might be getting a little too greedy. He reminded her who the kingpin was, and shifted his emphasis toward eliminating the source of the threat: Winston Tyler III.

Meanwhile, Tyler had also shifted his own emphasis. In the age-old conflict of intellect versus emotion, Tyler was becoming a slave to the latter. Like the smoker who knows it will kill him and still chooses not to quit, Tyler was choosing the illegal pennies over the big bucks of his financial business. This was primarily motivated by a distorted sense of revenge toward the establishment and certain politicians who had dissed him.

At home, he would lock his office door and count the shoeboxes full of hundred-dollar bills, like King Midas and his destructive golden touch. And it wasn't the money. It was something else—a symbol of his hubris and power. He was entrenched in delusion. Now he had to find a way to let the pathetic pretenders know how he had beaten them.

"Ernie, I really like you, which is why I'm telling you this. After my next big bonus, I'm adios." Sunny raised her martini in a gesture that said either "*salud*" or "see ya," or both.

"What the fuck, Sunny? There's never been a golden goose dropping eggs on us like this, at least on me. What's the problem?"

"Sometimes I think you live in a bubble, Ernie. Don't you see what's happening?"

"What?"

"Okay. One, this idiot Tyler has somehow flipped his lid, and I don't trust his volatility. Two, in some ways, so has the doctor. Three, the two of them are headed in different directions, and any check-and-balance system has gone *poof*. If this thing goes down, we go with it, so I'm looking at separation, and I mean *geographical* separation." She downed her drink, raised her arm to the bartender, and drew a circle in the air. "I'm looking at Melbourne."

"Wow." Ernie stared out the window. "They got any high-test hybrid weed down there?"

"David? It's Barbara."

"Hey, didn't think I'd hear from you this soon." A happy voice.

"Sorry. Guess I just wanted to hear your voice." It had been two days since her shopping spree. "When is your next business trip to New York?"

There was silence.

"Barbara, I'm feeling guilty. I have a confession."

Barbara felt cold. She said nothing and braced herself.

"I don't have any business in New York. I was taking my time coming home from sailing on Martha's Vineyard, and I made that up when you said you'd have dinner with me. Guess I was protecting myself against what happened at Sea-Tac. For a dinner with you, I'd jump on a plane whenever you could make it."

It was quiet. Barbara was choked up.

David filled the void. "Sorry about the fib, but it just came out."

After a while she said, "I will call you soon, David."

That, however, didn't happen.

CHAPTER 41

Bloomington
1971

"What I've got is good timing," Izzy said. "I've made a buddy with MPD, and he told me this story. It seems one of their cops was caught taking bribes. She's a single mom and having trouble making ends meet, so a few bucks on the side would make tickets go away. She got caught in a sting."

Izzy and Billy were sitting in a railroad car in Nordeast, Minneapolis, eating pizza.

"In any event, she's trying to bargain. She needs the job, and by all accounts, she's a good cop and tough. So, last year she comes across a guy she catches on a side street, in a most compromising position with a hooker. She takes a Ben Franklin and forgets about it until the news article comes out about his running for some council job. She recognizes his picture. Bingo." With a satisfied look, Izzy took a big chomp from his slice of the Broadway Special.

"Can we get MPD to bend on this?" Billy asked. "If we can get her to confront this asshole for her reinstatement, will she do it?" He was feeling victory in the making.

"Yeah, my guy said they would look for an excuse to keep her if she accepted their penance. They'll bend, and she'll be happy to confront him."

"She'll have to give him the hundo back, but I'll even spring for that."

"Then she'd be extra happy to do it."

"I owe you big, Izzy." Billy grabbed the check.

Billy and the lady cop were there an hour before the meeting. Today they were nominating for next year's positions. The building was stark and in need of an upgrade, like the big, open room where he had waited for his lecture from his grade school principle. He liked the cop. She was genuinely contrite, and most grateful for the second chance.

When Billy saw Anthony Binger headed for the meeting room, his pompous expression speaking volumes, Billy was pleased. It would be the long-awaited redemption.

"Mr. Binger?" Billy cut him off. "Could you step over here for a moment?"

"Who are you? No I can't. I have a meeting." Binger tried to skirt around Billy, who again blocked his way. "I don't know who you are, but if you don't get out of my way, I'll call security."

Billy gave him a glare that gave Binger pause. Then he whispered, "Unless you want that ugly face of yours all over the front page of the *Tribune*, I suggest you come with me."

They engaged in a stare-down that Billy would never lose. Binger blinked. They walked over to where the cop stood up. Billy noticed that Binger couldn't hide his recognition. She walked up to him and handed him a hundred-dollar bill. He backed away from it like it held the AIDS virus, and it fell to his feet.

"I see you recognize Officer Kutcher. She's undergoing some rehab with MPD for some, let's say *bad choices*. And you were one of those." No one spoke until Billy said, "So where does that leave us? Let me enlighten you, Councilman, with your two choices."

Binger's mind was racing. "Do you understand that I could sue MPD and the city for . . . blackmail, for one. My lawyer can figure it out." Binger was dismissive, but then he watched the imperturbable smile form on Billy's face.

"Indeed you can, Councilman. Actually, that is your second choice, so go ahead and make your call." When he didn't move, Billy added, "If you'd like, I'll tell you exactly how that will go."

Binger seemed to be processing how exactly that would go. Billy saw resignation in the subtle slump. Binger looked at the lady cop, and saw her intractable commitment. Eventually, he asked, "And what is the first choice?"

"Well, the good news is that you won't miss your meeting. However, you will want to add an agenda item . . . your immediate resignation."

Binger's eyes widened. "I can't do that. I've worked for a decade to become president. What would I say?"

Billy could detect fear, and that was when he took a step closer, lowered his voice and spoke methodically. "Tell me, Tony boy, is there something in my body language that says I give a fuck what you say?" He pierced his adversary with a look to kill. "Just do it or watch the ten o'clock news."

Binger, in his shock, absorbed the totality of his dilemma and slowly nodded. They began to walk in opposite directions, but after half a dozen steps, Billy stopped and turned around.

"Hey, Binger!" he called, loud enough for anyone to hear. "It was rude of me not to introduce myself. The name is Billy *Stone*." He let that sink in. "And I almost forgot to tell you, '*Hi, from my dad*.'" Billy watched the man's expression, and he knew he had hit home. With that, he and the lady cop left the building.

Billy sat on a lawn chair in the backyard, his mom and sister gone for the day. The sun was bright, offsetting the chill, and a light breeze was eliminating the last of the withered leaves that hung on to their branches for dear life. Billy watched them summersault and tumble before gliding to the ground, collecting in piles, taunting him with the next addition to his job jar. He was drinking a bottle of Hamm's, beer from a Saint Paul brewery that had been around for over a hundred years. His dad had liked Hamm's, as they sponsored the Twins.

Billy had thought that he would be on a high with the news of Anthony Binger's resignation and how the man would have to explain "personal considerations." Thing was, he wasn't on a high. It was more of a low, and he was trying to understand it.

He supposed part of it was like any longstanding, intense, emotional issue that is finally resolved: there comes a letdown. He also recognized that there was seldom great joy with pyrrhic victories. In this case, however, Billy suspected the source of his dispirit related to his self-concept. Had the mission of vindication diluted the strength of his honor and image? But then, shouldn't there always be a celebration when any injustice is rectified?

His next thought was, *No wonder there are philosophers.* Then he heard the phone ringing.

CHAPTER 42

Pine Ridge
1973

In 1968, Russell Means and Dennis Banks, as well as other Native leaders, founded the American Indian Movement (AIM), a political and civil rights organization. It was probably somewhat hyperbole to call it a militant group, at least when compared to groups like the Black Panthers.

In November of 1969, under the auspices of a treaty provision that granted unused federal land to the Indians, AIM members occupied Alcatraz Island in San Francisco Bay. They did so for the ensuing eighteen months. Again in 1972, for a short period, AIM members occupied the Bureau of Indian Affairs in Washington, DC, protesting certain programs that controlled development on reservations.

The grand event, however, took place in February 1973 when some two-hundred-plus Lakota activists and members of AIM, under the cover of night, rode into the historic village of Wounded Knee, South Dakota, in a caravan of trucks and cars, took the residents hostage, and began a seventy-one-day occupation. The occupants' demands, that the US government make good on all of the treaties from the nineteenth and twentieth centuries, were morally justified, but as always, it was form over substance.

The Native American arguments were again ignored and manipulated by the media-political complex. Some would argue that, as is often the case, the government overreacted—or at least reacted before understanding and analyzing the problem and providing appropriate response. The government's encirclement and use of indiscriminate machine-gun fire was certainly reminiscent of December 31, 1890. In any case, looking back through the lens of history, it was almost predictable.

As Peter found, the reservation had been in upheaval since he was young, and it had only gotten worse. Racism was prevalent, but combined with poor management and corruption within the tribal government, the Oglala Lakota tribal leaders looked for outside help. AIM responded.

Some critics, including a number of Indians, would later state that the occupation might have been both more effective and viewed differently, were it not for Russell Means. He was more than just an angry rebel who promoted the violence. He was a strong self-promotor who would later not only appear in movies, but would run for a governorship and for the presidency. Still, Means and the Wounded Knee siege was an inspiration to the indigenous people.

However, for the Pine Ridge Reservation, it was a failed venture that solved few problems. The federal government once again abandoned them, and it would be almost another four years before Peter would find himself in a position to influence change.

CHAPTER 43

Israel

FBI agent Israel Cohen had been at Wounded Knee during the siege. His intolerance for idiocy had reached a level of cynicism that affected his attitude about mankind. The smart-mouthed, blueblood, Jewish brat from Greenwich had morphed into an intrepid, worldly man of character with strong values. He had become a leader, and as such, understood the needs of the collective to be led. More than any other part of his being, he despised any form of injustice, and as a result, realized that such a world view was actually a Sisyphean curse. Indeed, the frailties of human nature itself would always prevent the expulsion of injustice from human existence. But that realization would not keep him from trying. Still, he accepted his own favorite shortcoming: he would always be a smart-mouth.

He could not communicate with Peter. He had watched the federal marshals and National Guard surround the town, just as the 7th Cavalry had surrounded the Lakota POWs eighty-three years earlier. Instead of Gatling guns, this time it was M-60s.

He approached one young soldier who had been firing at the

windows of a church. "Are you trying to prove that you got the biggest dick in the locker room?"

The soldier looked at him with a vacuous gaze.

"If you were to kill an innocent bystander, and you think for one second that *collateral damage* is a defense, you're smokin' funny cigarettes. I'll make sure that I'm a hostile witness at your court-martial." Izzy gave him a penetrating and defiant glare. "A word to the wise, soldier."

Sometime later, an officer from the Guard approached him. "Are you interfering in my command, Agent?"

Israel slowly absorbed the question before answering. "First, you make sure you fully understand the implications of what I said to your soldier. Secondly, go fuck yourself." Although the officer was bigger, Izzy's body language and look were enough to avert a reaction.

Israel recognized his own conflict of interest, and should probably have recused himself from the assignment. But if he could provide help and support to Peter and his family, he would stay, and so he did. On the question of the blindfolded Lady of Justice, Israel knew upon which scale he stood. His question was, why blindfold a lady who was already blind as a bat?

CHAPTER 44

The Years Pass By

There have probably been ten billion books and films and lectures and divine interventions about the secrets and meaning of life. You remember that mountain you climbed for years, where you skinned your knees and got bruises trying to get to the top just to talk to the shaggy-haired guru and learn the secret, only to hear some mundane truism you knew all along? Such revered intellects as Aristotle, Plato, and Socrates, of course, have their butts firmly planted in the tallest chairs of the philosophical heavens, but there are hundreds of Greeks, Romans, French, Germans, Italians, and prominent Far Eastern thinkers that spew forth the ideologies of existential objectivism, Sophism, epistemology, humanism, absurdism, and how about alethiology, ontology, and metaphysics? Had enough? There are lots more where that came from, and I apologize to all those I don't have room to list.

And then there are libraries full of all the crap about *tempus fugit* and how quickly time passes. The speed of the clock has never changed. It's just perception. *Whatever*. In the end, it just ain't that complicated. If you're lucky—or, for some people, *not* lucky—you get about seventy years to watch and experience all the bullshit fly by.

For me, I won the lottery when, as the fastest swimmer in that sperm pod, I hit the egg first, jumped inside, slammed the door, looked through the window, and gave the millions of other little fellas the bird. After that, and with some help from Mom and Dad and others, it was up to me to do what I had to do, and/or wanted to do. It was all in the attitude. No one's ever dealt a bad hand . . . It's always how you play the cards. But . . . you "gotta wanna" play. If you don't want to join in the fun, get the hell out of the way.

So, just for the heck of it, I mixed five paint colors together: white, light blue (blueblood), black, red, and yellow, and the result was really weird. Of course the hue, pigment, shade, tint, and tone changed dramatically depending on the predominance of any one or more of the colors, but it was still pretty weird—visually, that is. One had to conclude that they just don't mix, right? Wrong. That is just perception. There was no color like it. It was unduplicatable. It was the most beautiful color in the world. The perception had always been wrong. Sounds like a riddle: What happens when you mix a Jap, a Jew, a black, an Indian, and a white guy? Weird, huh? Nah . . . just a conditioned perception . . . a false reality. When you saw it, you believed it. When you believed it, you saw it. And of course, the Master Painter was God.

Billy picked up the phone on the seventh ring. "Hello?" He bottomed up his bottle of beer.

"Hello, who am I talking to?" The voice was strong, in command.

"This is Billy Stone."

"And how are you related to Marcie Stone, sir?"

"She's my mother." Billy paused. "What is this about . . . and who are you?"

"This is Captain Chapman from the Minneapolis Police Department, and I'm sorry to have to give you some bad news, Mr. Stone, but your mother was in a car accident."

There was an extended silence as Billy sat down, unable to process the message. Eventually he asked, "Will she be okay?" He silently screamed for the right answer.

He got the wrong answer.

"God could not be everywhere, therefore he made mothers." So said the poet's poet, Rudyard Kipling.

There is a big difference between a loved one dying unexpectedly and dying due to an extended illness, and it's mostly the shock effect. Extended illness provides opportunity to prepare, primarily emotionally. Billy was all too aware of how brittle life could be. War will do that. Still, he was shattered, a pain that he shackled in the deep well of his soul. On the surface, he had no choice but to show strength. His sister didn't have his fortitude or his wisdom, and her devastation was in dire need of his solidity.

Yes, his father's death had not been expected, but the ignominy of suicide that hung over his casket was palpable, though repressed. His mother, on the other hand, had been like a sparkler on the Fourth of July, providing that certain joy and uplift wherever she walked. People wanted to be around her, and people like that aren't supposed to die before their time, a time of sweet and sagacious wrinkles, gray hair, and cheek kisses that remind others that they are alive and just might live forever.

It was preordained that the funeral would take place under a cloudless sky with the sun god spreading his warm arms of welcome to the long line of cars along Thirty-Fourth Avenue, heading to the freshly dug grave next to Benjamin Stone in section nine of the Fort Snelling cemetery. Barbara and Billy rode in a black Lincoln behind the hearse. Billy's arm was around his sister's skinny shoulders, the loss of weight evident.

Billy was preoccupied with Barbara's health, both physical and mental. Mourning his mother was on the back burner, a cognitive decision he was postponing until he was alone. Barbara held the bouquet clutched in her small hands. Billy had a wreath beside him to place on his father's grave—to him, a symbol of forgiveness and closure. In the car behind him were the other four most important people in his life.

Scandinavians can be a rather woebegone fellowship, especially when it comes to things like funerals. The Irish, on the other hand, really have their shit together with the interment gig. Norwegians grieve the death while the Irish celebrate the life. They pile up turkey, ham, sauerkraut, and of course, potatoes, and they stuff themselves, slosh down beer and whiskey, sing songs, to include a few laments, and toast the "old bugger" or the "old girl." Marcie Stone, whose maiden name was Delaney, opted for the celebration, and it certainly eased the pain, until the next morning.

Billy mixed with everyone who came, more than twice as many as to his father's funeral, but this time there was no elephant in the room, unless one was physically describing the gentle giant Reuben James. Billy never let go of Barbara, who was the darling of the show, especially with his best friends. She clung to each of them as she did her brother, and they nurtured her away from that desolate place of deep anguish while steering her toward the more comfortable space of shared sadness and treasured memories.

"No wonder Billy loves you guys so much." Barbara looked at each of them with her teary-eyed smile.

"Who said I *loved* 'em? I said they were okay for a bunch of grunts." Billy's mocking grin didn't fully hide the flush.

That evening, the six of them barbecued in the backyard and got drunk in the process. There were plenty of tears, but the time was masked by the subtle defense mechanism of levity. They updated each other's résumés and spoke about coming events and political news.

"So now that Mr. Paranoid-schizophrenic has resigned, what happens next?" Israel threw out the question, looking at Billy.

Billy thought about it for some time. "To me, Izzy, Nixon was just another flavor of the Johnson regime. Vietnam was a political tool. The burning question is how does America rationalize the death of nearly sixty thousand soldiers?" Billy had their attention. "There's good news and there's bad news. I like to end with good news that really isn't that good, but so be it. So, here's the bad.

"If it weren't for the pussy, self-serving politicians like Kissinger, we would have won the war. Politicians negotiating anything is an oxymoron. They know nothing about war, and they know nothing about business. Their agenda is always votes, lots of votes, and nothing but the votes, so help me God. Worst of all, they don't really give a rip about the American people. Accordingly, America will always lose in any negotiation." Billy shook his head. "Kissinger was duped. Hanoi, with counsel from China and Russia, threw out the lure, and tricky Dick and Kissinger swallowed the bait."

"How you figure that, Gunny?" Reuben's interest was intense.

"To really understand it, Reub, you gotta go back to the early '50s and President Eisenhower. You remember the domino theory?"

"Kinda."

"Well, SEATO was a poor man's NATO, but the strategic thinking was that if Vietnam fell to the communists, the others would fall like dominoes. Cambodia, Thailand, Laos, the usual suspects. It was in March of '72 that the biggest what we would call *conventional* attack took place from the North. PAVN was backed with Soviet tanks, surface-to-air missiles, and constituted what amounted to almost twenty-three divisions of North Vietnamese regulars. Our ground forces had adiosed by then, and all the ground fighting fell on the South Vietnamese. We still had naval support, some advisers, and forward controllers, but our biggest contribution was massive air support. Credit goes to those ARVN troops, because by September, they were winning." Billy grabbed another beer.

All of his students were paying attention.

"The South Vietnamese marines took Quang Tri, just twenty miles from North Vietnam. In those six months, the North Vietnamese had lost over a hundred thousand troops, and Hanoi knew that they were cooked, so they sent their negotiators and kicked our ass. Kissinger might look smart and sound smart with the deep voice and German accent, but he gave the South to the commies."

Peter looked confused. "I don't get it. How do you mean?"

"Let me put it this way, Peter. If an attorney has a case won, he wins it for his client . . . He doesn't settle out of court, unless he's a half-wit or he gets a bigger chunk of the settlement than his normal fees or some other self-serving agenda. South Vietnam had the war won. US support was the leverage, and with the ill-conceived Paris Peace Accords, the 'cease-fire in place' provision left substantial communist troops in South Vietnam. Washington abandoned our ally. The US cut off support, and Congress cut aid from $2.8 billion to $700,000. The deathblow came from Congress with the Case-Church Amendment, which banned all US military operations in Indochina." There was anger in Billy's eyes. "So, sixty thousand dead American soldiers and our South Vietnamese allies lose their country because of the political idiots in Washington. So, there you have it, my friends."

"What the fuck, Billy? Where's the good news?" Izzy lifted his palms in the air and looked around.

Billy laughed, and then they all laughed.

"The good news is that there is plenty of beer and some big, fat steaks."

CHAPTER 45

***

Greenwich
2010

Dr. James Beloit should have been paying Clinton Hilliard much bigger bonuses than he was. If Hilliard had known how much money Beloit was raking in due to the inside information he was providing, he'd have extorted a mother lode that would give him his ticket to Aruba and the Richard Branson lifestyle he deserved. He knew he was involved in criminal activity, but money had a way of building a rationalization base that comfortably mitigated his guilt . . . not so much his fear.

Hilliard looked around his workspace and vindicated his transgression by profiling the other workers as to which ones were most likely doing what he was doing. The government was just plain stupid. They had no freakin' idea about what was goin' on. Waste and corruption everywhere and no control. And it was his hard-earned tax dollars that they were throwing away. So, *duh*, if you can't beat 'em, join 'em. He was putting away big bucks.

Beloit didn't have to prove any financial information to Hilliard. Everything was verbal, except for a copy of the cashier's check that Beloit sent directly to Hilliard's account in the Caymans. The income numbers he was giving Hilliard were about 40 percent of what he should have been receiving. Still, the numbers were impressive, as were Hilliard's checks, and their occasional lunches were celebratory, discounting the duplicity.

Hilliard was the true source code for Beloit's success. He was getting the constant policy changes from the CMS, the latest security memos, the reports on investigations, and anti-corruption strategies. The info kept Beloit ahead of the curve, and the life expectancy of his scam continued to extend. And then there was the weak link, or perhaps, links.

He could intuit a changed Sunny. It was subtle, but there. She had withdrawn, and he wondered if he should be concerned. Still, that paled in comparison to Winston Tyler. He could count on Ernie, however, and felt that he would be a key part of the Tyler solution.

Tyler had been *in the bag* when they had met yesterday. Apparently, Tyler's brother-in-law was coming to visit in a couple days, and that had him in a tizzy.

But that wasn't what bothered Beloit. Tyler kept talking about how he had a way to let the politicians know that he was the one who would make them look inept. He wasn't disclosing any plan, but it didn't take a psychiatrist to figure out that it related to a risk of exposing Beloit's scam.

Tyler was definitely not the same guy he had talked to initially. He had become an alcoholic goofball, and he needed to disappear. Beloit thought he might have an answer to that problem.

CHAPTER 46

The Years Pass By

The tumultuous '70s slipped by, and the '80s were much the same.

On second thought, that's not true. The Cold War was still hot (and heavy), which kept Israel busy at home and Akio even busier on foreign soil. Interestingly, Peter found himself in Washington, as he had been appointed to a primo position in the Bureau of Indian Affairs. Meanwhile, in the South, Selma, Alabama, celebrated their first black chief of police, and Billy, who had eschewed the many benefits of joining a large Minneapolis law firm, had hung his shingle in the small, historic town of Mendota, which in Lakota means the juncture of one river with another, in this case the Mississippi and the Minnesota Rivers.

Fort Snelling, named after its commander and architect, Josiah Snelling, was built in 1819 as a military fortification. You wanna talk about *out in the sticks*? Yeah, man, it was "nowheresville." Below the fort were a bunch of limestone caves, one of them named Fountain Cave, as a stream of cool, clear water ran through it and into the Mississippi. It was the perfect place for a pub.

So this fur trader of very dubious character named Pierre Parrant became Al Capone a century before Al Capone became Al Capone (my editor's going to want to scratch that, but, tough titty, I'm keepin' it). In any event, he was a bootlegger who found that local Indians and soldiers from Fort Snelling provided a lucrative market for whiskey, and so he built a bar. On top of shady, the guy was ugly. I mean *really* ugly—a surly, bushy-browed fella with only one good eye. His other eye was opal, with a weird, black ring around the pupil. He looked like a pig, so no surprise that his moniker became "Pig's Eye." Some claim he was the first resident of the community that surrounded his tavern, later named Saint Paul. He was the proprietor of the *hottest spot around*—well, okay, the *only* spot around—until 1840, when soldiers from the fort evicted him.

The famous brigadier general and explorer Zebulon Pike (you know, Pikes Peak?) had purchased a little island in the middle of the river just below the fort from the Mdewakanton Sioux, fifteen years before the fort was built. Minnesota creativity named the island Pike Island.

Just across the rivers, on the high bluff, several other interesting characters built homes. Another French trader named Jean-Baptiste Faribault lived on Pike Island in the 1820s, and found a better home site on that bluff in 1826. That house is still there for the kids to see on their field trips. He later moved south to Faribault, Minnesota. Now that is really a coincidence.

So, back on the field-trip bus and just down the street is the Henry Sibley House. Henry's dad, Solomon, was a most prominent judge in that area, and so Henry studied law under him. He later became a partner in the well-known American Fur Company located near his home in what was called Saint Peter. The name was later changed to Mendota, and Henry Sibley became the first governor of the newest state of Minnesota in 1858.

Oscar Wilde once said, "It is a very sad thing that nowadays there is so little useless information." In the spirit of that thought, I have taken a rather circuitous path in telling you where Billy hung his shingle.

Billy was pleasantly surprised at how many clients he got in such a short time. One of the reasons Billy had avoided the courtship of the big board law firms was because they were like the government. He had no interest in some Harvard grad telling him what cases and what clients he would represent. His loathing toward any kind of injustice was public information, and he made it clear that regardless of the legal aphorism that everyone deserved a defense, he would never represent someone that he was certain was guilty of a crime. He was a passionate litigator, and without his passion, could never successfully litigate. If you're innocent, I'm your man. If not, have a bad day.

Billy could appreciate the job of a prosecutor. There were a lot of assholes in the world, guilty bastards that deserved punishment, and a prosecutor's job was not easy. Way too many of these people walked away and shouldn't have, many for technical reasons having little to do with their guilt. But prosecution, to Billy, was more science, whereas defense was more an art form, and required artistic skills. One of Billy's early cases set the tone for his career.

His office was behind the reception desk, which was empty because he couldn't yet afford a receptionist. He heard a knock on the outside door. Although the main door was closed, a sign hung in the window: *W. Stone, LLB—Welcome—Enter.* He walked out, thinking whoever knocked must be polite.

The large man was black with short, curly gray hair and a pleasant smile. "Mr. Stone?"

"Yes, can I help you?"

"I hope so. Can I come in?"

"Oh . . . of course. I'm sorry." Billy was embarrassed. He held the door as the man walked in. "May I offer you a cup of coffee?"

"Actually, that sounds real good if you got some handy."

Billy grabbed the extra US Army cup and filled it, trying to guess the man's age . . . over fifty? Billy's desk was garage-sale vintage, but his two chairs were comfortable. When they had settled in, Billy asked him, "So how can I help you Mr. . . . ?"

"Wilson, Jim Wilson." After an evaluative look, he spoke again. "I guess I can see your dad in your face."

"You knew my dad?" Billy smiled at the man, hoping it was a good thing.

"I was sorry to hear of his passing. He was a bit of a hero to me. I fought with him in Korea. Naktong River." The man searched for signs of recognition.

Billy's smile faded to sadness.

The man continued. "Where he got his Star, you know."

Billy just nodded. "You know, Mr. Wilson, that dad took his own life."

There was a long pause this time.

"I did hear that. Yes, I did." A shorter pause. "He was a brave man, your father, a real stand-up man."

Billy looked out the window in thought. "I was pissed at him for a long time after that, Mr. Wilson. It took me a while to reconcile what he did, but I did forgive him."

The older man gave Billy a slight nod and a faint smile of understanding. Nothing was said for a while.

"So, I suppose you're not here for that," Billy said. "How can I be of assistance? And please call me Billy."

"Okay, Billy, and I'm Jim. It's about my daughter. She was raped." His pause signaled not to interrupt. "There's a problem, though . . . and I didn't know this until yesterday, but she was hooking . . . a prostitute." He let that hang in the air like a bad smell.

Billy was trying to process the disclosure. One could look at a raped prostitute as a twisted kind of oxymoron. All that came out was "That's . . . an interesting case . . . I guess." Back to the window stare, not looking at the older man. Finally, he said, "I think you're going to have to start from the beginning, Mr. Wilson."

And so, he did.

It was a small bar just off University Avenue and Dale in Saint Paul with the nebulous name the Blue Cock Tavern, with a blue chicken sign over the door. It was a Thursday, technically Friday, just before closing. Earlier, a football game had brought a rowdy group of fans, but when Latisha Wilson walked in, only three drunk, unsavory types remained. In retrospect, all the signals were there, and Latisha should have left, but one more trick would pay for a new purse. She ordered a drink and gave the unequivocal message of availability.

"So, whaddya say, baby?" the shortest loudmouth asked, looking to his pals for support. "How 'bout a threefer?"

Latisha didn't look at them.

"Better yet, why not three freebies?" he added with a nefarious grin.

The guy walked toward her. She realized she had better leave, dropped a five on the bar, and turned to go.

"Not so fast, bitch." The guy grabbed her, his hands roaming while his two buddies laughed.

The bartender just watched the scene unfold, a slight grin.

Latisha was scared. She couldn't get away as the other two joined the groping, which led to rape while the bartender watched. When it was finished, Latisha stumbled out, the three rapists had a final drink, toasting their conquest, and the bartender was told that if he wanted to remain in one piece, he had better keep his trap shut.

"I almost loaded up my forty-five and went to see that bartender," Jim Wilson said, "but I decided to come see you first."

"That was a good choice, Jim." Billy processed what he had heard. He thought, *Lawyers settle disputes, and there are lawyers that go to law school and those that don't.* He would probably connect with a few of those that didn't. "Tell me how to reach you, Jim. I need to think this through."

When Billy walked into the Blue Cock, he smiled. He could detect the faint odor of cannabis—one point for the good guys. The bartender was a smarmy-looking dude.

Billy introduced himself and got right to the point. "Were you working last Thursday night?"

"Yeah, so?"

"Tell me what happened just before closing."

"Whaddya think? Last call and closed the shop." The kid was snotty and dismissive.

Billy took a direct approach. "Cut with the 'tude, you little punk. Did you see the rape?" Billy leaned into the kid with threat in his voice.

The kid backed off, eyes wide, but didn't give in. "There wasn't any rape."

"If you saw it and did nothing, you're complicit, and you'll be spending your Christmas in Stillwater, so give me the names of the three assholes that raped Latisha Wilson." Billy raised his voice to intimidation level.

The punk absorbed the threat, and Billy detected fear, but not enough.

"If you're talkin' about the prick-tease hooker that was here, again, I say there was no rape."

Billy gave his killer stare for almost thirty seconds. He then gave the kid an evil smile, turned, and left.

Leroy Wood was an old acquaintance. Billy had heard that Leroy had gotten into trouble selling pot, so he called a friend that would know how to reach him. Wood had always been a cool guy, and Billy hoped that hadn't changed. The next day, he got a call.

"Hey, Stone, you made it back from that bullshit war in Nam. How you doin'?"

"Leroy, my man, you're right about the bullshit war. So, I'm reconnecting and wondered if I could buy you a beer."

"Always liked you, Stone—'specially when you buy."

They met at O'Gara's. After pleasantries and catch-up, Billy told Leroy about the rape.

"That place is crude, man . . . buncha assholes." Leroy sipped a White Russian.

"Do you think that bartender sells dope?" Billy had his fingers crossed.

"I ain't saying I know that, but there's some talk." Leroy's antenna was up.

"Here's the deal, Leroy. If you have any interest in making some points with the local cops, I have a way. If not, no big deal."

After thinking about that, Leroy replied, "Don't hurt to listen, man."

Two days later, Leroy went to the Blue Cock, sat at the bar, and ordered a drink with the twenty that Billy had given him. He felt his breast pocket, and hoped the microphone was working. After a couple drinks and some exchanges with the barkeep, Leroy quietly asked, "Hey, man, you know where a guy can pick up a little weed?"

The kid gave Leroy an evaluative look and thought it over. "You thinkin' dew, or somethin' else?"

"Lookin' for a woolah, man, just for me."

After a pause, the kid asked, "You know who the eighteenth president was?"

"Fuck no, man. I don't know who the current guy is."

"Well, it's Ulysses S. Grant."

Another pause before Leroy said, "Fifty bucks for one woolah? You shittin' me?"

"Goin' rate, man. I don't make the prices. I can get you one woolie for a Grant."

Bingo. Leroy smiled at the kid as Billy walked into the bar. The kid gave him a surprised glance and looked at Leroy, hate in his stare.

Billy pushed a button on the little recorder.

"Hey man, you know where a guy can pick up a little weed?"

Billy slapped Leroy on the back, smiled, and with an arrogant sangfroid, stated, "Well, I hope the owner of this dump is an understanding chap when he finds out you closed him down. He will, however, have to reach you in the hoosegow. On the other hand, a witness to a rape just might make this bad *woolie* go away."

Billy watched and waited. Finally, resignation became evident, and the kid nodded.

Jim Wilson came to Billy's office a week later.

"She'll still have scars, Jim, but the three rapists are going to jail. They knocked off a year with a plea, but Latisha can feel some vindication." Billy's smile was genuine and wide.

Jim gave him a nod. "Apple didn't fall too far from the Stone tree, Billy. I wanted to thank you with more than just a check, so I started singing your praises at the VFW, only to embarrass myself. Seems I'm the only one that didn't know you got a Silver Star. Now you're my extra hero." Wilson was almost contrite.

Billy actually blushed.

Wilson continued. "I am going to suggest you come down and join the V, however. You'd have a battalion of new clients." After a thought, he added, "One other thing, Billy. Latisha got herself a normal job at Burger King."

Billy gave a thumbs-up. "I'll keep that in mind, Jim. Thanks, and my best to your daughter."

As Wilson stood to leave, Billy spoke again.

"Here's a fun story, Jim. I get a call yesterday from Leroy. It seems he was stopped on the street by a black-and-white, and after he went into the usual position of surrender, the two cops laughed, slapped him on the back, and told him, 'You might have earned a free pass, Wood.'"

CHAPTER 47

The Years Go By

Weddings are a whole lot more fun than funerals. I understand that is a dumb statement, but when your short history is made up predominantly of funerals, it makes more sense.

So it was in two different locations, two different milieus, and two very different ceremonies. The first took place in a Baptist church in Selma, Alabama, and talk about a stentorian detonation of happy hymns and voices. Since I so love hyperbole, everyone was there. Yes, I know that everyone would encompass around six billion people, but it was so joyous that I'll say again that everyone was there. And you're not going to believe this, but the biblical Ezra and Esther's son, Reuben, married the beautiful, biblical Rachel, and once again, there was love in the air and everywhere else when it happened.

"How the hell did such a group of clowns turn out so good?" Ryan O'Flaherty said, hoisting his glass of champagne. "It must have been the influence of their esteemed commander. Oh yeah, almost forgot. That was me."

Smartass Israel smirked. "Can't remember, were you in Nam with us?"

"Saving your tight little Choate ass, Cohen." O'Flaherty snickered, pretending to be offended, before they all hoisted and giggled.

Reuben was Herculean handsome, and Rachel was adorable, a slight bulge in her lower tummy, confirmed when, eight months later, another Reuben came busting into the world. The difference was that this one would play football for Alabama. Ezra and Esther were two gray-haired children, hugging everyone in sight, including the servers.

Eleven months later, in the heart of the Pine Ridge Indian Reservation, under the stars near a raging bonfire, again it was O'Flaherty. "Jesus, I can't get away from you guys. What the hell? Some of us work for a living."

"We all agree with that," Israel quipped. "So what are you doing these days, Mr. Rockefeller?"

"Trying to fund the extravagant salaries of government agencies. Oops! Sorry, Cohen."

Peter's mom and dad were dressed in traditional native garb, as was Peter and his bride. The music was different, drums and tambourines, and you felt the presence of the Great Spirit. Native American spirituality was what all the gods of all man-made religions agreed was the true template. Mother Earth, nonjudgmental, all-inclusive, and all-forgiving—what's not to love? The smoke from the great bonfire took the collective prayers and good wishes toward the heavens and the happy hunting grounds. Beer, whiskey, and hugs were still a big part of the ceremony.

The next get-together would be in Bakersfield, California. Sadly, it would not be a wedding.

CHAPTER 48

Greenwich
2010

Barbara's fantasies about David were deliciously painful, like nostalgia always is. What could be and what might have been, a lethal thought pattern. Her routine at home was just plain painful. Her father-in-law was a grumpy old malcontent who needed care, and her husband was worse, a man possessed—with what, she wasn't sure. Her jailbird son had developed a nasty attitude, and she envisioned his future as a juxtaposition of his father's.

On the asset side of the balance sheet, she had Shotsy, her brother was coming to town, and in the mist of her fantasy stood David. Like a good quarterback, she took what the defense gave her.

Beloit took Ernie to dinner. If he'd been aware of the close relationship that had formed between Ernie and Sunny, he wouldn't have taken the risk.

"You know, I'm getting the impression that our friend and colleague, Miss Sunshine, is getting cold feet. You notice anything?" Beloit studied his reaction.

"Boy, I don't see that, Dr. Beloit." Ernie was both defensive and protective in his reply, but uncomfortable.

"Okay, but let me know if you do. The other thing I wanted to talk to you about is a bit more delicate." Beloit proceeded to tell Ernie about what was happening to Winston Tyler, and how it was posing a major threat to their accumulating fortune. He tiptoed into forbidden territory. "Even if we pulled the plug on our operation today, I believe he could still blow the whole deal. His ego is out of control." Beloit's language was designed to include Ernie as a partner. "So the question is, what do we do about it? You got any ideas?" Beloit wanted Ernie to get some skin in his game.

"Hadn't really thought about it, Doctor. I haven't been that involved with Mr. Tyler. What are you thinking?"

"I'm thinking he's got to go . . . maybe disappear. You and I wouldn't look good wearing orange jumpsuits, and I've never had the urge to see Leavenworth, Kansas."

Ernie had difficulty grasping the innuendo of what he had heard. Was this guy talking about murder? Really? Ernie chose silence.

"So, Ernie, do you know any guys who might take care of something like that?" Beloit was trying to be opaque, but that was difficult when asking someone if they knew an assassin.

Ernie's anxiety was palpable. "Boy, I really have to think about that, Dr. Beloit . . . Yes, sir . . . I need to think about that."

"Holy shit, Sunny, he's asking if I know a fucking hit man. He's planning on taking out Tyler."

"That's it for me. Color me gone. I never bargained for this shit. You won't see me after Thursday."

"Well, I'm sure as hell not getting involved, either. We get paid Thursday. If you're going to Melbourne, can I go with you?"

"Up to you, but I'm getting plane reservations tonight." After several minutes of deep thought, she added, "And I think we ought to get an anonymous tip to Mrs. Tyler before we leave."

Barbara's brother was coming tomorrow. So what? He had bigger plans. All the people that had been discounting Winston Tyler, the dismissive assholes, they would see who the kingpin was, and that included that arrogant Beloit. He hadn't been sitting on his ass—hell no. He'd been planning, calculating, and had discovered that he could take them all down. Beloit thought he had Winston by the gonads. Well, think again, Doctor.

Tyler had been working on the explosive revelation. The incompetent politicians couldn't even control the corruption in the Medicare program. Millions of taxpayer dollars were being scammed, and the political idiots couldn't even figure it out. They'd be impeached or resign, and Tyler would be the whistleblower hero. The people would try and recruit him. Who knows? Maybe he would have to move to Washington, DC.

Tyler had dissected his position from every possible angle. He didn't see where he could be found to be complicit in Beloit's scam. He owned the property and received rent. Period. He could deny any knowledge and involvement in the terrible corruption that his tenant was involved in, and when he did find out, he would be outraged, and that is why he came forward. As far as all the cash, he could get rid of it. If not, so what if he converted his rent to cash? He was on the verge of becoming *somebody*.

CHAPTER 49

The Years Go By

Daisuke Yamada was buried with full military honors. In attendance were members of the iconic 442nd, as well as the Bakersfield National Guard, the police department, and members of the top brass of Chevrolet. Akio stood with his family, all stoical, processing internally. Missing was Israel Cohen, who was involved in an undercover operation with the FBI. He had sent a huge flower arrangement and a note to the family. It had made Akio's mother cry when hidden from view.

Reuben was there with his wife and two kids, a lithesome boy and a pretty girl in a blue dress. Peter and his wife brought their baby. They had finally timed things right after trying to conceive for three years. He was back on the reservation and had been elected tribal chief. Billy held hands with an attractive redhead. He had a girlfriend, and it had lasted for over two years.

Billy fought to hold back tears, not just for Akio's father, whom he hadn't known, but for his own father and for the intense feelings he held for all veterans. World War II vets were special. *The Greatest Generation*. And he would always have the same conditioned response when the lonesome bugler played "Taps."

Akio didn't have a girlfriend. If he'd had the time, he probably would have had five, but the old saw prevailed . . . It's tough to hit a moving target. Still, he hugged his extended family as if they were his own, and they were. And everyone loved Mia, Billy's redhead. They fawned over Peter's little papoose and marveled at the strength, beauty, and manners of Reub's children. Love was there, and all was good, except for one strange thing: a vision came to Billy of his own funeral. He looked around and wondered who would come. Would people speak about his life, and would they cry? Would there be a grave near his folks? Who would get the flag? Would Barbara be okay? What about the cold, cold ground, and would he hear the final bugle call, the doleful timbre of those twenty-four notes . . . "Taps."

Several years later, Israel's father passed away. Billy and the other squad members got a letter from Israel saying that the funeral was a small, private gathering, not to come, and instead of "sending flowers that would be dead in two days, maybe make a donation to disabled vets instead."

The next horse to go down on the carousel of life was Peter's mother. This time Billy couldn't make the funeral, as he was in the middle of a court case defending several veterans' families that weren't receiving benefits for the delayed effects of Agent Orange. Izzy was there.

Akio was in Colombia, involved in the hunt for Pablo Escobar, the world's most famous drug dealer with a net worth of, some say,

$30 billion. Bill Clinton was president at that time, creating an embarrassing world image of America with his sexual proclivities.

Reuben James, his wife, daughter, and aging parents were the proudest people in the stands, cheering on the Crimson Tide and their all-conference running back, Joshua James, as he fulfilled his father's sidetracked destiny.

And the seasons went round and round. Everything came and went. There were good things and bad things, most traceable to the good and evil in humanity as a whole. As people died, they were replaced by 1.3 new people. Technology was quickly changing the world, especially the Internet. If the president farted during a speech to Congress, the Chinese general secretary was laughing about it five minutes later. Orwell was a dinosaur, and democracy was becoming passé, and to some degree, it was every man for himself. Cracks were forming in the foundation of the great United States of America. The Supreme Court was becoming a political tool, and the jurisprudence system was losing its teeth. Politics had reached a new level of nastiness, and self-serving political candidates were reaching their lowest levels of competency in a century. Sadly, the great system of checks and balances that kept the nation on the up-and-up had become farce, that being the media. The chasm between the news and the truth was measured in miles, not inches and a wink between reporters.

The name of Lord Woodhouselee, aka Alexander Tytler, that had remained dormant for some time, was being whispered among conspiracy theorists and bantered about in political science classrooms. Tytler, a Scottish intellect and clairvoyant, was born in 1747. He claimed that democracies have a lifespan of around 200 years. He designed a circle defining the various stages that democracies go through, from bondage to bondage, and the eight phases in between. These include spiritual faith, courage, liberty, abundance, selfishness, complacency, apathy, and dependence before spiraling back into bondage. America, in its 225 years, has experienced every stage, and is currently in the very throes of dependency—so say the pundits. So, get ready to restart the Tytler Cycle. What's missing is a group of real leaders. *Washington, Jefferson, Adams, Franklin, Lincoln, where are you when we need you?* That is the cry of the doom and gloomers . . . Oh, and the realists.

During the last decade of the twentieth century and the first of the new millennium, one of the highlights for the old squad included the wedding of Billy Stone and Mia Christensen. What it lacked in extravagance, it more than made up for in joyous celebration. Everybody came. (Yeah, I know, the hyperbole thing.)

Billy's buddies weren't used to his ponytail. It had just happened, and Mia liked it. If it was a statement, it said, "Nobody owns me."

Izzy had done a wolf call, followed by, "Ma'am, could you point me to the ladies' room?"

"Hey, Corporal, aren't you familiar with political correctness, or at least the latest fashion trends?"

Peter loved it, Akio appeared not to notice, and Reuben figured it must be cool, as Billy could do no wrong. Regardless, he looked very handsome in his tux. Mia had to get a girlfriend for her maid of honor, as Billy had already grabbed his sister to be his best man. He couldn't pick a favorite from his best friends, so he ignored the contradiction of terms, and Barbara just loved it. Un-tradition was alive and well.

Billy knew that things weren't good with Barbara and the Tyler household. Only Barbara had come to the wedding—not that

that was a bad thing, as far as Billy was concerned, as he considered Winston a dickhead, and William was a spoiled little prick, and so there would certainly be less tension. His concern was for his little Button Nose sister. Whatever travails Barbara was suffering, they were lost in her excitement at seeing her brother.

Billy recalled when his sister had called him from one of her fashion shows in New York and told him about meeting Winston Tyler. He could tell that she was a bit enchanted by the man's alleged lofty position in the high-test financial community of Greenwich, his background and family history, but he could also intuit the absence of passion. He sensed that a sinkhole awaited the relationship as, instead of support for her boundless energy, this man would use restraint.

After meeting him, Billy knew that Tyler had never experienced a woman like Barbara, genuine and showing him unfiltered attention and respect. Instinctively, he felt the man's insecurity. Billy had met enough spoiled jerks along the way, and so a gentle sadness replaced the elation he had felt for her finding a partner. The extravagant wedding, months later, only reinforced his deduction.

As he aged, Billy found that seeing his old squad members was more exhilarating and meaningful than ever, but there was a subliminal sentiment that the number of reunions was now finite and would surely come to an end. When they left, it was with a troubling sense of loss, while at the same time, his life had reached a level of comfort he had never felt before. Happy and sad were such strange and competitive bedfellows.

Billy's law practice was booming. He had expanded his space in Mendota, and had not only added a receptionist, but had two young lawyers, a paralegal, and a legal assistant. Two of the larger

Twin Cities law firms had made overtures to merge, but Billy had no interest. He had grown to like his ponytail. Though not exclusively, most of his clients were vets or their families. He had joined the VFW, and was actually on their board. He ate dinner with Jim Wilson on occasion, with warm greetings to the assistant manager, Latisha Wilson. Both he and Mia had joined a bowling league and a fitness center. Mia had received a master's degree in child psychology, and was employed by the Bloomington School District. They were only missing one piece to this beautiful puzzle, so one night after a bowling tournament, they looked at each other and said, "Let's have a kid."

It is normally not the good news that makes us change our priorities. It's the tragedies. That probably needs definition. It's the tragedies that put things in proper perspective. So it was when Billy got the call from Peter in 2010. The ending had begun. He set the phone down, shut his door, and slowly laid his head in his hands. A part of him died. He drove home. When Mia came home, he hugged her and said, "I'm going to Greenwich, Connecticut, for a funeral."

CHAPTER 50

⁓

Greenwich
2010

D r. James Beloit was not a man who panicked. Ernie had told him he had no such source "in regard to their discussion," and Beloit was now concerned whether he had opened a door with Ernie that posed a threat. Tyler had been coming by often, but he'd heard neither hide nor hair from him in several days, and that was also bothersome. Sunny barely acknowledged him anymore.

The web he was weaving was creating an element of paranoia. His mind had gone to a dark place, and he was spending time sleuthing out the many ways to kill someone. Car accidents, poison, fire—it was an ugly place indeed. There was another option, which was to take the money and run. He had followed Hilliard's lead and opened an account in the Caymans, and he had enough dough to hide and live comfortably, but at this point, it was all conjecture and based on fear. He absolutely hated having reached this point. He should have known better. But then, maybe he was overreacting. He still had time to see where the chips landed, but he would be prepared.

Sunny and Ernie would be headed to Australia early Friday morning. They had purchased tickets with cash, but since they didn't have fake passports, they worried that they could be traced and extradited if things went bad.

Ernie came up with what he was sure was the perfect solution. "I've been doing some research on Australia, and we can disappear and make some good bread to boot. They have this huge, open space called the Outback where nobody lives, and you can't find jack-shit out there anyway. So I started checking into the climate conditions, and I'm telling you, it's perfect for growing pot. We could develop a new strain and head to town a couple times a month, sell the shit, and get back to the farm."

Ernie's visage was pure excitement, like he had just discovered the Internet, but apparently, he had done a poor job of managing his expectations in regard to Sunny's response. She stared at him, mouth half-open, like he had just sprouted a second nose.

"Are you fucking for real, Ernie? You think I've been working my ass off and taking these risks to become a desert hermit? *Little House on the Outback*, that what you're thinkin'? Plus, if we got caught down there, we'd never see the light of day. Fuck that. I'm going to bask in the sun, drink rum all day, and dance all night until the cops grab me or the money runs out." She shook her head. "Sometimes I wonder if some extraterrestrials dropped you off on their way to Saturn . . . or Uranus."

Ernie's head drooped, but then a smiled returned. "On second thought, that sounds pretty cool, too."

Barbara was becoming clinically depressed. The old man was always looking for old stuff that had disappeared or been thrown away years ago. He constantly talked to himself, sometimes in very animated ways, and he only wore the same old pajamas and bathrobe that smelled. He wouldn't let her wash them.

Her husband was either out getting drunk or locked in his office. He ignored his father, but like his father, she could hear him talking to himself, or the wall, but certainly the signature of someone who was very loosely wrapped.

On top of that, she had fallen in love, and that presented additional problems. The best news . . . Billy would be here tomorrow.

Barbara's brother would be here tomorrow. He would need to have it be as normal a day as possible. Get up, go to work, stay moderately sober, bide his time for a couple of days, and then make his call to the press. Billy Stone could be a tough character, and was not only overly protective of his sister, but he was intimidating. Tyler could tell that the guy didn't like him, but it was a two-way street. Tyler had also convinced his son, William, that Stone was a bad apple. Hopefully Stone would be gone most of the time, and if not, Tyler would make life miserable as long as Barbara didn't see it.

Today he would have a couple snorts at lunch and then stop by and get the lay of the land with Dr. Know-It-All. He had written the news release, and he knew he would be shaking up the damn establishment, big-time.

CHAPTER 51

Billy

Billy hadn't seen his sister for almost two years. He missed her, and he couldn't wait to see little Shotsy. His niece was a miniature Barbara, sweet and full of life. Billy would give her a present when he saw her. The last time, he had presented her with a matching ring and bracelet. She had jumped on him and pulled his ponytail. Like his own son, Jimmy, Shotsy was the offspring of aging parents. She would now be eight.

Billy had stopped by Best Buy on the way to the airport. He didn't know much about the games and handheld devices that kids used these days, but the Millennial was most helpful in suggesting the small device that played a game popular with young girls. After going through security and settling in his seat, Billy looked around, smiled, and went to cynic mode.

The weapon of choice for the 9/11 terrorists had been plastic box cutters. He wondered how every passenger on this plane would feel if they knew that the person sitting next to them had between four and nine lethal weapons. He took off his glasses and turned them around. A pair of glasses could be made to hold two thin knives in each of the temples. The glass lenses could be sharpened to a knife blade and made to remove quickly. Everyone had plastic credit cards whose edge could be sharpened to a knife blade, and a clever belt buckle could also disguise a knife. Yet the overreacting idiots in Washington preferred to spend over 75 billion taxpayer dollars on airport security. He giggled when he thought about the fact that most of these weapons didn't even go through scanners, but were put in the little plastic baskets. Government waste was alive and well. At least they had created the perception of security.

Billy leaned back into the seat and sighed.

Every NBA team has a sixth man. There is even a sixth-man award. Captain Ryan O'Flaherty had been their sixth man, and he would be missed. He had deserved his Bronze Star, but mostly, he had been a leader, someone Billy would follow into enemy fire. His men had always come first, the mission close behind. He was tough but fair, and he never asked his men to perform a task that he hadn't done or wouldn't do. Unlike the so-called leaders in Washington, Captain O'Flaherty really had been one, and now he was gone.

Barbara and Shotsy picked him up at noon. As usual, JFK was a maelstrom of activity. His sister held him way past normal hug-time while Shotsy hugged his leg. Billy drove and Shotsy sat in the back. She squealed with joy when she opened her new toy, then remained quiet as she figured it out. He looked at his sister and saw the smile, but also a certain melancholy in her eyes.

"I think you should talk to me, Button." Billy waited for a response.

Barbara gave a quick shake of the head and scrunched her

face. The expression said, "I'm happy at the moment and don't want to go there."

"Okay, then tell me something good." Billy smiled.

"Well . . . the Vikings are looking good." Her lame deflection.

"That bad, huh? Okay, so I'll tell you about my latest." Billy proceeded to chat about Mia and Jimmy. He had never told anyone, but he had named his son in honor of Reuben. He hadn't even told him. Like a parent with four sons, they were all different personalities, but you loved them equally, as he did his squad. Still, there was something about Reuben James that prompted Billy to hope his boy could become like this great man. Billy was proud of his son. He was a good kid, a good student, and a baseball prodigy, though he was only fourteen.

His feelings were mixed about the military. Yes, he had enlisted, but at the time, he would have been conscripted anyway. With today's all-volunteer service, he might still do what he did, but it was different with his son. Some of the best things in his life had come from his time in the service, but so, too, had some of the worst. He had been lucky. He didn't want that risk for his only child, nor did his wife. The reality was, there would always be a war. There was only a handful of days in history when a war was not taking place somewhere in the world. It was in man's DNA, the dark side of human nature. Eric Bogle said it well. Billy recalled the last verse of his song, "Green Fields of France."

I can't help wonder why
Do those that lie here know why did they die
And did they believe when they answered the call
Did they really believe that this war would end war

Well the sorrow the suffering the glory the pain
The killing the dying was all done in vain
For young Willy McBride it all happened again
And again, and again, and again, and again.

He told Barbara about his law practice and the good things that were happening in his life. He understood that it could make his sister feel worse, but it was an act of tough love. He wanted to tell her that she always had choices. She didn't have to face a future of suffering and denial.

"You're the sweetest girl I've ever known, Button, so do what you need to do to be happy."

Except for giggles from the back seat, the rest of the drive was quiet. Billy could tell that his sister was processing what he had said.

Barbara's husband wasn't home, but the old man was.

"You remind me of Minnie Pearl," he said.

Billy laughed. "All I need is a price tag hanging from my hat? Right?" Billy was aware that the old bird was in the advanced stages of some sort of dementia. Nothing he said was offensive.

"That's it, young man. Most folks don't know Minnie Pearl. Marie and I go to see her once in a while. You want to buy a new hat, there are lots of hundred-dollar bills upstairs."

Billy nodded and looked at his sister. Her expression spoke volumes. The old man sat down in a chair and stared out the window. Barbara nodded toward the kitchen.

"It's not easy, Billy. I get no help from Winston." Barbara

pulled the stew from the freezer and showed it to her brother, smiling. "See what I made for you?"

"You never forget, sis. Love your stew." He looked around, grabbed a cup of coffee, and said, "What's with the hundred-dollar bills?"

Barbara shook her head, thought for a minute, and said, "I wonder if Winston is following in his father's footsteps. He's gotten a little crazy over the past couple of months. And, yes, he's apparently keeping all sorts of cash in his office. It's a mystery."

"That's weird, sis. Anything else strange?"

"Other than he's drunk half the time, I suppose not." Her tone was derisive.

Billy was quiet until he said, "I don't have to tell you I've never liked the man. And at this point, I don't trust him. More importantly, I don't trust him with you." He let that hang.

"And I guess I don't have to tell you that I am not happy. But for the moment, I don't want to talk about that and spoil our time together. Okay?"

Billy agreed. Twenty minutes later, his cell phone rang. He smiled and answered.

"Hey, secret agent man, what's up?"

"Well, counselor, I can tell you what's not up these days. I haven't had a date in six months." Izzy would never change. "But it could be time for a quid pro quo. How about lunch tomorrow? Wake is tomorrow eve and funeral the next day. I need you alone."

"I'm good with that, Iz. Where and when?"

"Like da' gangstas say, Billy, I know where you live. Pick you up at noon."

For dinner that night, the stew was terrific, but the company was horrific. The old man was basically unintelligible, occasionally conversing with his friends from the Eisenhower era. William was mute with only snide, judgmental looks. Winston was two sheets to the wind, and Barbara was flustered in her fruitless attempts to make it pleasant. Shotsy was the saving grace.

As Barbara washed dishes and Billy dried, he thought he heard his sister mutter, "Fuck 'em all."

Billy evaluated Israel as he drove to the restaurant. His hair was salt-and-pepper now, and his crow's feet were pronounced. His eyes were aged. The one-time dynamo was more subdued. He somehow remembered a quote by Raphael: "Time is a vindictive bandit to steal the beauty of our former selves. We are left with sagging, rippled flesh and burning gums with empty sockets." Only Izzy's smart mouth was unchanged.

"Your father-in-law's a dickhead, Billy."

"Is that supposed to be an 'aha' moment?"

"I don't say 'aha.' I say 'no shit.' We'll get into that at lunch, but your sister's always been way too good for that prick."

"I think she's beginning to see that, Izzy, and the kid is a bad seed."

Izzy gave Billy a scary look and a scary voice . . . "*Spawn*."

They both had beers. Izzy ordered onion rings and set the menus aside.

"What do you know about Medicare fraud?" he asked Billy.

"Just what I've read, which isn't much. Hard to separate one fraud from the next anymore. Why?"

"This will knock your socks off. Over fifty billion dollars last year and climbing. There's very little oversight, and few crimes are easier to get away with. It's a titanic problem."

"Sounds that way, but what's it got to do with me?"

"I need you to tell me where you stored all that loot." Israel stared at Billy with a serious look until he broke up laughing.

"Once a schmuck, always a schmuck." Billy implied relief and managed a grin.

"Okay, so seriously, the FBI is involved now. We got a court order to tap into all phones in the Medicare office. There was a lot of shit going down, and a lot that required some investigation, but one guy in particular raised the eyebrows of the brass, a guy named Clinton Hilliard." Izzy paused to gnaw on a ring and drink half his beer. When the waiter came by, he signaled for another round. "It seems this guy is passing on confidential information to a local clinic, specifically a doctor named James Beloit. So, this info is the kind of shit that would allow someone to avoid scrutiny and investigation. What we've found so far, the clinic looks pretty clean, but that's just superficial. The guy is rackin' up big bucks, like a million and a half, but there's a pile of red flags." Israel finished the rings and told the waiter to bring two specials.

"I haven't even looked at the menu." Billy looked at Izzy, who waved the waiter away.

"Trust me, you'll love it." Israel dismissed Billy's concern and moved on.

Billy made the hand gesture of someone who'd been dismissed.

"Anyway, this Beloit is using account numbers of doctors and patients that can't be found, might not exist, or are dead. Big overcharges, double claims, lots of warning signs, but the guy is clever . . . covers his ass. My guess is that he's got another set of books that would take a forensic whiz months to analyze, and that assumes we can give a judge enough evidence to issue an order. And can we hold him? There's so much fucking red tape. What we know is that if the prick is guilty, he'll be in the wind as soon as he suspects we're comin'."

The waiter dropped off the food. Billy stared at what looked like a big pile of red and brown leftovers.

"Don't look at it, Stone," Israel said. "Just dig in."

And Billy did. He was pleasantly surprised, but wasn't about to give his friend any satisfaction. "Looks like shit," he grumbled, "but it tastes all right. Beer helps."

Israel smiled. "Told ya you'd love it."

They ate.

When finished, Izzy continued. "So, why am I telling you this fascinating tale? Well, most all of these fraud cases involve phony storefronts. Most are drive-by obvious—a sign over an empty space, some even abandoned properties, but Beloit's place is first class. Looks like a real clinic with real people and visible equipment. So, where's the weak link?" Izzy downed his beer and thought about one more. He opted for coffee. "Guess who owns the property? And guess who drops into the clinic almost every day?"

"Don't I get to spin the wheel first to see what I win?" Billy asked.

Izzy ignored the sarcasm. "Winston Tyler." He let that hover.

"Really?" Billy processed the implications. He remembered the reference to *lots of hundred-dollar bills.* "How do you know he's there every day?"

"We've been watching the place for a couple of weeks. You know, a stakeout, a couple people sittin' in a car for hours, drinkin' coffee and eatin' apple fritters."

"Yeah, I saw the movie. So, you think Tyler's involved in the scam?"

"Kinda looks that way, but that's where you come in, the quid pro quo. If Tyler turns on Beloit for a plea, we can grab the guy. The bad news is that your sister's hubby might be goin' to the crowbar hotel for a vacation."

"That's the bad news?" Billy smirked.

"Well, being the diplomatic, nonjudgmental guy I am . . ."

The two were silent for a while. Billy was deep in thought about what this development meant. He was looking at it through the eyes of his sister. In the end, he concluded that, at minimum, it was not a bad thing.

"I need to think this through, Izzy. I need some alone time with Barbara, and on top of that, we have a funeral. So, how about you pick me up again in a few hours for the wake?" Another pause. "Where are the guys staying?"

"I talked to Peter, and they're at the Hilton. We'll meet 'em there."

There are few dry eyes when a vet watches the missing man flyby. Aircraft fly in a V-shape, with the flight leader at the point and his wingman on his left. The second-element leader and his wingman fly to his right. The formation flies over a ceremony, low enough to be clearly seen, and the second-element leader abruptly pulls up out of the formation while the rest of the formation continues in level flight until all aircraft are out of sight. A salute to a fallen comrade. That didn't happen at the wake, but it seemed that way.

Aside from the squad, there were other members of the old unit. Once they arrived at the local VFW, things lightened up and whiskey flowed. Their platoon leader, First Lieutenant Roberts, hugged Billy, a boilermaker in one hand, " . . . the fuck, that Paddy-Mick was a keeper, Sarge. Kept me alive." He moved on to the next hug.

Billy felt vulnerable. He watched his men. Time was taking its toll on all of them, less so on Peter and Akio. Perhaps that was a genetic thing. He pictured the kind of wonderful world it would be if God would start over with only this group and their families, with exponential growth in their offspring until one day all peoples were strong and united and people didn't know what that strange word meant . . . *war*. He'd had his share of Jim Beam, and he found himself hugging each of them, saying stupid things like thank God they had been born.

When he got to Reuben, he looked into that big, black, beautiful face and put his hands on his friend's cheeks. "I named my son after you, Reub. You're the finest man I've ever known."

Reuben didn't know what to do or say, but his eyes watered.

Another damned Irish funeral. Hell, another funeral.

"So, here's my take, Billy—sort of Shakespearian. Once we get past shittin' and suckin' on a bottle, we go to the circus with Mom and Dad. Next, we get boners and chase girls until we have to pay bills. Then we set our sights on becoming *somebody* and gettin' fancy shit to show the world that we've made it when we go to weddings and fawn over little kids. Then we discover that all of the first part is just bullshit, and we become enlightened. By that time, it's too late and we're already going to funerals and back to shittin' in our pants and eatin' applesauce. *Poof.*" Izzy made an explosive gesture with his hands. "Life is backwards."

"Gee, thanks for that bit of poetic insight, Izzy." Billy was glad for the comic relief.

Billy couldn't get away from a preoccupation with Tyler and his potential involvement in corruption. He had analyzed his options for an approach to Tyler, and had decided to take it head on, and bluff. The guy was a weak-kneed spoiled brat, and Billy felt it would work. If not, so be it. First, however, he needed time with his sister. It was April 30. Tomorrow was May Day.

The restaurant was really nice. It was old-world. Two bartenders with white shirts and black bow ties. A long bar of polished mahogany in front of a big mirror with bottles of every kind of booze ever invented. Barbara looked stunning, and she had really gone the extra mile. Billy wore a pair of slacks and an open-necked shirt. He had gone the extra block. He felt underdressed. If Oscar saw him, he would call him undereducated. They sat in a booth, and both ordered Gray Goose martinis. Billy should have told the waitress to "keep 'em comin'."

"What's the occasion?" Barbara raised her drink.

They clinked and sipped.

"When did you get so suspicious? Can't a guy take his sister, who he adores, out to eat?"

"I know you, soldier."

"Well, okay, I do have something important to talk to you about, but it'll wait till we get to the stingers."

Barbara's salmon was delicious, and Billy's lamb was to die for. The waitress brought Billy a stinger and Barbara a Baileys. Too full for dessert. Billy went right after it.

"I'm not going to beat around the bush, Button. Your husband may be involved in criminal activity."

She was stunned. "What in God's name are you talking about, Billy?"

Billy told her what Israel had told him. When he had finished, he gave her an inquisitive look. "Level with me, Button. How do you really feel about that?"

She was quiet for a long time. Billy went to the restroom to give her some space.

When he returned, she said, "Here are my questions: What do you think will happen to him? Why do you have to be involved? And if you're wondering whether I feel sorry for him . . . no, I don't. 'Stupid is as stupid does,' to quote Mr. Gump." She maintained a thoughtful expression until admitting, "I don't love the man, Billy. I'm not sure I even like him."

"I'm not surprised by your feelings, so let's look at the cause and effect. First of all, even if I didn't owe Izzy, I'd still help him. Secondly, because you're involved, I'm involved. Thirdly, I'm the right guy to get this done." He downed the last of the cognac. "As far as what happens to Winston, that depends on how helpful he is, assuming he actually does have two arms in this tar baby."

Billy paid the bill, and they walked out arm in arm.

William had become involved with a group of teenage white-collar druggies. Most of them were just users like William, but two were dealers, as well. They were known as *potrepeneurs,* only they weren't just dealing in pot. It was primarily crack cocaine, and those two had formed a relationship with a *Samson,* whose contact was from the Sinaloa Mexican drug cartel. They were amazed at not only how much amidone and cocaine, the all-American drug, was available, but how easy it was to get. It came across the Mexican border in truckloads. Over fences, under fences, through fences—didn't seem to matter. There was no security. Multiple networks had been put together, and the product was selling big-time on the East Coast.

William's group was the by-product of overindulgent parents who often produce such spoiled brats. Even the two dealers didn't need the money, although it turned out to be a most lucrative revenue stream. They were all in it for the rush, the excitement, and the challenge. There are cardinal rules that dealers live by under normal circumstances, but when it ain't the money, who gives a shit? So, in relatively short order, all of them got hooked on the drug.

William paid in cash. He had a ton of it after searching his father's office one afternoon when his dad and his bitch mom weren't home. Only his goofy grandpa and a maid were around, and he had been looking for some booze in his dad's desk. When he opened the closet and saw the dozen stacks of shoeboxes, he opened one and couldn't believe what he was looking at: piles of *Benjamins.* Every box was filled.

What the fuck is goin' on? he thought to himself. The more he tried to figure it out, the more confused he became, so he concluded, *Who gives a rip? I think I'll just help myself,* and he did. He took two bills from each of the first ten boxes. He guessed that his old man would just think he had miscounted, especially because he was usually in the bag anymore. He knew that he now had an easy source of funding for his habit. But the drugs weren't enough for William. He wanted something even more exciting. He had also found a loaded pistol in his dad's desk. That might come in handy, but first, he had another idea.

William and Roger Breton had been hanging at Roger's parents' home. They were on a cruise, so it was the perfect place to get crazy.

"Here's my idea, Rog. What would you say if we could do a rape and never get caught?"

"You fuckin' nuts, Willy?"

"Think about it, man. Put some bitch in her place and scare the shit out of her, and she'd never say a word. Talk about an adrenalin buzz. Come on."

"What if she's not scared and calls the cops?"

"I got that covered. Let's go. Tell you on the way."

They drove to a shopping center twenty miles west of Port Chester, New York. They were wacky, but enough in control to drive. They parked in shadows, away from other cars, but with a clear view of shoppers going to their cars. It was eight-thirty p.m. and dark. They had the windows open and shared some weed.

After about an hour, a lady walked to a big SUV with a cart full of groceries.

"Okay now, Rog. We don't want her to see our car and our faces. I got condoms, so no DNA shit. We get her in the back of her SUV. You drive while I do it, and then we switch. We drive near our car, I get out, get the car, and pick you up where she can't see what we're driving. Got it?"

"I don't know, man. I don't really like it."

"Think of the rush, man. We can do anything we want and won't get caught. Come on."

They left their car and walked to where the woman was loading up the SUV. They put on plastic surgeon's gloves. William looked around. When he was sure no one was nearby, he caught her by surprise, wrapped a cloth around the woman's eyes and mouth, and shoved her in the back. Her keys were in her sweater. He gave them to Roger. He pulled the back down, and Roger drove out of the lot. William's face was covered in case she removed her own cover. He told her that if she ever said anything, they would find her and kill her. Then he raped her.

When he was finished, he told Roger to find a place to switch, but Roger declined. William lost it.

"You motherfucker, I'm not doin' this alone. Pull the fuck over. We had a deal."

After a minute, Roger pulled over and they switched places, but Roger couldn't do it, so he pretended. He made grunting sounds and then said, "Okay, let's go."

William got close to the mall and parked. Before getting out, he turned to the woman, who wasn't moving. "Don't forget what I said, bitch. We'll find you."

On the drive back to Greenwich, Roger was quiet while William kept saying "Shit man, talk about a Rocky Mountain high."

William checked the papers every day for a week . . . nothing.

When Billy and Barbara got home, Shotsy was in bed, the old man was in his room, William was nowhere to be found, and Tyler was gone. The maid left.

"When are you going to do it, Billy?"

"In the morning, when he's in his office." Billy felt the apprehension, but he felt something else, as well. He couldn't put his finger on it. He checked his watch. It was just after eight o'clock, still early. The guys wouldn't be leaving until tomorrow night. Time to see them once more and coordinate tomorrow with Izzy.

He took Barbara's car and left for the Hilton. His thoughts were going faster than the car. He thought he was controlling the speed of his spinning mind, like a cerebral lazy Susan, but was it delusion? Do we really control anything? But we do influence. Both Israel and Akio had grown up in the same kind of environment that William had, but look how they had turned out. Reuben and Peter had found an inner strength that came from their parents, that guided them through a world of adversity and injustice, and then there was himself, a product of good parenting, little adversity, never a victim, living in a rose-colored bubble, until Vietnam. Still, he turned out okay. Were all the studies of analytical, social predictability just more bullshit? How about philosophical abstractions, metaphysical theories, and concepts? Did they fall under the heading of bovine defecation, too, or was there substance? Did the masses simply create icons out of these goateed thinkers because of their own shortcomings? To paraphrase Voltaire, if there were no delusion, it would be necessary for man to invent it.

What he was beginning to think was that mankind was just not comfortable with reality, because reality sucked, and a yellow brick road was so much more colorful and fun. God had to have a tremendous sense of gallows humor when he looked down on his silly creation called *man*. And to really stir up the soup, he created woman. And he gave them love. But after a while, he must have gotten bored, so he threw in a little hate, but even that was too pat, so spice it up with money, religion, greed, lust, power. God had gone on a terror, laughing and watching the self-destruction, shaking his head and asking himself if he had screwed up and should maybe think about starting the man gig all over again.

Billy had missed his turn, and in the process, confirmed his question about control. There wasn't any, so he called Mia and Jimmy to bring meaningful substance to his own reality. After a status report, they all said, "I love you." Now he was grounded, except for that little, ugly thing that was crawling around his boundaries, whatever it was.

They did one of their favorite things. They sat around, drank beer, and laughed about old times. Highlights were Izzy's smart-aleck remarks about taking on a battalion of Cong by himself, Reuben's two bullets in his ass, Akio's appearance from the tunnel, and Peter's crazy attack in the rice paddies.

Billy told Israel to be ready for a cell phone call after his confrontation with Tyler. They said their goodbyes until next time.

They didn't know there would never be a next time.

CHAPTER 52

May Day

Billy and Barbara were in the kitchen drinking coffee. It was early, and the house was quiet.

"I'm worried about Shotsy."

"She's tough, sis, just like her mom." There was tension in the air, and Billy needed to defuse.

"There'll be a lot of changes, Billy."

"In your case, Button, good changes."

They sipped coffee, each with a different picture of the future until they heard movement above. When the door to Tyler's office closed, Billy went up the stairs.

Billy didn't knock. The door wasn't locked, so he walked in, shut the door, and stood in front of Tyler's desk, forcing him to look up, an authoritative figure. He had to take control from the start.

"This isn't the Army, Stone. In civilian life, we knock. What do you want?" Tyler acted put out, but uncomfortable.

"Funny you should put it that way, Tyler. In the Army, we're trained to knock on the door of one who deserves respect. That's why I didn't."

They stared at each other.

"I don't need your sarcasm, Stone. I'm busy. So, what is it you want?"

"Time to talk." Billy walked over to the closet and opened it.

"What the hell do you think you're doing? Get away from there." Tyler started to get up when Billy whirled toward him.

"Sit down and shut up." Billy was in full intimidation mode now.

Tyler sat back down.

"Know this, Tyler: you are going to prison. The question will be, depending on the extent of your cooperation, for how long and whether it will be a country club facility or general lockup. So, speak only when spoken to, and answer my questions truthfully. You understand?"

Winston Tyler was in shock. He was trying to process what was happening here. Finally, he tried to speak. "How dare you . . ."

Billy came closer, wagging his pointy finger back and forth. Tyler went silent.

"The FBI not only has proof that you have been conspiring with Dr. James Beloit to bilk hundreds of thousands of dollars from the Medicare system, but there are witnesses. If you want to doubt me, I'll make a call and walk out of here. Know that I'm your best hope for a lighter sentence, and that is *only* because you are, unfortunately, married to my sister." Billy pulled out his cell phone and scrolled for Izzy's number. "What say you, Tyler?" After ten seconds, Billy put his finger to the call button.

"Hold it. What kind of deal are we talking about?" Tyler tried to appear as though he had even a sliver of control, but it quickly faded. "I was just the damned landlord, Stone."

Billy shook his head. "That really how you want to plead?

Winston . . . you're dumber than I thought you were." Billy put his finger back, and Tyler caved.

"All right, so understand that I wasn't doing this for the money. It was Beloit's idea and his people. I just saw it as a way to prove those son's of bitches politicians were incompetent losers. You get that?"

"Actually, you have no idea how much we agree on that issue." Billy sat down across from Tyler. "You just chose a very stupid way to show it, and now you got to pay the piper."

They looked at each other, Billy relieved, Tyler hopeful.

"So," Billy said, "here's how this is going down. It goes quickly and quietly if you strike a deal with the FBI. You get the best deal available, and with your testimony, Beloit gets a long prison sentence. They'll pick him up now. I call my agent pal, he comes here, and you give him a full statement. You agree?"

Tyler was still looking for any escape route and took his time.

"I'm calling him now regardless," Billy added, "but if you don't agree, I wouldn't want to be in your shoes." Billy hit the send button. Izzy picked up after one ring. "Tell your people to pick up Beloit and come on over. Bring a pen and paper." He disconnected.

Tyler said nothing while they waited.

Finally, a knock on the door.

While Tyler wrote his statement, Izzy was on the phone with the agents who were picking up Beloit. It seemed that the doctor had sniffed out the stakeout and had slipped out the back of the clinic, but that exit was covered, and a black-and-white blocked him in. They had him in custody. He was chirping like a bird, putting it all on Tyler. What Izzy found most interesting was that Beloit's two key employees, a man and a woman, didn't show up for work that day.

Israel was also talking to the agent in charge at the MECS office. Hilliard had been ambushed. They had cuffed him and marched him out in front of everyone, hopefully sending a warning signal to anyone with similar ideas.

Billy was back in the kitchen with his sister and his coffee mug. Her face showed a mixture of sadness and confusion, and she absorbed his words in silence.

When someone is killed by the destruction of a hurricane, it is a tragedy, but sometimes there is a choice involved. Afterward, people might say, "Damn, why didn't he listen? He had plenty of warning." Or when a soldier dies in combat, "He always knew it could happen." Other tragedies are harder to fathom, more unforgivable, as when a child is killed by an errant bullet in a drive-by shooting. Webster defines tragedy as this: "An event causing great suffering, destruction, and stress."

Then there are some people who are not supposed to die at all. To all those who know them, who take their lives for granted because they know that no matter where they are and what challenges they face, that person is available to them to make things good again, there is a subliminal suspicion that those few will live forever because of their imposing, even sacred, presence in the world. But the real world isn't that way, is it?

Billy and Barbara looked up as Israel and a cuffed Winston Tyler entered the kitchen. Barbara just stared at her husband.

"How could you be such an idiot?" She waited.

Winston stared back with acrimonious eyes.

Right then, William walked into the kitchen. He had a wild look, like he was on something, with palpable anger.

"Hey, Dad, what the hell is goin' on?" He saw the cuffs and glared at Billy, Israel, and his mother.

"They betrayed me, son, and now I'm going to prison." Tyler looked at his son like he could help.

"Who, Dad? Who betrayed you?"

"Who do you think? Your mother and her damned brother." Tyler nodded toward them.

They both shot him menacing glares that said, "What the hell are you talking about?" but they said nothing.

Wide-eyed, William turned and ran. They heard footsteps on the stairs and assumed he was headed to his room. In less than a minute, the pounding on the stairs returned, and William burst into the kitchen, only he had a pistol in his hand. He pointed it at his mother.

Israel was too far away. It would have been suicide for him to take any action, so he made the decision to let it play out. He would regret that decision until he passed away, nine years later.

"You never supported Dad, you and your bastard brother." William was not in control.

Billy slowly moved toward his sister until he was directly between her and her son. He put his arms behind and pulled her to his back.

"Don't you ever point a gun toward your mother. Now put that goddam gun down." Billy was furious. He started to walk toward William with his hand out for the pistol, when the loud bang shook the walls.

No one moved for a lifetime, until Billy's legs went out from under him. Along with the glass table, he fell to the floor, his face forming a strange look of curiosity. Barbara fell to the floor beside her brother.

"Billy . . . Billy, are you okay? Please be okay." Tears poured from her eyes.

Israel jumped on William, ripping the gun from his hand, rage in his eyes. He shoved the barrel into the kid's mouth, breaking his front tooth, and shoved it far down his throat. William was gagging and choking on the tooth chip. Israel didn't care. He pulled the hammer back, and then came under a semblance of control.

"You try anything, and I'll shove this gun up your ass and pull the trigger." Israel cracked William in the head, but the kid was choking so hard, he rolled onto his stomach.

Israel stood up, looked at Tyler, and said, "You did this, you son of a bitch," and shoved him ass over teakettle. With his hands cuffed behind him, Tyler couldn't break the fall. Then Israel knelt next to Billy, speed-dialed 911, and yelled for help. He ripped open Billy's shirt and saw the damage. Billy was mostly lucid.

"Not how I planned it, Izzy." Billy's breath was shallow, a wheezing drawl. "You tell the guys I loved 'em . . . Best thing that ever happened to me. And check on Mia and Jimmy . . . huh?"

"You tell 'em yourself, Chief. First we need a medic."

"Button? Lean over here . . . You go get happy, little sis. And this won't make sense now, but for yourself, you need to forgive your son. My love to Mia and Ji . . ." Billy's head fell to the side . . . and he died.

The bullet had shattered the left coronary artery. Billy had bled out quickly. Barbara was vibrating beyond control. She was massaging her brother's head, shaking him to wake up, screaming for help.

Israel had seen enough death to know that Billy was gone, and with him, a huge piece of himself. Tears dripped from his nose as he leaned over to kiss Billy's forehead and whisper something. He closed Billy's eyes with his thumbs. He was so torn. He wanted to kill Tyler and his son, but only touching Billy kept him from doing it.

The medics arrived. Israel looked at them and shook his head in the negative. The cops arrived, and he pointed to Tyler and William. "Lock up these assholes. I'll come by when I find some time."

Israel just held his arm firmly around Barbara. Shotsy was at school. The old man came down the stairs, and one of the cops took him back to his room after Israel's instructions. Barbara, Israel, and Billy stayed that way for a long time. Izzy asked a female cop to stay with Barbara as he walked to the living room. He dialed Peter's cell.

"Peter, I can't talk now, but you guys have to cancel your flights. I'll be there in ninety minutes." Israel hung up on Peter. He couldn't answer any questions over the phone . . . He just couldn't.

He thanked the cop and took Barbara to the couch. The medics had removed the body. Barbara had calmed a bit. After a while, he told her he would take care of Shotsy. She gave him the name of a neighbor friend. Israel called the woman and explained enough to get a commitment from her to come over. When she arrived, Izzy explained and asked her to make arrangements to pick up Shotsy from school, and then he left. He needed to be alone.

In the life of a hero, it seems that tragedy is inevitable—at least that has been a common thread that has run through the fabric of history. Billy would never have considered himself a hero. Real heroes never do. But when the song of Billy Stone ended so suddenly, there would be an echo that would sound for a generation to follow. Israel knew his life would be affected. What he couldn't know was to what extent. And for the moment, he would endure the pain with added burden. How could he tell them?

Maybe he should retire. The work had lost its sizzle. Too political anymore. What the hell, maybe go back to San Francisco? But those flowers had died years ago, along with the summer of love. Kesey and Cassady were gone. The only one that might still be there would be Moonbeam, and she probably didn't look so hot these days.

But he was just repressing and dodging pain while at the same time knowing the paradox that such avoidance only increased it. He pulled into a dive bar and had a double Jameson, hoisting to Billy before tossing it down the old gullet. It felt good, kicking and fighting all the way down.

Israel parked near the entrance of the Hilton in a handicap spot. If they moved it, he would arrest them. He liked his recalcitrant temper. The whiskey had propped up his mettle, which faded when he entered room 719. He seemed to hear Billy telling him, "Don't fuck around, Izzy. Tell 'em and move along, little doggie."

"It is so painful to tell you this, but Billy is dead."

Israel looked at each of them. No reaction. Nothing.

Israel had never had a dog, but he knew a lot of dog lovers. When their dogs died, they would lose it . . . emotional mush. All would cry, some would bawl, and some would even wail. Yet when parents of these same people died, they didn't cry, couldn't cry. They might try—they were supposed to—but no, and that would cause a lingering guilt. Some would pretend to forgive and forget, but those were just words. It didn't mean they wouldn't grieve. They just couldn't cry. Izzy had concluded that with humans, there were always conditions to relationships, resentments maybe, small seeds of discontent. But dogs and pets? Never conditions, innocent behavior, no judgment, just pure, unfiltered love, and the sense of loss was in turn magnified. With Billy, however, it was more like losing "Old Shep." At the moment, it was just disbelief.

"What are you talking about, Izzy? That's not possible." Akio waited.

"We got a confession out of Tyler and arrested him. I think his son might be a crackhead, but he went berserk, got hold of his father's gun, and shot Billy. He died almost immediately." He watched as disbelief segued into the reality of truth and subsequent emotional response.

It went as Israel suspected it would. It was ingrained in the culture and genetic matrix of both the Japanese and Native Americans to be stoical in times of grief and tragedy, but the emotion was clear in the eyes and facial reactions of Peter and Akio. The news was absorbed and processed within.

All three, on the other hand, showed personal trauma when Reuben broke down. It was like seeing the prodigious Mount

Saint Helens erupt and crumble. His face in his hands, his shoulders quaking, he seemed to gasp for breath. He was a child grasping for a fragment of untruth, but forced to accept evanescent hope.

Billy Stone's funeral was different from so many others. Too many are heavy on the form and light on the substance. Not so at this one. It took place in the same church in Bloomington as Billy's mom's and dad's. The young priest was really with it. There wasn't a Mass. The priest kept it short but honest.

"I knew a lot more *about* Billy Stone than I knew him," he said. "I regret not having gotten to know him. Winston Churchill said, 'We make a living by what we get; we make a life by what we give,' and as I've been told by so many, Billy Stone gave it all. On the other side of the globe, a Buddhist monk said, 'When you are born, you cry and the world rejoices. When you die, you rejoice and the world cries.' My guess is that, in his new home, Billy Stone is busy sharing his strengths, his undying loyalty, and his love. His spirit will remain within all of you."

Israel Cohen stood right next to the coffin. Peter Akecheta stood next to Israel. There was an empty space, and then came Akio Yamada. Lastly, stood Reuben James. As the priest finished, the four men turned toward the casket, in slow motion, slowly raising their arms in a salute, which they held for a long period of silence, except for the dull melody of muffled tears. It ended with the Irish lament, popularized in the production *Riverdance*, "*Caoineadh Cu Chulainn.*"

Barbara and Shotsy sat in the front row, both crying. They

sat next to Mia and Jimmy. Jimmy had the same proud, resolute strength in his face as his father. Although it was a bit strange, the only other person in the front row sitting next to Barbara was an elderly, gray-haired black man with his strong hand resting on her shoulder. His daughter would have been with him, but she was getting the reception ready at the VFW, which she managed.

The burial at Fort Snelling was a sad redundancy. The grave was in the newer section, far away from his parents'. Outside of a strong spring wind, the weather was fine. Most of the cars left to go directly to the V.

The church ceremony was unconventional. The reception was crazy . . . *Everybody came.* In the end, the bill for what turned out to be a gala affair was over double the budget, but the VFW gladly absorbed the overdraft. The reception morphed into a festivity as a result of a bunch of things, but as usual, the primary culprit was John Barleycorn.

Latisha Wilson was standing in a circle with her dad and Leroy Wood. For a small-time doper, Wood was a real personality, but he sure had lots of stories. They were laughing. When the four squad members joined the group, it became a contest of funny anecdotes and stories. After Barbara and young Jimmy dropped in and started laughing, protocol and conventional behaviors disappeared.

They all knew it was what Billy would have wanted. Without saying it, Billy's reception also set the tone for their individual and collective attitudes for the future. Of course, there would be heavy hearts when they thought about him, but Billy somehow told each of them in different ways that life was meant to be treasured and enjoyed, so, "Miss me, but let me go."

They all would miss him, but they couldn't let him go.

CHAPTER 53

As Time Goes By

B arbara and Shotsy moved back to Minnesota. She filed for divorce from Winston, and it didn't take long for it to move through the system. He was serving a ten-year stint in a minimum-security facility. She wanted nothing to do with her husband's business, but received credit for the asset in the settlement. She ended up opting for 75 percent of the proceeds from the sale of the house. Ironically, the buyer was the Winston Tyler Trust. The old man, Winston Tyler II, didn't change a thing. A full-time nurse and her husband moved in, were paid something, paid no rent, and took care of him. Basically, he got along just fine for the ensuing four years until his death. He wondered what happened to all the people, but not often and not for long.

There were a half-dozen people at his funeral, three of them lawyers and accountants. What happened after that, Barbara didn't know, nor did she care. She had her money in a savings account. Shotsy never brought up her father or her grandfather.

William had posed a different kind of anxiety, at least for a while. She had tried to process Billy's dying words, but it didn't reconcile. She blamed her husband for instigating Billy's death, but her son had pulled the trigger. When she later was told that another druggie friend of William's had plea-bargained drug charges for information on a rape case involving her son, she shut the door on forgiveness. He had been tried as an adult, and was serving life in Sing Sing. She couldn't muster a desire to visit him, and she carried no guilt.

Most of her efforts were directed to her daughter. What remained went to Mia and her nephew. Jimmy became a doppelganger of his father, and it usually made Barbara cry. She had a lot of friends, like Jim and Latisha Wilson and others from the VFW, but something was missing, and it related to what Billy had also said just before he died.

So on the anniversary of Billy's death, her pain called upon her to pick up the phone. She hoped the number was still good.

"Hello?"

"Hi, David. Can we talk?"

At the same time, there was another call taking place—a conference call. Izzy, Peter, Akio, and Reuben had been talking for an hour. Basically, all four were doing well. Izzy and Akio had remained bachelors. They enjoyed their freedom, didn't have time for domestic tranquility, and liked the variety of dating and occasional girlfriends. In truth, each knew they were so set in their ways that no female would put up with them for long.

Peter and Reuben loved family life, and tried to give of themselves as much as they could. Peter could have remained the tribal chief until he died, had he wanted to, but he and his wife got the itch to travel, and so he didn't run for reelection this past year. Billy's death had affected him in ways he hadn't understood for months.

It would have been surprising to have grown up on the Pine Ridge Indian Reservation and not had a deep resentment for white people. Yes, the military gave him the exposure to an environment that was a world apart, and it could have completely destroyed his belief in humanity, but it hadn't. His perception of the Japanese was only that they were bad people who ambushed America and committed atrocities. His perception of black people was that they, too, were victims of white supremacy, but still looked down on Indians.

But white people had stolen his people's land and murdered his uncle and hundreds of innocent, unarmed women and children. His parents had taught him to be tolerant, but the Indian community had taught him differently. From the standpoint of historical perspective, they hadn't been wrong, but his squad had proven how false those teachings could be, and no man had ever influenced him so essentially as had Billy Stone. Without Billy Stone, integrity, loyalty, commitment, and fortitude would only have been words and concepts. Accordingly, he and his squad members had collectively come to represent the vision of a true world community.

Peter and his wife had set their itinerary for their first travels: Greenwich, Connecticut; Selma, Alabama; Bakersfield, California; and Fort Snelling, Saint Paul, Minnesota.

Later today, May Day, early evening, he would drive up to the bluff, alone. He would build a small fire. He would chant and dance and sprinkle tobacco on the fire and send the smoke to his friend in the other world of the Great Spirit.

Special Agent Israel Cohen had retired, but a funny thing happened on the way to his retirement party. He got a call from the FBI director, offering him a two-year consulting contract. Irony springs eternal. Over the past decade, Izzy had developed a strong skill set and some critical contacts in the special area of bank and government fraud, and now his employer really needed him. He would be paid more, control his own schedule, could have other clients, and still receive all the government benefits. He could hear Billy: "Whaddya thinkin'? Unless you got an IQ of less than ten, jump on it, smartass." He did.

He thought back to that trip to San Francisco, the call from his father, and the decision he made on the way home, and he thanked his God for the wisdom. Vietnam sucked, America was breaking, and Billy Stone was dead, but Israel Cohen had become a man of respect, and self-respect, thanks to his squad.

Could he have kept that kid from shooting Billy? He had replayed it a hundred times, and every time, Billy whispered to him, "Just shut that smart mouth of yours, Izzy. You're responsible for the effort, not the outcome, and you always gave it your best shot."

When Akio wasn't in some other country or at Langley, he was alone in that big old house in Bakersfield. He had avoided it to date, but would be forced to retire soon and would need to fill the hole. Most everyone will reprioritize after a traumatic experience, when confidence in the predictability of life is shaken, and

Akio adventitiously found himself immersed in an effort to understand spirituality, the concepts, the history, and the definition of his own rather enigmatic interpretation. He had found that he aligned closely with Peter on spirituality.

Although not ardent in their practice, Akio's parents had been Shinto, which means "the way of the gods." The *kami*, or "spirits," refer to the energy that is generating the *essence* of life's phenomena that manifests in multiple forms. Rocks, trees, rivers, animals, and people all possess the nature of kami. Most importantly, kami and people are not separate. They exist within the same world, and share its interrelated complexity. Peter and Akio agreed that, in many ways, their spiritual beliefs were like Siamese twins.

Akio had also realized one day that he was drinking too much. Like the others, Akio sensed the kami of Billy Stone that brought solution through self-development, and he made some changes. He decided to join a study group on world religion, and as only sweet happenstance can bring in the mystical chain of consequence, Akio sat next to a friendly, attractive, and seemingly successful Japanese widow. If you're wondering if what you are hoping would happen, happened? Yup, it happened.

Reuben was a little different story. The other three could intuit an emotional withdrawal, and Reuben never could hide his feelings. Billy's death had affected all of them, but none as deeply as Reuben.

The old man's name was Johnny Biggs. He was black—African black—but then, he *was* a descendant of the Masai. He, too, had been a warrior. He was six foot six, maybe now a touch less, as he had celebrated his eighty-fifth birthday a week ago, April 24. Unless the weather was prohibitive, Johnny would take a walk every day along the bank of the Alabama River, near the Edmund Pettus Bridge. He would stretch out that lithesome, athletic body and walk to the old cast-iron bench, where he rested and watched the river roll by before heading home.

It was a gorgeous day, the spring festival, May Day. He didn't remember much from the late 1930s—something about Germany and England feudin' and fussin'—but he did remember that his mom and Aunt Bertie would hide candy, or eggs, or something like that on May Day. Didn't matter. Summer was comin'.

When Johnny was seventeen, he was the best basketball player in Dallas County, Alabama. There were blacks and even a few whites that claimed to have seen him single-handedly beat three white kids in the city park, starters on the Selma High team. They made him swear not to tell anyone. He never did. No reason to. Fact was, he had done it, and that was good enough for him. He became the star of some Negro League team, but would have been an All-American at any college. He had learned a trade, and was a most respected man in his community. To Johnny, injustices were like water off a duck's back, and he just kept rollin' on down the line. His smile was infectious, and kids gravitated to him, white and black alike. Life was a real trip. He wanted to squeeze out as much as he could.

When Johnny got close to his bench, he noticed that someone was already sitting there. His eyesight wasn't what it used to be, and it was late afternoon, so he walked closer. When he got to within fifteen yards of the bench, he was sure he recognized the man those big, broad shoulders belonged to. *Damned if it ain't Chief James. Chief Reuben James, best damned police chief Selma ever had.*

He smiled and started to approach, but hesitated when he noticed that the chief's shoulders were trembling and his head was in his hands, shaking from side to side. Could he have heard a muffled kind of moan?

He stopped. It seemed that Chief James was real sad. He hoped that the chief was okay, but he didn't want to interfere and embarrass him. Slowly, Johnny Biggs turned and walked back along the river. He would see him in the coffee shop in the next few days and check on him. Now that Chief James was retired, he was taking some leisure time. Johnny Biggs stopped down the way and looked back, then turned and headed for home.

EPILOGUE

What a day to be lying on a reclining beach chair sucking on mojitos, watching beautiful young bodies boarding in the surf. The wind was steady, providing good waves for the surfboards while keeping the sweating sun-god worshippers relatively cool.

"What do you think, Trixie? Be nice to be young jocks like those dudes, huh?" The man had a chic goatee, big red sunglasses, and matching swim trunks.

"Cut with the Trixie shit, Bartholomew. It's been three years. I think I'd prefer Mildred." The woman wore a middle-aged bikini, her face covered in cream.

"My guys told me they have quite a football team, and they got me two tickets. You want to go?"

"I didn't know they had a football team here. Who do they play?" She looked at him as if he was in la-la land, which he was.

"Over here, they call it football. In the US, it's soccer. My guys know their shit."

"I'm sure they do, and I think you smoke most of it."

"I like to think I make weed while the sun shines . . . Get it?" The man was having a good time.

"No, maybe you can help me out. It's just too fucking clever for me." Her sarcasm was part of the fun.

"So . . . do you think those agents ever quit, or did they go looking for us in the Outback?" Ernie giggled at the mental picture.

"Hopefully, the Outback for about a year, Bart, but that's nine thousand seven hundred miles away, so who gives a shit?" Sunny finished her drink. "I need another one. And you go to the football game. I'm going dancing."

Even though it had been short notice, Ernie had still been able to reach his guy in Brooklyn to get two counterfeit English passports and matching driver's licenses in two days. It had cost a mint, but what the hell—they were loaded. They used their tickets and real IDs to fly from JFK to Melbourne. Sunny's fake passport and license were in the name of Trixie Williams, and Ernie was Bartholomew Williams, a nice, married British couple. After leaving the Melbourne Airport, they took a cab to the train station and slept on the boring trip to Sydney. There, they bought two tickets to San Jose, Costa Rica. The Williams couple was now on holiday. Cheerio, mate, the bee's knees, wouldn't you say?

As Ernie left the beach, he blew Sunny a kiss. "Dance your ass off, Trixie."

She gave Ernie the finger. "Hope your team loses, Bartholomew."

That's it, folks.

CPSIA information can be obtained
at www.ICGtesting.com
Printed in the USA
LVOW08s0224200317

527770LV00001B/109/P